MW01469810

NEFERTITI'S LEGACY

A Lost Pharaoh Chronicles Complement, Book III

LAUREN LEE MEREWETHER

LLMBOOKS
PUBLISHING

LLMBOOKS
PUBLISHING

eBook ISBN: 978-1961759213
Paperback ISBN: 978-1961759220, 979-8643873297

CONTENTS

DISCLAIMER

While the author has gone to great lengths to ensure sensitive subject matters are dealt with in a compassionate and respectful manner, they may be troubling for some readers. This book contains violence and adult scenes and themes.

Nefertiti's Legacy will contain spoilers for the following books:

- *The Lost Pharaoh Chronicles* complete quadrilogy (Books I - IV)
- *King's Daughter* (Complement, Book II)
- *A New Dawn* (The free bonus ending for *King's Daughter*)

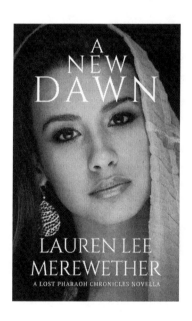

THE LOST PHARAOH CHRONICLES TIMELINE

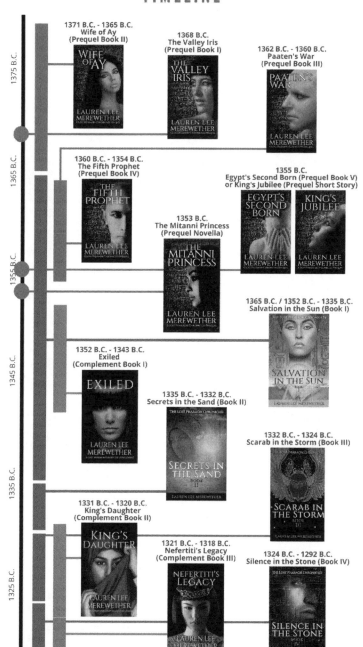

1375 B.C.

1371 B.C. - 1365 B.C.
Wife of Ay (Prequel Book II)

1368 B.C.
The Valley Iris (Prequel Book I)

1362 B.C. - 1360 B.C.
Paaten's War (Prequel Book III)

1365 B.C.

1360 B.C. - 1354 B.C.
The Fifth Prophet (Prequel Book IV)

1355 B.C.
Egypt's Second Born (Prequel Book V) or King's Jubilee (Prequel Short Story)

1353 B.C.
The Mitanni Princess (Prequel Novella)

1355 B.C.

1365 B.C. / 1352 B.C. - 1335 B.C.
Salvation in the Sun (Book I)

1345 B.C.

1352 B.C. - 1343 B.C.
Exiled (Complement Book I)

1335 B.C. - 1332 B.C.
Secrets in the Sand (Book II)

1332 B.C. - 1324 B.C.
Scarab in the Storm (Book III)

1335 B.C.

1331 B.C. - 1320 B.C.
King's Daughter (Complement Book II)

1321 B.C. - 1318 B.C.
Nefertiti's Legacy (Complement Book III)

1324 B.C. - 1292 B.C.
Silence in the Stone (Book IV)

1325 B.C.

THE LOST PHARAOH CHRONICLES COMPLEMENT COLLECTION

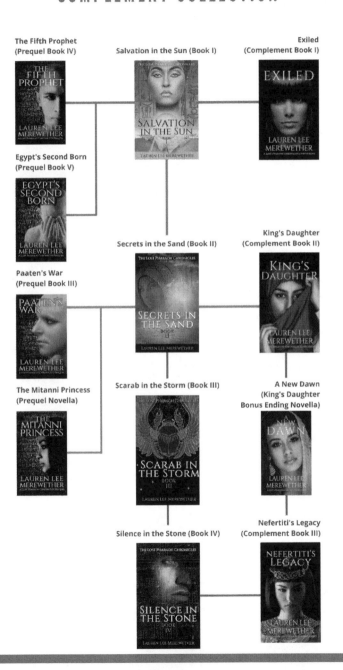

The Fifth Prophet (Prequel Book IV)

Salvation in the Sun (Book I)

Exiled (Complement Book I)

Egypt's Second Born (Prequel Book V)

Paaten's War (Prequel Book III)

Secrets in the Sand (Book II)

King's Daughter (Complement Book II)

The Mitanni Princess (Prequel Novella)

Scarab in the Storm (Book III)

A New Dawn (King's Daughter Bonus Ending Novella)

Silence in the Stone (Book IV)

Nefertiti's Legacy (Complement Book III)

PROLOGUE: SEEKING FREEDOM

MALKATA, 1321 B.C.

ANKHESENAMUN STOOD LOOKING OVER THE NILE toward Waset. The wail lifted from the city and carried on its breeze to her bedchamber in Malkata's royal harem. Her chin lowered and her fingers laced together over her belly as she listened to the wail's ebb and flow. The same wail had lifted when her previous husband was declared one with Re, as it had for her mother before him and their father before her mother.

Her eyes narrowed in thought as her gaze fell to the floor. The wail for her father had been a sham: planned, forced, and, although loud, short-lived. No one missed him. No one wanted to remember him. Even Tut, his own son and her late husband, had disowned him.

The wail for her mother . . . she was not sure if it had been a sham or not. There seemed to be a true sadness that accompanied the wails, but she did not know if the sadness was for the loss of her mother or about the sad state of Egypt. Her mother had reversed many of her father's and her uncle's decrees, but she had made the foolish decision to secure a Hittite prince when she found she was with Horemheb's child.

A decision made in haste, but it would not have stopped Pawah from killing you. The image of her mother's lifeless body on the council room floor supplied her belly with momentary upset. *Mother, rest your ka.*

Her mind turned numb as she tried to push past the memory of her parents. *Such a tangled mess they were in: Father losing his mind in his unending rituals to the Aten disc, Mother doing her best to hold Egypt together in Father's absence, and eventually Mother taking poison to Father on the threat from Pawah.*

A cold chill swept down her spine as that name sprang into her mind. His face haunted her dreams. A brief burning sensation struck her lips as she thought of Pawah's forced kiss in her parent's throne room and his groping hand. It was then she had realized the depth of corruption in her father's sun city, Aketaten. No one in the throne room had come to her aid as Pawah threatened her life. Tears built on the edge of her eyes and threatened to pour down her cheeks.

He took everything from me, even Tut and my daughters.

The wail from Waset intensified in the moment, only to wane once more. "Was the wail for Tut genuine?" Her whisper barely made it to her ears. She had thought so. *He was a good King. He did what my mother did not do; he moved into this palace, Malkata—the palace of my grandfather, Egypt's Magnificent King, Amenhotep III. He defended Egypt as the divinely appointed.* Her eyes rose in defiance, and she looked out of her window to the god Re as he sat on his sun-barge in the sky. *Yet you allowed him to die at the hand of Pawah, your Fifth Prophet.*

She gazed over her shoulder at all of the faience statues of the gods strewn over the floor of her royal harem bedchamber. She had never picked them up after she had swiped them all from their place on the top of her chest. She had never told her stewards to do so either, so there they rested in a mockery of her life. Her curse to the gods after Tut's murder rushed over her once again:

"I want no part of you if all you do is take and never give. You only punish. You never reward. You trick with your gift of ba-en-pet—you lie! All of you, even the Aten disc!" Her fists slammed into the table as her head wrenched up. *"Show me! Show me you are gods!"* Her fisted hand dropped into her lap. *"I want no part of you."*

That day came back in clear memory. The gods had been silent. They had not answered.

"All this death because my father decided to worship one of you, the Aten, instead of all of you? Have we not paid enough for his heresy?"

The wail in Waset yet again drew her attention. The same wail had come the night she held her first-born daughter, born already on the journey west. It

3

had come again when she held her second-born daughter, also already journeying to the afterlife, the Field of Reeds. Those wails had seemed genuine; they had seemed real. It was not until much later that she discovered Pawah had also orchestrated their murders. He took her children from her by forcing the hand of her own steward and cupbearer to slip boiled poppy and silphium into her nightly wine.

A shaky breath passed over her lips. "It was all a game to him," she whispered in realization. He had almost persuaded Tut, along with his list of "witness-es," that she had killed her daughters. He had almost persuaded Tut she was unfaithful to him with his Tutor, Sennedjem, after spending every day in his training yard learning to defend herself from Pawah. A red boil of anger burned her ears. Pawah had driven a wedge between her and Tut. All of the lies, the doubt, the distrust, the years of isolation—they surfaced in her memory. *How can one man bring so much destruction, so much death?*

"I want to forget. I want to remember no more," she whispered low in her throat. The tears that had courageously held onto the brink of her eyes finally fell and ran down her cheeks in a single stream. "This will be the last time I cry for all that the gods have allowed Pawah to take from me."

She wet her lips with a small lick, tasting the salt from her tears. Her hands folded behind her back as she stood straight and tall.

The wail came again. Was *this* wail genuine? She

turned her back on the window. "Egypt weeps for royal wife and Queen Ankhesenamun. An empty sarcophagus shall be placed in my grandfather's tomb in the Valley of the Kings."

Her grandfather, Pharaoh Ay, wanted to name a Hereditary Prince she wanted to marry, but her options were Horemheb, her mother's lover; Nakht-min, Master of Pharaoh's Horses; or the elderly Nakht, Vizier. Her grandfather had named Nakhtmin as his successor, but Horemheb was rightfully appointed by Tut. The weight of her duty as Heredi-tary Princess crashed around her. *Why, Grandfather, did you do that? Marriage to me would seal either man's place on the throne, and it would prevent any struggle between the two powerful men.*

"But I cannot do it."

Sennedjem's face appeared in her mind. A pang of guilt stabbed her belly. "I am so sorry," she whispered to Tut's ka. Her eyes pressed close. "I was never unfaithful to you, but you are gone and I am alone here. He has agreed to go with me to Canaan."

The accusations of infidelity sprang upon her again.

"He has been faithful to you, Tut. He has been good to me since your passing; I only ever knew of his feelings toward me because I told him I had wanted my grandfather to name him Hereditary Prince. But it was a foolish idea; no one would accept him as Pharaoh. But I am glad I asked him to go to Canaan. I am glad to leave. He is a good man, Tut. He honored you and my grandfather, who is my husband now."

Her chin drooped.

"Forgive me. I am so tired of being the royal wife passed from Pharaoh to Pharaoh. First, married to our father, then you, now my grandfather, next Nakhtmin or Horemheb"—a heavy sigh fell from her mouth—"and the next after him, for I will surely outlive either one . . . I will be doomed to the royal harem, alone and forgotten, with Sennedjem in the training yard as a precious bait." Her fingers brushed her lips as she thought of Sennedjem's kiss in the prior month when she had asked him to leave Egypt with her.

She had kissed a man who was not her husband. Had Pawah's accusations of infidelity come true in the moment? Was she all that he had said? Her grandfather had released her in secret from her marriage to him, had he not? However, the declaration of her journey to the Field of Reeds had not come until that morning. But did it matter?

The memory of Sennedjem's breath upon her lips caused her pause. She relished his kiss as she relived it. In the moment, she had forgotten about Tut, but when she walked away from Sennedjem, the turmoil in the aftermath of those accusations washed over her. A sudden piercing pain pricked her heart.

"Is it wrong of me to find a future with the very man with whom I was accused of being unfaithful?"

She did not know, but she drove the question away to be answered on a different day.

Her grandfather had spent the past month preparing her and Sennedjem's clandestine journey to Canaan. He planned to leave Sennedjem's tomb intact since Sennedjem's wife lay there, but in the year after they left, he would erase Sennedjem's name to arouse no suspicions or rumors.

Sennedjem.

Her finger rested on her bottom lip. The past month had been one of the longest in her life. She had not left her bedchamber in the name of appearing to be ill and traveling to the Field of Reeds. Her royal guard, Hori, knew she was alive, as did one of her stewards.

"The whole of Egypt thinks me gone now." Her hands drifted to her sides, and her shoulders pulled upright. "I will own my life, and it will not be spent here in the royal harem, isolated and out of mind."

Three of Pharaoh's trusted Fleetsmen would take her and Sennedjem to Per-Amun. Once there, they would meet a man named Panhey who would teach them Akkadian, the language of the Canaanite city-states.

It seems so simple. She would find her last living sister in Canaan, and there, she would rebuild her family again.

Her mother had wanted her to leave Egypt so many years ago with Nefe and General Paaten, but she had stayed to save her husband, her Tut, from that monster Pawah. In the end, she had still failed him. Warm tears built in her eyes. Pawah . . . he had taken her father, her mother, her husband and her two daughters. The man responsible for those deaths was dead; yes, dead for an Egyptian: burned and fed to the Nile's predators. Even more well-deserved, she thought, Pawah had suffered impalement, a truly agonizing death. It was a truth that soothed her ka for only a moment.

The wail pressed against her ears; its slow moan of sorrow bore into her ka as a reminder of the pain and agony she had endured thus far. She scanned the dark interior of her nearly empty royal harem bedchamber, the epitome of what her life had become. "I shall leave Egypt with Sennedjem to find joy again with my sister Nefe, and I will forget this life of misery. It matters not to me if this wail for my passing is genuine or false."

CHAPTER 1
SEEKING FAREWELL

SHE DID NOT WANT TO RELEASE HER. THE MEMORY of her mother impressed upon her mind with a long inhale of Mut's lotus blossom scent. Ankhesenamun tightened her arms around her. On the way to Per-Amun, she had wished to stop in Men-nefer to say goodbye to her last friends in Egypt.

"I wish you the best in Canaan, Ankhesenamun," Mut whispered in her ear, drawing her back to the present.

Her eyes opened, and she pressed her forehead against her mother's sister, her friend, her aunt, her Mut. She wanted to tell her that Horemheb did love her, but she refrained. Mut would find out in time. A smile grew upon her face as she envisioned a happy future for Mut. She refused to look at Mut's thick gold bracelets that covered her scars. Pawah had given those to her.

Ankhesenamun should have killed him when she

had the chance in the quiet corridor of Malkata, but she wanted him to suffer impalement for all he had done. She never told Mut she had had the opportunity to end his life years ago, thus preventing him from torturing her later. Why add to Mut's pain when she could keep her guilt to herself? Why ruin the image of Mut's only friend? She glanced at Horemheb. *Perhaps he will become a better friend to her in time than I have been all of these years.*

"I shall miss you," Ankhesenamun whispered and stroked Mut's cheek.

"And I, you." Mut shook her head. "I am glad for you. You get to start over."

So do you, Ankhesenamun thought and lifted Mut's chin. She said, "Anyone can start over."

Her eyes drifted to Horemheb, who stood behind Mut. He dipped his chin before making himself known to Mut by placing a hand on her shoulder.

Mut dropped her arms, and Ankhesenamun stepped away. She locked eyes with Mut one last time. *Mut is the last person in Egypt I needed to see, and I have said my goodbye. She will be safe and loved by Horemheb. She will have a good life. There is nothing left for me here in this land.* And with that thought, she knew she could leave Egypt.

Sennedjem spoke. "Thank you for the horse, General Horemheb. You did not have to do that—"

"Yes, I did. May it help you on your journey." Horemheb's gaze fell upon Ankhesenamun.

She recalled their conversation in the stables just

a few hours prior, and she nodded her head to him in reassurance. *Live your life, Horemheb. No more guilt about my mother and returning in the place of my Tut. Love your wife. Be a good man. I will live my life in accord with Tut's last words to me: Be happy; find someone who loves me as he did in the end and who will come to love me even more.* She gave Horemheb a soft smile. He had given her half of her mother's letter to him. It lay rolled up, hidden in her belt. It would be the only thing of sentimental value she would be taking from this land, and part of her did not want the reminder. She pushed past the thought. *We shall both be happy now, Horemheb.*

He seemed to read her thoughts as he released a steady breath. "Where will you settle in Canaan?"

Ankhesenamun paused to look at both of them. "I will not stop until I see or find out what became of my sister, the last of my family." Ankhesenamun shrugged. "I may never find her, but I will never stop searching." It had been ten years since Nefe had left with General Paaten, her mother's steward Aitye, and the man named Atinuk. She hoped they all were alive and thriving in whatever life they had found for themselves; she hoped one day, she could be alongside them, embracing Nefe as she just had Mut. Her heart swelled as she took a small step backward in line with Sennedjem.

"May Amun-Re bless you, Ankhesenamun." Horemheb turned his attention to Sennedjem. "Protect her."

Sennedjem's fingers slid into her hand. "With my life."

The people believed she had traveled to the Field of Reeds. She stood before the General and his wife as a woman of no regard, dressed as an officer's wife: long linen dress, no gold-beaded collar, and, since it was the cold season, a long, thick linen cloak. Gold beading adorned her wig, but it was not like the elaborate detailing of the one she had worn as a royal wife. No empyreal vulture headdress sat upon her head to signal her birthright as a royal woman.

The thought brought a smile to her lips. She was free. Free to forget her past life and all of the pain it had brought her. Sennedjem stood beside her in lieu of Tut, but she could see her future with him—an unknown future where nothing was clear. She had not even the faintest notion of what could happen. Fear gripped her heart, but as she stood before her last friends in Egypt, she knew this was what she wanted: to seize her own life and make it count for something; to maybe one day love again and have family in her arms once more. It was worth giving up her birthright.

Her hand squeezed Sennedjem's hand in hers—the man with whom her late husband had thought her unfaithful. The sick irony of it all forced a tear from her eye.

No more of that.

She pushed Tut from her mind. She had cursed the gods for Tut. She had cursed Egypt for him. But no more. She set in her mind to leave Egypt and to forget the past.

"Be in peace, my friends."

"Be in peace," Mut whispered.

THEY LEFT HOREMHEB'S MEN-NEFER ESTATE AS THE sun dipped low in the west. The horse trotted along beside them as the gold and copper clanked and water sloshed alongside the bags of grain.

"At dinner, I saw you share a look with General Horemheb regarding your mother's blanket that you gave to Mut." Sennedjem's hand gripped up on the horse's reins as he reached for her hand with the other. "Are you disappointed you will not marry him and be a sister-wife with Mut? Why did you not ask your grandfather to keep the Hereditary Prince appointment bestowed upon Horemheb?"

Ankhesenamun softly grinned as she shook her head. "No, Sennedjem. I am afraid it is not that simple." She moved his hand to wrap around her waist. She slid an arm around his lower back and spun around in front of him—something she could have never done outside of the closed doors of her royal apartment. The horse's trot stopped as Sennedjem pulled her close. It was the first time they had been able to be alone like this since their kiss in his training yard out of sight of the royal guards. She would enjoy her new Freetown outside of the palace walls.

He waited for her to speak.

She pushed his heavy linen cloak away from his strong jawline before she answered. "Horemheb loved my mother. She was going to have his son. I never wanted to marry him, Sennedjem."

Sennedjem's jaw fell agape. "I did not know."

"No one knew except for my grandfather."

"So many secrets, it seems." Sennedjem cupped her face and blocked the increasingly chilly winds from her cheek. "That is why he did not want Horemheb to marry you, and so named another Hereditary Prince?"

Ankhesenamun shook her head. She loved her grandfather. She always would, but in the moment of recounting his decisions, he seemed weak to her. Almost petty.

"Among other things," she answered.

"Would you have stayed at Malkata if Horemheb remained Hereditary Prince?"

She kissed the inside of his hand. "I would have wanted to leave. There were so many memories of Tut and my daughters there. I could not . . . " Her voice trailed off. She pushed her thoughts away. "I would have wanted to leave."

He searched her eyes. She felt he wanted to say something, but it never passed his lips. She guessed at his intentions.

"It is too late for me to go back, but your name has not yet been erased."

He pressed a kiss to her forehead. "I want to go with you, Ankhesenamun. I never believed I could have a future with you." He peered over his shoulder to Horemheb's estate in the distance. "I never would have kissed you if this future were not a possibility." He returned his gaze to her.

"My mother was willing to live a celibate life married to Tut." She paused. "My grandfather gave me this escape because he could not give my mother the same. She loved Horemheb, Sennedjem, and she was willing to give him up for Egypt."

"She was an honorable Pharaoh," he whispered.

"Do you think me weak for not choosing the same path as she?"

Sennedjem shook his head. "You are anything but weak." He lifted her chin.

"Do you think ill of me for choosing a life with you despite all the accusations of infidelity? The Fleetsmen seem to think so. I hear them at night when they think I am sleeping." Their whispers had brought tears to her eyes as she huddled on the lounger of the barge. Even two years after Tut had been murdered, the rumors were still fresh on their minds. Sennedjem had been "appointed" to be her protector in her voluntary exile, but it did not stop the suspicions. Pawah's actions still haunted her.

His gaze locked with hers; his eyes intensified.

"What matters is that you were faithful to your husband, and I was faithful to my oath to the throne. You never held me in that regard until after Pharaoh Tutankhamun was no longer in this life. Those accusations were made by a madman vying for the throne. I do not think ill of you. The Fleetsmen should not either."

She whispered, "Are you sure you are here with me because you want to be? Or are you only here to fulfill your oath to the throne to protect me?"

"Yes, Ankhesenamun. I am here because I want this life with you." He lowered his lips to hers but stopped before they touched. He saw the glisten in her eyes.

"Even if it means you may never be reconciled with your wife and child in the Field of Reeds?" she asked.

He pressed his forehead to hers and winced. "Even if it means you will never be reconciled with your daughters and Pharaoh Tutankhamun?"

The pang of guilt from cursing the gods wrapped around her heart. Tut's and her daughters' faces passed before her. Her heart would weigh heavy on the scales of Ma'at. She would never see them again in the afterlife anyway. "I will never be reconciled with Tut. He is to be one with Re."

"And your daughters?"

She cupped his cheek; she could not tell him she had cursed the gods, not yet. "Please do not speak of them. I cannot bear to think of them. What of you? You did not answer me."

"I loved Sadeh, and I still do, but my wife and my child, they have each other. I need you, Ankhesenamun. I am thirty-four years old; I spent four years in a haze after Sadeh and my child traveled to the Field of Reeds. That haze cleared when I found a purpose in my life again: to teach you to defend yourself against Pawah—"

She pressed a finger to his lips before letting her hand drop to his waist. She could not hear that name anymore; that name put a hole through her heart.

He rubbed her back and looked off toward the sunset over her head. "You are my purpose, Ankhesenamun." His hands lingered on her back before he pressed his lips to hers. Quick smiles passed over them both, but hers held a tinge of sorrow. He must have noticed her sadness, for his kiss multiplied into many quick, stealing kisses over her face and neck until she giggled.

He pulled away, beaming. The sun's rays caught him in the eyes, and their deep brown color became as honey.

She traced his face. "Thank you," she whispered. Her heart lifted in her chest at the sudden playfulness; it had given her a short respite from the past.

He stole one more kiss before looking to the west. "The sun is setting, and we must return to the barge. We can be together again once we reach Per-Amun."

She sighed. Three of Pharaoh's Fleetsmen waited for them on their barge. His hands on her body and his many kisses warmed her heart on land, but she would feel alone again on the barge since, in front of the Fleetsmen, Sennedjem would treat her as he did in Malkata. The Fleetsmen kept a full day and night schedule, so she and Sennedjem could never be together or even speak much. It was still at least two decans, twenty days, to Per-Amun.

Just two more decans; then I can talk to someone like this forever. I will not have to be isolated and lonely anymore. She thought as she moved out of his way. They walked together hand-in-hand. "I still feel selfish for asking you to come with me."

He squeezed her hand. "I am glad you asked me to come with you."

She glanced at the profile of his face. "But you are leaving Sadeh and your unborn for me."

"We all make choices, Ankhesenamun." He pulled her under his arm. "And I choose you for the rest of my life."

She smiled, pulling up against the weight of guilt at the corners of her mouth. *Am I being unfair to him? I can see a future with him, but I cannot say I love him. I kissed him. I enjoyed his kiss. I want more of his touch. Have I led him to believe we will be married? I am grateful to him for all the kindness and dedication he has shown me . . .* Tut's face entered her mind. *Forget this old life. Live a new life with Sennedjem. He cares for me. He loves me. One day I will love him.* She rubbed his chest as they walked.

"And I choose you," she said.

CHAPTER 2

SEEKING HONOR

SENNEDJEM PEERED OVER HIS SHOULDER AT THE boat's cabin at the stern. Its four sides of dark drapes blocked his view of Ankhesenamun. Her silhouette was the only outline he could make out in the cabin.

The worst part of the journey thus far was not being able to touch her or speak to her with the Pharaoh's Fleetsmen aboard the modest vessel.

The Fleetsmen were bound to silence from Pharaoh Ay, yet he still wanted them to think he was merely a protector of the Hereditary Princess. It was silly and perhaps even unnecessary, but he felt he needed it to be that way with them. The action of leaving Egypt was desertion, but if it were construed as part of his oath to Pharaoh Ay, then it would not seem as dishonorable.

"Overseer of the Tutors," Khui said, acknowledging him as he joined him near the barge's edge.

"Fleetsman," Sennedjem said in return.

They both looked out over the serene Nile as the barge gently rocked in the current, pulling it along toward Lower Egypt.

"You look at her too much," Khui muttered and popped a date into his mouth. He offered one to Sennedjem.

How to respond to that statement? He politely declined with a slight wave of his hand. The rocking of the barge had always made him a bit queasy when he had to travel by boat with Pharaoh's Army. Only meat had settled his stomach. The sweetness in the date always made it worse.

"She is a selfish Queen," Khui mumbled. "Do you agree?"

Sennedjem pushed off of the side of the barge to stand up straight. "She has been through more than anyone still living. She is afforded this right to leave by Pharaoh."

The Fleetsman continued to lean on the side of the barge. "She puts Egypt in a weak state. I disagree with Pharaoh in this matter." He gestured to the two other Fleetsmen near the stern. "All of us do."

"She has journeyed west in the eyes of Egypt. She cannot put Egypt in a weak state." He winced. *How else to defend her without becoming petty?*

Khui straightened up and popped another date in his mouth. "The truth is that she lives. There will be an empty throne when the time comes. Most of the army supports General Horemheb. Pharaoh Ay did not have the authority to strip Pharaoh Tutankhamun's appointment of the General in the absence of an heir. We will not stand for Nakhtmin as Pharaoh."

"You speak of conspiracy, Khui."

Sennedjem received a glower in Khui's sidelong gaze at him.

"I speak of duty and honor." Khui turned and squared his shoulders to Sennedjem. "If our Queen were like her mother, we would not have a possible civil war when Pharaoh Ay journeys to Re. The blood of Egypt will be on her hands for running away."

"I am her Protector, appointed by Pharaoh Ay. You will keep these comments about her to yourself," Sennedjem said, standing toe-to-toe with the Fleetsman.

"You do not outrank me, Overseer of the Tutors." Khui smirked. "Or should I say, former Captain of the Troop."

There was a time that jab would have prompted him to anger, but he had accepted his resignation, his mistakes, and his past. They had led him to where he was today with Ankhesenamun.

"Yes, *Fleetsman*, 'former.'"

His face held no expression as he reminded the man of his lowest rank in Pharaoh's Armies. Khui was not even the captain of this three-man vessel.

Khui narrowed his eyes and leaned into Sennedjem's face. "Deserter."

"I resigned," Sennedjem corrected him. "Now, I

am under oath to Pharaoh Ay to protect his grand-daughter while in Canaan." Sennedjem stood still, making no movement that would agitate Khui further.

"His granddaughter?" A burst of hot air flew from Khui's nostrils. "His wife. Yes, you will *protect* her. What other Egyptian man will there be for her in Canaan? Your heart will weigh heavy in the afterlife should your body make it back to Egypt. You will take Pharaoh's wife for yourself. I already see how you stare at her."

I do not see it that way, Khui, Sennedjem thought and let Khui smirk and lean back before speaking. "Pharaoh's wife is in her tomb, and I do not stare at her."

Khui scoffed. "It is your heart, Overseer. Perhaps the rumors were true of you and her when she was Pharaoh Tutankhamun's Chief Royal Wife." He pushed past him to rejoin the other Fleetsmen.

"She and I were faithful to our oaths." He eyed Khui as Khui rejoined his troop without further word. His gaze fell to the cabin before he turned his attention back to the Nile. He was clear in his mind and purpose. Khui's words had been expected from the murmurings he had overheard during the past month of travel. They were almost to Per-Amun, and then he and Ankhesenamun could continue their journey alone. He would be able to speak to her without considering the Fleetsmen's prying ears and eyes. A twinge of guilt did gnaw at his stomach, though: guilt of leaving Egypt in a potential power struggle for the throne, made worse by the gentle rock of the barge. He smacked his lips as he tried to settle his stomach.

I hate boats. The horse neighed and drew his attention away from the water. *Especially with animals.* His thoughts drifted to his time in Pharaoh's Army when they transported men and chariots with the horses to the Hittite-Egyptian border. His knees had wobbled when they finally unloaded at Kubna.

The smell of the horse and donkey themselves were not horrible, but their dung was especially bad on a boat. The barge had several clay pots full of animal dung on the opposite side of where Sennedjem stood, but the odor still reached his nostrils.

He put his fist to his mouth to block a small belch and force the bile back down to his stomach. *Almost to Per-Amun. Once we learn Akkadian, we will set out for Canaan, and I will never have to step aboard a water vessel again.*

He breathed out of his mouth as he looked forward to the future. He peered over his shoulder again to Ankhesenamun's cabin. Her silhouette lay in the lounger on her side, perhaps facing him. He smiled just in case she could see him before he turned to look out at the Nile again.

"I cannot wait to start my life with her," he whispered.

His eyes lifted to the skies as the amulets of Isis

and Hathor bounced on his chest under his nobleman's tunic. "Isis—Goddess of Marriage—grant us happiness in Canaan. Let my reasoning for her annulled marriage to Pharaoh be valid so that we speak the declarations of innocence in truth before the gods on the journey to the afterlife. Hathor—Goddess of Love—I know Ankhesenamun longs for Pharaoh Tutankhamun. I know she has much to overcome. I know she does not love me as I love her." His whisper dropped low. "But let me help her overcome and show her how much I care for her, so one day I may have her love in return."

He pressed the amulets against his chest and hoped the goddesses heard his plea even though he had not opened their mouths. He had no shrine for them as he did in the Tutors' apartment at Malkata.

"The Queen emerges," Ibebi, the Fleetsman on the steering perch called out. Khui and Theti, the third Fleetsman, stopped what they were doing and dipped their chins at her. Sennedjem turned around and did the same.

Ankhesenamun stood in her noble's long linen dress. She peered around at them all. "I am no longer the Queen," she said. "You do not have to treat me as such."

Khui and Theti shared a knowing glance before Theti ventured to say, "You are still the grand-daughter of Pharaoh Ay even if you reject your birthright." A callous undertone accompanied his words.

Sennedjem became the object of her eyes, and he gave her a reassuring nod. *She hears them. She has to. This barge is small enough, and the breeze carries.* "Tell them," he mouthed.

She squared her shoulders to Theti. "I know you, all of you, do not agree with Pharaoh Ay and this gift he is giving me." She glanced among the three Fleetsmen. "Do you think I do not hear your mumblings when you believe me to be asleep at night?" Her jawline grew taut. "I do. Despite what you say, I *never* betrayed Pharaoh Tutankhamun. He and my daughters were ripped from me by Amun-Re's former Fifth Prophet." Sennedjem sensed a break in her voice. "That is why I leave. I am not running. I am not afraid. I am not weak. My grandfather allowed me to start over and let Egypt's problems be Egypt's problems."

They shuffled and shifted their weight.

"My family has suffered enough because of my father."

Khui opened his mouth to retort, but she beat him to speaking.

"I know you hate him. He is still my father, even though we have disowned him. Please speak no more of him. Speak no more of the previous Pharaoh. Speak no more of Pawah. Speak no more of my family."

She stared at Khui. "You will leave Overseer of the Tutors Sennedjem alone. You will keep your mumblings to yourself. I know you disagree with Pharaoh's decree and with my actions."

Sennedjem stared coolly at Khui and watched him fidget as Ankhesenamun continued to chide him.

"I never asked for the title of Hereditary Prince to be removed from General Horemheb. He was my friend. He did his best to protect my mother. I want him to have every honor. And somehow, I hope the throne does fall to him when Pharaoh goes to Re."

She turned to stare at Ibebi. "Thank you all for your oath of silence to Pharaoh Ay. Please extend your oath to not speaking of these subjects again."

Her gaze fixed on each Fleetsman in turn. They remained silent as she turned and reentered her cabin. Its dark drapes gave her a false sense of privacy. Her shoulders visibly dropped from her silhouette.

She has endured so much. She has never stopped fighting, Sennedjem thought. The image of her stepping into his training yard ten years ago came to the forefront of his memory. She had ripped her royal dress along her leg line, grabbed a training stick, and ordered him to teach her to fight. . . . It had been a long ten years. She had lost much, but now she stood, perhaps, even stronger than ever. *Even the fiercest warrior needs to rest. This is her rest. No one should live with such a burden on their shoulders. These Fleetsman do not agree, but she deserves to be able to live a life away from this.*

Khui threw Sennedjem an annoyed glare, but Sennedjem only grinned in response. *Shut your mouth, Khui,* his eyes said. *That was the Queen's command, you rumormonger.* Sennedjem spun around to look out over the Nile once more. *At least I do not have to row, but Khui and Theti will have to on the return journey.* He smirked at their coming labor despite his stomach upset. In Sennedjem's mind, the problems of Egypt were no longer his or Ankhesenamun's concern.

CHAPTER 3

SEEKING PANHEY

THE GLIMMERING STREAKS OF DAWN PAINTED THE horizon. The three Pharaoh's Fleetsmen docked the barge at the stone pier in Per-Amun. The trip had been mostly in silence, as Sennedjem did not want to speak about private matters in front of the men. Khui let the stone anchor down, and the captain of the barge nodded his head to Ankhesenamun.

"My Queen," Ibebi whispered, as not to draw attention. "This is as far as Pharaoh Ay commanded us to take you. You are now in the hands of Sennedjem, the former Overseer of the Tutors."

"Your loyalty to the crown is appreciated." She acknowledged the three Fleetsmen. "Thank you for keeping this secret."

Their behavior had been more refined since she had chided them; there had not been another encounter like the one with Khui.

"Be well. Be safe." Ibebi eyed Sennedjem. "May

you find peace in this life."

They helped unload the horse and the donkey laden with riches gifted by Horemheb and Pharaoh Ay. They trod down the long stone pier, making sure the horse's step was sure. People gaped at the horse. Sennedjem wondered how he would hide such an oddity—an official having a horse for leisure. Only the highest elite of their society owned horses for pleasure, and even then, most were used in Pharaoh's Chariotry. He gripped up on the reins of the two beasts he commanded.

They stepped out of the docks and into the markets, watching the people go about their busy lives. Even though they tried to stay to the edge of the commotion, many people reached up to pet the horse's mane. It grew increasingly agitated, and, at the next person to reach up, Sennedjem spoke. "Do not touch my horse, Mistress of the House. He does not do well with many strangers touching him. He may be about to rear and run off. He could hurt many people in the process."

She withdrew her hand. "I have never seen a horse this close." She reached back out to touch him.

"Please." He gripped up on the reins just in case Horemheb's horse decided he could take no more.

"Mistress of the House," a deep voice said behind Sennedjem. The flash of red and white fluttered under a long linen cloak. A pair of Medjay approached. "The man asked you not to touch his horse. Be on your way."

The woman quickly tucked her hands underneath her cloak and scurried away under the watchful eye of the Medjay.

Sennedjem tensed and swallowed, expecting the worst. *The Medjay: ruthless enforcers of Pharaoh's Law.* He dipped his chin in gratitude to them. "Thank you," he said.

Ankhesenamun turned her head toward the donkey to hide her face. She took the reins from Sennedjem.

"A horse?" one Medjay asked, running his eyes the length of Sennedjem's attire. "How do you own a horse? You do not look like anyone important enough to own a horse."

Sennedjem cleared his throat. They were right. *What to say? The truth? Will it give away Ankhesenamun's identity?* He knew if he paused any longer, the Medjay would grow suspicious. "I am not anyone important enough to own a horse. My wife and I came from General Horemheb's estate in Men-nefer. He gifted us this horse—"

"Why would the General gift you a horse?" The Medjay crossed his arms and widened his stance.

"I was . . . I helped him at the Hittite border." Sennedjem pushed the stutter away. The lie did not slide easily from his lips.

The other Medjay swished his cloak and rested his hand on his khopesh.

"Are you a horse thief?"

"No." The truth came out bold and firm. "General

Horemheb gifted us this horse."

The question came again: "Why would he give you a horse?"

"Because I helped him at the Hittite border."

"What did you do to warrant a horse?"

"I saved him from an enemy strike." He squared his shoulders to the Medjay, as if daring them to call him a liar.

The Medjay tilted his head and pursed his lip as he sized Sennedjem up. "I do not believe you."

"Whether you believe it or not, it is the truth." Sennedjem gripped up on the reins of the horse.

"Where are you headed, Citizen?" The questions came like lightning strikes: quick and frightening.

"To the house of Panhey."

"What business do you have at the house of Panhey?"

"He is going to help us trade this horse."

Sennedjem paused, hoping what he had said made sense. They were supposed to trade half of the gold from Pharaoh Ay to Panhey for lessons in Akkadian. If Panhey were a trader, then perhaps he would trade many things . . . like a horse?

The Medjay looked at each other. The one uncrossed his arms as he looked at Ankhesenamun before returning his gaze to Sennedjem.

Sennedjem held his breath. *Are they going to accept his answer? Do they recognize their Queen in the clothes of an official's wife?*

"Very well. Thank you for your service to Egypt

and to General Horemheb." They nodded to him and gestured for him to move along.

"Thank you for your service to Pharaoh." Sennedjem nodded in return as he walked past them with Ankhesenamun close behind.

The Medjay eyed them as they walked off until Sennedjem peered back and saw them speaking with another person.

"How are we supposed to find Panhey here?" she whispered.

It is a good question, but I have a more pressing action I need to take, now that we are free of the Fleetsmen. He lifted her chin and placed a soft kiss on her lips.

She blushed and looked around. Her grin was contagious. There was no reason for her to blush except that she had never been kissed when other people were around.

He confessed, "I have wanted to do that since we boarded the barge at Men-nefer."

"I have wanted you to as well," she whispered. Her rosy cheeks intensified their color.

He looked up and around at the people before answering her question. "It seemed the Medjay knew who Panhey is; perhaps he is well known here and we need only to ask."

She nodded as a passerby gaped at the horse.

Sennedjem extended his hand toward him. "In peace, Citizen."

"In peace, Official," the man acknowledged him.

"I have not been to Per-Amun before and am

looking for the house of Panhey. Are you able to help your fellow Egyptian?"

"Ah, Panhey," the man snorted. "Yes." He pointed sharply to the southeast. "Follow the walkway to the outskirts of Per-Amun. There is a row of small nobles' houses. Panhey lives in the third house." He shook his head. "You will *not* miss it."

A certain unease passed over Sennedjem's stomach at the mocking undertone in the man's voice. *What could be wrong with this Panhey?*

"We are indebted. However, if I may ask, why do you say his name with such disdain, Citizen?" Sennedjem tilted his head.

"Have you met the man before?"

Sennedjem shook his head, as did Ankhesenamun.

The man scoffed. "Then, well, you are in for a surprise." He chuckled. "Best of luck, Official, Mistress of the House." He dipped his chin to Ankhesenamun as he continued on his way.

"That does not sound promising," Ankhesenamun said as she looked off down the walkway.

Sennedjem chuckled, trying to keep the mood light. "It does not, but we need him to teach us the language of the Canaanites. We will have to endure him, and perhaps it will not be as bad as the Citizen implied."

But his stomach turned over as he stepped with sure foot toward the house of Panhey. *Surely, if Pharaoh Ay sends his granddaughter to him, he is an honorable man,* he reassured himself.

CHAPTER 4

SEEKING CLEANLINESS

THEY LOOKED UPON THE HALF STONE, HALF mudbrick single-story small estate. The half-wall mudbrick-enclosed courtyard with a wood-framed reed gate sat in front of a long row house. A reed pavilion sat on its roof. An out-of-kilter slatted wood door and two windows with drooping reed mats for curtains faced them. Some chickens, two goats, and a donkey meandered in the modest courtyard.

"The Per-Amun estates look very different from those at Men-nefer," Ankhesenamun said, covering her nose.

"Waset too." Sennedjem narrowed his eyes at the smell of animal feces in the courtyard. He looked at the other estates, where servants tended the court-yards and the animals were corralled into stable-like structures. His attention again fell to the third house in the row of small estates. No servants could be seen.

"Why would my grandfather send us here, Ro-en?" She pressed the donkey's head near hers. She stroked Ro-en's long nose.

"Let us find out." Sennedjem attempted to push the gate open, but it fell off its hinge, causing the chickens to flap away.

"Who is it?!" a roar came from within the home. The door of the house flew open, and an unkempt man appeared before them. He appeared not to have shaved in days, and his shendyt held asymmetrically under a large semi-gray-haired belly with a poorly tied belt. Sennedjem hoped the shendyt did not fall in the presence of Ankhesenamun.

"What do you want?" the man's gruffness extended to his voice.

"Are you—"

"You broke the cursed gate." The man shoved a hand toward the gate and threw the other into the air as he stepped out into the courtyard. "What did you do? Rip it from its hinge?"

Sennedjem noticed the stares of the servants in the other estates.

He kept a calm voice. "No. I merely opened it." Sennedjem's heart sank into his stomach. *Please, Hathor, Bastet, Isis—do not let this be the place we must live until we learn Akkadian.*

"You did not *merely* open it for it to rip—"

"Are you Panhey?" Ankhesenamun blurted out behind Sennedjem. "We have been sent to find a citizen of Per-Amun named Panhey."

A gruff laugh erupted from the man's throat and ended in a loud, cackling cough. "Who sends you to me?" he asked through the ending fragments of his cough. At last, he seemed to notice the horse.

The servants from the other estates were now fully immersed in the happenings of the third house of the nobles' estates.

"Perhaps we can come in to discuss?" Sennedjem asked, but the imagined intensified smell almost caused him to retch.

"Ha!" Panhey waved them in and turned around.

Sennedjem winced at seeing the man's drooping shendyt that revealed part of his backside as he limped back inside. Panhey's hand scratched his lower back before he unsuccessfully yanked up on his belt.

Sennedjem whispered to Ankhesenamun. "I can go in alone if you want to stay out here with the horse and donkey?"

Her hand had not left her nose. She nodded. "Thank you, Sennedjem."

"Come into the courtyard, though. I will return immediately if you call out." He guided the horse and the donkey into the courtyard and found a clean spot for her to stand. Then he carefully stepped into the man's house.

"Hurry up. I am an old man and not getting any younger," Panhey called from within the home.

Sennedjem cleared his throat and tried to take minimal breaths inside the man's stale house. No matter what strategy he tried, he could not escape the smells of beer and body odor. The sunlight streamed in a dim haze through the wall vents.

"Order is a principle of Ma'at," he whispered under his breath as his eyes darted among the filth, cups, clothes, and other basic items strewn about the house.

He found Panhey sitting at his low table on a stained cushion. Panhey reclined against the wall with a leg propped up. His shendyt fell over his groin, but it was evident he was not wearing a loincloth. Panhey gulped another large intake of beer straight from his small amphora. A large belch sounded and echoed in the small inner hall. "So what did you want?" He licked and smacked his lips. "Who sends you to Panhey?" He rubbed his fingers over his unshaven chest.

"Pharaoh Ay sends us to you."

"Ay?" He laughed.

"Pharaoh Ay," Sennedjem clarified.

Panhey spat at Sennedjem's feet. "Ay." He shook his head and took another swig of beer. "Why would *Pharaoh* send you here?"

Sennedjem pulled the papyrus from his belt and handed it to Panhey as he eyed an empty cup on the table. "This is from his scribe."

Panhey slammed his amphora on the table, which knocked the cup to the floor. He yanked the letter from Sennedjem's hand. "As if I can still read," he muttered under his breath. He narrowed his eyes, opened his eyes wide, held the papyrus close, and moved it far away until he finally found a spot where he could apparently read. "Something about his granddaughter . . . Ankhesenamun . . . " He wiped his mouth and stared at Sennedjem. "Is she not in the Field of Reeds?"

"She is outside." Sennedjem responded.

His eyes grew wide. "The Royal Wife, Hereditary Princess, Daughter of the King, is outside my estate?"

Sennedjem nodded.

"*Hmph*." He found his spot and continued to decipher the words from his youth. "Akkadian?"

"We were told to give you one hundred deben gold for your help."

He let his hand holding the letter fall into his lap. He stared at Sennedjem again before he let out a loud, mocking laugh. "I thought that old man had forgotten about me."

Sennedjem wanted answers. "How do you know Pharaoh Ay? Are you able to house us and teach us Akkadian, or shall we find someone else?"

"It is no business of yours," the man laughed through a cough, but, at Sennedjem's stare, he cleared his throat. "Yes, you can stay here, and I will teach you Akkadian."

Sennedjem looked around. "The Queen is not familiar with such . . . living quarters. Perhaps we can hire some servants to clean—"

He laughed again. "You and her majesty will clean and take care of the animals while you stay and learn

Akkadian from me. Do you think Canaan will be easy and will cater to royalty?"

Sennedjem narrowed his eyes at him. "It will not be as this filth."

"*Ebaburu nāṣiru.*" Panhey chuckled. "You clean it, Protector."

Sennedjem gritted his teeth.

"First lesson." Panhey scratched his belly and took another swig of beer. He crumpled up the royal papyrus and tossed it on the table.

Sennedjem took another carefully orchestrated breath. "Where is your broom?"

"In Akkadian." Panhey smirked.

This man, along with the stench of the house, caused Sennedjem's stomach to roil. "I do not know Akkadian."

"Then find the *qātu* yourself, *nāṣiru.*"

"*Nāṣiru.* Protector? *Qātu.* Broom?" Sennedjem asked.

"Ah, the quicker you learn, the quicker you can get out." He pointed toward the back of the house. "The *qātu* is *kīdānu.*"

"What is that? Outside?"

Panhey winked at him. "Quick study." He stretched his leg out. "What I would give to be young again."

Sennedjem shook his head. "Perhaps if you lived by the principles of Ma'at, you would not be as you are." He turned to go to the courtyard at the front of the house.

"Wrong way to the *qātu*," Panhey called after him.

"I must tell your second guest what has happened; then I will clean your dirty house."

Panhey chuckled. "Good. Good," he muttered under his breath.

Sennedjem stepped into the sunlight; it nearly blinded him in comparison to the dark and repugnant interior of the home. The feces aroma in the court-yard was almost a reprieve.

Another yell came from the interior of the home. "You will have to get rid of the horse. There is a rich landowner, the Nomarch of the province, who owns all the land of the ports and markets. Continue on the path and find the largest estate. His name is Amenemhab."

Sennedjem lifted his gaze to the skies. "Bastet, give me patience in this man's home," he muttered.

Ankhesenamun's knuckles were white around Ro-en's reins. "Please tell me this is the wrong Panhey," she whispered.

He sighed. He wished as much. "No. We are to stay here. He wants us to clean to earn our keep."

"But we have one hundred deben—"

"That is his deal. He does not want servants to do it. He wants to get us acclimated to life in Canaan."

"Surely Canaan will not be this . . . " She chewed her lip to search for a polite term.

He said it for her. "Filthy?"

She nodded.

"Well, I have learned four words already. The

quicker we learn, the quicker we can leave. I do not think he wants anyone here, and I know we would rather be elsewhere."

Her shoulders drooped as she looked around the unsightly courtyard.

He covered her hand with his, feeling her disgust in his belly. "I will begin to clean if you want to stay here with the animals. We will need to trade the horse as well."

"It is our horse. What if we trade for servants to clean? Although I hate to use Horemheb's horse for this." She shook her head. "But I am not sure we can make it to Canaan with a horse, anyway. They seem to be rare, so it would draw a lot of attention."

Sennedjem smiled at her reasoning. "There is man named Amenemhab who lives further up the way. Let us go see what he will trade for; I assume the horse will probably trade for twenty servants for a year."

"We do not need a year. We can keep it clean once it is cleaned."

"Yes, and the longer anyone is around, the greater the chance of someone finding out who you are. And I will keep it clean," he offered, not wanting her to have to touch the man's dirt.

"Sennedjem, I am no longer royalty. I should learn these things."

He kissed her forehead. *Perhaps you are right, but I still do not want you to touch anything in that house.*

Her cheeks blushed on contact.

"You are going to have to stop doing that when I kiss you," he teased.

"I am sorry; I have never been touched before out in the open," she whispered as she looked toward the servants in the nearby estate.

He smoothed the back of his hand over her brow. "Much will change, Ankhesenamun."

"I know. Let us go trade the horse."

———

SENNEDJEM AND ANKHESENAMUN DEPARTED Amenemhab's grand sprawling estate, which was on a hill facing the sea. Wisps of salty sea air drifted to them as they descended back down the path to the small nobles' estates. Their donkey was laden with double the gold and silver they originally had. Additionally, twenty servants accompanied them, rented for three days.

As Sennedjem led them into Panhey's estate, he could sense the disgust among them. A few of them curled their lips as they envisioned the large task before them. "Start inside. Work your way out. My wife and I will help. The owner—"

"Wait," one male servant said. "This is the estate of Panhey?"

"It seems everyone in Per-Amun knows of Panhey," Ankhesenamun muttered under her breath.

The servant shook his head. "God Huh—give us long life after this." He boldly entered the courtyard, only to firmly step in horse dung. He turned to the rest of the servants. "Watch your step."

They all filed into the courtyard, each looking around at the grotesque landscape, almost afraid to start cleaning.

Panhey yelled from within. "Who is it?!"

Sennedjem pushed past the crowd of servants and opened the door before Panhey could swing it open. The two men stood toe-to-toe.

"I thought I said no servants," Panhey wagged a finger in Sennedjem's face.

"We will be helping to clean as well, per your agreement. Our horse traded for these servants. You can keep all of your payment." Sennedjem slapped Panhey's finger from his face.

"You fool. I cannot teach you with others here." Panhey's voice dropped low as he peered around Sennedjem to the servants in the courtyard.

"I will gladly spend three more days here in a clean house rather than learn while we clean it alone, and I am sure . . . "—he cleared his throat, not knowing if the servants could hear him or not—"my wife would as well."

"Your wife? I thought she was—"

"She is my wife." Sennedjem narrowed his eyes at Panhey and stepped forward, backing Panhey farther into his home. *Shut your mouth, you fool,* he mouthed.

Panhey coughed in Sennedjem's face. The stench of beer and tooth rot almost made him lose his breakfast. "Yes, well then," Panhey said, "your *wife* and your servants should start cleaning. The sooner you all can leave, the better." He turned and walked through the outer hall of his home and into his inner hall to sit down at the low table.

Sennedjem yelled over his shoulder after he quelled his stomach. "Let us clean. The broom is in the back."

Ankhesenamun sent two servants away with a few deben copper and silver to trade for more cleaning tools. Sennedjem approached her just as she asked them to return as quickly as they could.

"There should be a storehouse or cellar in the back of the house. We can unload the donkey there."

She nodded and examined the path to the back of the house. He followed her gaze and then hung his head at the grotesque path. He wiped his face with his hand. "Disgusting."

He called over two more servants and pointed to the well. "Bring back as much water as you can. We are going to need it."

They nodded and grabbed a few empty buckets before heading to the well. Sennedjem turned to Ankhesenamun, picked her up, and set her on Ro-en's back. "You only thought this adventure started when we left Malkata, did you not?" he whispered so low no one else could hear.

She chuckled and took a deep breath. "I am almost acclimated to the smell now."

"Do not do that," he laughed and patted her hand. He took the reins of the donkey and led them through the slush; he did not even want to guess at what he was walking through as it squished through his leather sandals and onto his toes. "In all of my days in Pharaoh's Army, I have never walked through this much filth or dirt or grime."

The back of the house came into sight as they trudged through the mess; the servants were already cleaning out the kitchen and the cellar. One dipped his chin to Sennedjem. "We have disobeyed, Official. You ordered us to start within the home, but we thought it would be best to work back to front. Then we would leave when we were finished."

"Think nothing of it, Citizen."

Sennedjem did not let Ankhesenamun off of Ro-en's back as he cleared out the cellar with a servant. Finally, he allowed Ankhesenamun to dismount to help store their trade goods from the donkey's back. He pulled her cloak from her shoulders and draped it over Ro-en. "I will take him back to the front so his hooves can be washed. Perhaps you can help those who are inside?"

She nodded in agreement and entered the house through the back. Sennedjem returned to the front of the house just as the servants arrived with the buckets full of water. "They are starting in the back," he motioned. "The path on the outside of the house will need to be scraped out."

The servants looked at his feet and the donkey's hooves. "Here," they splashed water on his feet. "You should probably throw those sandals away once we are done here."

"Yes. You as well," he said as they walked past.

Sennedjem looked at the servants coming and going through the estate and patted Ro-en's neck. He was about to run his hand over his mouth, but in the moment, he realized all that he had touched and lowered his hand. He scanned the filth that needed to be cleaned.

"You are lucky to be a donkey," he whispered to Ro-en as he tied the reins to the post. He put his hands on his hips and took in a deep breath in preparation for the task ahead. But due to the smell, he regretted his deep breath and spat it out as quickly as he could. "The sooner we get it done and learn Akkadian, the sooner we can leave," he muttered under his breath and walked off to help clean.

THE THIRD DAY ENDED, AND THE SERVANTS Sennedjem had sent to the markets to trade for new sandals returned. They bathed in Panhey's bath chamber attached to the kitchen, even dousing Panhey to rid him of his smell.

"Now get out," Panhey waved them all off.

Ankhesenamun waved her blistered hands as the servants left with the baskets of filth to be burned. Panhey slapped a hand on Sennedjem's shoulder and the other on Ankhesenamun's shoulder. "Now we can learn." He shook their shoulders.

Ankhesenamun winced, causing Sennedjem to remove Panhey's hand from her shoulder.

"*Nāṣiru*," Panhey scoffed and then turned and laughed. "You may want to think of another name, Princess. You do not want your *husband* to refer to you only as his wife."

"It was Queen," she muttered under her breath.

"I do not think you will get much acknowledgment from him, but he is right, my Queen." Sennedjem took her hand and led her into the freshly cleaned house. The stench was all but gone, and they no longer had to preplan their steps as they walked across the floor. "We should probably choose Canaanite names as well."

"I do not know any Canaanite names."

"Perhaps Panhey can be of help in that regard." Sennedjem tilted his head toward the cleanly-shaven old man.

She nodded. "In the meantime, what name should I be called until we leave this place?"

Sennedjem thought of all the women he knew, which was not many. "How about Khumit?"

"Khumit?" She lifted her brow. "You came up with that quickly. Where is that name from?"

"The wife of a friend I knew in Pharaoh's Army."

"I see," she said, eyeing him, "and what will your name be?"

"Sennedjem." He wrapped an arm around her

shoulder. "My name is not as uncommon or as known as Ankhesenamun, the royal woman, wife of Pharaoh Akhenaten, Tutankhamun and Ay. Besides, no one misses Sennedjem, Overseer of the Tutors." He smirked in a truthful jest.

She peered up at him. The sadness in her eyes caused his smile to fade.

"No one shall miss me either," she said, averting her gaze from his. "Everyone hated my father. They are probably glad the last of his line is gone."

Sennedjem stopped at the door of the house and faced her, lifting her chin. "Many miss the Chief Royal Wife of their great King Tutankhamun." He wrapped her in an embrace at the sight of a wet glistening in her eyes. "What is it?"

"I do not want to remember, Sennedjem. It is all too painful."

He rested his chin on the top of her head and rubbed her back. "And now we can leave. We can leave it all behind. We can move forward."

She nodded into his chest. He loved her warmth against him, but Panhey's gruff call came from within the house: "Make us food, *Nāṣiru* and his *wife*."

He sighed. "As soon as we learn Akkadian and leave Egypt." He gestured toward the house. "Shall we learn to cook?"

She giggled and pushed the braids of her wig to the side of her face. She looked into the home while the glisten in her eyes disappeared. "Might as well."

She smiled, shrugged, and stepped over the threshold.

Sennedjem watched her enter the home. *That was an abrupt change: tearful to happy.* He rubbed his lip in thought before he followed her to the kitchen in the back.

CHAPTER 5

SEEKING KNOWLEDGE

PANHEY SLAMMED A FIST INTO HIS TABLE. "DO NOT speak Egyptian." He gulped down the rest of his beer and wiped his mouth with his forearm. "I want you out of my house as soon as possible. The quickest way to learn a language is complete immersion."

Sennedjem shifted on his feet, and his jaw grew taut.

"Now," Panhey spoke in Akkadian. "Make dinner. I want beans, bread, and fish. Repeat back to me what I want."

Sennedjem opened his mouth to speak.

"No, not you. Her." Panhey pointed a finger to Ankhesenamun. "Princess. Queen."

She licked her lips, and a flutter in her chest temporarily overpowered her voice. *We have been here seven months learning this backward language; I would not hate this as much if he were not so demeaning.* She closed her eyes, ending the thought, and began to stutter in

Akkadian. "You want . . . beans, bread, and fish . . . for dinner."

"Quit speaking like a child. You sound dim in the head." Panhey tapped his temple and smiled and began the conversation again in Akkadian. "What are you going to do?"

Ankhesenamun took a deep breath and also shifted on her feet. "You want me to—"

"No, shut your mouth—"

"Do not speak to her like that," Sennedjem said, taking a step in front of Ankhesenamun.

"Ah, the Protector." Panhey chuckled. "Step aside. She has to learn the language. She wants this life, so she must do this without you."

"I am with her."

"And what if you die in Canaan? Get taken as a slave? Find a pretty woman?" Panhey winked at Sennedjem and threw his empty cup at his chest.

Sennedjem caught it before it hit his chest and lobbed it back at Panhey. It bounced off his fat belly and fell into the cushions by his leg. "You know nothing of a man's oath."

"Neither do you, *husband*. Did you not make an oath to protect Pharaoh and his family? This woman has disowned Pharaoh. She is no longer worthy of your oath. You stay with her for another reason, do you not? I see you hold her hand. Yet is she not a royal wife of Pharaoh? I even saw you kiss her a few times—"

"Now it is your turn to stay your tongue."

Panhey chuckled. "You are the quick study; she is slow. She will not last in Canaan. She will return here in less than a year if she is not taken as a bed slave to one of the city-state Kings. She at least has a pretty face. It may keep her alive."

Ankhesenamun stepped forward. "I have more than a pretty face." She shook her head at her error in Akkadian. "I am more than a pretty face," she corrected herself.

"Then act like it, you dim woman!" Panhey paused and then laughed. "Did you understand everything I said, Princess?"

Most of it . . . half of it. But she uttered a small "Yes."

He propped his leg up as he leaned his head back, eyeing her.

She averted her gaze to avoid having to look at what he was exposing. *I have not seen many male organs, but his is disgusting every time he does that.*

He chuckled. "No, you did not; otherwise, you would have said something much sooner. Go make my dinner like a good woman; take your Protector with you. He will have to do everything for you since you cannot."

She glared at him. "I will make your dinner . . . " She wished she knew what insult to say in Akkadian, so she switched to Egyptian. "You lazy fool with scattered senses."

He picked up his empty cup near his leg. "Do not

speak Egyptian." He launched it toward Ankhesenamun's head, but Sennedjem again caught it in midair.

"You will do well not to threaten Ankhesenamun."

He glared at Sennedjem. "Yet you do not even call her by her title? You are not a man of good word."

Ankhesenamun interjected. "He is a man of good word."

"Yet he takes the wife of another man, and not even any man . . . he takes the wife of Pharaoh?" Panhey shook his head. "You have been here almost two seasons; you cannot keep your infidelity from me."

Ankhesenamun's nostrils flared. It was not that she had not envisioned being with Sennedjem, but they had still not lain together. She again did not know how to respond in Akkadian and so spoke in Egyptian. "My grandfather annulled our marriage the day he said I could leave, and he put an empty sarcophagus in his tomb. I am no adulteress—"

"Are you finished, your majesty?" Panhey flicked a crumb of breakfast at her.

She bent down and pointed a finger in his face. "Do not—"

"Do not speak Egyptian!" He shot up and pushed her back out of his face. Sennedjem grabbed his wrist and sent a heavy hand into Panhey's chest, forcing him back down.

"You will not touch her."

"Is she only reserved for you, Protector?" Panhey laughed.

Sennedjem lifted his chin and eyed him. "She can be with whomever she wants to be. She is a free woman, unmarried now."

"Well, at least Ammit will not have your heart if you manage to journey to the Field of Reeds in Canaan," he mocked.

"You should be more worried about your heart, Panhey." Sennedjem ushered Ankhesenamun toward the back of the house. "We will make your dinner."

"Good. Make sure you cook the fish right this time," Panhey yelled after them as they passed through the bedchamber and into the outdoor kitchen.

Ankhesenamun pulled the soaked beans from their storage and threw them into the pot while Sennedjem began the fire in the oven. "I wish for a bath," she muttered in Akkadian as she took a knife and prepared the fish for cooking.

"I will give you a bath if you give me a bath," Sennedjem chuckled.

She smiled at the noble's way of bathing, dousing water on each other. She had always been bathed in a bath well. But that life ended, and her heart settled. *I am not a dim woman*, she thought. *I can learn. I learned how to fight from Sennedjem. I learned to read and write and perform dena in the royal harem. I learned the ways of the priestesses of the temple of the Aten and the temple of Isis.*

I am a learned woman. I will learn to speak the Akkadian tongue.

"Do not let Panhey get the best of you," Sennedjem said as he wrapped his arms around her to guide her in cutting the knife and holding the fish. "He is an old, ill-tempered man living a miserable existence."

"Why did my grandfather send us here?" It was a question she had asked herself many times, but this time, she spoke it aloud to Sennedjem.

He shrugged. "Perhaps he is the only loyal man Pharaoh Ay knows who speaks Akkadian. Panhey has yet to tell us how he knows your grandfather. I can tell he is not Egyptian, though."

"How can you tell that?" she whispered and leaned back into Sennedjem's broad chest.

"When he sleeps, he speaks of Baal."

She took out the fish's innards. "I have heard him as well. What is Baal?"

"I think it is a Canaanite god."

"How do you know that?"

He grabbed an oil, garlic, and thyme mixture to spread inside the cleaned fish. "I was on a campaign with General Paaten, and we had gone to see what remained of Egypt's vassal states. I had seen and heard of the temples of Baal in some city-states."

She let him finish preparing the fish as she rinsed the knife and her hands in the nearby water bowl. "Then how is he here, living as a lower Egyptian noble?"

"I have not figured that out yet; I doubt we ever will. As free as the man is with insults, he remains close-lipped about his relationship with your grandfather." He plated the fish and washed his hands in the water bowl as well.

Ankhesenamun did not care about Panhey's background story. She wanted to master the language and then leave the man's house. A sigh passed her lips. "Do you think I am being unfaithful, as he says?"

He stood behind her once again and lowered his lips to her ear to whisper. "No, nor do I ever think you would be unfaithful to your husband."

"I am no longer married?"

"Ankhesenamun, royal wife of Pharaoh Ay, has traveled west. You are no longer married."

She smirked as she looked at the fish in front of her. "You speak objectively?"

He nibbled her ear, at which she giggled. "I may have some bias, but I also believe it is the truth. I do not see kissing you as kissing another man's wife. I would not do it if I did."

"Well, you did kiss me the one time in the royal harem's training yard."

He chuckled. "You had asked me to run away with you at the permission of your grandfather. I do not count that."

"I suppose," she teased with an exaggerated upturn of her nose. "You did not touch me again until after the word was given that I passed from illness, so I will believe y—"

A shadow appeared behind them from the torch-lights. "Do not speak Egyptian!"

Sennedjem stepped away from Ankhesenamun. "We were speaking Akkadian, old man."

Sennedjem was speaking Akkadian. I was speaking Egyptian. Ankhesenamun hung her head with the thought. *Am I ever going to learn this?*

As Panhey spoke, Sennedjem grabbed the plate of fish and slid it into the oven. He added the beans in the bronze cooking pot to the oven as well.

"You see there, Protector." Panhey scratched his round, hairy belly. "I heard that you kissed her. Both of you are despicable to Pharaoh. You both should be arrested, beaten, and killed for your actions." His bony old finger pointed at the both of them, alternating between them with each phrase he spoke.

Sennedjem spun around to face Panhey. "Go wait for your dinner. We have done nothing wrong; we have committed no crime."

Panhey used both hands to push away Sennedjem's words. "Why do I even concern myself with you?" But he turned away as Sennedjem had ordered and returned to his stained cushion inside.

"How can I not speak Egyptian? I do not know Akkadian." Ankhesenamun sat down to wait for the fish to cook and the beans to warm. It would not be long until dinner was ready, and she would have to go back in there with Panhey. She lifted the cloth over the bread that had been baked that morning. It tempted her to pinch a few pieces off, but Panhey would surely notice.

Sennedjem sat beside her. "It will come."

"It seems easier for you." She leaned her head against his shoulder.

"I have been around the Canaanite people more in my travels with Pharaoh's Army. Perhaps I remember some of their words." He shrugged. "You will learn, Ankhesenamun, despite what Panhey tells you. You know everything that I am saying in Akkadian right now, but you only respond in Egyptian."

Her mind drifted to Panhey's latest tirade, and asked, "What would I do if you were to be killed or taken? Would you ever leave me for a pretty woman?"

"You are a fighter, Ankhesenamun. You would find a way to your sister. You would live a good life." He slid his hand into hers. "And you are a pretty woman; *my* pretty woman, if I may be so bold to say."

She kissed his shoulder. "You may."

"And I hope seeing Panhey's"—he cleared his throat, and his cheeks turned a hue of pink; he winced and gestured to his groin with his eyes—"does not cause you too much heartache or makes you not want to be with me."

She licked and bit her bottom lip as her gaze fell to Sennedjem's awkward half-grin, half-grimace when she failed to laugh. There was clearly a request behind his attempted joke, but she did not know what to say. Had they been alone, had perhaps there been no accusation of infidelity from Pawah, Tut, the

Fleetsmen, and now Panhey, or even had someone she loved not left her or been hurt or killed, she would have already married Sennedjem. Even her dreams were of Sennedjem, when they were not of Pawah slaying her family. However, her dreams of Sennedjem always ended the same: with him murdered or executed. She knew he loved her; she knew he wanted to be with her, she knew she wanted the same, but she could not . . . yet.

Her silence made his half-grin falter.

What to say?

She returned her gaze to his eyes. She had stolen a few glances at his body when they bathed each other, and she smiled wide as the words entered her mind. "You are nothing like Panhey." She grasped his chin and kissed him on the lips. "And one day, we will be together."

His failing half-grin stretched in full across his face. "Well, I am glad you think I am nothing like Panhey." They both chuckled low so Panhey would not hear.

"The fish smells done," came a yell from within the house.

She sighed as Sennedjem glanced into the oven. He stood up, helping her to stand as well. "Grab the bread and the wine. I will bring the fish and beans," he said. But as she turned to complete her task, Sennedjem kept hold of her hand and spun her back into him. "If you will, my Queen," he whispered, "grab the bread and the wine."

She smiled. "I shall."

She watched him bend over to retrieve the fish and beans from the oven, taking note of his broad muscular back, narrow waist and firm backside, unfortunately hidden under his perfectly white shendyt. Her thoughts ended there. They still had some time at Panhey's since she could not learn the language. She quickly grabbed the amphora of wine and the bread and joined Sennedjem before returning to the inner hall with the dinner they had prepared.

They placed everything on the table, and Ankhesenamun poured the wine.

Panhey eyed her. "Tell me what you are doing in Akkadian, Princess."

She did not like the way he called her "Princess." She was Queen, not Princess, if he was going to use her title. There was also a mocking tone underlying it, rather than a revered one. She winced. *I hate this*.

A deep breath filled her lungs, and she stammered, "I am pouring wine."

"And?"

Ankhesenamun licked her lip before speaking. *I will show him I can do this*. She stole a glance to Sennedjem, who gave her a reassuring nod. "I am sitting down to eat this meal of fish, beans, and bread that we have prepared."

"And what were you doing with your Protector in the outdoor kitchen?" Panhey scratched his once-again unshaven gray chest hair.

She shot him a glare. "We were talking."

"And?"

"And preparing a meal."

"And?"

"That is enough. That is all we were doing," Sennedjem said, dropping a hand to the table and causing the wine in the cups to ripple.

"Sure, it was," Panhey chuckled. He grabbed a piece of bread and stuffed it into his mouth.

Ankhesenamun envisioned taking Panhey's cup of wine and throwing it into his smug face, but instead, she tightened her grip on the amphora.

Sennedjem sighed. "We have nothing to prove or disprove to you."

"That is right. You do not." Panhey eyed Ankhesenamun. "Tell me what you did today, Princess. In Akkadian, since I must remind you ad nauseam."

She flicked her gaze to the ceiling and then licked her lips to speak the dreadful language once again. *I hate this.*

DINNER WAS LIKE ALL THE OTHERS HAD BEEN FOR the past seven months of their stay: brutal. Then it ended like it had every time before, with Panhey dismissing them to clean up while the lazy fool went to bed.

"I am tired, and I will sleep. It will be an early morning; you will do well to sleep." Panhey stood up and eyed the two of them. "Clean up dinner before you go to bed. Speak only in Akkadian. If I hear Egyptian whispers, I will kick you out into the streets of Per-Amun to begin your journey this very night."

"I understand," she said.

Panhey smiled. "Good, and make sure to bathe. You stink." Then he made his way to the adjacent bedchamber and fell into his bed.

"*I* stink?" Ankhesenamun narrowed her eyes at the fat, old, repugnant man. She rose to her knees, gathered the platter and the cups, and marched extra loudly through the bedchambers to the outdoor kitchen. *See if he can sleep through this.* She clanged everything together while she cleaned it all up. She marched off to feed Ro-en in the almost-empty stables at the back of the small estate.

Sennedjem had retrieved the hand broom made of braided reeds and swept out all of the food crumbs and loose sand that had blown in through the day. After he was finished, he left the house to pull well water for their baths.

When Ankhesenamun was done with her outdoor chores, she returned to the inner hall and pulled down the box bed they had traded for the first night they were there.

She mumbled in Egyptian under her breath as she completed her tasks, until Sennedjem grabbed her hand. "Your bath awaits, my Queen."

"Thank you, Protector," she responded in Akkadian.

He smiled. "See, you understand and can speak it just fine when you do not have Panhey around."

She smiled, and the tension in her shoulders melted away. They walked through Panhey's bedchamber on their way to the bath chamber. Panhey chuckled. "Enjoy bathing," he muttered, his eyes barely open as slits.

"Go to sleep, you dirty man. You could use a bath too." Ankhesenamun shook her head at him.

"Speak Akkadian, you dim woman."

Sennedjem kept a firm grip on her shoulder and led her to the bath chamber. A slab of stone was in its corner, along with a drain to send the water back to the ground outside. She undressed and noticed Sennedjem trying not to look at her as she knelt on the slab. Sennedjem poured two buckets of water over her, and then she did the same for him. They shaved and oiled themselves before they dressed for the night.

"You are nothing like Panhey," she whispered with a smirk, making an implied confession of where her eyes had been drawn while he bathed.

He leaned in close. "I looked too." He smirked and grabbed her hand to sneak back into the dark house.

Panhey's thunderous snoring shook the house, so they moved their box bed into the outer hall to put more distance between them, although it seemed like a futile effort.

She lay down, and he slid in beside her under the

LAUREN LEE MEREWETHER

linen sheet. He warmed her after her cold bath. His hand cupped her cheek. "I love you, Ankhesenamun," he whispered in Egyptian.

She smiled. She wanted to say it back, but she could not. Her heart still missed Tut. She covered his hand with hers and kissed his palm. She wrapped her arm around him, and he pulled her close to him. Their boxed bed was meant for one person, but if they shared it, neither of them had to sleep on a straw cot on the floor.

He kissed her forehead, and she lifted her face to his. "Thank you for coming with me. We have not left Egypt yet if you want to turn back."

"Turn back to what, Ankhesenamun?" His brow furrowed. "I want a life with you."

He had told her he loved her every night they had been there, and she had yet to return his sentiment.

"I have been unfair to you," she said.

He sighed at the conversation that came up every now and again. "How so?"

She shivered in his arms, which caused him to tighten his embrace around her. It was time to confess to him something she had not yet. "I asked you to come with me, and yet I do not love you as you love me."

He grinned in the soft moonlight that fell from the wall vents. "I know that, Ankhesenamun."

What? How can he know that and still give up his life in Egypt and chance his afterlife? She strengthened her grip upon his bicep. "But why?" Her chest tightened.

64

"Why would you risk your afterlife with Sadeh for me, who cannot even tell you I love you? I told you I only wanted you to come if you wanted to and not because of your oath to protect Pharaoh's family. I—"

Panhey stirred in his sleep in the adjacent room.

Sennedjem peered over his shoulder to make sure the man still slept before he turned again to Ankhesenamun. He caressed her cheek as a genuine smile appeared on his lips and the soft light brightened his eyes. "I have had over ten years to mourn and grieve my wife and to fall in love again with a woman who saw me as nothing but a Tutor. But you, you have had two years since Tut, if I may call him Tut"—he waited for her objection but she gave none—"since Tut was murdered. You were forced to marry your grandfather as soon as word of his journey west came. You chose exile from your home rather than marrying a fourth Pharaoh and perhaps a fifth . . . all of this, in your twenty-five years of life."

A glisten appeared in his eyes as he recounted the hardships she had endured.

"If you could see a life with me enough to return my kiss that day you asked me to leave Egypt with you, then one day, I hope you will return my love." He placed a soft, gentle kiss on her forehead and then her mouth. "And that is enough for me," he whispered on her lips.

Her face flushed, and tears pricked her eyes. *Tut is gone. Tut wanted me to be happy. Is it wrong to love Sennedjem after all the accusations of infidelity?*

No. Tut is gone. They are all gone. Everyone I ever loved is gone or will be soon. She thought of her grandfather, who was well-aged. Word had traveled to Per-Amun that her grandmother had been sick and would soon journey west; she knew her grandfather would only follow her in the years to come. She had asked Sennedjem to come with her but was it wrong of her to have done so?

Not if she saw a future with him. One day . . . Was she being unfair to him? Was she taking him away from Sadeh and his child? He could never see them again.

She closed her eyes as Sennedjem's lips moved over hers and his hand stroked her neck. She breathed him in and returned his kiss. A fluttering raced across her belly as she sank into his embrace. She imagined gripping the back of his neck and conveying her desires and urges upon his mouth and body, but Panhey's loud snores in the other room and a stab of guilt in her heart kept her mind solely focused on his soft kisses.

CHAPTER 6

SEEKING PER-AMUN

THE PER-AMUN MARKETS BUSTLED WITH PEOPLE, both Egyptian and foreign. It had been exactly one year since they had arrived at the Per-Amun port.

Panhey's belt is actually tied correctly, Ankhesenamun noticed as she peered at his presentable clothing. *I am tired of seeing so much of him.*

Panhey stood in between her and Sennedjem and pointed to a couple of Canaanites conversing with a merchant. He murmured to them, "You can tell they do not speak Egyptian. Perhaps you two should go translate for them." Then he pushed Sennedjem and Ankhesenamun in their backs. "Get going."

She grabbed Sennedjem's hand to keep from losing him in the crowds, and he led her to the merchant. To her surprise, she understood everything the Canaanites were saying.

"This woman is trying to take us for fools. Five

deben silver for a tunic?" the Canaanite man said and sneered.

"I hate Egyptians. They think they are so much better than the rest of us," said the apparent wife of the man who spoke.

Sennedjem nudged Ankhesenamun, who froze; her mind went numb. *What do I say? How to say "In peace" in Akkadian?*

The Canaanites noticed the two of them staring.

In very butchered Egyptian, the man said, "What do you want?"

At Ankhesenamun's silence, Sennedjem spoke in Akkadian, "Greetings."

The man's jaw fell open, and he took a step back. "You know my language?"

"We are learning to speak your language." Sennedjem gestured to Ankhesenamun. "My wife and I. We are Sennedjem and Khumit."

The woman glanced at her husband before her eyes darted between them. "What do you want, Sennedjem?"

"We noticed there may be misunderstandings here between you and the merchant. Would you like us to translate for you?" Sennedjem asked.

Ankhesenamun could understand, but her tongue was firmly rooted to the top of her mouth. *How will these foreign words proceed out of my mouth? Will I stutter, as I have in the past with Panhey? Will I immediately sound like a foreigner? I will look like an incompetent fool.*

"What do you think, Aqhat?" the woman asked

her husband. "Are these Egyptians only acting in their fellow Egyptian's interest?"

Just say something! Get it over with, Ankhesenamun thought before sputtering, "We are not."

Ankhesenamun hoped she had applied the correct suffix to the correct prefix of the Akkadian word phrase. "We are simply trying to—" She cut herself off; she forgot the word. She took a deep breath and began again. "We are simply trying to increase our learning."

"Your knowledge?" Aqhat asked, tilting his head at her.

"Yes."

Sennedjem smiled at her before nodding in response to the Canaanite man.

"What is your fee?" Aqhat asked, crossing his arms.

"Nothing. We simply wish to learn and to increase our knowledge," Sennedjem replied.

Hmph. His wife mimicked her husband.

"You said the merchant woman wanted five deben silver for the tunic?" Ankhesenamun asked, with hesitancy in her voice.

"See, Arsiya"—Aqhat gestured toward Ankhesenamun—"the Egyptians do not always think themselves better than non-Egyptians. Some actually want to help out of the goodness of their hearts."

Hmph. Arsiya narrowed her eyes at Ankhesenamun before her gaze rested on something behind Ankhesenamun.

Sennedjem followed Arsiya's line of sight and peered over his shoulder. He quickly pushed Ankhesenamun toward the merchant booth to turn the woman's head away from what she appeared to be observing.

"Sennedjem, what are you doing?" Ankhesenamun asked in an Egyptian whisper.

He smiled at Aqhat and Arsiya before he said through clenched teeth, "A statue of you and Tut stands over there." He nodded and returned to Akkadian. "What do you want us to say to the merchant woman?"

A tight grip wrenched Ankhesenamun's vocal chords as she peered over to the statues. Tut seemed to look straight at her and Sennedjem. His stone eyes burrowed through her. Her yearslong defense against the accusations surged in her memory: *I did not betray you.* Yet, here she was in Per-Amun, about to flee Egypt with Sennedjem. She closed her eyes and repeated her reminder. *Tut is gone.*

She returned her gaze to the Canaanites.

"I want you to tell her she is ill in the head if she thinks this tunic is worth five deben silver." Aqhat pointed to the tunic up for trade.

Sennedjem patted Ankhesenamun's shoulder. "Would you like to try?"

She nodded and stepped forward. Aqhat and Arsiya drew near to her, and their overbearing body odor stifled her senses. *Canaanites do not bathe as often as Egyptians, it seems.* She breathed through her mouth and hoped she would at least have a bath every day once they left Egypt. She turned her head to the merchant woman.

"In peace, Mistress of the House."

"In peace," the woman's gruff voice came back.

"These Canaanites are confused. They want to confirm you ask five deben silver for this tunic?" Ankhesenamun pointed.

The merchant woman's brow rose. "Yes."

"They do not believe it is worth five deben silver."

The merchant woman laughed, and Aqhat and Arsiya glared at Ankhesenamun, who tried to ignore them.

"Tell them I meant five kite silver. When I heard you say 'deben' I thought these fools wanted to give me their trade goods," the merchant woman laughed.

Ankhesenamun politely chuckled. "I will tell them five kite silver."

She turned to Aqhat and Arsiya, who were uncomfortably close to her. She took a step backward, only to have them take a step forward. Sennedjem snickered behind them, and Ankhesenamun gave him an unamused stare before she spoke. "The merchant says you misunderstood. She wants five kite silver."

"Kite? It is not worth five kite silver. Tell her we will give her two kite silver. No more," Aqhat said as he crossed his arms and stuck his long, curly beard out at her.

Ankhesenamun turned her head at the repulsive

growth of hair. Her eyes grew wide at the merchant woman, who also snickered. "They will give you two kite silver, no more."

The woman laughed. "Between you and me, it is only worth one, but I will take two from these fools."

Ankhesenamun smiled politely. She turned to Aqhat. "She agrees."

Arsiya eyed the merchant woman. "She agreed too quickly. It must mean we can trade for less because it is worth less."

Aqhat nodded his head. "Agreed. Tell her we will give her one and one-half kite silver."

Ankhesenamun sighed. "You are putting me in a difficult situation." She chewed her lip, trying to remember how to say the words. "She just told me it was worth less than two, and now it looks like I am divulging what she told me in confidence."

"Did she say how much it was worth?"

She sighed again and then turned to the merchant woman without answering them. She was not going to lie for these two Canaanites. "They said you agreed too quickly and now offer one and one-half kite silver."

"You are supposed to be on my side, Egyptian." The merchant woman's finger shook at her. "I will deal with you no more." She pointed at Sennedjem. "What did they say?"

"They said as my wife told you. You agreed too quickly, and they thought the price was too high." Sennedjem gestured toward the tunic.

"Fine. I will take one and one-half kite silver for the tunic," the merchant woman said.

Ankhesenamun nodded toward Aqhat and Arsiya as she leaned away from them.

Arsiya clapped, and Aqhat threw his trade goods at the merchant woman to weigh while he grabbed the tunic. He wagged a finger in Ankhesenamun's face. "That is one thing I will give to the Egyptians. They make the softest and nicest clothes in all the land. I only wish I could trade for silk."

Sennedjem found her gaze. "As do I."

They made their way back to Panhey, who stood rocking on his heels with a smug grin plastered on his face. "The dim woman did better than I thought she would. I think it is about time you leave my home and set out for Canaan. You will need Canaanite clothes. Go trade for some and meet me at my house. I will show you a map of Canaan, and you can be on your way tomorrow at first light."

Ankhesenamun smiled and glanced at Sennedjem. *Finally.*

Yet a tickle of unease settled into her stomach. *Finally.*

"And I suppose I shall tell you." Panhey leaned over and sniffed Ankhesenamun's perfumed wig just before he whispered in her ear, "I was a spy for your grandfather when Pawah lived. It was a mutually beneficial relationship, as you can tell from my estate—"

That makes some sense, but still . . . she thought...*surely my grandfather knew someone more civilized than Panhey to teach us Akkadian. Perhaps not. Spies must be loyal, or they lose their worth. At least the secret of my sham death is safe with Panhey.*

"—so, you see, nothing gets by me, you unfaithful wretch."

What? Pawah's name and his accusation boiled her blood, and she shoved him in the chest, away from her. Her finger pointed in his face. "I have never been unfai—"

He chuckled, cutting her off, and he rubbed the spot where she hit him in a slow, circular motion. His lips puckered, kissing the air twice. "You only thought I was sleeping."

Sennedjem stepped between her and Panhey. "Leave." The one-word command was said with the authority she assumed he wielded as a former Captain of the Troop.

Panhey laughed and patted Sennedjem on the shoulder. "I think that is what you will be doing, tomorrow, first light." He winked at Ankhesenamun as Sennedjem removed Panhey's hand from his shoulder.

"Her husband still lives, boy," Panhey muttered as he stared at Sennedjem. "And I do not see a decree of divorce."

"What is it to you?" Sennedjem asked, keeping a firm stance. "We have been through this time and again."

Ankhesenamun only stood watching Sennedjem

defend her honor from Panhey, a man who meant nothing to her. But the whispers of infidelity from the Fleetsmen and the servants and Tut and Pawah from long ago came rushing upon her once more. She almost thrust her hands over her ears to keep those whispers at bay.

I must get out of Egypt. Once I leave Egypt, none of this will matter any more.

Sennedjem was speaking. " . . . You know nothing, you old fool."

Panhey scoffed. "I know more than you do, *nāṣiru.*" He spun on his heels and left them there.

A few of the passersby peered over at them, but Sennedjem waved them off as if nothing had happened. He turned to Ankhesenamun and placed his hands on the sides of her arms. "That man is old and lonely." He pressed his forehead to hers. "Do not listen to his worthless words."

"But is he right?" she asked and closed her eyes in thought.

"No," came the answer. "You may have no formal decree of divorce, but your grandfather declared you on your journey west. It is the same. You have no husband now."

She drew in a deep breath.

His tone turned playful. "Unless you want to count me as your husband. You have already told several people today at the markets that you were my wife. "

Her eyes popped open to witness the smug smirk on his face.

"And I know it has been a year, Ankhesenamun, but I am not ready for that type of arrangement just yet."

That tease.

"Sure, Sennedjem." She tapped his chest as he stole a quick kiss.

He leaned over and sniffed her wig before he whispered in her ear. "Should I start sniffing your perfume too?"

She laughed and unsuccessfully pushed him away in jest. Her mind, though, was stuck on Panhey's rough voice speaking Pawah's name and the accusation of infidelity. "No. Please do not do that." A shiver crawled down her spine as she remembered Panhey's hot breath in her ear.

His hands slid down her arms, and he took her hands in his. "We need Canaanite clothes. Shall you accompany me to those merchants over there to trade for some?"

Panhey's words replayed in her ear: *"When Pawah lived . . . You unfaithful wretch."*

A smile hid her thoughts. "I shall."

While they approached a merchant, her gaze drifted to her statue that stood alongside her late husband. That statue mocked her grief. A grimace contorted her face as she stared at it, reliving the stoppage of time when the messenger brought word of Tut's passing on the battlefield. The urge to vomit tasted fresh on her tongue once again as she envisioned holding her two daughters killed by Pawah through her own former steward and cupbearer. No tears fell as she stared at that statue, but the grinding of her teeth pulsed in her ears.

She finally had to turn away. That was what she had been doing for the past year: turning away, running, and leaving the pain of the past behind her. She did not want to remember. Her heart ripped open again, wishing Tut were with her; wishing her daughters were playing around her in the royal harem; wishing her mother were there, as well as her sisters and her father. She wished Sennedjem were living with his wife and child. That life was so clear to her in the moment, yet it quickly faded. The fleeting happiness it brought revealed the pain she had buried beneath her new life. It bubbled to the surface within her. She had cursed the gods previously in the privacy of her royal harem bedchamber, and she nearly cursed them again as she stood in the markets of Per-Amun.

But as fast as the pain ascended to the surface of her emotions, it descended just as quickly. At the sight of Sennedjem trading for a few pairs of Canaanite leather shoes, she came back to her present life once again. That pain was behind her, or it would be soon, once she left this land. She did not ever have to see a statue of Tut or her mother or her father or herself ever again. She would never have to be reminded of her life in Egypt. The salty air of the Mediterranean Sea whisked by her, carried by a sudden breeze. *Yes, I will forget this place.* She linked her arm with Sennedjem's and leaned her head into his shoulder to play the part of his wife for the merchants.

With the next breath, she envisioned the future she had planned over the last few months: finding Nefe in Canaan, setting up a house with Sennedjem and having their children play with Nefe's children, and growing old and dying after a carefree life with her husband and her sister. But after that, she would cease to exist, as her heart would not make the journey to the afterlife. She glanced to Sennedjem, who stole a quick look at her before returning to barter for a Canaanite tunic. Her past pains seemed to melt away. *It is easier to forget. It is easier to run away. It is easier to start over.* She pushed her family and Tut away once more. *I want this life. I want to live it with Sennedjem. He wants to live it with me.* Her embrace tightened upon his arm. *As he says, it is enough for me.* A peace settled within her.

"You have the late Queen's resemblance," the merchantman said, his voice pulling her from her thoughts.

Sennedjem's arm tensed in her grasp.

She turned her head to the merchant, grabbing at any words she could think of to form a coherent sentence: "Thank you, but there should be no comparison to our late Queen."

The merchant nodded his head. "You are probably right." He chuckled with a nod and a half-grin.

His gaze drifted off toward the statues in the distance. "She was a good Queen. I was hesitant when Pharaoh Tutankhamun took the throne with her by his side. They were the children of Akhenaten . . . " His eyebrows raised as his voice trailed off. "But Pharaoh Tutankhamun brought Egypt back to the rightful gods. He restored much to the land and continued what Pharaoh Neferneferuaten had started. I hope their names shall live forever. May they find peace in the afterlife with their daughters."

Ankhesenamun's lips pressed tightly together; she had to respond, but how? She wanted to forget. She needed to forget. She did not want the nightmares anymore. She was glad at least her mother, Tut and her daughters were held in good memory by the people—well, at least by this man—but she wanted this conversation to end.

Sennedjem's hand pressed over hers on his bicep. "We wish the same as well."

Her eyes lifted to his in gratitude. *Thank you for speaking when I could not,* they said.

"I am glad that Pawah got what he deserved." The merchant shook his head. "He deserved much worse. To murder the divinely appointed, a young king who did so much for Egypt?" He tapped a fist into his palm. "The Amun priesthood's judgment is forever impaired in the eyes of the people for letting in such a foul creature to tend to our premier god."

At the mention of Pawah's name, Ankhesenamun turned her face into Sennedjem's shoulder to keep her emotions at bay. She never wanted to hear that man's name again.

"Oh, I apologize, Mistress of the House," the merchant soothed after he ended his small tirade. "I do not mean to cause you discomfort with the mention of that demon."

Sennedjem spoke for her once again, and her ka rejoiced in his careful understanding of her feelings. "We keep his name alive by speaking it. My wife does not wish for him to be remembered."

The merchant nodded. "Of course. Well, in any case, I am glad he can longer hurt the royal family or anyone else, for that matter." He eyed Ankhesena-mun. "I apologize again. I will give you this Canaanite head wrap. No trade."

She smiled at him. "You are too kind. We shall trade; we are not here to take."

"Then I shall make you a deal: one half shat copper."

"You are most generous, Citizen," Sennedjem said and handed him a full shat copper. "Keep the difference."

The merchant nodded his head. "You two are good people. May you be blessed. May you have peace." He tucked the shat copper away and then turned his attention to other traders.

They loaded Ro-en with their trades and began the long walk to Panhey's estate as the sun dipped low in the western sky. Sennedjem took her hand in his as he led Ro-en down the road. "Tomorrow, we shall head to Canaan."

"I wonder if the skies are as beautiful in the evening there as they are here." Her eyes lifted to the rows of pink and yellow that billowed up into purple and dark-blue clouds. But before Sennedjem could respond, she said, "Thank you for speaking for me today."

"I am here for you." He looked up as well. "Whatever you need, I will be here."

She sighed.

"What is wrong?" he asked.

She stopped and turned to him. "I want to forget, Sennedjem." She shrugged, not knowing what else to do. "Is it wrong of me? Do you think ill of me? Remembering them is how they have immortality in this life. It is their honor as royalty—their names are always spoken; their images are always worshiped. But I want nothing more than to forget." Hot tears burned her eyes as she met his gaze.

Sennedjem pulled her close. "I think you worry too much about what other people think of you." He grinned.

She pushed him on his chest, and his grin fell. "I am serious. It seems running away is the answer. That is what my mother wanted me to do almost ten years ago. Did she want me to forget as well?"

He paused for a moment to think about what to say. "When I lost Sadeh, I did not want to remember either.

It was easier not to remember her. But when I was reminded of her, I hated myself for the times I spent not remembering her, not acknowledging her existence, and not celebrating her life." He dipped his chin and tilted his head. "I found that once I could remember and smile, then life seemed to move forward."

"My life is moving forward, and I do not want to remember. I cannot remember and smile. Every memory brings me pain of what I have lost." She crossed her arms.

"Is it moving forward, though?" His brow furrowed, and he jangled the reins to settle Ro-en's hoofing.

What an odd question; I just told him it is.

"I am leaving Egypt with you," she stammered, second-guessing herself. "I have learned Akkadian . . . for the most part." She shifted her weight under his gaze.

Why is he looking at me like that?

He lifted his chin, and a slow grin spread on his mouth after a few moments. "You are right. I see that it is moving forward."

She snorted and shook her head. "You are a horrible liar. What do you wish to say?"

He rubbed his chin. "One day, you will understand what I am saying. I will wait for you to understand. It took me a long time." He chuckled in a soft sorrow. "And apparently, as Panhey says, I am a quick study."

She scoffed, glad for the change in subject, although he never really answered her first question or any of her subsequent questions. "I do not want to remember Panhey either. *Any* of him." She circled her hand in front of her face as if erasing every single image of his body in one fell swoop.

Sennedjem tucked her under his arm as they continued to Panhey's estate. "I would rather you not remember him either," he teased. "I do not want those images in your head when you envision me as an old man," he whispered, leaning low to her ear.

She laughed. "They are in the furthest reaches of my mind." She wished the memories of her family would go there too. She glanced back toward the statues of herself and Tut in the fading sunlight. *Those people are gone. My life starts over tomorrow. They will stay in Egypt where they belong, and I will go with Sennedjem to find Nefe and my new life in Canaan.*

She wrapped an arm around Sennedjem's waist and let a smile grow on her face.

CHAPTER 7

SEEKING EXILE

A LONG LINE OF DONKEYS AND CAMELS DEPARTED from Per-Amun, heading north along the Mediterranean Sea coastline. Sennedjem and Ankhesenamun walked among the caravan's family units, and Ro-en trotted beside Sennedjem.

They fell in step alongside the caravan with a full picture of where they were going. They both had committed the map of Egypt's vassal Canaanite city-states to memory. Her grandfather had encouraged her to find refuge in one of those vassal city-states, telling her that if a hostile city-state rose up in an attempt to take over Canaan, Egypt would come to their aid. He had said General Paaten would have known to seek refuge in one of the city-states with Nefe.

But there were so many city-states.

Ankhesenamun looked out at the vast sea.

How do you find one fish in a sea of millions?

A deep breath soothed the anxious fit before it began.

"Are you sad to leave?" Sennedjem shook her hand in his.

"No," she returned her gaze to him. "I am worried we will never find Nefe."

Sennedjem pulled her into a side embrace as they walked.

"We will never know if we do not look." He stared in the direction they were walking. "Do not be discouraged. We have not even started searching yet. Knowing General Paaten, I do not think he would have chosen Azzati . . . or *Hazzatu* in Akkadian?"

She nodded, sure of that name.

"Yes, he would not have chosen Hazzatu. He would be considered a deserter if he were found alive, and the Egyptian army heavily travels that strip of Canaan lying along the sea."

"Then why are we going to Hazzatu?" she asked, thinking it would be a waste of their time.

He chuckled. "We have to stop at Hazzatu. The longest stretch without any cities is from Per-Amun to Hazzatu; we must restock on water and supplies there."

She flicked her eyes to the sky as she chided herself for asking an ignorant question. "So we will not go to Surru, Berytus, or Kubna?"

His lips pressed together in a half-smirk while he shook his head. "We can, but it seems they would not be good places for the former General to live in hiding. He would be identified too easily."

"Do you think he would go to one of the Egyptian administrative centers such as Makedo . . . " she struggled to remember its Akkadian name. "I mean, Magidda?"

He shrugged. "He might go to Magidda; it is not fully in the path of Pharaoh's Army, but the army does go there a fair amount, especially with the Canaan rivals desiring its wealth."

All of the city-states ran together, and they stretched from Addar, southeast of Hazzatu, to Labana, far north of Damaski and Baal-gad. So much land. So many cities.

"Ah, Sennedjem and Khumit!" The Egyptian names spoken with a heavy Akkadian accent jolted her from her thoughts. She peered to the other side of Ro-en. The Canaanite man from the market had turned to them as Sennedjem steadied Ro-en. "You are dressed as Canaanites?"

"Aqhat," Ankhesenamun said, remembering his name.

Aqhat pointed to his family in the caravan line as they slowly made their way alongside them. "We did not realize you were learning Akkadian to journey to Canaan." He laughed, and his small belly laughed with him. "Where are you headed? You may join our caravan if you would like. There is safety in a caravan."

The last statement opened a pit in Ankhesena-mun's stomach. "Safety?"

"Well, in this area, there are not many threats, but when we get into the hillier country, there are raiders. They usually stay away from the larger caravans, though."

"Where are you headed, Aqhat?" Sennedjem asked, switching the conversation fully to Akkadian. He squeezed Ankhesenamun's hand. A tiny tickle of hesitation brushed her innards. She knew why he did it, but she still felt unready.

"Oh," he chuckled, "my family and I are merchants. We go through the lands once every few years and trade with all of the city-states. Then, we return to our home in Magidda to trade exotic items such as Egyptian linen." He smiled warmly at Ankhesenamun. "Thanks to this woman, we were able to get a good deal on a tunic, and it will trade for much more in Magidda." He dipped his chin at her. "We are grateful."

She returned the gesture. He spoke much faster than he had at the markets, and now she had trouble keeping up with him.

"If you are still offering, we would be happy to join your caravan and experience your merchant life," Sennedjem said. "We do not know much about Canaan. We want to travel through the Egyptian vassal states and see what they are like before returning to our home in Hut-Waret."

She understood Sennedjem more than she understood Aqhat; perhaps it was a dialect or accent that differed in Aqhat's speech.

"Ah, travel for pleasure? You must be nobles."

Sennedjem laughed. "There are no nobles of that magnitude in Hut-Waret. No," he shook his head, and Ankhesenamun could sense the hesitation in his voice as he came up with a lie.

Her eyes grew wide before pressing shut. All this time, they had not thought up a reason for why they were leaving Egypt or a backstory for their fictitious personas. They did not think they would have to answer such questions, she supposed, as she considered a response as well. But Sennedjem spoke before she could formulate a good story.

"We are merchants. We trade quality papyrus and other woven-reed items, but our previously fertile lands are no longer fertile. We traded our land to those who needed to build homes, and we have decided to travel to see what we want to do now that our livelihood is gone."

Aqhat's smile faded. "I am sorry to hear about such misfortune. You are free to travel with us. We will be going from Hazzatu to Urusalim, then north to Sakmu, before we return to Magidda. Of course, we will stop at all the city-states on the way."

Sennedjem peered over to Ankhesenamun and smiled.

She smiled too. That was probably a quarter of the land they needed to search. But what about Addar and the cities south of Urusalim? Would they have to leave Magidda and return to them? Or just assume Nefe was not there? It was close to the uninhabitable desert, according to Panhey's map. It would be a hard life to live there. She realized Sennedjem was speaking to her and was waiting for a response.

She froze, her eyes big. She had not heard the question.

He cleared his throat. "Do you want to join them, Khumit?"

Who is Khumit? Her brow furrowed at the silent question. *Oh, I am Khumit. That was the name we chose for me.*

She quickly nodded. "Yes, that would wonderful." She turned to Aqhat. "Thank you for your hospitality."

"Anytime for those who helped us in the Per-Amun markets. Consider it our trade for your hospitality." Aqhat gestured for them to fall into step alongside his family, who drew ahead of them.

Sennedjem jiggled Ro-en's reins as they slowed in their step to align with the caravan.

"Now, if I may ask, where did you learn Akkadian?" Aqhat posed the question to both of them but looked at Sennedjem. "It is quite good."

He looks at Sennedjem because Sennedjem is better at speaking the language than I am. Ankhesenamun's chest filled with a heavy sigh. *Seems I cannot do much outside of the palace.*

"A man we traded with in Egypt." Sennedjem stole

a playful glance to Ankhesenamun. "He is a master of languages."

She tried not to laugh.

"Ah, well. He must be, since you speak so well. Or is it that you are the master of languages, Sennedjem?" Aqhat slapped him on the back.

"I would not call myself that," he said.

Arsiya peered over at them. "Good to see you again," she called out.

"You as well," Ankhesenamun said, noticing that the judging stare Arsiya gave her at the markets was gone.

Aqhat hit his head. "How inconsiderate of me: you have not met the other members of our family. My wife, Arsiya, you know. She spoke highly of you to our caravan after the markets. The whole caravan knows of you, Sennedjem and Khumit." He gestured toward his wife. "She carries our son, Beth-shadon, and my daughters, Shapash and Ishat, walk beside her."

Shapash smiled but hid behind her mother's long tunic.

Memory pricked Ankhesenamun's heart when she found Shapash's eyes. *My eldest daughter would probably be around Shapash's age.* Her jawline grew taut as she stared at Shapash peeking out at her. She had to turn away to keep her tears at bay.

Aqhat was still speaking. "The sister of my wife, Hurriya, and her husband, Heth, are there." He turned and pointed to the couple behind them.

They waved, and Sennedjem returned the greeting.

"The little one strapped to Hurriya is Sidon, their son. The boy beside Heth is their older son, Ug." Aqhat's hand dropped. The rest of the caravan is not related to us, but they are good friends. I will introduce you to all of them when we make camp for the night."

"We are most grateful," Sennedjem said.

Ankhesenamun squeezed his hand. *I am so thankful he is with me. And to think, I was going to come alone!* A chuckle lightened her heart. In its lifted state, she turned her attention to Aqhat's daughters once again. Looking at Ishat and Shapash skip along was like watching a memory of her and Nefe playing together as youngsters.

I am coming, Nefe, she thought. *Finally, after all these years, I am coming.*

CHAPTER 8

SEEKING FRIENDSHIP

THE SUN WAS SETTING IN THE WEST, BEHIND THEM. It had been a few days since they had joined the caravan. They stopped to make camp, deciding they would make the rest of the journey to Hazzatu the next day. The caravan knew Ankhesenamun and Sennedjem as Khumit and Sennedjem, the Egyptians, seeking a new way to support themselves after their misfortune.

Most of the caravan had been friendly, Ankhesenamun decided as she sat in Hurriya's tent along with Arsiya. She looked at the two women who seemed to like her, and she liked them. She had always wanted friends. The only friends she had were her sister Nefe, whom she had not seen since she fled Egypt, and Mut, whom she left in Mennefer.

She smoothed out her long Canaanite tunic that reached her ankles. It was thick and opaque wool, unlike the translucent and lightweight silk and linen she was used to wearing in the palace.

"Do you want to hold him, Khumit?" Hurriya asked her, drawing her attention to Sidon, the baby boy. Ankhesenamun had offered to help care for the children earlier in the day to make herself seem like a typical woman, but they had been hesitant. They had seen through her charade. But in the privacy of the tent, at least, Hurriya and Arsiya were giving her a chance. They seemed genuine enough not to laugh at her . . . in front of her, at least.

She nodded and tried not to be awkward in handling the wiggly, little thing. *I have already embarrassed myself many times with them. How can they not laugh at me? I can barely speak their language, cook, or set up a tent, and now, I can barely hold a child.*

Hurriya handed her a nearby small clay pot as Ankhesenamun adjusted Sidon in her hold.

She looked inside it. *Empty.* She looked for any markings. *None.* She stared at Hurriya. "What is this for?"

Hurriya glanced at Arsiya, and they both chuckled. "Have you no children of your own or never cared for a child before?"

Ankhesenamun's chest constricted at the question. She winced, feeling the sting of holding her two daughters' lifeless bodies.

"Oh, well," Hurriya said, assuming a negative answer. She slid the clay pot under Sidon's little bottom. "When he presses his lips together and a twitch overcomes his nose, that means he must, as we say, *ezû*."

"*Ezû*." She did not know that word. "What is that?"

Hurriya squinted and peered to Arsiya. "How else do you say *ezû*?"

Arsiya shrugged. "Wait until Sidon does it, and then she will know."

Ankhesenamun looked at the clay pot firmly placed under Sidon's bottom. "Oh." She realized what it was. "I see." She held it to his bottom for fear his excrement might get on her tunic.

Hurriya laughed. "He does not need to go now. You wait until he has to go, and then you raise the clay pot."

Her brow wrinkled in concern. "But how will I know?"

Arsiya placed a gentle hand on Ankhesenamun's forearm. "Each child is different, but they will let you know."

Hurriya pointed at Sidon's face. "See, he needs to go."

Almost as soon as she had finished speaking, the clay pot filled, and a slight stench came over the small space between Sidon and Ankhesenamun. "What do I do with it now?"

"We need to wipe him, and then you wash out the pot and the linen." Arsiya handed Ankhesenamun a small linen cloth.

"Where do I wash it out?"

"At the edge of the caravan. Here, use this water from the sea so we do not waste our drinking water washing it." Hurriya reached back and grabbed a small amphora from their sling, and placed it near Ankhesenamun's leg. She studied Ankhesenamun's face before offering, "But I can do it. Sidon is my child."

"No, I said I could care for him . . . for today," she added quickly. But as she held Sidon and the clay pot under his bottom, she wondered how she would remove the clay pot, wipe him, and then wash everything. She chewed her lip as Arsiya and Hurriya stared at her.

"Did you not have siblings or watch your mother care for children? Did your mother not teach you?" Arsiya asked, sensing Ankhesenamun's discomfort.

Visions of her sisters playing in the courtyards of the palace's royal harem passed through her mind. She had no memory of the wet nurses tending to her younger sisters. "No. I had no other siblings, and my mother never cared for other children. I grew up with no other children. I never cared for children . . . " Her voice trailed off as her ramblings became evident. *Quit being awkward,* she told herself. "I do not know what to do," she confessed.

They both stared at her in disbelief. In that moment, she felt completely inadequate, as if she were lacking as a woman and in what women should know.

"Please do not laugh at me," she whispered.

Arsiya leaned forward and clasped her hand over Ankhesenamun's that held Sidon. "We do not laugh at you, Khumit. You do not know what you do not know. You can always learn, especially when you have a child of your own."

She pressed Sidon to lie against Ankhesenamun's lap and helped her to remove the clay pot, using the linen rag to make sure the mess stayed put. She folded it over and wiped his bottom. She laid the dirty side down on the edge of the pot and placed it aside. "See, it is not hard."

Ankhesenamun nodded. "How do you wash the pot while holding him?" She glanced at the long linen wraps that she had seen Hurriya wearing earlier in the day that securely strapped Sidon to her chest.

"Yes," Hurriya said, noticing her glance. "You strap the baby to your chest, and, when they are older, to your back. It leaves your hands free to do what you need to do for the rest of the family."

Ankhesenamun pressed her lips together as a soft burn touched her cheeks. "Please do not laugh at me."

Hurriya smiled. "We do not laugh. I had never considered there was a woman who had not been taught how to care for children at an early age. It surprises me, but I do not laugh at you, Khumit. We are here to teach you."

"I am grateful," Ankhesenamun said with a dip of her chin. "I do not know many things about the home."

"Why is that?" Arsiya asked.

Her eyes darted between the two women about her age. She should have had children by now, as they did, but she only had the two daughters that Pawah murdered. The thought of him rendered her mute and caused hot tears to form in her eyes.

"We do not need to know," Hurriya quickly responded upon seeing the change in Ankhesenamun's face.

Ankhesenamun nodded and handed Sidon back to Hurriya. "I will go wash this." She left quickly with the pot and the amphora of salty sea water.

Forget. Please, she begged of herself.

THE DESIRE TO SWIPE AWAY THE FOUL AIR IN FRONT of her nose came over her as she cleaned out Sidon's clay pot. "This is not pleasant." She gritted her teeth and attempted to perform the entire task without taking another breath.

Sennedjem walked up beside her and watched her with a smile. "What are you doing?" he asked, cajoling her to speak.

Curse you, Sennedjem. You know what I am doing.

She did not open her mouth to speak the thought but simply nodded her head toward the clay pot.

"Cleaning out an infant's pot?"

She nodded.

"How do you feel about it?"

She cut a glare over to him as he smirked. The urge to thrust the pot into his chest for him to perform the task almost dominated her restraint.

He must have sensed it, too, for he took a large step away from her.

She braved a breath as she rinsed it clean and wrung the linen out.

"Coward," she hissed.

He only grinned, crossed his arms, and shrugged.

She spun around to go back to Hurriya's tent. He followed close on her heels. "Where are you going?" she muttered.

"With you," he said. "Wherever you go, my Queen."

She stopped and faced him. Her eyes glanced around. "You must not call me that, Sennedjem." Her whisper was barely audible.

He popped a peck on her lips. "I can call you whatever I want."

Her eyes narrowed at him. *He is in a happy mood. I wonder why.*

"Is that your term of endearment for me?"

"Yes, my Queen."

"Then, next time, *you* clean the infant's pot." She jabbed a finger in his chest. She huffed and continued on her way.

He snickered and fell into step beside her. "I did not realize royal women did not learn anything about the home," his whisper came.

"Why would we?" Ankhesenamun stopped, again

seeing her lifeless daughters flash before her. Her voice no longer held a playful tone. "The stations of wet nurse and nurse were beneath us. They took care of the children." The searing pain spread to her fingers and toes. *Forget. Please forget.*

Sennedjem heard the shift, and his grin faded. "What is wrong?"

She shrugged, clamping her teeth down hard atop a rigid jaw. Tears glistened in her eyes, and then she averted her gaze. "Nothing." She turned to go, but he grabbed her wrist and stared into her eyes.

"Something," he whispered.

She yanked her wrist from his light grasp. "I said, 'Nothing.'" She spoke through her clenched teeth.

"Your daughters?" he asked as she turned again from him.

She stopped in her step. Her eyes pressed shut. *How can I forget my children?* she wanted to cry.

Sennedjem's hand smoothed over her shoulder and down her back as she realized he now stood before her, wrapping her up in his arms. "It is good to remember," he whispered in her ear.

"I cannot, and it is not good." She pushed past him. "It will never be good." She ducked into the tent with Hurriya and Arsiya.

"Is that Sennedjem?" Arsiya called from inside upon seeing him standing there when Ankhesenamun entered.

Ankhesenamun looked at the tent flap. "Yes."

"Sennedjem," Hurriya called.

Sennedjem ducked down but stayed outside as he held the flap open. "I am here."

"Did you know your wife is good with children?" Hurriya asked.

Good? How can she say that? I barely knew how to clean an infant's mess. Ankhesenamun's brow furrowed, and her gaze fell. *Are they mocking me?*

Sennedjem stared at the side of her face. "We have never had children, but I assumed my wife would be good with children." He grinned a sad smile at Ankhesenamun.

Arsiya seemed to notice, and her eyes darted back and forth between the two of them.

"Are you going to have children?" Hurriya asked.

A dark stab to her heart nearly took Ankhesenamun's breath away. She opened her mouth to speak, but nothing came out.

Sennedjem spoke for her, and she silently thanked him. He always knew when she needed him.

"I misspoke; we have had two children. Daughters. They were stillborn. We are trying to move past our sorrow. When we have done so, we may try again."

Ankhesenamun heard the slight uptick in Sennedjem's voice. Had it been a statement or a question? She recalled his mention of wanting a wife and children in the royal harem at Malkata. *It is a question to me,* she assumed. She saw that future with him, but it seemed far away. She nodded, nonetheless.

His half-smile beamed at her and made her take a

deep breath. *I can see that future with him*, she told herself.

Hurriya sighed and rubbed Ankhesenamun's back. "Sweet woman; I know this pain. I have had three children who no longer live in this life."

Arsiya nodded along. "I have had one. It is hard to lose your children, Khumit. But birthing new life is hard, and it is dangerous. So many things can go wrong."

Except my children were murdered. Ankhesenamun took a cool breath and nodded politely at their attempts at comfort.

Hurriya looked at Sennedjem. "You both deserve a living child, Khumit and Sennedjem. You are good people, and you would be good parents."

One day, maybe. Ankhesenamun glanced at Ishat, Shapash, Sidon and Beth-shadon. *If I knew how to care for children,* she thought. Her heart longed for her daughters, but simultaneously, she wondered how she could love the children she would have in the future if they reminded her of her two daughters taken by Pawah.

Forget Pawah. Pawah is dead. She paused. *But his actions live on. My children are still not with me.*

"The sun is set, Khumit," Sennedjem said. "Perhaps we should go to our own tent."

Arsiya chuckled. "You have a lean-to, not a tent. You should trade for a tent. It is more private." She winked at Ankhesenamun, who pressed her lips together and then averted her gaze. The lean-to

Sennedjem had assembled for them like he had done every night, was simple: two small rods driven into the sandy earth, a blanket draped over them, and the blanket's edges secured to the ground with rocks. It barely provided a barrier from the weather elements over their heads.

Hurriya jabbed her sister with her elbow. "Not in front of Sennedjem." She shook her head and dipped her chin to him. "Our tribe does not speak of such blatancies in front of mixed company."

Sennedjem peered in and looked at Arsiya and Hurriya. "We are Egyptians. It makes no difference to me."

"See?" Arsiya jabbed her sister back.

Ankhesenamun chuckled, finding their sisterly banter funny. "Our lean-to will be fine for now, Sennedjem. We will make sure no one sees us kiss."

"Just kiss?" Arsiya smiled a knowing grin.

"Yes." Ankhesenamun glanced at Sennedjem. *I am not ready for that,* she thought.

He seemed to read her mind, and he nodded with an understanding smile.

"Yes, that is something that is different in Canaan," Arsiya wagged a finger. "In Egypt, I noticed, couples hold hands and kiss in the common areas. Not so in Canaan." She pointed at Ankhesenamun. "Especially you, Khumit. You will be labeled a *šamḫatu.*" She searched for another meaning Ankhesenamun could understand: "a harlot."

Hurriya continued. "Even though having relations

is a form of worship of some goddesses in Canaan, you are not a priestess, and you will not be honored."

Ankhesenamun licked her lip in hesitation. "I cannot even hold my husband's hand?"

Hurriya shook her head in opposition but then seemed to think some more on the question before nodding her head. "In this caravan, you can. We all know you are Egyptian, but I would not once we enter the city-states. In some of those city-states, you should not say you are Egyptian either. Some of them hate Egyptians, and you could be killed in the streets."

Killed in the streets?

Sennedjem grinned. "They could try to kill us." He cocked his head. "We are both fighters."

A small, soft chuckle escaped her. He knew what to say to make her feel better. He had spent almost ten years teaching her how to fight. Even though she thought her skills were laughable, he had often told her that they were good. She hoped he had not lied to her, now that she might need them again.

"Fighters?" Hurriya asked, her eyes once again darting between the two foreigners.

Oh, no. We are supposed to be papyrus merchants, Ankhesenamun thought as Sennedjem winced.

Ankhesenamun tilted her head as she spoke a lie. "Yes. Sennedjem was a member of Pharaoh's Army, but he resigned when he married me. He did not want to be away from me as much as a soldier would have to be away from his wife."

The sisters looked at each other and covered their hearts with their hands. "What a sweet husband." Arsiya wagged her finger at Ankhesenamun. "Khumit, you had better keep him. I know Egyptians allow divorce, but you had better never rid yourself of him."

Ankhesenamun looked at Sennedjem. "I have no plans to."

A warm smile came over his face.

"So you know how to fight as well?" Hurriya asked, breaking her connection with Sennedjem.

She nodded. "Yes. Sennedjem taught me."

"Really?" She turned her gaze to Sennedjem. "Would you be able to teach our husbands and the other men of the camp? It would help when we go into the lands of the raiders."

He nodded. "I can do that."

"Good, good." She nodded and patted Sidon on the belly, causing him to squeal.

Ankhesenamun looked at the two little families in the tent and smiled. She could see herself with Nefe interacting like Arsiya and Hurriya: their children playing together while they sat and joked with new friends. The vision brought a warm smile to her face. But finding Nefe would be the hard part.

She whispered, "Sleep well."

"You too," Arsiya said. "Oh, and Khumit, women in Canaan do not fight. Do not let anyone outside our caravan know you are able to fight like a man. Most of the men would not take offense at these things, as we know you are Egyptian and have Egyptian ways, but some may. If you did so in a city-state, you would probably be dragged to a temple of Chemosh and sacrificed. Or you would be stoned or burned or killed in another manner for not being like other women."

"Is that all?" Ankhesenamun asked, recounting the number of ways she could die in Canaan for simply kissing or defending herself: being sacrificed, stoned, or burned.

"Yes." Arsiya nodded, not understanding the derision behind Ankhesenamun's words.

A heavy sigh escaped her chest. "Well then, sleep well."

"You too, Khumit."

CHAPTER 9

SEEKING HAZZATU

THE SANDS OF HAZZATU SWEPT INTO THE RIPPLING waves of the sea. The scent of salt in the air was fresh and crisp. Ankhesenamun stood facing the water. As the sea breeze whipped over and underneath each of her outspread arms, she obliged the urge to lift her hands above her head. The setting sun warmed one side of her face while the shadows encompassed the other side, chilled from the sea breeze.

The stark contrast between the chill and the warmth reminds me of my life: wanting to embrace the new day, only to have the biting sting of nightmares in its wake.

She closed her eyes and wanted to pray, but to which god? Who would listen to her after she cursed them for allowing Tut to be killed?

That secret gnawed at her belly, as did the fruitless hunt for her sister that she and Sennedjem had undertaken in Hazzatu that day. No one had ever heard of or remembered a man named Paaten or Atinuk or a woman named Aitye. She had been too afraid to mention Nefe's name. For surely, Neferneferuaten Tasherit would draw attention, as would Ankhesenamun.

Her fingers stretched to the sky until her back finally loosened, and then her arms fell with a thud to her sides.

Sennedjem told me they were probably not in Hazzatu. I allowed myself to become too hopeful. I thought we would at least find someone who remembered them in their journey onward, but today yielded nothing.

Her body bristled as the crisp breeze whipped underneath her headdress and the hem of her long, itchy tunic. The market behind her still bustled, but soon, she heard the shouts of merchants telling people to come back tomorrow.

"Where are you, Nefe?" she whispered. The panorama of the vast sea awaited her as she opened her eyes.

Familiar steps approached.

"Did you want to get a tent?" Sennedjem's soft voice tickled her ear. She wished he would speak in Egyptian to her when they were alone, but she knew why he did not. She still needed the practice. "A merchant is willing to trade one for a good deal."

Tension swept into her shoulders. A tent meant privacy . . .

"How will we carry it?" she asked, still looking out at the sea.

"It is small. Ro-en could carry it without difficulty; I could even carry it, if Ro-en tired."

She peered over her shoulder at him. "Do you think we will need the trade goods for something else on our search? Would it be better to trade for this now or to be better prepared for the future?"

He rubbed his mouth. "We can always trade the tent for a lean-to again if we need the trade goods." He looked back at the merchant and raised his hand to alert him he was coming. His hand brushed her arm.

"Whatever you think is best, Protector." Ankhesenamun turned back toward the sea as he walked away with a furrowed brow. She assumed he would look back at her, wondering why she was not excited about a tent. *Why would I not be excited about a tent? It provides much more privacy than we have now. It would provide more protection from wildlife and elements. The men who keep watch at night would not be able to watch us sleep.* She gulped. *We could be together . . .*

She remembered back to her last visit to Mennefer. As Horemheb loaded the horse, he told her Tut's last words to her as well.

"Horemheb even said he thought Tut would be happy for me as long as Sennedjem loves me and takes care of me."

Tut wanted me to find someone who loves me as he did . . . . someone who can grow to love me even more.

"After all the accusations, after all the lies of infidelity, is it wrong of me to find happiness with

Sennedjem?" She shook her head, recounting
Horemheb's answer to the same question. "It is not
wrong . . ."

But what?

An answer would not come. Her heart was
conflicted, and it confused her senses. The calm of
the sea lost its effect as she stared into a great
unknown.

What now?

Someone touched her arm and startled her.

Her body quivered in the crisp sea breeze once
more as she turned to see who it was. "Oh, Sennedjem." He had strapped a large roll of thickly woven
brown fabric and a large wooden pole to Ro-en.

"We have a tent." He grinned and brushed her
generous tunic sleeve with his, careful not to hold her
hand. "The sun is almost set. We need to return to
the camp, so I can set it up before nightfall."

She nodded but said nothing. Her feet began to
walk toward the edge of the city where the caravan
was staying for a few days. Tomorrow they would try
the ports, but Ankhesenamun knew that would be in
vain. So many people come and go through the ports.
No one would remember anyone from ten years ago
who may have passed through once.

Sennedjem walked beside her. "Are you feeling
well?"

"I need to lie down. I am tired from today," she
said softly.

Sennedjem looked off toward the center of

Hazzatu, where the Egyptian administrative buildings were. "It is only the first city, Ankhesenamun," he whispered in Egyptian.

It is good to hear that language again, but I need to forget that past. I need to practice speaking Akkadian so I can better find my sister.

"There are many cities out there. We will find her," he whispered again in their native tongue.

"I know," she responded in Akkadian. "I am just tired."

He maneuvered Ro-en to the opposite side so that the small donkey blocked the city's view of them as they walked along the shoreline. His hand snuck to hers, and he peered over at her. "Then we can sleep well tonight, and tomorrow we can start at the ports, well-rested."

"That sounds perfect, Sennedjem." The tension in her shoulders slipped away since she knew that night would be restful. The boxed bed at Panhey's was uncomfortable, but the thin cot on the ground, vulnerable to the weather elements, was unbearable, especially compared to sleeping in a bed with a head-rest and a linen-wrapped wool mattress at Malkata.

That luxury would probably never come again. Most Canaanites slept on the floor atop cots or large cushions. She peered at Ro-en, wondering if he could carry better, thicker cots.

"I also got us a thicker cot to sleep on." Sennedjem smirked.

How does he seem to know what I am thinking?

Her gaze lifted to his. "Thank you," she whispered. She chased the ache from her back by rolling her shoulders. "Even on the barge, there was a lounger for me to sleep on."

He chuckled. "Yes, my Queen."

She popped him in the chest with a playful flick of her hand. "Do not say such things."

"Yes, my Queen."

She only shook her head in response.

They came upon the campsite just as the last of the sun was shining out over the horizon. Sennedjem quickly unloaded Ro-en and began to set up the tent. He built up a small altar of rocks in a tall circle and then put the wooden pole into the middle so it stood tall.

"Ankhesenamun, can you help me?" he asked, and she walked over to him.

He lifted the large piece of cloth over the top of the pole, and they spread out their tent, securing the perimeter with rocks. He took out two poles half the size of the middle pole and secured them in the same way on one edge of the circular tent to give it a little bit of headroom and an entrance.

She stood back and looked at it.

It was indeed small, but at least it was almost triple the size of their lean-to. It would certainly provide them much more protection from the chilly sea winds.

His arm wrapped around her just as the sunset. "I will make some dinner."

He set out to make the fire while Ankhesenamun grabbed the small cooking pot and the satchel containing beans, spices, and an amphora of salt water. They had been lucky to be by the sea all this time. They could save their drinking water by cooking with seawater. Its salts also helped to flavor the food. She unpacked the fish and the vegetables Sennedjem had traded for in the market and helped him prepare their meal.

SHE HANDED HIM A BOWL OF FISH AND BEANS, AND she sat next to him, ready to eat. She looked up at Shapash and the other children playing outside of Arsiya's tent as the fire blazed and the family finished up dinner.

"Do you want children someday?" Sennedjem's question hung in the air as she watched Shapash.

Ankhesenamun cleared her throat. "Someday." Her chin quickly dropped, and she focused on her food. She still felt Sennedjem's stare upon the side of her face. "What do you want to ask me?"

"We will find Nefe," he said and rubbed her knee. He leaned over and kissed her temple before beginning to eat once more.

She pulled at her food. The meat of the fish flaked off easily. *Sennedjem is a good cook—much better than I am.* It looked appetizing, but at the same time, she felt she had lost her appetite.

What is wrong with me? I am in Canaan. I am searching for my sister. Sennedjem is with me. We will be fine. We will find her. She nodded her head and began to eat as well.

After they ate, she cleaned while he leaned down to kiss her. "The men want me to teach them another lesson," he said. "I will come to you when we are finished. The thicker cot is already in the tent. I snuck it in there while you were cleaning." His grin was contagious. "Sleep well. If you are still awake when I return, I will tell you goodnight properly."

She smirked, revisiting their evenings in Panhey's house. "I will do my best to stay awake."

He shook his head. "I want you to get some sleep. We have another long day tomorrow."

"Yes, Protector," she whispered with a smile.

He leaned in for one more kiss before he left. She finished cleaning up and patted Ro-en on the nose as he grazed the ruddy plants. "Sleep well, Ro-en." She unloaded him and brought their sling of goods into the tent for safekeeping. She found the cot Sennedjem had rolled out. She tried to move it out of the way as she positioned their travel slings within the tent, but it did not budge.

"Poor Ro-en," she muttered as she shuffled the slings to the empty side of the tent. The pole did not allow for the cot to be fully centered in the tent, but the tent was still better than the lean-to. She stood up next to the pole; the cot looked soft, and it beckoned her. She fell into the cot, knees first, and then flat on her belly.

Indeed, it was soft.

She repositioned herself and propped her head up with their long blanket roll. "Some semblance of luxury," she whispered. Her mind emptied of the day's; no, the month's; nay, the year's; rather, the decade's cares. She thought of nothing except the desire to sleep and hoped she would not have to endure another nightmare.

CHAPTER 10
SEEKING URUSALIM

"WELCOME TO URUSALIM," A MAN STANDING NEXT to the city gate shouted at the caravan. "You are entering the reign of Chieftain Abdi-Heba." His long white tunic and purple robe depicted his regal designation. "Thieves will be punished by the removal of a hand. Murderers will be stoned. Welcome, all traders."

Sennedjem brushed Ankhesenamun's hand. "Do not steal anything, my Queen," he whispered. "I would miss holding your hand."

Her deep brown pools peered up at him. "Do not kill anyone. I would miss holding you at night."

He forced his hand to stay by his side and chuckled instead. If they had been in Per-Amun, he would have wrapped his arm around her shoulders and pulled her close.

Aqhat pulled his donkey up beside Ro-en.

"Sennedjem, the men of the caravan were discussing last night that we want you to teach us more fighting while the women cook the dinner." He slashed the air with his hand with a hard grunt. "You are a good teacher. You should not sell papyrus. You should teach fighting." He slashed again with another grunt.

Sennedjem laughed. "Of course, friend. After we are done trading in Urusalim, we will meet back at the campsite."

"While the sun is still in the sky, Sennedjem. It is too dark to truly see you and learn what you teach when the sun is gone." Aqhat patted his donkey on the neck. "And since Shalim is the god of this city, we do not want to interfere with his worship."

Sennedjem opened his mouth to ask what he meant, but Aqhat kept talking.

"Shalim is our god of the setting sun, and the city of Urusalim is named for him," Aqhat said. "Worship of him begins at sunset. We need you to teach us before then."

Sennedjem nodded along as Aqhat continued. "And, Khumit—Arsiya and Hurriya want you to go to their tent when you are done in the city." He looked around at the men in the caravan. "Why do you even come to Urusalim?"

She opened her mouth to respond, but Aqhat continued. "Only the men go to the city-states to trade, but you have come with Sennedjem in every city. Is this an Egyptian custom?"

"Arsiya came with you in Per-Amun," Ankhese-namun quickly threw into the conversation as Aqhat took a breath between sentences.

"Well, yes, because there were women in that market."

Ankhesenamun gestured to the marketplace, where the merchants sat under their fabric awnings. "There are women here too . . . "

Sennedjem followed her gesture. *Man. Man. Man. Man. I do not see any women.*

Aqhat pointed. "There is a woman, but she draws water from the well for her family. Women stay in the home. Men go."

Ankhesenamun's brow knitted. "Go where?"

"Everywhere," Aqhat chuckled. "If you are trying to hide the fact that you are Egyptian, you should not go into the cities. Everyone knows you are an Egyptian woman if you do. I assume you are trying to hide it since you dress like us. Sennedjem, you can be here, but Khumit should not be."

Sennedjem waited for Aqhat to continue speaking. He had almost tuned him out, but the silence drew his attention. Aqhat's face boasted raised eyebrows and wide eyes while he waited for Sennedjem's response.

"Ah, well." *What had he asked me?* "Ankhes—"

"—Khumit—" Ankhesenamun blurted.

His heart skipped a beat at his blunder. "Khumit should come with me. I need to make sure she is safe.

She is my wife, after all. She is my partner in business. She needs to be here." He rambled, and he knew it. To keep from further rambling, he shut his mouth.

"She would probably be safer in the caravan."

"Are there raiders here? You speak of the lands of raiders quite often," Sennedjem asked.

"No, their lands are north of here." Aqhat pointed off in a general direction of south, but then he realigned himself and pointed north. "All I say is this: women do not perform men's responsibilities here."

"Is this city safe for Egyptians?"

Aqhat leaned toward them and raised his hand to block others from seeing his mouth. "Any city-state that does not have an Egyptian administrative center is probably not as safe as you think it should be."

"I see. Well, we have business to do, and, hopefully, no one will bother two travelers."

Aqhat shook his head. "We cannot protect you should a chieftain or even a mob take you for this reason or that."

"Thank you for the warning, but we will be fine. We were fine in Gerar, Libnah, and, well, all the city-states between Hazzatu and Urusalim; we will be fine here too."

"Suit yourself," he murmured with a defeated shrug.

Sennedjem waved him off as they took to the side streets. They began knocking on doors and asking those who answered if they had ever encountered anyone by the name of Atinuk, Aitye, or Paaten. As with Hazzatu, Gerar, Gath, Libnah, Lakisha, Makkedah, Jarmuth, and Ekron before, no one remembered those people or knew their names. Ankhesenamun's shoulders drooped lower with every door.

———

THEY STEPPED OUT OF THE SIDE STREETS AND INTO the markets. Ankhesenamun scanned the open area, taking in its dreariness and comparing it to the day of searching.

Aqhat and other members of the caravan stood on the other side of the grand courtyard filled with merchant's tents. The marketplace, although large and bustling, lacked the vibrancy and splendor of that of Per-Amun. Ceramic pots, woven baskets, barley and grain, white and brown tunics, and other craft trades were laid about the ground to entice traders. The markets seemed ordinary—even the columns that upheld a small overhang remained plain, unpainted, and unplastered. No tales of greatness were engraved on their surfaces; no elaborate colors of red, blue, or yellow adorned the cylinders; natural white stone was the only feature. Each marketplace was the same as every other city-state they had been to.

These Canaanites know how to forget their history . . .

by not writing it down or, in the very least, plastering it over the walls for all to see and remember.

The two thicker stone entry pillars to the Canaanite temples of the god Shalim and of the goddess Anat faced the market.

A sea of people formed one blur in front of her. "We will never find her," she muttered to herself.

"We will be here three days, Ankhesenamun," Sennedjem whispered, overhearing her. "We can search the rest of the city later."

"I agree. Let us trade for our supplies and go back to the campsite," she said, staring at the goddess's temple for a long time. *I wonder if the Canaanite gods would have saved their King?* The thought of Tut stabbed her in the belly. *Forget. Have peace.*

"Their goddess is Anat. She is like our Hathor," Sennedjem whispered in her ear as he stood behind her.

She only nodded before walking toward the markets. *I cursed Hathor. I cursed all of them. Sennedjem prays every morning and night to Hathor and Isis, and I cannot do so. But maybe, when I see Nefe again, I will rescind my curse. I may worship them again . . . one day. But if I never find Nefe, I want no part of them.*

She stepped up to a merchant booth and found the eyes of the merchantman, noticing how his polite smile faded. "Greetings. We are looking for a family member. Do you know of a man named Atinuk or a woman named Aitye?"

He peered up at her in silence with a demeaning

scowl on his face. The darkness in his eyes swallowed any sunlight that befell them. The gurgle in the back of his throat made her step backward just as he spat at her feet. "Woman," he muttered and sneered.

Sennedjem appeared beside her and gently guided her back to Ro-en as he spoke. "Greetings. Do those names sound familiar to you? We are looking for a family member."

He responded to Sennedjem with a grunt and a headshake. "But you look like you want to trade?" He held up an intricately formed grain-colored ceramic vase.

Ankhesenamun thought it was like everything else in this marketplace—lacking.

"Perhaps later," Sennedjem politely declined and ushered Ankhesenamun on. She peered over her shoulder at the merchant and saw the same sneer form on his face as he watched them walk onward. Her gaze shifted to the wandering eyes watching her, the one oddity of the plain place.

Even as Chief Royal Wife, I have never had so many eyes on me. These men truly hate me for being a woman in a man's place.

But a new thought came upon her. Her chin lifted and her nose turned up. *It matters not to me what these petty men think. I will find Nefe, regardless of them.*

They asked every merchant they came upon if they had heard of those they sought, but each time the answer was "no." She stood next to Ro-en while

Sennedjem traded and inquired, and with every head-shake, her stare grew more vacant.

The lingering temple of Anat in the background of the marketplace weighed heavy on her mind. *I want no part of you, Hathor, goddess of deception and lies. I want no part of you, all of you gods and goddesses of Egypt.*

CHAPTER 11

SEEKING ADVICE

Sennedjem left her to prepare dinner; he went to teach the caravan men while the sun was high in the sky. Ankhesenamun covered the bread in the bowl as a shadow appeared over her. She peered up to see Shapash.

"Greetings, Khumit," Shapash said and waved.

"Greetings, Shapash."

"My mother said you should have made the bread in the morning. It will not be ready by the time to eat dinner." Her shoulders swung.

"Is that so?" A pink tint graced her cheeks. "Well, tell your mother that I was making bread for tomorrow."

A big smile came upon Shapash's face as she spun around and ran off.

Ankhesenamun chuckled at her and pushed away the thought that her eldest daughter might have done the same. Her gaze fell on the fish in front of her. "So we shall have only fish tonight, Sennedjem." She glanced at the bread. "Cooking is hard, and I will never be good at it."

She held the fish up by the tail before laying it down before her. Her fingers slipped around the knife's handle, and its blade captured her attention. A sudden memory forced itself upon her: Pawah's hands on her neck in the hall of Malkata. She had wriggled loose using Sennedjem's teachings. In her mind, the handle of the hidden dagger from her belt became the handle of the knife she held to ready the fish. She had slid her blade up Pawah's chest and chin. His bright red blood oozed from the slice. Her heart beat faster as she remembered. The desire to plunge that blade deep into Pawah's chest rushed through her hand once again. *But I wanted him to suffer.* Her knuckles went white around the knife in her hand, just as they had with the dagger three years ago. Her chest rose and fell with a steady breath. *Forget.*

Her gaze returned to the fish; its empty eyes stared off into a void. *Just like my mother's . . . Just like Tut's . . .*

She sighed and sat back on her heels, unable to relinquish the memory. A hot rage flushed over her face. *I should have killed him then.* As she thought back to standing over Pawah's body, the knife twirled in her hand: a useless trick Sennedjem had taught her.

"I got my wish," she whispered. "I know you suffered in agonizing pain," she spoke to her memory of Pawah, but her chin quivered. She slammed the knife through the fish. "If I had killed you then, Mut would have never been harmed by you." A hot tear rolled down her cheek as the swirling rage rekindled once again in her chest and roiling stomach. She had withheld her anger. She had withheld her rage. Mut had paid the price. "Even in death, Pawah, you still haunt me."

Her eyes closed as another tear chased its twin. She spoke to the memory of that evil creature: "If you were alive in the afterlife, I know you would be pleased with yourself."

The weight of Pawah's deeds fell upon her rigid back, causing it to slump. Her grip on the knife loosened until her hand dropped into her lap. "Never again will I hold back from killing a murderer," she whispered to herself.

She sat and stared at the fish with a knife in its gut. The knowledge of how to prepare a fish had left her. In a fleeting moment, she desired Sennedjem's arms around her and his hands guiding hers in holding the knife to prepare the fish, as he had at Panhey's estate.

Sennedjem. Her chest rose with a deep breath. She looked out over the hill where the men were learning how to fight. She could not see them, but she heard their grunts, snorts, and mocking laughs of each other. An image of Sennedjem in his shendyt standing before her in the Malkata's training yard came to her. It was the day she had come to tell him she would be married to the next Pharaoh succeeding her grandfather. Whoever that was would not be as lenient with her visits to the training yard. She had come then to say goodbye to him, but the words had never crossed her lips. He was her friend. He was loyal.

He still is.

Her chin rolled to her chest. *And yet I refuse him night after night. Any other man would have left me by now, but he still stays with me.* Another source of guilt pressed into her heart.

A small shadow appeared next to her again. She snapped her head to the person standing there, and a warm smile crossed her lips.

"My mother says you can have some of our bread," Shapash said.

"Your mother is most kind," Ankhesenamun replied.

"But you have to come get it," Shapash pointed to their tent.

Ankhesenamun chuckled. "I will," she said, standing up.

Shapash took her hand, and they walked side by side to Arsiya's tent. Ankhesenamun peered down at Shapash, taking in her dark hair and dark eyes. "My daughter"—her voice broke—"my daughter would have been about your age." Her whisper barely made it over her tongue.

Shapash looked up at her. "Then we can be friends!"

Ankhesenamun patted her hand. "Yes," she said softly. "You could have been friends."

Shapash wrapped her arms around Ankhesenamun's thighs and squeezed. "I wish she could be here. I want to meet her."

She rubbed her neck. *Why did I say anything? She must not understand.* She looked up to the sun-filled sky. "She is not here, Shapash."

"Oh." Shapash's hands dropped from their embrace. "Does she not like us?"

Ankhesenamun knelt in front of the small girl. "She would love you," she whispered, lifting Shapash's chin. "I miss her. She is in the afterlife."

Shapash nodded as if she knew the pain. "The land of Mot."

"Is that your afterlife?"

"It is where the dead go," Shapash shrugged. "They do not live here anymore." It was said so matter-of-factly, it caused Ankhesenamun to fall back to her heel.

"Yes, they are not here anymore."

Shapash pursed her lips and pulled on Ankhesenamun's arm. "We need to get you some bread"—she ducked inside the open tent flap—"since you do not know how to take care of a home."

Arsiya called from within the tent. "I said something like that to her, Khumit; she is only repeating and in poor recollection. I meant no harm by my words."

Ankhesenamun shook her head. *I am running out*

of excuses for why I do not know how to do any of this work. She entered the tent. "Greetings, Arsiya."

"I truly meant no harm with my words, Khumit," she said and shook her head. "Here, come sit."

Ankhesenamun swallowed as she did what was requested of her. She liked Arsiya and her sister Hurriya, but they made her feel inadequate.

Arsiya stared at her and tapped her lip. "I have figured something out."

"What have you figured out?" She shifted under her stare.

"You and Sennedjem are rich. You have lots of servants, and this is why you do not know these things." Her eyes grew wide. "You only say you are merchants."

What to say to that? She chewed her lip. "Rich?" she asked and tilted her head in question.

Arsiya laughed and laid a playful slap on Ankhesenamun's shoulder. "I knew it." She called Hurriya. "Hurriya, come quick!"

Not a moment after, Hurriya appeared at the entrance to Arsiya's tent. "What is it?"

"Do you know how we spoke the other day about Khumit and Sennedjem?" Arsiya nodded her head toward Ankhesenamun.

"Yes," Hurriya said, her eyes growing bright as she ducked inside and plopped down before them. "Are you rich, Khumit?"

Her gaze fell to her hands as they wrung. *What to say?*

"Silence is enough of an answer." Hurriya laughed. "Why are you sleeping in a tent on a caravan in Canaan when you are rich enough not to have to run a house?" she asked through heaving laughs as she wiped the tears from her eyes.

"We are not rich," Ankhesenamun said. Her eyes darted between the two sisters as she tried to formulate an answer.

Hurriya's laughter died down as the two sisters threw her a disbelieving stare.

"Not anymore," she whispered, forcing her hands to still.

A warm hand fell upon hers. Arsiya's dark brown eyes met her gaze. "What happened, Khumit? Why are you in Canaan, really?"

"We have lost everyone." Ankhesenamun began, her voice sticking to her constricted throat. She had not wanted to say it, but it was said now. *How to tell? What to tell?* "We sold everything we had and left. We decided to visit Hazzatu but decided we would go with you when we came upon your caravan. Perhaps we will go back to Egypt once you reach Magidda, but we do not see a future there at this time."

"Is this because you lost your two daughters?"

The question punched her in the stomach. She had not been ready for it and nearly lost her composure. She wanted to blurt *Because I lost my whole family! They were taken from me.*

"Dear Khumit," Arsiya cupped her cheek while her head tilted from sympathy, "you cannot run from your past. You must face it. Only then can you live in the present and plan for the future." Arsiya patted her hand.

"I do not know how to do that," Ankhesenamun whispered, letting some tears escape.

Hurriya scooted closer and wrapped her large arms around her. "My friend," she crooned. "It is different for each mother." She loosened her tight embrace and sat back. "My sister"—she gestured to Arsiya—"she grieved for a long time and wished to be alone. Then one day, she emerged a new woman. For me, I wanted to surround myself with my family. I needed them. I needed to hear laughter." She shook Ankhesenamun's shoulder. "What do you wish? What do you need?"

Ankhesenamun's gaze fell between Hurriya and Arsiya as she debated telling them. "I wish to forget."

They shared a glance before Arsiya took Ankhesenamun's hand. "If that is what you truly need, then I wish it for you."

Hurriya pressed her lips together into a smile.

They do not think I should forget. Sennedjem has told me the same. What am I not seeing?

She pulled her hand from Arsiya's. "What is it that you are not telling me?"

"I could never forget my child, but perhaps it is because I have living children?" Arsiya glanced at Ishat and Shapash taking care of Beth-shadon. "When I put sackcloth on my body, I was grieving my loss. But in my mind, I committed my son's lost life to my heart. I decided he would live through me."

Arsiya's words knocked Ankhesenamun into a haze. Her face fell sullen and sallow. Her body stilled. She repeated her words in her mind: *I committed my son's lost life to my heart; I decided he would live through me.*

It sounded so easy to do. Tears pricked her eyes as her daughters' faces flashed in memory. "I will commit them to my heart," she said, her voice barely a whisper. "My daughters will live through me."

Both sisters' lips spread wide into kind and supportive smiles. "Good," Arsiya whispered in return.

That day she was haunted by their memory; the next day, she would not be anymore.

"Thank you." Ankhesenamun dipped her chin in gratitude.

Arsiya held a sad chuckle on her breath as she reached over to a bowl on the side of the tent. "Here is your bread, my friend. Enjoy it with Sennedjem tonight." She wrapped a small chunk in a piece of linen and placed it into Ankhesenamun's hand. She leaned in close. "Enjoy him tonight, too." The corner of her mouth popped into a grin. "Loving your husband will make it better."

Ankhesenamun's cheeks flooded red.

Hurriya chuckled. "We talk about this in front of your husband, and you do not blush. But here, in the presence of only women, you blush." She shook her head. "Egyptians are funny."

Ankhesenamun chuckled politely but fiddled with the bread in her hand until it drew her attention. The thoughts plagued her: *I am attracted to Sennedjem. I am deeply attracted to him. I want to be with him. I want a family with him. I want a future with him. But* . . . she did not know what had held her back every night since they had been together.

"Oh my." Hurriya's chuckle turned into concerned silence.

She closed her eyes, knowing they had guessed as much. These women were like seers. They were both able to see through her—it seemed as though they were almost able to read her mind.

"Sennedjem is a patient man. He must truly love you." Arsiya reached over and rubbed Ankhesena-mun's back.

"He does," she whispered. She stirred to leave. "Thank you for the bread and the private words."

"Where are you going, Khumit?" Hurriya asked as Ankhesenamun stepped past her.

A quick glance at the bread bowl gave her an answer. "I saw your dinner was ready. I will go summon your men to eat."

"Thank you, Khumit," Arsiya said. "We are sorry if we—"

She turned around. "Do not be sorry. I needed to hear your words. Thank you." She held a momentary gaze with each woman. She glanced at Shapash and

Ishat. "My daughters will live through me," she whispered with a smile.

The sisters' eyes brightened in response before she stepped outside of the tent. She felt like a new woman emerged from that tent, just as Hurriya said Arsiya emerged a new woman after her grieving, but . . . there was still something heavy in her heart.

She told herself to think nothing of it.

She scanned the caravan's family units, and a fresh breath filled her chest. With a sure step, she went toward the hill where the men were learning to fight.

Loving your husband makes it better. She recalled the times she had been with Tut. It was true. But a heavy weight plopped into the pit of her belly. *Do not think of Tut. Think of Sennedjem.*

The image of Sennedjem in his shendyt standing before her in the Malkata's training yard came to her once again. She had watched him teach the noble boys, four at a time, training each one with care. Her chest swelled as she remembered his muscular physique and the sweat rolling off his well-oiled body in the Egyptian sun at Malkata's royal harem.

She reached the top of the hill and admired Sennedjem as he taught the caravan men.

Previously, when he stood in his training yard, she had likened him to bait in a trap. She was her grandfather's wife. She would be married to the next Pharaoh and not to Sennedjem, the only man with whom she could envision sharing a life. But here, he stood in front of her, in Canaan. They were free.

There was no more trap. She nodded in assurance of herself.

Is it wrong for me to be with him? She closed her eyes. *No. Tut is gone. Tut wanted me to be happy, and I can be happy with Sennedjem.*

She licked her bottom lip while opening her eyes. "Men, your wives say your dinner awaits," she called out.

CHAPTER 12

SEEKING LESSONS

THE MEN SENNEDJEM TAUGHT BEGAN THE WALK back to their tents to join their families for dinner. Each of them was exhausted but proud. Sennedjem poured water into his mouth and wiped his forehead. Ankhesenamun approached him once they were more or less alone. She missed seeing his bare chest and muscular legs in his Overseer of the Tutors shendyt. Instead, he was covered head to toe in a long Canaanite tunic and headdress.

"Sennedjem, could you teach me another lesson? We are not in Egypt anymore, and Aqhat says there could be raiders out here that I may need to defend myself against." Ankhesenamun clasped her hands behind her back and tilted her head upon speaking her request.

"Yes, but Canaanites do not think it is proper for a woman to learn how to fight," he whispered and stepped closer to her. He looked around to make sure no one was looking in the moment and then dropped a quick kiss upon her lips. "They do not like kissing in the common areas either."

She chuckled and liked the way he made her laugh. "So, will you teach me?"

"Come with me," he gestured with a nod of his head. He took Ro-en by the reins and led him over the other side of a hill out of sight of the caravan. He wrapped Ro-en's reins around a small but thick-trunked olive tree. He kicked away some of the loose rocks to even out their small makeshift training yard.

"What will it be, my Queen?" He lifted an eyebrow while he came to stand in front of her. He untied her belt securing her hidden dagger and placed it over Ro-en's back along with his belt, still removed from his prior training. They both made it a priority to keep their daggers sharp and could not risk the accidental injury if they kept their belts on during the lesson. "Daggers, hand-to-hand, long sticks?"

"What do you think is the biggest threat out here?" she asked him.

He put his hands on his hips and looked out over the rolling hills at the vast nothingness. "We have yet to see the constant threats Aqhat keeps talking about, but besides those . . . I would say, no water. Lack of drinking water is our biggest threat out here," he chuckled. "So I am glad we stocked up at the river outside of Urusalim." He pointed to some greenery in the distance. "At least it looks like there is another river over there. That must be the Jordan River the caravan keeps speaking of."

She flicked him in the arm. "I am serious. I heard about the caravans being raided when my father was on the throne." She shrugged. "I barely fought off Pawah." She closed her eyes and pushed past that name. "How can I fight off many men if a raid were to happen?"

He stooped down and grabbed a small wooden branch. He studied it before pulling her into an embrace. "Well, now you have me by your side if someone were to attack you." He smoothed a hand over her brow and down her cheek; its soothing warmth relaxed her.

He lowered his head, but instead of giving her a kiss, he spun her around. His arm gripped under her neck, but, just as he had taught her, her chin pressed down to keep his forearm from making contact with her throat. His wooden branch pressed against her chest.

"First lesson in caravan raiding."

She smiled at his change of subject. She pushed Pawah, that horrible demon of a man, to the farthest place in her mind and focused on the position of her body in Sennedjem's grip.

She held onto the arm under her neck, not wanting to move. Even though their impromptu training dagger was just a wooden branch, Ankhese-namun had already experienced its hard jab against her skin in past lessons.

He whispered in her ear. "What do you do?"

"I cannot do anything. The blade would render me immobile."

Tsk, tsk, tsk. "I thought I taught you better than that." He kissed the side of her head. "Think." He choked up on his grip on the wooden stick. "Both of your arms are free, along with your legs."

She looked twice. Yes, they were free. She was trying to pull his arm away from her neck, but her arms were indeed free. She gripped his hand, holding the branch, and pushed it away from her while she leaned back. Then as quickly as she leaned back, she hurled herself forward with a large lunge, lifting his feet up and flipping him to the ground.

He groaned. "I will feel that in the morning." He rubbed his hip, but a wide smirk and sparkling eyes looked up at her. "See, you are a fighter. You could easily fight off a horde of men." He hopped up, clearly having faked his entire painful performance.

She pushed his arm. "I would believe you more if I actually hurt you."

He chuckled and pushed her arm back. "You would have if I had not been expecting it. If I were a brute of a man attacking you, I would not expect such a defense from a woman. Consider it an advantage."

She pursed her lips and cocked her head. "I will."

He grabbed a nearby rock. "Now, if I had two daggers." He held up his rock and his stick and walked behind her again. He gently wrapped one arm across her body, holding the rock near her neck, and with the other, he held the stick over her chest. She arched her neck to keep the hot rock from touching her skin. But Sennedjem took advantage and turned his nose into her neck, kissing it with a soft peck. "If one were here under your throat and the other were here hovering over your chest, you have very few options." He swayed a little with her as he kissed her neck once more.

I wish he would be serious. I wish he would not be serious. Part of her liked being wrapped up in his arms, but part of her wanted a proper lesson.

"Then I would suggest teaching me what my options are if I allow myself to get into this situation." She let out an annoyed sigh.

He stopped swaying and stopped his nuzzling.

At least he understands me. I am not playing here. I want to know how to fight, just as in Aketaten—

She pushed the thought away. *I want no more of my life in Egypt. Forget it. I want to learn more about how to defend myself and my future family with Sennedjem.*

Sennedjem cleared his throat. "Well, one option is to try to talk yourself out of his grip calmly. The second option is to do what he says. The third and last option is to try to get out of the hold and most likely be stabbed or get your neck slit."

She pushed out of his arms, and the singe of the hot rock against her neck caused her head to twitch. "Then why"—she rubbed her neck and let out a soft grunt—"would you even try to teach me that?"

He held up both hands and shrugged. "So that you do not try to escape and get yourself killed." He pressed his lips together, as if he wanted to say more but would not chance it.

She narrowed her eyes at him. "You just wanted to wrap me in your arms again."

A sheepish grin and flushed hue graced his cheeks. "I am sorry, Ankhesenamun. I am tired from teaching the men from the caravan, but if you want a lesson, I will teach you. I apologize that I did not take you seriously before."

She stooped down and grabbed another wooden branch.

Taking her cue, he nodded and said, "So, daggers?" He tossed the rock aside. "The dagger is for close contact, as you know." He twirled his wooden branch in his hand.

Her mind was not there. It drifted back to the impossible situation to get out of as he continued speaking: "Keep it available at all times, hidden, so that you can surprise your att—"

"So if you had a dagger to my neck and to my chest, I could not do anything, even with two free hands and two free legs?"

He took a deep breath. "Anytime there is a blade to your neck, you are better off not fighting. One wrong nick, and you could suffer a fatal injury."

She stood, arms crossed. "But there is absolutely nothing I could do?" She refused to believe that.

He shrugged as he squinted up at the sun in

thought. "If the attacker did not seem to be a well-trained soldier *and*"—he held up a finger for emphasis—"was distracted, then perhaps you could slip your hand into your belt and grab your dagger. Turn it backward and stab him in the belly." He shook his head though. "But you would need to be faster than he is with his blade across your neck." His lips pressed together once more.

"Anything else?" She tapped her foot. *He clearly has more to tell me.*

"Nothing gets past you, my Queen." He sighed. "If he is really distracted and seemingly not very strong, you can grab his wrist that holds the dagger to your neck. Pull it down while twisting away from him, blocking the other dagger to your chest with your arm." He demonstrated. "It will twist his arm behind his back enough for you to knock the dagger from his hand. Then, hopefully, you will have time to duck a coming swing from the other dagger."

She nodded. "I could do that."

"No," he shook his head with vehement emphasis. "Daggers to the neck are no good. Daggers to the neck and the chest"—he shook his head once more—"only the prideful try it, and rarely do they succeed."

Her eyes ran the length of him. "I will not be prideful then," she told him.

"Good." He tossed his wooden stick to the side of their makeshift training yard. "Now if I am an archer and you see me drawing an arrow, what do you do?"

He pulled an imaginary arrow from a quiver and quickly nocked it in his imaginary bow.

Without thinking, she sent her wooden branch sailing, hitting him square in the chest. It bounced off his tunic.

He pursed his lips and nodded. "Good. You have disabled me, but you are now without a weapon." She looked at him wide-eyed. "Which means if I am the only one coming after you, you are fine. You would simply retrieve your dagger from my body. If I am not, then you will need to do some hand-to-hand combat." He stooped down and picked up her branch before rushing her, branch fully drawn and ready to strike.

He thrust the branch at her midsection. She hopped back and parried his attacking hand as she stepped into his space. Her elbow thrust up, stopping short of just tapping his chin.

"Good." He kissed her elbow since her long, loose sleeve had fallen down over her bicep. "And thank you for holding your attack."

Her breathing deepened as she lowered her arm and lifted her face to him. He stood so close to her, and her tongue involuntarily licked her lip. Her gaze fell to his chest, and she wished he were in his shendyt or in the bath. She cleared her throat and blinked away the imaginings that rushed upon her. *Curse him. I was serious about this, or at least I thought I was. No! I am serious about refreshing my skills and learning something new.*

"You know all of this," he said, breaking her from her thoughts. He pushed her linen headdress away from her forehead and lifted her chin so that their eyes met. His hand slipped to her neck in a light grasp. He let his forearm graze her chest as he stepped a bit closer. "If your attacker grabs you by the neck, what do you do?"

His lips hovered over hers.

Curse you, Sennedjem.

She reached up, wrapping her arms around his neck and attacked his mouth, throwing her weight into him. He seemingly lost his balance, and they fell to the ground, but somehow, Ankhesenamun noticed, he fluidly rolled and ended up on top of her.

"I hope you do not do that with every attacker," he chuckled between kisses. "Good defense, though."

"Should I throw myself at every attacker? Would it stop the attack?" she whispered in a playful chuckle.

He pulled away and looked at her with an incredulous stare and a shake of his head. "No."

"I was not serious." She sat up—a bit perturbed—and pushed him off of her.

He lay on his back and folded his hands behind his head. He smirked. "I thought you were serious."

"I was . . ." she stammered. "Not about that, but about . . . " She shook her head at her lapse in judgment, letting herself get distracted. She could not even look at the man and his silly smirking. Her surroundings drew her gaze. Vast nothingness.

Sennedjem is right. The biggest threat out here is no water, and there is even a river in the distance. She followed its path running straight north.

"I was trying to be a good Tutor," Sennedjem cut into her thoughts, "and you, well, you had your mind on other things, apparently."

That tease!

She pulled her fist back and turned to him as if she were going to punch him in jest. But he was too quick and sat up, blocking her hand by getting an arm in the crook of her elbow and pushing her onto her back. He cradled her neck and head in his other hand so it would not hit the rocky ground. He outlined her face with his eyes. "I had my mind on other things, too," he whispered.

Her headdress had fallen off and lay next to her head. He rubbed her growing locks of hair, slowly and smoothly running his fingers through them. "You should always keep your elbow down when you are about to strike with your fist," he whispered and lowered his lips to her neck. "It makes for an easy block if you do not."

She lifted her chin, allowing him to nuzzle her neck a little more. "But I still knocked you down, Tutor, twice."

He hummed in acknowledgment as his free hand ran down her arm and then up her sleeve. "Besting the Tutor now." His hum and whisper tickled her neck. "I do not like the clothes of Canaan." He pulled his headdress off, revealing a head of short, matted hair.

She smiled in agreement and ran her hands down his back.

He placed a soft kiss upon her lips. "I love you, my Queen," he whispered before giving her another kiss and smoothing his hand up her arm.

The heartthrob in her chest only intensified at the tingling sensation of his touch.

He pulled back to gaze into her eyes. "I want to be with you."

It was not a question this time, she noticed. It was a statement. She would not be haunted any more. A slow, beaming grin grew across her face. "And I, you," she whispered and lifted her head to kiss him once more.

He took a satisfying breath, and a smile spread over his lips. Soon, they were lost in a world of each other, ignoring the rock of the ground underneath them, and the heat of the sun above them, and the soft chatter of the caravan off in the far distance. When the hem of her tunic slowly slipped up and bared her knee, she was knocked from that world of growing excitement.

She had only ever known one man and that was Tut. *Tut*. Yet here she was with Sennedjem. The lies of infidelity and murder rang in her ears and pulsed in her chest. Pawah's face flashed in memory. Her breathing shallowed and quickened. A different type of tingling took hold of her chest. *Push past. Forget that demon.*

The feel of Sennedjem's mouth upon hers grew in intensity. Her hands stilled on the back of his neck and in his hair. *I want Sennedjem.* She pressed her mouth harder into his kiss. *I want a family with him. I want this life with him.* She pictured their children somewhere in Canaan. Her two murdered daughters joined them. Murdered. By Pawah. Then, in a moment, Pawah's forced kiss was upon her lips in the throne room of Aketaten, the day he threatened her life, the day she sought out Sennedjem to learn to fight, thus beginning the horrible accusations. Pawah enveloped her mind. A wave of nausea rippled in the pit of her belly as her throat constricted; her breath became trapped in her chest. She sat up, throwing Sennedjem off of her. She closed her eyes and forced herself to breathe. *Forget. Forget. Please forget.*

"What is it? What is wrong? Are you hurt?" His stream of questions came quickly.

She shook her head. "I just . . . I needed . . . " She gulped down air. "I am sorry." She could not bear to look at Sennedjem; he was probably completely perplexed at her rejection of him. She covered her eyes and pretended to catch her breath while she wiped the hot tears from her cheeks. He pulled her into his lap and let her lean against his chest. He rubbed her arms and let her cry.

"After all this, I am still embarrassed to cry in front of you."

He kissed her temple and settled his breath as well. "You have no reason for that. Have I hurt you, Ankhesenamun?"

"No, Sennedjem."

"Are you remembering Panhey's body?"

A surge of laughter sprang from her lips amid her tears. "No. No." She shook the image of the old man's propped leg away. "But thank you for putting that image back into my mind."

"Oh, thank you? So you liked what he showed you?" he teased.

She shuddered and shook her head. Her lips curled back. "No." A last chuckle escaped before she rested her cheek against his chest, letting her body sink into his warm embrace. Her heart felt light, and in the moment, it was just her and Sennedjem. She felt safe again. The past was gone. He pulled her up into a hug, and she nuzzled her nose into his neck.

"What is wrong? Why do you cry?" His whisper tickled her ear, along with the wisps of her hair that fell there, before he pulled her back to look at her.

Tears glistened in her eyes, and then, she averted her gaze. She covered her mouth with her hand. In an instant, the past returned, gripping her vocal cords. *I do not want to tell him.*

A small shadow fell beside them. "I saw you kissing," a young voice said behind them. They both turned to see who it was. None other than Shapash stood there swinging her arms. "I did not want to bother you, but are you done kissing?"

Ankhesenamun's cheeks turned red. *She saw us?*

Sennedjem looked at Ankhesenamun. "Are we finished kissing?" he asked with a playful smile.

"Yes." She peered at him and saw a momentary wave of disappointment cross his eyes.

He turned back to the girl and nodded.

"My mother looks for you, Khumit." She turned and shouted in the direction of the caravan. "Mother! She is here."

Arsiya came upon them as Sennedjem helped her up. She took one look at their dusty tunics and their headdresses in their hands. "Oh, it can wait. You continue." Her eyes lit as she scooped up her child. "You Egyptians have different beliefs on lying with each other outside of the home."

"We were just . . . sparring," Ankhesenamun said, stepping forward and trying to defend her honor in front of these Canaanite peoples.

Sennedjem picked up a small branch and twirled it in his hand. "Gathering firewood," he said at the same time as Ankhesenamun said "sparring."

Ankhesenamun's jaw grew tight. *So many things Canaanite women are discredited for: fighting, loving . . . doing basically anything.*

Arsiya's eyes darted between them. "Of course, whatever you call it. Shapash and I have something for you when you are done *sparring* or *gathering firewood*." She threw Ankhesenamun a wide-toothed grin. "Sometimes I wish I were an Egyptian," she muttered under her breath and then turned back toward the caravan.

Ankhesenamun bit her lip and shook her head. "That was embarrassing."

His brow furrowed. "Why?"

"Because." She pointed at Arsiya hurriedly walking away. "A five-year-old child was spying on us."

He dropped the wood stick and turned her to face him. "Well, at least we are alone again." A half-grin appeared on his face. "No spies."

She shook her head and pulled from his embrace. "Perhaps we should just gather firewood as you said, so no one makes any other assumptions about us out here." She looked to the sun in the west and stooped down to grab some branches. "The sun is setting as well. We should probably gather firewood. We have none for tonight, and I left the fish uncooked."

Sennedjem popped his neck with a quick twist of his head. "As you wish, Ankhesenamun."

She peered up at him. "Are you mad at me?"

He stooped and found her gaze. His eyes did not hold anger but, rather, concern. "No, I am not mad." He kissed her forehead and began gathering the small wooden sticks alongside her.

CHAPTER 13

SEEKING BELONGING

THE LIGHT FROM THE CAMPFIRE FLICKERED AGAINST the night shadows. They had been walking for four decans, stopping at every city-state between Urusalim and the next city-state, Gibeon. The torchlights from the city of Gibeon brightened the dark sky in the distant horizon while some of the men from the caravan kept watch for the raiders in the lands.

Sennedjem handed her a bowl of bean-and-salted beef soup, complete with leeks, peas, and radishes. Its aroma caused her eyes to close in anticipation, and a warm smile grew on her lips to match the heat of the meal.

He sat down next to her and pulled the shoulder of her tunic down to kiss her soft skin. His eyes popped up to meet hers as she chuckled at his antics. Her smile slowly faded as she studied his face.

"What is it?" he asked.

She peered off at the caravan family units huddled

by their campfires. She took note
fling her brother around while her
family dinner. The small braide
Shapash had given Ankhesenamu
her wrist. Her toe dug into the
thought about what to say to him.

"I always felt safe in your training yard, and then
the feeling changed. Your training yard became a trap
for me, and you were the bait; every dream I had that
was not of . . . " she could not say Tut's name. *Forget.*

"Was of me?" he asked, bypassing what she could
not say.

She nodded. "I was a royal wife of Pharaoh Ay. My
dreams of you always ended the same: your enduring
the punishment for having a wife of Pharaoh."

"Well, we do not have to worry about that
anymore, just as you do not have to worry about any
of it anymore."

She hung her head. *I know, but I cannot escape that
life, no matter how far I run from it,* she thought. *And you
remind of what I want to forget.*

"Look where we are," he said, cutting into her
thoughts. "Look how far we have come. Look how
much closer we are to finding your sister."

She looked back up at Shapash, also taking note of
the other couples and families in the caravan. "These
people . . . I know we are planning to say goodbye to
them after we reach Magidda, but I feel as if maybe
we should not leave them. We could be happy with
them. We do not have to hide from them or lie to

much." She noticed Arsiya's smile and Hurriya's ⸺n at her son's coo. "We could have a family."

His head dropped. "We could." He kissed her shoulder again and teased, "You would have to lie with me first."

She chuckled at his jab, but its truth struck her heart. "Well, yes . . . " Her gaze returned to Shapash, and again she could not help but think her oldest daughter would be around her age. Ishat shuffled over and took their brother from Shapash. She saw herself and Nefe in the two sisters as well. "I just want a family again." She bit the insides of her cheeks. "They were all taken from me. And I need not remember that to move forward." It made sense to her. She nodded. *I do not have to relive that pain in that way.*

He grasped her hand and drew her attention away from the family units in the caravan. "Are you sure you are moving forward, Ankhesenamun?" The firelight danced in his eyes as he searched her face for the truth.

"Yes." She shrugged and ducked her chin. *I hate when he does that. Clearly, he does not think I am moving forward, and yet, he does not tell me what he truly sees.*

"When you asked me to come with you to Canaan, I thought it was to find your sister and to live a life outside of the restrictions of Egyptian royalty." He kissed her hand. "But if you want to stay in Magidda with Arsiya and Hurriya and have a family, I will do as you wish . . . as you command."

Her shoulders slumped. "I do not want to command you, Sennedjem." Her face lifted to the dark skies as she filled her chest with the smoky campfire air. "I do not know what I want." She leaned over into Sennedjem's chest, and he wrapped an arm around her.

"Yes, you do."

She peered up and into his eyes. She wanted him; she wanted Tut. She wanted her daughters. She wanted a child with Sennedjem. She wanted her mother. She wanted a life with her deceased family, but she wanted a life with Sennedjem and Nefe. She wanted a family. She wanted to be strong to save them from anyone who dared take them from her. She wanted her faith back. She wanted to believe she would have an afterlife. She wanted to forget, yet part of her wanted to remember. But every good memory was tainted with the horrid ending of her life in Egypt. All of those desires jumbled together in her heart. They conflicted with each other. It was painful to know some of them would never come to fruition. Others were painful to remember; reliving the past was too difficult to bear.

"No, I do not." The whisper came out low and soft.

"Is that why you cannot move forward?"

She shook her head. "I just have to forget. I have to forget everything. If nothing haunts me, then I can be free." She lifted her head to look Sennedjem in the eyes. "Is that what you did when you lost Sadeh and your child?"

A sad half-grin appeared on his lips. "Each person has to grieve in their own way. It seems you are still grieving."

"I want to stop. I want to be with you, but I . . . " What was holding her back? He loved her. He wanted this life with her. "How do I forget?"

He shrugged. "Maybe you do not forget?"

Her brow furrowed, and an unease settled into her chest. *He does not understand. I thought he would. Out of everyone I know, I thought he would understand what I need to do.*

She leaned out of his embrace and began to eat her dinner. "Thank you for cooking," she whispered.

He stared at her for a moment, studying the profile of her face, until he finally picked up his bowl and ate as well.

CHAPTER 14

SEEKING GIBEON

THE LARGE WALLS OF GIBEON TOWERED OVER THEM as they walked through the entrance of the city. The fertile, flat land boasted springs of fresh water. Ankhesenamun's clean tunic brushed against her freshly bathed body, and she walked tall with a renewed sense of well-being.

A soft smile held on her lips. *Who knew a bath could change so much?* She had scrubbed her tunic along with Sennedjem's to rid them of the odor that had developed. Her fingers still ached from scrubbing as she rested her hand on Ro-en's neck. Arsiya and Hurriya had accompanied her to wash their family's clothes as well. As they washed together, she stared at the multiple, filthy little tunics, and, at that moment, she wished never to have children. Laughing along with Arsiya and Hurriya as they teased each other and seeing Ishat and Shapash splash in the water had been a much-needed respite.

Watching the pair of sisters interact made her long for Nefe. Even as she walked into the main street of Gibeon, there was a new steadfastness in her step. *I will find someone who knows something today. I feel it. I know it. The last six months have not been good to me, so surely, today must be good.*

"You seem lost in your thoughts," Sennedjem said as he peered over Ro-en's neck.

She patted the donkey's mane. "I am."

"What are you thinking about?"

"I envision someone knowing something about my sister." She stared at the street bustling with well-off people.

A large presence appeared next to her. "You stare at the people's wealth, Khumit?" Aqhat leaned over to whisper.

"No, I—"

"This is one of the royal cities of Canaan. It is a rich city, mostly due to the fertile plains and the springs. There are no poor Hivites who live here."

"Hivites?"

"Yes, yes. That is what they call themselves."

"Not Gibeonites?"

"No, no. Hivites." He annunciated each of the two syllables with a gesture of each hand.

She peered over to Sennedjem, who pressed his mouth into a thin line and shrugged his shoulders.

"The Hivites are friendly to the Egyptians. They are rich and can provide food and protection for themselves. You have less to worry about here than anywhere else we have been; well, except Hazzatu."

"Oh, I see," Ankhesenamun said, politely nodding along as she listened to the man's rambles; every now and then, he had good information to take in.

"Yes, yes." He looked around the white plastered walls that lined the streets. "But Magidda is much richer." He laughed. "That is where we live."

She nodded, allowing the man to boast of his home city-state. His voice got lost in the street chatter as she entered the markets. Purple fabrics dripped from the merchant's booths, and silver-entwined leather belts dangled as an enticing trade. Vibrant vegetables and fruits lined the streets as people pushed through the crowds. The air seemed fresh as it filled her lungs, just as her clothes felt fresh against her skin. She took in this clean city, and a hesitant smile hung on her lips. "Today, we find someone who knows something," she reassured herself.

Sennedjem's presence stood next to her. "Shall we begin?"

Her tepid smile turned bold. "We shall."

A BOWL OF FIGS, DATES, AND APRICOTS RESTED IN her hands as the warmth of the fire soaked into her expressionless face. Sennedjem was talking, but she was not listening.

I was so sure we would find someone today. How is it possible to have traveled to so many cities, yet no one knows anything regarding the whereabouts of my sister? Her eyes closed. The smell of the day began to latch onto her clothes once again. She wanted another bath. The bowl sagged in her grasp.

"Ankhesenamun . . . " Sennedjem's voice called to her and then faded to silence.

I suppose I should answer him.

"Yes?" she said, opening her eyes.

"I asked if you are excited for our dinner? We have not eaten like this in a long time." He held their second bowl of goat meat, lentils, and peas.

The savory aroma of the freshly cooked meat did make her mouth water, despite the disappointment of the day. "I am."

He walked up to her and sat down on the rock next to hers; he placed both bowls of food on the ground before taking her hands in his.

"We will find her."

Her heart tore in two: one half was uplifted, while the other half plopped into her stomach. "I know," she said and forced a smile. *But where is she? Is she even alive?* she asked herself.

"Today, we did not find anyone, but maybe we will learn something tomorrow," he offered. "We will be here for a while, according to Aqhat. Lots of trading to do in Gibeon."

"I was so sure," Ankhesenamun blurted out. Her

head dropped, chin to chest. "I was so sure, Sennedjem."

He wrapped his arm around her and kissed her temple. "Perhaps it was the city's wealth. It is quite a city of awe. That, and you had just taken a bath." He dipped the top of his head toward the spring nearby. A smug smile arose on his face.

"Are you saying I needed a bath?" she teased.

He leaned forward, pressing his forehead to hers. "We both needed a bath," he chuckled in a low voice and gave her a sweet kiss on the lips.

"You were probably just feeling renewed from the spring waters today." He stroked her cheek. "We will look tomorrow and the next day and the day after that until we find her."

She nodded and took a deep breath. "Thank you, Sennedjem. What would I do without you?"

He pulled away with a teasing smile and opened his mouth to speak. But his teasing smugness faded, and his brow knitted. "You would be here as you are, searching for your sister. You would get along just fine without me. Remember? I told you, you are a fighter." He squeezed her hand. "You would do just fine without me."

"You do not mean that," she whispered, blushing for some reason unknown to her.

He leaned over, picked up the bowls of food, and set them between them. He poured the water to clean her hands and then his. "I meant every word, Ankhesenamun." He found her gaze. "It is I who would not know what to do without you. I would probably still be in the training yard, going about my mundane life, still in a haze from losing Sadeh and my child to the afterlife. Drifting without purpose, excelling at my career as a Tutor because I felt I was too incompetent to lead a troop." He shook his head.

"You are not incompetent, Sennedjem. You would have found your way."

"Maybe," he said. "It helps when you can feel valuable to someone, even if they do not need you."

"I need you," she said.

His gaze fell to her lips for a quick moment. His teasing smile returned. "No, you want me." He nodded in assurance of himself.

She chuckled and picked up a fig. "I need you for cooking, of course."

He snatched her hand and kissed her fingers before stealing her fig from her grasp. He put the whole fruit in his mouth and muttered, "My payment."

Her eyes lit. "Quite the trade, Sennedjem. A whole meal for one fig. There must be a reason why you gave me such a good deal."

"*Ah, ah, ah,* I did not say my payment was complete," he said and licked the sweetness of the fig from his lips.

"What more do you require?" She pulled her hand from his light grip.

The shadows of the fire cast across his face. The fire's flames danced in his eyes, softening them to a honey-brown color. His teasing smile simmered to a playful grin as he admired her face. "What more are you willing to trade?"

Her gaze fell to his lips, down his broad chest, and then to his defined stomach, hidden under the layers of Canaanite tunics and robes. She lifted her eyes to meet his once again. Her lips parted, but no words came through them. *I want to be with Sennedjem. Why can I not allow myself to be? He is, in essence, my husband. He is the only one who will ever know my true identity. He stays by my side. He cares for me; he loves me. What is wrong with me?*

Tears welled in her eyes, and she averted her gaze. She grabbed the next thing she could find. "This date." She held up the fruit, blinking away any tears that might have fallen otherwise. Her lips pressed into a fragile smile after a momentary droop in his head.

"Take it," he said, his teasing smile returning. "I will just take this bowl of goat meat." He picked up the bowl and bit into the hot, savory meat.

"Not a fair trade," she whispered and leaned forward to take a bite as well.

They spent the remainder of their meal teasing one another with their playful banter. After they had cleaned, they bathed each other again in the night at the nearby spring. They snuck back to their tent, holding hands under the stars. The caravan was asleep; no one stood watch. There were no threats to the caravan there at the city of Gibeon.

Sennedjem lay down on the cot next to her after changing out of his tunic, and she ran her hand down his arm. *I am glad he does not sleep in his sleeping tunic —that itchy thing.* The light from their fire fell into the tent and illuminated his freshly cleansed skin.

He rubbed her arm and caressed her shoulder, slowly moving his way up to her cheek. He kissed her on her forehead and then her lips as he scooted closer to her.

She chuckled at his familiar antics as she had every night before. A desire formed in her heart: *I hope he does this with me every night for the rest of our lives.*

"Two baths in one day," she murmured. "I almost feel like a Queen again."

"You will always be a Queen, Ankhesenamun," he said, brushing her cheek with his hand.

"Please, I do not want to remember." She closed her eyes tight, wishing she had not brought it up. Tut, her daughters, her mother and her whole family passed before her memory once more. "It is too painful," she whispered. "It is easier to forget than to be reminded of the pain every day." She opened her eyes and found Sennedjem staring at her with a furrowed brow.

"I never want you to be in pain," he told her and grasped her chin, leading her lips to his.

I love his kisses. They come when I need them the most. She returned his act with a playful bite of his bottom lip.

He stopped in a bout of surprise, and a wide smile emerged. "Are you not tired?"

She laughed. "I wanted a good kiss to end the day."

He pressed his body closer to her and tightened his embrace about her. "Then I shall oblige," he whispered before his hungry lips took their fill.

Her mind cleared as she forced the rumors to stay away. She allowed her mind and her body to get lost in Sennedjem's embrace. But as their hands roamed and Sennedjem's kisses dipped lower to her neck, the barriers she had put up against the rumors came crashing down. The rumors returned like careening water and quenched the joyous fire growing in her heart.

Not again. Focus. Forget. I am with Sennedjem. I want to be here.

Pawah's imagined taunt rang in her ears: *"You are close to making the rumors true, royal wife of Pharaoh Ay and Chief Royal Wife of Pharaoh Tutankhamun. Have you warmed the bed of your guards too? How many times have you dishonored the bed of Pharaoh and the throne of Egypt?"* The whispers of Malkata and of the Fleetsmen resounded in her memory as Tut appeared on his throne while Pawah spoke to him about her. *"Kill her, Tut. She is not worthy of you nor of Egypt. Is it not why she runs away and beds the Overseer of the Tutors? Is it not why she leaves Egypt to civil unrest? It is because she is selfish. She murdered her daughters! Believe me!"*

Her breath hitched as Sennedjem placed heated

kisses on her collarbone. His roaming hands stilled and pressed on her back as a tear emerged from the corner of her eye. *Pawah, get out of my mind. How do you still have this hold over me?*

The once-budding joy was now stabbed and bleeding in the depths of her belly.

Slowly, he lifted his face to hers with his brow furrowed. His eyes questioned her. He moved his hand to her cheek and wiped away the tear that had slid from her eye.

Out of her own fears, she expected him to tease her or to become angry like she believed any other man would who found himself in that moment, but he simply brushed the back of his hand over her cheek and brow as he calmed his breath. The previously unknown tension left her shoulders, and her brow smoothed.

"I never want you to be in pain, Ankhesenamun," he whispered breathlessly. "Especially with me." He pressed his lips once again to her lips before he laid his head down beside hers. He stroked her cheek and her brow while she snuggled against his chest, unable to look him in the eye.

He loves me so. One day, I shall forget them all, and then our time will not be plagued by Pawah. I promise. I hope. One day.

She feigned sleep until it became so under his soothing touch.

SOMETHING WOKE HER. HER EYES POPPED OPEN. Sennedjem was not beside her. The thump of her heart surged to a rapid beat.

Has he left me?

Her gaze snapped to the shadow at the front of the tent outlined by their dwindling fire. Sennedjem knelt at the edge of their cot facing toward their sack of trade goods on the opposite side of the tent. His amulets of Hathor and Isis were set before him. He was in the worship position: forehead to the ground, hands on either side of his head, and palms down. She closed her eyes again to give him his privacy in prayer like she had done most nights, but this time, she could not help but tune into his soft mumblings:

" . . . does not love me . . . help me show her I care . . . help her overcome her past . . . help her move forward . . . even if she never loves me . . . enough for me . . . find her sister . . . keep our hearts light . . . live by the principles of Ma'at . . . "

After a few more moments of prayer and worship, he sat up, and she heard the clink of his faience amulets as he slid them back over his neck. He lay down next to her and brushed her cheek with his lips. "I love you, Ankhesenamun." His whisper barely made it to her ears. He pulled back, seemingly to gaze at her.

She pretended to sleep but let one corner of her mouth rise enough to where she could feel his beaming smile in response. The shared blanket roll shifted under her head, and soon his rhythmic breathing signaled he was asleep.

Her eyes opened, and she sat up. She stared at his dark shadow in the tent-filtered moonlight. *It feels good to be loved again; is it so wrong to be happy with him?*

All of the death and pain from the past sucked the answer away. Her mother's scream the day she was murdered came to the forefront of her memory. "My mother wanted me to be with Nefe. She wanted me to live a happy life away from all the strife in Egypt," she whispered. She pulled her knees to her chest and wrapped her arms around her legs. Her forehead rested on her knee. "Tut wanted me to be happy too with someone who would love me more than he did."

The question came again: *Is it so wrong to be happy with Sennedjem?*

"No," she whispered and softly knocked her forehead against her knee.

Then why am I afraid to love him? Why can I not forget?

"Once I find Nefe, I will be able to. Wherever she is in Canaan is where I will start my life and be rid of my past forever. I will never have to relive that pain ever again." She closed her eyes and believed the truth she had set in her heart.

CHAPTER 15

SEEKING SAKMU

"THE RESIDENTS HERE ARE NOT A FRIENDLY people," Aqhat whispered to Sennedjem as they walked through the second gates of Sakmu.

It seems the farther north we go, the people become less and less friendly to the Egyptians, Sennedjem thought. Since Urusalim, they had traveled to Anathoth, Gibeon, Beit-El, Silu, Tappuah, and now, Sakmu. It seemed the cities were growing more dangerous too.

"The Habiru are friends to this city and its King Labayu."

Sennedjem peered over to his friend. "Who are the Habiru?"

"I believe the Egyptians call them the Apiru. They came and captured many Canaanite city-states. They slaughtered them and drove their peoples out. Some of those dispersed peoples remain here, living among them. Some of those dispersed Canaanites now live in raiding parties because the Habiru took

167

their homes. It is why a few of us stay awake at night to keep watch for men who approach."

Sennedjem nodded. "They are the raiders."

"Yes. Some of the raiders are known to be ruthless."

"How so?"

"During the raids, they capture the women, children and men—those they do not kill. They sell them to Sakmu to become work slaves, temple slaves used in their worship, or sacrifices to Baal." He gestured toward a temple to the goddess Qadeshtu. "She is the goddess of pleasure and desire. Worship of her means lying with all of the temple slaves, priestesses, and priests."

Sennedjem's belly knotted as his eyes fell on Ankhesenamun. He only wanted one woman, and even if she never gave herself to him, he did not want another. In Egypt, monogamous marriage was the most common unless the man was an elite noble or Pharaoh; even then, there was only one chief wife.

"My family and I are of a mixed faith," Aqhat continued. "We do not worship some of the Canaanite gods, like Qadeshtu."

"Why?" Sennedjem asked, thinking it odd to worship only a subset of the gods. Never in his life had he worshiped only a few of the Egyptian gods and rejected others. He imagined worshipping Hathor but rejecting Pakhet. *What kind of faith is that? Well, I can only worship Hathor and Isis now, but I do not reject the others like Aqhat's family does.* He thought some more about it as Aqhat continued talking.

"Ah." Aqhat shook his head. "My grandfather came from the Habiru and married a woman of Gazru. They left her homeland and settled in Magidda. The Habiru worship one god; they have different ways. Some of those ways and beliefs have carried on through my family."

Sennedjem bobbed his head even though it seemed silly to him. Either worship the god of the Habiru or the gods of Canaan. Would it not anger the god or the gods if loyalty to them were split?

"Oh, another thing about the city of Sakmu: They hate the Egyptians," he whispered low. "Do not let anyone here know you are Egyptian. They will take advantage of you, and since there are only two of you, they may capture you and trade you as servants or slaves."

"Duly noted," Sennedjem said, envisioning a horrible life in the temple of Qadeshtu for him and Ankhesenamun.

Aqhat leaned even closer to Sennedjem. "Did you know the city of Sakmu and its allies were going to rise up against Egypt when the boy King was killed in war?"

He peered over at Ankhesenamun, whose attention now focused on their conversation.

"No, I did not. Why did they not follow through with their plan?"

Aqhat chuckled and shook his head. "General

Horemheb crushed the Hittites. The Hittites! Of all the warring elites, Egypt forced the Hittites into surrender and treaty. And there was a rumor that the gods of Egypt sent Horemheb back to this world from their afterlife in order to defeat Egypt's enemies."

Aqhat jabbed him in the arm with his elbow.

"They were scared; what do you think? They did not want to rise up against the empire that defeated the Hittites and whose leader was divinely reborn." He swatted his hand in the air. "They fear Egypt's General, and he is to be the next Pharaoh. I doubt they will think about rising up again in the foreseeable future."

But Horemheb was not Hereditary Prince anymore. Sennedjem considered telling Aqhat the news, but he did not want to start any rumors if it meant more uprisings for whoever succeeded Pharaoh Ay. Thus, he decided to change the subject. "Did Sakmu attack Egypt's vassal states during the reign of Pharaoh Akhenaten?" As soon as the question left his mouth, he wished he could pull it back.

Aqhat nodded. "In part, but the Hittites and the various raider tribes also attacked, knowing that worthless Pharaoh would not come to the aid of its tributary states."

Ankhesenamun shrank back, and Sennedjem chewed his lip. "I see," he said.

"Tell me, Sennedjem. You were a man during

Akhenaten's rule, were you not? How did you feel about him as your divine King?"

How to respond to that? He knew how he felt, but he did not want to portray Egypt negatively. He opened his mouth to come up with something to say, but Aqhat continued speaking as usual.

"We in Canaan did not have much regard for him. He left us to fend for ourselves against our enemies, yet he still demanded our wealth as tributes. All we had was the Weputy at Magidda. We were fortunate because we were an Egyptian administrative center, so we had some protection. However, the other city-states that were not administrative centers were completely abandoned and left to defend themselves."

Sennedjem nodded along and then stopped when Aqhat looked at him.

"So what were your thoughts, Sennedjem?" He peered to Ankhesenamun, who walked beside him. "Khumit?"

Sennedjem cleared his throat. His words would sting Ankhesenamun's heart, but he believed it was the right course of action to provide an answer. If he refused, Aqhat would assume they were in favor of Akhenaten.

"Khumit and I were not fond of his orders, especially restricting worship to the Aten alone after declaring the Aten as the premier god of Egypt. I knew foreign relations were not as . . . " He searched for the word, but his Akkadian vocabulary was failing him.

"Good?" Aqhat chuckled.

Sure, he thought. It met the objective of the answer. He nodded.

"Yes, not as good as his father's, Pharaoh Amen-hotep III—"

"You mean nonexistent," Aqhat corrected. "Akhenaten's foreign relations were *nonexistent* until his wife sat upon the throne in his stead as Coregent. Even then, it seemed Egypt's economy was too far gone to salvage, much less to send much aid to Canaan."

"Yes." Sennedjem wanted this conversation to end quickly. He was running out of things to say, and Ankhesenamun had turned her head away. Her shoulders drooped from the weight of the conversation. He had not realized how invested Canaan was in Egypt's politics, but it seemed they knew everything.

"We did not care much for that Pharaoh," Aqhat said. "I was actually happy when he went to the land of Mot or wherever the land of the dead is for the Egyptians."

Sennedjem swallowed at the word "dead." It was something he was still familiarizing himself with in Canaan. They did not care for the afterlife that much. They wanted the dead to stay dead and not haunt the living.

"And I am not usually happy when someone dies," Aqhat continued. "I just hoped his successor would be good to Egypt's vassal states, but then, that horrible Smenkare came along. He actually killed his own people!" His whisper got louder, but he looked around, ensuring no one paid attention to him. He let out a breath and wiped his forehead. "I apologize. I get worked up thinking about that time. It was a hard time for all of my family, my wife's family, all of our friends, and trading partners. We only went on two trade caravans during Akhenaten's entire reign. It was too dangerous to go."

Sennedjem nodded. In that moment, he realized how much Aqhat talked, and he wished the man would still his tongue. He grabbed Ankhesenamun's hand to help her through whatever Aqhat had to say. He pulled her under his arm, letting her head rest on his chest as they walked. Her arm slipped around his waist, and the other held Ro-en's reins.

"Then Akhenaten's wife took the throne after Smenkare died." He put his hand over his mouth and whispered even lower. "If you ask me, I think the Egyptians killed their divine leader to rid the throne of Smenkare. Do you think so? Do you know if they did?"

Sennedjem cleared his throat once more. While they were at Panhey's estate, Ankhesenamun had told him everything her mother had told her. He knew that both Akhenaten and Smenkare were "rid from the throne" by fellow Egyptians led by Pawah, but he could not diminish Egypt further in the eyes of the Canaanites.

He waited for Aqhat to continue speaking, but instead, the burly Canaanite only looked at him, waiting for a response.

"I"—he pursed his lips and shrugged—"I only heard he started his journey to the afterlife with his wife, the Queen Meritaten."

"Yes, the same night." Aqhat's eyes grew big. "It did not seem to be a coincidence, and if you ask me, I think Akhenaten was killed too."

Sennedjem nodded in consideration of Aqhat's conspiracy theories as Ankhesenamun squeezed his waist. "Yes, well, it is all in the past, and Akhenaten was disowned by his son, the late Pharaoh Tutankhamun."

"Yes, yes," Aqhat said with a quick bounce of his head. "Good thing too."

Sennedjem waited for Aqhat to say more, but nothing else came from his mouth. As they approached the city's markets, Sennedjem said, "We will return to the caravan before nightfall. Enjoy trading for the day." He hurried Ankhesenamun away as Aqhat waved with a finger in the air.

"Sennedjem. Sennedjem!" he called out with concern in his voice, but then he covered his mouth and looked around.

What was Aqhat worried about? Sennedjem noticed a man lingering in the shadows and staring at him after Aqhat's call. The man glared at them before spitting in their direction.

"Egyptians," the man whispered. The beginning of Aqhat's long conversation rushed back to him.

"This city does not like Egyptians," Sennedjem muttered under his breath. He pulled Ankhesenamun along faster to get out of that man's sight. When they were far enough off, Sennedjem pulled Ankhesenamun aside out of the Sakmu's main street. He pushed the few errant strands of her hair that had fallen over her forehead back underneath her head-dress. A whispering couple of women stared at them from an inner room across the street. He couldn't touch her either. The thought made him re-position Ro-en to block them from the women's view.

He lifted her chin. "I am sorry, Ankhesenamun. I should have not asked about anything. I did not realize he would—"

She pressed a finger to his lips. "I loved my father, Sennedjem. I know what he did was enough for my mother to help kill him." A glisten appeared in her watery eyes. "I just never realized the depth and reach of his actions, and it hurts me to hear it." She pressed her forehead into his chest. "I wish to forget. Help me forget."

He stroked her back. "I know." He saw a few men staring at her. "We should probably not touch. They may think you are a harlot," he whispered to Ankhesenamun.

She pulled away from him, keeping her head down.

"Let us ask and see if they know of Paaten,

Atinuk, or Aitye. We will go to the markets before the night comes to trade for more water and food"— he glanced at his feet—"and perhaps new sandals."

She nodded and added, "We should use Aqhat and Arsiya's names as well, since Aqhat told us this city does not like Egyptians."

"Agreed, and, on second thought, we should only ask about Atinuk or Aitye. Neither is an Egyptian name." He gave her a reassuring nod. *Please let someone here know something, for Ankhesenamun's sake.* They walked up to one of the men staring at them to begin their search for Nefe in this city.

"Greetings, *bēl*," Sennedjem said. "We are looking for some family that may have come through here a few years ago or that may be living here. Do you remember or know of anyone named Atinuk or Aitye?"

"Go to Mot, you filthy nomad," the man said and spat at his feet before turning to leave with his group.

He shook off the man's spit from his foot. He whispered to Ankhesenamun, "This is my opinion: Paaten would not have chosen this place to live with the King's Daughter."

She looked at the cracking mudbrick walls and the narrow streets. "Or would this be the perfect place to hide an Egyptian princess?"

He dipped his chin in response. "You are right, Ankhesenamun. We must consider every option. Let us continue our search in Sakmu."

CHAPTER 16

SEEKING HEALING

Sᴇɴɴᴇᴅᴊᴇᴍ ʀᴇᴛᴜʀɴᴇᴅ ᴛʜᴇɪʀ ʙᴏᴡʟs ᴛᴏ ᴏɴᴇ ᴏғ their travel sacks after rinsing them with clean water. He grabbed a handful of beans and placed them in the cooking pot resting on the embers of the fire for them to cook through the night. Ankhesenamun gave Ro-en's head a pat and stroked his nose. "Sleep well," she whispered to him before she herself lay down in their tent.

Sennedjem came inside and took off his tunic, crawled over to her, and whispered, "I do not have to keep watch tonight." He gestured to the two dark figures standing on the outside ring of family unit tents. "Which means more time with you."

They faced each other. Their heads shared the rolled blanket they used as a headrest. He preferred the headrests in Egypt that kept his neck cool at night, but he would gladly take the rolled-up blanket as opposed to having his head rest on the ground.

Like every night since they had traded for their private tent, he rubbed her arm and caressed her shoulder, moving his way up to her cheek. He kissed her on her forehead and then her lips as he scooted closer to her until he was comfortable. He kicked his sandals off his feet at the end of the cot. As he stretched his toes, he winced.

It has been a long day, he thought as he recalled their endless wandering throughout Tahnaka. They had probably asked at least a hundred people if anyone remembered a man named Atinuk or Paaten or a woman named Aitye. After searching, they barely had enough daylight left to trade for their needed items and get back to the caravan before the sun set.

He watched Ankhesenamun's eyes close. She had barely said anything to him all day. He wondered if she was mad, but she did not seem mad. Usually, she would chuckle or laugh at his nightly routine of getting comfortable on the rocky hillside they had to call a bed.

"What are you thinking, Ankhesenamun?" he whispered. "You seem far away."

She released a heavy sigh, and her eyelids slowly rose. She traced his face with her eyes. "Do you think we will ever find Nefe?"

He pressed his lips into a forced smile that he hoped seemed genuine to her. "She is out here some-where. We have much of Canaan left to search."

"We have been to Hazzatu, Gerar, Gath, Libnah,

Lakisha, Makkedah, Jarmuth, Ekron, Urusalim, Anathoth, Gibeon, Beit-El, Silu, Tappuah, Sakmu, Burkuna, Ibleam, Gina, and now Tahnaka. Tomorrow, Magidda. Then, we have to say goodbye to Arsiya and Hurriya and Shapash." She wiped below her dry eyes, ostensibly practicing for the tears just starting to form.

He pulled her closer to him and kissed her forehead once more. "Which are you dreading more—not finding your sister or saying goodbye to our new friends?"

She drew in a deep breath but said nothing. Soon, he heard sniffles.

"What is it, Ankhesenamun?"

"Do you think we will find Nefe?" Her fingers dug into his side. "If you think this is a fool's errand, then perhaps we should remain in Magidda."

He rubbed her back and then pushed her away to look at her face. "It matters not what I think." He searched her eyes. "Someday, at the end of your life, will you look back and regret not looking for your sister? Or will you regret not staying in Magidda?"

Her bottom lip quivered, and a shaky breath escaped it. "I cannot tell you. I want my sister. I want my family. But it has been almost twelve years since she left Egypt; no one will remember them if they simply traveled through a city on their way to somewhere else. We will have to come upon the city they are in, that is, if they still live, and hope they have not changed their names."

Her eyes fluttered closed. She pressed her lips together and shook her head. "How can you find one specific grain in a full silo?"

"By looking," Sennedjem whispered. "Intently. Which is what we have done for the past nine months."

"Will I spend my entire life looking?" Her eyes remained closed.

Even though the question was innocuous, Sennedjem felt a slight wince come to his eye. He was in her life too. They were to spend *their* lives looking. Perhaps it was because she did not love him yet.

"I cannot answer that for you, Ankhesenamun." He chewed on his lip when her brow furrowed. *What does she need me to say to her? What does she need me to do?*

He stared at her while her eyes remained closed. "I love you, Ankhesenamun. I will—"

"So you want to stay in Magidda?" Her eyes popped open.

He chuckled at her quick response, reasoning perhaps she might want to stay and have a family, as she said the night before they arrived in Gibeon. However, she still had not told him she loved him, and they still had not lain with each other.

He pushed past it to answer her question. "I want, above all, for you to be happy. I want you to have joy and peace in whatever life you have. I want, at the end of your long, happy life, for you to look back and say what we did here in Canaan is enough for you to have no regrets."

She smoothed his cheek with her hand. "How long do we look?"

That question made him think she wanted to search for her sister rather than to have a family with him, but this time she had said "we." A certain contentment settled his stomach.

"Until you believe we have looked enough," his answer came.

She studied his face as he continued after her silence.

"Do you believe we have looked enough?" he asked. "If the answer is no, then we say goodbye to this caravan and continue looking. If the day comes later when you think we have looked enough, we can always come back to Magidda, find Aqhat and Arsiya again, and start a life together then. We know where they are."

Her growing black locks fell over her forehead and at the base of her neck. He brushed them aside so her head and neck would be cool.

"What do you believe, Ankhesenamun? Have we looked enough? Or shall we continue to seek?"

"There is still much of Canaan to search," she whispered and cupped his cheek. "Thank you, Sennedjem. Where would I be without you?"

She would be in Malkata, married to her grandfather, or in Canaan, alone, seeking her sister by herself. He smiled instead of voicing those thoughts. "You would fare just as well without me. You are a fighter. You endure."

Her lips finally curled up for the first time that day. They parted and touched his lips, which he received with pleasure. He had not told her he wanted her since Urusalim, but he knew he would be dishonest if he said he had not thought about it every night since. He cleared his throat as he replayed what happened under the sun that day they practiced sparring and in their tent at Gibeon, trying to figure out what went wrong. *She had been in tears. She sobbed. Does the past bear on her mind enough to keep me away? At Gibeon, a tear slid from her eye.* It seemed every time their encounters became too passionate, she would stop, either from fear or pain or sorrow. He knew she needed to work through her past, and it seemed she enjoyed the time they had together, up until a certain moment. In the beginning, he had thought that hitch of breath was evidence of her pleasure, but in the time since, he knew it to be the rush of thoughts that kept her from him.

He noticed her hands running down his body.

Say something. Ask.

"Ankhesenamun," he whispered.

She hummed in acknowledgment as she kissed his lips while he spoke.

"Why do you kiss me but nothing more? Why do you tell me you want to be with me but then push me away?"

Her kisses stopped, and she audibly swallowed. She studied his face as he studied hers. A wave of fear passed over her eyes, and a red hue graced her cheeks. Silence drifted between them for a long while until she opened her mouth to speak. But as soon as it opened, she pressed it closed again. Tears glistened in her eyes, and then she averted her gaze: a tell of hers when she did not want to tell him the whole truth.

"I feel exposed, Sennedjem. They can hear us. Children can sneak up. I never had to worry about anything in the palace. Tut and I were behind closed doors; servants were gone." She closed her eyes momentarily, and her brow furrowed.

He thinned his lips while she relived her desire to forget her late husband. He rolled to lie on his back. "What if I used our extra tunics to make a tent flap on our tent?" he asked in vain, knowing that was not the reason.

She shook her head.

"Is that the only reason why you do not want to be with me?" His mind jumped to every other time they had almost been together since they left Panhey's house. They were no longer in Egypt. No one knew who she was. No one could assign blame or accuse her and him of infidelity.

"I want to be with you, Sennedjem. I just cannot right now." Her breath caught in her chest.

Yet, she speaks of having a family in the near future. He closed his eyes to think. *I know she is grieving. Am I pushing her too quickly? Am I helping her at all? Am I being a detriment to her?*

It has been almost two years since we left Malkata, and

almost five years since Tut was murdered. He chided himself. *Grief has no timetable.*

He thought some more. *When she asked me to come with her to Canaan, had I erroneously thought she saw a future with me? Was she simply asking me to come to protect her?* He tried to remember back. He had seen a longing in her eye. She had kissed him back with passion, not a false promise.

I know she does not love me as I love her. But will she ever?

He turned his face to her and traced her profile by the amber light of the fire outside the tent.

If she can never accept what happened and move beyond her grief, she will never love me. Maybe I should not kiss her anymore. The thought gnawed at his stomach, and he licked his bottom lip to taste her once more. *For a while, at least. It will help her heal, and I will not be triggering memories every time our kisses grow into something more. I can do that for her.*

"Can you say something?" Her soft whisper ended in a crack in her voice.

His thoughts made him pause. *Maybe do not be so quick to leave her alone. First, confirm what you believe she is truly experiencing when she kisses you.*

"I know you are hurting, Ankhesenamun. I know you are still grieving. I know you need time to heal. I am sorry if I have pushed you into a relationship with me, or if you feel I am—"

She shook her head. "No, I just—"

He knew she would make up a half-true answer,

so he did not let her finish. "After one of Panhey's ill-made comments, you asked me if I would leave you if I found a pretty Canaanite woman. I told you I would never leave you."

"I know. I—"

"So if the question were put to you, how would you respond? You could meet a nice, handsome Canaanite man and fall in love with him . . . "

She shook her head.

" . . . he who is *not* the last reminder of a time you would rather forget."

Her head stilled in its shake, and after a few moments, she took a deep breath. He knew he had correctly assumed her hesitation. She remained mute, so he continued.

"I know you do not love me as I love you, Ankhesenamun. But if you will never love me, please tell me."

There was a longing in her eye, but it never formed into words. *Perhaps one day, then? Or never? I need to know,* he begged with his eyes.

"Regardless of your answer," he said instead, "you asked me to come with you to protect you in Canaan. I agreed. You have my word; I will never leave your side. I give my life to protect you. I will admire you from afar as I would have done at Malkata. You will always have my love, and that is enough for me, as I have told you. But it will be easier for you and for me, if you tell me now whether or not you truly see a romantic future with me."

She swallowed audibly again but said nothing. She wrung her hands atop her belly.

His heart fell into the pit of his stomach as he tried to corral his false hopes and keep his breath steady. Having kissed her, it would be so hard to watch her love another. He closed his eyes and turned his face away from her, trying his best not to envision her with someone else.

"Why do you always say that is enough for you?" she finally asked.

He thought: *Because . . . it may not be, but at least I know I can live through whatever life gives me. It may not be what I want, but I never know what the future may hold.* He drew a deep breath. *It is enough for me even though it will be hard, and it will hurt.* He turned his face to the tent ceiling once more.

"I choose to live in whatever life I am given," he said. He reached for her hand, but before he touched her silky smooth skin, he retracted and placed his arm by his side again. "It is enough for me to be happy knowing I can protect you and knowing I love you."

She rolled to her side and wrapped an arm over his chest. Her forehead pressed against his shoulder. "Every time . . . " Her voice trailed off and ended in a sigh. "You are a reminder of everything."

He nodded, unable to look at her, or touch her like he wanted to. She had confirmed his conjecture. "I know I am."

"And I just want to forget." She kissed him on his shoulder.

"Ankhesenamun," he said, sitting up and bringing her with him, "you will never truly forget, and if you can, I would consider you a daughter goddess of Thoth and Seshat."

Tears glistened in her eyes.

His chin dipped to lock his gaze with hers. "Can you see a future with me?" he asked her once more.

She chewed her lip. "I do not know, Sennedjem." But she quickly added, "Yes, I want that, but right now, I cannot escape the memories that come upon me."

His shoulders drooped, along with his gaze. "I see." A thick lump slid down his throat as he realized he might never truly be with her. He bit the insides of his cheeks.

"But Sennedjem, I do want you." She leaned into his chest and kissed his neck. Her arms wrapped around him. "I want a life with you."

But you cannot be with me because I am a reminder of the pain Pawah gave to you and your family, he thought and wished that man could be impaled again just to experience agony once more. He pulled her arms from around his chest and gently lifted her off of him.

"What if, for now, we act as a runaway Queen and her Protector?" He leaned to give her forehead a kiss, but refrained and pulled back. He wanted to run his fingers through her hair, caress her cheek, run his hands down her back . . . but he stilled and swallowed the second lump in his throat at her silence and inaction. *No objections.* He nodded in self-assurance. *This is for the best. She has to accept what has happened to her; that is the only way she will come to move forward and maybe one day love me.*

A tear ran down her cheek. He stared at that tear and wanted to wipe it away but again refrained. "Sleep now, my Queen," he whispered, returning his gaze to her eyes. "I will help the men keep watch during the night." He stood up, letting her hands fall from his chest and arm. He dipped his chin in respect to her before pulling his tunic over his head. He secured his headdress upon his head with the band, tying the knot in the back. His hands dropped to his sides as she watched him. "Dream of a happy time, my Queen."

Another tear ran down her cheek, and he had to turn away to keep his resolve. He shuffled into his sandals and walked to the two other men who were keeping watch over the caravan during the night.

Hathor, Isis, Goddesses of Love and Marriage—please let this be the right decision.

CHAPTER 17

SEEKING DEFENSE

SHE TOSSED FROM ONE SIDE TO THE OTHER. THE thick cot was not as comfortable as it once had been. She turned back to the other side. "What is wrong with me?" Her eyes popped open.

She plopped over to her back and stared at the spiral ceiling of the tent. "Just forget. It is not that hard to do. Live your life with Sennedjem."

In the darkness lit only by the small fires outside the tent, she remembered back to every night before. It seemed as if Sennedjem did not think she could forget. She could speak Sadeh's name without Sennedjem's even batting an eye. How could he do that? He had not forgotten Sadeh. He spoke of her in memory and in love, but never with a tear in his eye.

"How can that be?"

Her arms crossed over her chest.

"I wish you were here, Mother," she whispered. "I thought I understood. I thought I could do this." Her eyes closed, and she took a deep breath. The blanket roll underneath her neck enveloped her relaxing shoulders. "What would you tell me to do, Mother? How did you live with Meritaten's murder? Knowing your hand in it? Knowing Pawah's hand in it?" She searched the furthest recesses of her mind for an answer. "How did you press onward?"

Her eyes rolled back and forth under her eyelids. "Should I not forget? But how can I not remember? Every time I think of anyone"—the images of her father, mother, sisters, Tut, and her daughters all came into view; each loved one lay under Pawah's foot, which was squashing them from existence—"I only feel Pawah. I feel his hand around my throat. I feel his lips upon mine. I feel the turmoil he set in my heart. I feel anger."

Her hands clenched into fists.

"I feel fear. I feel helplessness."

Her brow furrowed, and her lips turned into a scowl accompanied by a short, swift intake of air.

"I feel *hate*."

The same dagger with which she slit Pawah's chest and chin remained concealed in her belt beside their cot. Her fists tightened, and her nails dug into her palms. The urge to stab him over and over again revisited her. He was lying motionless in the corridor of Malkata after he had attacked her. She could have done it, but she did not.

"I hate him, Mother. How can he still cause me so much pain three years after he was put to death?"

Her teeth ground and caused her ears to ache.

"I should have run away with Nefe, but I would have still lost you and Tut to that man. How can he make my heart so heavy? How can he still hold this much over me even when he is dead—impaled, burned, and fed to the Nile crocodiles?" A slight chill slithered down the back of her neck. "I hate remembering, Mother. I only see what and who I have lost. Like you." A shaky breath passed over her quivering lips. "I want to remember the times you held me in your arms, but all I see is your ashen body with that fatal wound to your chest." Her eyes shut tight, and she whimpered, "I hear your scream."

Her voice got lost in her throat, and she turned back onto her side. Their sack of trade goods lay opposite her. "I am overwhelmed. I just want peace."

The worn blanket roll cradled her head. "I want peace," she whispered and tried to clear her mind.

A new day means new beginnings, she had told her mother. It was a lie. She had seen bright and happy futures with everyone she had lost, even with Sennedjem for a moment. But now that future seemed dismal. Would Pawah plague her the rest of her life?

"I am tired. I want to sleep. I do not want to dream. I want to sleep." Her eyes closed. Sennedjem appeared in his training yard at Malkata. Her brow furrowed and changed the image's setting to Canaan.

Do not remember Egypt.

She tried to focus only on him. She forced every

thought to relive his kiss upon her lips, but, in the end, he was right. Sennedjem was a reminder, and her past always made an ugly appearance.

"Think of someone else. No . . . do not think at all." Her breath shook, and she readjusted her head on the blanket roll. "Just sleep." Her eyes closed, and she fell into a restless sleep.

Tut's face appeared, and his hand brushed her cheek. His warm smile turned cold as Pawah loomed over his shoulder and whispered to him, "She bedded the Overseer of the Tutors and murdered your children, Tut."

The smack of Tut's cane caused her leg to burn. The whispers of the palace and the Fleetsmen rushed toward her in a frenzied wave of unrecognizable chatter. Pawah pointed his finger in her face. "Kill her." He stood over her mother, father, uncle, sister, daughters, and Tut. "Kill them all," he laughed. Then he stabbed her with a quick thrust in the same way he had stabbed her mother.

She gasped for air as she awoke from her nightmare. Her hand clutched her heaving chest, ensuring no damage was done. The dryness in her mouth spread to her throat. A scream sounded once more; she sat up. *Am I still dreaming?* Another scream. *It is coming from the caravan.*

She grabbed her belt as more screams came. She crawled out of her tent and witnessed chaos unfolding within the campground of the caravan. Tents were being torn to pieces by men pillaging them, women and children were running in every direction, and the caravan men were engaged in combat with the outsiders. As she surveyed the scene, she saw three men at Arsiya's tent and two men heading straight for her. Time seemed to race as fast as a war horse heading into battle. The smell of burning tents and the nauseating smell of men's sweat plagued her stomach.

No. Not Arsiya. Not Ishat and Shapash and Beth-shadon.

The men were almost upon her, and just as they raised a sword, time slowed to a lazy gait. Her heartbeat pulsed in her ears as the scene before her silenced.

Fight! Her fingers instinctively wrapped around a long branch that lay on the outside of her fire pit; she swung it upward like a sword, thrusting the fire into their eyes. The screams of the caravan came in full force once again. Their howls of pain and loss of control played to her advantage. Her short sleeping tunic allowed full use of her legs, and she kicked one of the men in the head, jolting him to the ground. She left him writhing in pain as she smacked him in the face again with the fiery branch. The other man staggered on his feet. She let out a warrior's yell as she wound up again and smacked him on the other side of the face, sending him to the ground alongside his fellow raider. Her breath became shallow, and her arms shook with energy. As she watched the men lying on the ground, the briefest of images flashed in her mind: Pawah lying on the floor of Malkata as she stood over him with her dagger firmly secured in her hand.

"Anat," they called out to her. "She is Anat, goddess of war. Spare our lives. Spare us!"

Their screams pulled her to the present. *Arsiya's tent.* She picked the sword up off the earth along with her fiery branch, spat at the two men writhing on the ground, and sprinted toward her friend's tent. The chaos around her flared larger. A caravan man fell in front of her and a raider nearly stabbed him, but she blocked his strike, allowing the caravan man to kick out the knee of his assailant. The screams of the children in Arsiya's tent pulled her forward. She glanced around as she ran, searching for Sennedjem, but she did not see him amid the pillaging. Running at full speed, she hit the first man at Arsiya's tent over the back of the head with the branch, taking him by surprise. The force of her blow knocked him sideways, but he did not fall to the ground. She swung the sword, slicing his leg to send him down, but it was too late. The two other men had noticed her and came out just as the tent lit aflame.

"Arsiya," she cried, hoping they were still alive. "Get yourself and your children to safety." One of them swung his sword down hard over the top of her head. She blocked it with her blade and thrust the fiery branch into his face.

The impending strike from the second man caused her to turn and block it with her sword. She swung the fire branch overhead to keep them from attacking her back in mid-turn. While she drew their attention, she saw Arsiya leave the flaming tent, carrying Beth-shadon and ushering Ishat and Shapash by their arms.

They are alive. Ankhesenamun struck with the fiery branch with a renewed vigor and caught one of the men's tunics on fire. She ducked from the sword strike of the other and rebounded with a strike of her own. As both men were recovering from her strikes, she gestured Arsiya toward her. "Hide. Hide in my tent." She pointed with the sword. The raider who had been set on fire threw his tunic on the ground and advanced.

Thunk.

Ankhesenamun heard a swift swoosh of air as Arsiya fell by her feet. She froze when she saw the arrow protruding from her back. *Was that arrow meant for me?* Her muscles squeezed rigidly in fright as she looked off into the direction from whence the arrow came.

Her body anticipated the strike from the oncoming raider, and she raised her sword upward even though her attention searched for the arrow's owner. The two bronze swords clanged together, and, in that instant, she spotted the archer nocking another arrow. She dropped underneath the raider's next sweeping strike and ducked underneath his arm, placing him directly between herself and the archer.

The raider's face contorted, and he fell to his

knees, having been struck by his fellow archer's arrow. She looked up once more and witnessed the archer nocking yet another arrow. *I am vulnerable.* There was no cover to hide behind, but a familiar tunic flashed in the firelight. *Sennedjem.* She turned to fight anyone else who dared hurt her friends, knowing he would take care of the archer. Two raiders came at her, swords raised.

Thunk. Thunk.

She watched them fall to their knees with arrows in their chests. A horn blew in the distance, and the few remaining raiders took off running with whatever trade goods and possessions they could carry.

"You cowards," she yelled as she kicked dirt in their direction. "We did it. We fought them off." She wiped her mouth with her forearm and licked her lips to quench her voracious thirst. Her heavy breath compressed from her chest as she tried to regain her composure.

She froze.

Still.

"Arsiya," she whispered and turned to where she had fallen.

Images of her mother's body rushed back to her as she stood at the feet of Arsiya's lifeless body. Her vacant eyes peered up at Ankhesenamun. Beth-shadon cried underneath her. *The baby.* She ran to Arsiya's side, fell to her knees, and pulled Beth-shadon free. She clutched him in her arms as she stared at Arsiya—mind blank, save for her mother's scream ringing in her ears.

Hurriya came running. "No. No. No. No." She slid to her knees and screamed over Arsiya's body. Hurriya's hands searched for a place to touch her, but they could never quite make contact with her tunic. "Arsiya!" Her son Ug came holding Sidon—he fell quiet and still.

Ankhesenamun's mouth remained agape, and her blank stare upon the sisters blurred as tears fell from her eyes. In the ring that pierced her ears, she heard a small yelp that drew her attention. *Please. Please do not be Ishat or Shapash.* Her eyes closed as she turned her head toward the sound. She opened her eyes to the visage she begged not to see.

Ishat pulled her brother Beth-shadon from Ankhesenamun's hands and called for her father in an agonizing scream. "Papa! Help!"

When Ankhesenamun's hands were free of the babe, she crawled to the young girl. She gripped Shapash's struggling body, pulling her close to her chest as she sat back and rocked with her.

Shapash's little broken voice whimpered, "Mama."

Shh. Shh. Ankhesenamun locked eyes with her, unable to look at Arsiya's body. Tears flowed from her eyes, and a coursing, surging, violent stream of hate attacked her voice, rendering her mute. She choked out a broken hum she remembered from somewhere in an attempt to console her little friend.

"Where is Mama?" Shapash rasped as her eyes fluttered closed.

"She is with you," Ankhesenamun forced out; tears blurred her vision. Her lip quivered as she watched Shapash's chest struggle to rise and abruptly fall.

"It hurts, Khumit," she whispered through hitching breaths.

It hurts me too, Shapash. The thought lived on her tongue. Her tears dripped onto Shapash's neck. Ankhesenamun gripped her tighter, pulling her closer, as she had done with her daughters. "It will not hurt much longer, my sweet one."

In a few more moments, Shapash lay still: her eyes closed and her body no longer in pain. Ankhesenamun held her close, looking at the pillaged caravan. Other family units surrounded their lifeless members. The smell of smoke burned her lungs as the harsh orange and red of the flame hungrily ate a few of the tents. Her body and chest grew cold and still. Her stare focused on nothing. No more tears fell from her eyes, but her cheeks glistened in the firelight from tears past. A hungry pit settled deep within her stomach. The wails and screams of those around her slowed and silenced in her ears until one sharp yell broke through: "There is a survivor of the raiding party." With a quick dart of her eye, she saw Heth drag a raider to the center of the caravan.

Ankhesenamun, with muscles drawn tight and teeth bared, slowly laid Shapash on the ground with the utmost respect for her little body. She stood. A haze overtook her mind as she surveyed what remained of the family units mourning their fallen loved ones until her gaze fell on the surviving raider. The tears on her cheeks turned hot while she squared her shoulders to him. *He took them. He killed them. He should pay with his life.* With a purposeful stride, she approached. Her hand slid to her belt, and when she came within the circle of men, she grasped the handle of her hidden dagger and thrust it toward the man's chest with a rage-filled yell.

But someone caught her hand and stopped the blade in place just as its tip made contact with the raider's tunic. She tried to force the dagger through the raider's chest with renewed effort. But the man who held her was stronger than she. Another yell escaped her lips, and her face buckled into a grimace as she realized the man had pinned her against his chest and was dragging her away from the raider. He spun her around, and Sennedjem stood before her. He slid the dagger from her hand and dropped it to the ground.

Him? Sennedjem? He keeps me from this? Does he not see the savagery?

With a curl of her lip, she lifted her elbow and drew her arm back to punch him in the chest, but he blocked, locking her arm under his. He leaned in close as his gaze fixed with hers. His bloodshot eyes stared back at her, but his pressed mouth spoke with the empathy he held for her and the others.

"Ankhes—"

"That man does not deserve life!" she yelled in his face, but he kept a firm lock on her as she squirmed. "Do you not see the blood?" Spittle formed in the corners of her mouth. Shapash's blood covered her hands and soaked through her linen tunic at the chest. Shapash's soft face of death blurred with those of her daughters. Arsiya's arrow-pierced body merged with that of her stabbed mother. Images of Tut wrapped in his sarcophagus plagued her mind. She had been weaponless, skill-less, helpless to do anything about their murders and their murderers, but this time . . . *this* time, she had a weapon, she had defense skills; she could have saved them.

"That man killed my daughters! He killed them! Shapash and Arsiya—he took them from this life. He killed my mother! He took Aqhat's wife and child from him. Do you see how much pain he has caused us? Do you not see this, Sennedjem? He took them all!" Her heartbeat rendered her chest incapable of breath but the words continued in thought: *I want him to hurt. I want him to pay. I will avenge them all.* She struggled in Sennedjem's lock, but he held her still as she finally secured a swift intake of air and pushed the final words out. "He does not deserve life." She spat at his chest; his face blurred in her hot tears. "He took my family. He killed them. He took them all."

Sennedjem's brow furrowed. "That man is not Pawah." It was a simple statement, spoken low and with the deepest of care.

Her belly knotted. A harsh pounding reverberated in her ears. Her dry throat rasped from rushed breaths. Rage shook her body.

"Killing out of righteous anger"—Sennedjem's voice broke—"is still a form of murder, my Queen," he whispered so only she could hear. He lowered his forehead to hers while tears pricked his eyes. "Do not stain your ka with this."

A guttural roar seared its way up through her hard-pumping chest and squeezed through a constricted throat, and what remained of it flung off her tongue and past her lips as a small breathless cry.

His tears fell down his cheeks as she crumpled in his grip. He unlocked her arm and drew her into his chest, squeezing his arms about her.

"Sennedjem." Her cries choked her words. Her fists curled the fabric of his tunic within their grips as an openmouthed sob burst forth from her inner depths.

CHAPTER 18

SEEKING MAGIDDA

THE REMAINING MEMBERS OF THE CARAVAN SLOWLY walked through the gates of Magidda after plodding up the long entry road to the hill on which the city sat. Sennedjem and Ankhesenamun walked side by side, each carrying what was left of their belongings since Ro-en had been stolen, along with most of their trade goods. The thick city walls of grandiose stone and the soldiers that lined the entrance spoke of Magidda's great and mighty status. But even such grandeur could not lift the spirits of those walking through its gate.

Ankhesenamun's eyes drifted to Aqhat in his tunic made of black, coarse goat hair. He had called it "sackcloth." Aqhat had told them every detail of each city they had stepped foot in thus far, but now, as they entered his home city, he only plodded along next to his camel in silence. Beth-shadon was strapped to his chest, and Ishat walked beside him, holding her sister's blanket. His defeated head hung with chin to chest.

When the news of Tut had come that horrid day, she found herself walking in the same manner. His wife and daughter were killed, as were Tut and her daughters. Her eyes drifted to Ishat. *Her mother and sister were killed, as were my mother and sister.* As the busy streets of Magidda pressed against her, she saw herself in both Aqhat and Ishat. Tears welled in her eyes, and an ugly grimace covered her face. Their sorrow became hers once more and nestled firmly on her shoulders, weighing her head down until her chin touched her chest too.

Hurriya's strained-but-joyous voice carried on in the background, but no one responded to her incessant talking.

" . . . Shapash was so good with Sidon . . . I remember when she held the clay pot for the first time . . . Her laugh was so pure . . . "

They are gone, Hurriya. Can you not see we are mourning? she wanted to ask.

" . . . They brought joy to my heart . . . "

But as she thought, a brief memory came upon her: Hurriya wanted others to speak and to laugh. It was her way of grieving. She took a deep breath, knowing then what she must do.

"Please be strong," Ankhesenamun whispered to herself. She lifted her head and pressed her lips into a weak smile. She turned to Sennedjem as they walked. "I will be with Hurriya."

He glanced back over his shoulder before finding her gaze again. He seemed to know her intentions, because a sad half-grin appeared on his lips. "Yes, my Queen," he whispered.

Another deep breath filled her lungs as she slowed her gait to walk alongside Hurriya.

"Khumit," Hurriya said and patted her arm. "Have you been to Magidda before?"

Ankhesenamun shook her head.

"Well, our home, Magidda, and its sister city, Hasura, are on the trade route between Egypt and the Mitanni, Assyrian and Babylonian empires. We are known for our ivory." She pointed to the elephant tusks decorating the palace gate as they walked past its black basalt steps. "Our King Biridiya lives there." She whispered low. "Shapash always teased us, saying she would marry his son and live in the palace," she chuckled.

Ankhesenamun forced some words out so Hurriya would not be the only one speaking, "Yes, I could see her saying something like that."

Hurriya softly laughed again. "And Arsiya, she would always tell her, 'Be content, my little Shapash.'"

Ankhesenamun smiled at Hurriya's strained but cheery tone. "I could see that too." Her heart lifted at Hurriya's stories.

How can she speak of them and smile? How am I able to

*smile at these stories so soon? Were they not killed? How is
she not plagued by the manner of their demise? How can she
be this way? How can she grieve in this way?*

Hurriya nodded her head and continued remi-
niscing until the caravan began to disband; one by
one, each family unit separated from the group and
left toward its home. They passed by a large and
sprawling two-story building.

Hurriya pointed. "This should interest you,
Khumit. This is the Egyptian Administrative Center."
Her arm fell back to her side. "This building is
rumored to contain lots of traded ivory and riches
ready for the next transport to Egypt."

She stopped walking and turned to Ankhesenamun. "Are you to return to Egypt now that you have
been throughout the land of Canaan? Have you
observed enough for your merchant business?"

Hurriya's chin quivered.

Ankhesenamun realized that if she were to stop
speaking, she would cry. It seemed she did not want
to cry, though, because she kept speaking.

"I know you and Sennedjem probably want to get
back to Egypt," she nodded along. "You could be safe
under the protection of an Egyptian caravan headed
to Pharaoh's markets." Her lips drew wide into a
smile that could break at any moment.

"I do not think we will return just yet."

"I think you should stay with Aqhat." The words
bubbled out of her mouth before a cry could. "My

mother lives with us, as his mother lives with them. They will need extra help now that . . . " Her voice trailed off, and her eyes grew moist with unshed tears. "It will be winter soon, too; you will not want to leave here in the cold time of the year. The days are bearable, but at night, the winds feel like they could take your life."

Ankhesenamun could only nod.

"Well," Hurriya looked up to the sky to keep her tears from falling. "I shall speak to Aqhat and let him know that you have decided not to return just yet."

"That would be wonderful, Hurriya," Ankhesenamun's voice wavered through a tight chest.

Hurriya stepped closer, and in one fell swoop, she wrapped both arms around Ankhesenamun and squeezed tight. "Thank you," she whispered.

"I miss them too." Ankhesenamun returned her embrace.

THEY PASSED THROUGH THE DOORWAY OF AQHAT'S home into an open-air courtyard lined by covered storage on each side. Another doorway into the sheltered quarters was straight ahead of them. Aqhat led his camel to the corner of the courtyard where a stable of sorts stood.

A twinge of sorrow pricked Ankhesenamun's already numb heart as she thought of Ro-en off with the raiders. Ishat grabbed Ankhesenamun's hand and leaned into her leg. "I miss mama."

"I miss her too," she whispered.

Ishat pulled her inside their home, where an old woman sat on a woven rug near the hearth. The old woman stared at her with a piercing gaze. Ankhesenamun shifted her weight and looked around to take in their temporary dwelling. The second story of the one-roomed home was accessed by three ladders, each leading to a sleeping loft—two on the sides of the home and one in the back over a doorway leading to an outside kitchen and storage area. Sennedjem and Aqhat followed them inside.

"Where is Arsiya?" The old woman's frail voice nearly shattered upon speaking. The warmth of the home's hearth vanished as her gaze scanned the four people and the baby standing in front of her, coming to rest upon Aqhat's sackcloth. "And Shapash?"

"In the land of Mot." Aqhat's equally weak voice came from behind her. He pushed past Ankhesenamun and Sennedjem and darted through the doorway to the outdoor kitchen. Red rashes ran along the back of his neck from the rub of sackcloth against his skin. Soon his sorrowful wail lifted into the sky and resounded into the small home.

The wail's ebb and flow summoned the wails of Waset from Ankhesenamun's memory. *So much sorrow. So much grieving. I came to Canaan to rid myself of death, and yet it has found me again.* Her gaze fell. Aqhat's and

Ishat's pain were her own, and yet she could not bring herself to relive it, even for their sake.

The old woman struggled to her knees before standing before them. She reached out her hand to Ishat. "Come, my little one. We shall grieve alongside your father."

Ishat squeezed Ankhesenamun's hand before joining the old woman. "Go to the baskets by the chest and retrieve our sackcloth, my little one."

While Ishat obeyed the command, the woman lifted her countenance to the strangers in her home. "I am Kotharat, the mother of Aqhat. Who are you?"

Sennedjem cleared his throat before responding. "I am Sennedjem, and this is my wife, Khumit."

"Khumit?" Kotharat tilted her head. "Egyptian . . . dressed as a Canaanite?" She looked them up and down but said nothing more as Ishat returned and handed her the sackcloth.

"Aqhat offered his home to us for the winter, and then we will journey onward," Sennedjem explained.

She raised her hand to silence him. "Aqhat is the master of this home. You have no need to explain yourself to me." She draped the sackcloth over her shoulder and laid a smaller cloth over Ishat's small frame. "Let us take these and join your father and brother, my little one. We shall mourn your mother and your sister."

Ankhesenamun's hand slid into Sennedjem's without a further thought. Her mind drifted to the dancing mourners at her sisters' and father's funerary parades to Aketaten's royal tombs. Their rich wails and loud screams had sounded all the day. The sistrums' warm prattle danced on the arid breeze, along with their musicians' feet.

And to think, that mourning was all a mockery of the dead, a cover for their joy at the passing of my father.

Had Waset really mourned for their Queen Ankhesenamun, or were there beams of happiness hiding behind their forlorn mud-caked faces?

Do I even care?

Sennedjem's stare upon her face drew her attention. His eyes held a woeful darkness.

I mourned my family in Egypt, she wanted to say. *I feel I should mourn my friends in Canaan, yet I do not feel the need to mourn. I have nothing more to give. I am tired. I am numb. I am empty.*

However, Ishat's scream plagued her ears. Its depth of tone commanded her feet to lead them both outside and kneel next to their friends and wail alongside them.

TWO MONTHS PASSED, AND ANKHESENAMUN AND Sennedjem continued to grieve with their friends. The cool winter air brushed Ankhesenamun's cheeks as she sat outside in the courtyard. She looked up to the sun, attempting to replace the chill from the breeze with the sun's warmth. As she closed her eyes, she envisioned her family standing around her in the open-roofed temple of the Aten in Aketaten, giving worship and praise to the sun-disc god. But it was gone in an instant. She opened her eyes, finding herself still in the small courtyard of the home.

The interior of Aqhat's home had become small and cramped, so she spent much time in the courtyard. It reminded her of the palace courtyards where she had spent most of her time in Egypt. That and the training yard. Her chest tightened at the thought.

I made it so easy for Pawah to accuse me. But I won his game, did I not? Tut believed me in the end . . . well, even if he did not believe me, he forgave me nonetheless. The corners of her mouth turned down. She had won the game but lost the war. Tut and her daughters had still ended up in their sarcophagi.

Even though her long woolen sleeves protected her arms from the cold, the memories of the past caused her to shiver. *I am alive, and they are dead. All of them, except Nefe . . . and Sennedjem.*

She peered over her shoulder to look at Sennedjem behind her; he was helping Aqhat remove food from storage in the back kitchen so the women could cook it. A sigh left her lips as she turned her face to the sun again before she had to go back inside.

I miss his touch. The drifting thought took her to the hill at Urusalim and their tent at Gibeon. *Why do I still feel unfaithful? Why do I still feel like Pawah wins if I live my life with Sennedjem? He is the last reminder of a time I have to forget, as he said. How to separate him from the past?*

The questions repeated in her mind until they became a cacophony of unrecognizable thoughts swirling around in her head.

No tears came to her eyes as she stared up at the sun, now covered by clouds. *Please, cloud, cover my past as you do the sun. I am trying to forget so I can move forward. I need to forget. I have to. I cannot live like this.* Her head lowered into her hand to end the memories while her fingers smoothed her brow just as Sennedjem had done for her the past two years.

Her mind had almost cleared until a small voice broke her focus, and a hand touched her shoulder.

"Khumit?"

She forced a smile. "Yes, Ishat?"

"Father wants us to help Grandmother prepare this evening's meal while he and Sennedjem go to the markets to trade." The brittleness of her voice matched the fragility in her eyes.

I felt like that once. Maybe I still do.

Ankhesenamun patted Ishat's hand upon her shoulder. "I will come." But she made no attempt to stand as she locked eyes with the girl and took note of her quivering chin.

I still feel as you do, she thought.

"I will tell Grandmother," Ishat whispered and turned to leave, but Ankhesenamun held on to her hand.

"What else do you wish to say, Ishat?"

Ishat's quivering chin turned into a blubbering cry. "I miss Mother and Shapash."

"I do too," she said and pulled Ishat into her lap. She glanced inside the home. Kotharat was a kind woman, but she did not seem to be as forlorn as Aqhat and Ishat. She had mostly left Ankhesenamun to comfort Ishat, rather than to tend to her grand-daughter's sorrow herself.

Perhaps she has seen many travel to the land of Mot. Perhaps her heart has grown callous. One day I hope mine does too. I cannot endure much more.

Ishat's arms wrapped around Ankhesenamun's neck, and her cheek pressed against her shoulder.

"I must confess something, Khumit," she whispered as her tears soaked through the wool of Ankhesenamun's shoulder sleeve.

Ankhesenamun looked at the sun still hidden behind the clouds. She had so much to confess too.

"You do not need to say anything to me."

"I must. I cannot sleep. Grandmother and Father will think ill of me," she whimpered and tightened her embrace about Ankhesenamun's neck.

"They love you. They will never think ill of you." She rubbed Ishat's back, half-hoping the girl would tell her family what she felt needed to be confessed instead of her. With every comfort she gave Ishat, the probability of finding Nefe only diminished in her eyes as Magidda started to feel more like home. However, she concluded through her twisted web of thoughts that finding Nefe would equal the peace she sought—the peace her mother wanted her to have. Ishat's warmth flooded her chest in the cool, crisp air. *Maybe peace can come eventually in Magidda as well. Ishat needs me here.*

"They will," Ishat said in a barely audible whisper. "Mother told me not to let go of Shapash as we ran, but Shapash got away from me, running another way, and Mother ran after her. I stood still, afraid. I could not move." Tight fists wrenched Ankhesenamun's tunic, and Ishat forced her face into Ankhesenamun's neck. "I saw the arrow pierce Mother; I saw the fleeing raider strike Shapash down." Her voice broke and tired out.

Ankhesenamun remembered her own mother's body with that ghastly dagger wound to her chest. Her mother's screams mixed with those of the members of the caravan during the raiders' attack.

Ishat needs me to say something. What do I say? Do I tell her about my life? Do I tell her I am still grieving all these years later? Do I tell her I am still afraid?

"Why would your father and grandmother think ill of you because of that?" The question barely made it over her lips.

"Because . . . they died because I did not do as Mother said."

Ankhesenamun shook her head. "No, they were killed by cowardly raiders." She pulled Ishat off of her chest to look her in the eyes. "Do not bear that burden."

"But I—"

"Your mother told me something when I was grieving, my child. She said, 'I decided my son would live through me.' And now, your brother, your mother, and Shapash all live through you. They would not want you to bear that burden."

"Even if—"

"Even if." Ankhesenamun lowered her forehead to Ishat's. "Think no more of it, little one. Do as your father and grandmother: remember them. Recount the laughter and the smiles. Their deaths only bring pain, and you, my beautiful," she tapped the underside of Ishat's chin, "are too young for that much pain."

Ishat winced, and her gaze fell. "But it hurts."

"I know it does," she whispered, cupping Ishat's cheeks. "But . . ."

"But what?" They locked eyes once more.

"You can do nothing to change what happened." She stroked some wayward hairs from Ishat's face and tucked them back under her headdress. "You can only change yourself."

The words repeated in her mind in a slow, measured cadence as she realized she spoke to herself.

Ishat crumpled in her arms and cried. "I miss them," she whimpered.

"I do too." Ankhesenamun rocked the girl back and forth and stroked her back, trying to steady her heartbeat. Each member of her family passed before her in a slow reenactment of their lives together, worshipping and dancing before the Aten.

It seemed such a simple time back then, and yet, I can do nothing to change the events of the past. But how can I remember and smile? Even now, I only feel sorrow and wish to forget that life.

The sun no longer warmed her face as it sat hiding behind the cloud; the cool air pricked her tear-moistened face.

CHAPTER 19

SEEKING COMFORT

Sennedjem leaned against the doorway to the inner courtyard and watched Ankhesenamun rock back and forth with Ishat, slowly stroking the young girl's back as she cried.

Aqhat stood next to him. "I never thanked you for saving my life," he said.

Sennedjem winced and crossed his arms. "Please do not thank me, my friend. I was too late in saving your wife and daughter." The image of the archer releasing the arrow meant for Ankhesenamun came to mind. If Arsiya had not had been there, he would be in Aqhat's place picking up the pieces of his life alone.

"You were saving Hurriya and Sidon." Aqhat sighed. "You and Khumit were saving our families while Heth and I—"

"We were all fighting off the raiders," Sennedjem

said. "We were all doing the best we could; I am sorry I was not quicker in dispatching the archer."

"Do not apologize. He was aiming for Khumit. I know you tried your hardest to make it in time." Aqhat sighed and followed Sennedjem's gaze to Ankhesenamun.

I tried my hardest, but it still does not bring back his wife. I could have saved his daughter, but I was too focused on helping Ankhesenamun and did not see Shapash in the raider's path.

"My Arsiya told me of your marital sorrows," he whispered, his voice low and weak.

Sennedjem shifted his weight off of the doorway and furrowed his brow, uncertain if he heard him correctly. "Sorrows?"

"Khumit does not wish to lie with you because of your stillborn daughters." Aqhat turned to face Sennedjem, leaning his full back against the doorframe. "You are a good man."

Sennedjem pursed his lips. "If you think so." The guilt of pushing Ankhesenamun away, perhaps at a time she needed him most, gnawed at his belly. But how could he have known the raiders were going to attack that night? They were so close to Magidda, and they had had no trouble from raiders the entire journey.

"My Arsiya . . . the first child we had was stillborn." Aqhat nodded, his face sullen. "She did not speak more than what was necessary for almost a year.

She seemed to go about her life in a haze or a fog of sorts." His gaze rose to the roofline of the open court-yard; his shoulders and head leaned fully back into the doorframe. "It was a sad time. I thought I would never have my wife back, but then, one day, she began talking to me again. I could not understand. We had lost a child. Yes, it was painful, but I could not under-stand her pain." He sighed. "But now," his voice broke. "Losing Shapash." He choked and could not speak.

In that moment, Sennedjem realized what he had been missing in trying to help Ankhesenamun, and Aqhat confirmed it. He would probably never under-stand what she felt; he had not lived through the murder of his loved one and his child.

"Losing Arsiya. They were taken from us."

Sennedjem peered over to the man, afraid Aqhat's sorrow would become his own. Aqhat's tears ran down his cheeks and into his full beard with his eyes still averted to the roof. "It is different. It is a different hurt." His arms crossed. "I . . . " His voice trailed off for a moment. "The night the raiders attacked, I did not go with Arsiya to pray and worship with the children before they went to sleep. I wanted to stay with the men and continue my conversation with Heth." His head shook. "I convinced myself it was for only one night; I can miss one night with them." A lone finger pointed upward and bounced against his lip. It curled back into his fist. "Oh, what I would give to have held them both in my arms that night."

Sennedjem's gaze returned to Ankhesenamun. "Khumit's first husband was killed, as well as her mother," he said, trying to help the conversation. "I do not know how to comfort her, and I do not know how to comfort you."

Aqhat chuckled at the sorrowful situation, but his chuckle ended with a grimace soon after. "I do not know how to be comforted. Perhaps I do not want to be comforted." His gaze finally fell before he looked out to the courtyard. "I do not know how to comfort Ishat."

Sennedjem's eyes welled with tears. "You all have been through so much," he whispered. "She does not want to remember them. All she can see is the pain."

Aqhat nodded. "I do not know if I could forget Arsiya and Shapash. I only hear their laughter and see their smiles. Every corner of this home holds their memory. It is when I realize I will never hear or see it again that I become sorrowful." He clutched his chest. "I need those memories to live."

Sennedjem chewed his lip. That was what he had been trying to tell Ankhesenamun, but she would not see it. He wanted to ask Aqhat to speak with her, but he could not bring himself to do it. The man had just lost his wife and daughter to raiders. "They are good memories. You will treasure them always."

"Yes, I will." Aqhat's head dropped.

They stood in silence for a moment.

Aqhat stood up straight and placed a hand on Sennedjem's shoulder and patted it. "I am glad you are here. Stay as long as you like before you journey onward." He looked out to the courtyard. "I am glad Ishat has Khumit. I am not glad Khumit's mother was killed, but I am glad she may help Ishat understand her feelings."

Sennedjem's brow furrowed. "And maybe Ishat will help Khumit understand hers." He stood up straight as well and squared his shoulders to Aqhat. "I will do whatever I can do to help your family."

"Your presence here helps us heal," he whispered weakly, but he said no more as tears once again built in his eyes. He turned and left to go inside the home.

Sennedjem watched his dark shadow disappear and climb the ladder to his bedroom above the hearth. "What to say? How to help?" he whispered to himself and slightly shook his head in uncertainty.

Kotharat stared at him as she sat on the woven rug by the hearth. He dipped his chin to her and then returned his gaze to Ankhesenamun and Ishat. He knew Kotharat still stared at him. She had said nothing to him since their first day there. She only stared at him and Ankhesenamun. He had heard her whispering to Aqhat a few nights after they had arrived; she had spoken to Ankhesenamun a few times but never to him directly. The crisp winter air sent a shiver up his leg and arms. He crossed his arms over his chest and leaned on the doorway once more, stealing a glance back at Kotharat, who still stared at him.

What is she thinking? Why does she stare? Surely, living

in Magidda, I cannot be the first Egyptian man she has seen. He looked down at his long, thick wool tunic and robe, girded with thick fabric belting. *Maybe I am the first Egyptian she has seen dressed as a Canaanite.* He rubbed his head of hair under his headdress. *And who is not clean-shaven.* He dropped his head back and popped his neck before Ankhesenamun captivated his attention once again. *How to comfort her? How to help her heal?*

ANOTHER MONTH PASSED, AND SENNEDJEM crawled up the ladder to their bedroom on the side of the house. Kotharat and Ishat slept on the other side, and Aqhat slept at the back with his sons. Ankhesenamun lay on her side on the cot, facing away from him. He crawled next to her and lay down on his back. His hands folded across his belly. She had not spoken to him more than what was needed since he had stopped her from killing that raider. She had withdrawn inside herself. After the month's events, he wanted nothing more than to console her, but she had pushed him away.

He sat up and touched her arm. *I am only her Protector right now*, he reminded himself. But he pulled her to face him. Her cheeks glistened in the candlelight below. He held the desire to wipe them away captive in his chest. *What do I say?*

He studied her face, and she studied his, until she rolled back to face the wall.

He touched her arm again.

"Sennedjem, please do not touch me anymore." Her soft whisper came in a firm command.

He lifted his hand from her smooth skin and dropped his chin to his chest. "As you wish, my Queen."

He debated telling her he had found a man who knew of a Paaten that lived within the city, but when he had tracked him down earlier that day, he found a young man who worked in the Egyptian Administration Center. Obviously, he was not the former General. He did not know if it would bring her hope or sorrow. He opened his mouth to speak, but he hesitated. If it brought her sorrow, what would he do? He lay back down next to her. His thumbs circled each other as his hands lay folded atop his belly. He looked across the hearth room to Ishat and Kotharat in the room opposite theirs. Kotharat's gentle humming brought comfort to his ears as she sang Ishat to sleep.

We have not found one person who knew of Atinuk, Aitye, or Paaten until today. Perhaps it will give her hope. He swallowed the lump in his throat. *And if not, maybe Kotharat's humming will soothe her.*

His amulets grew heavy on his chest. *Goddess Hathor, Goddess of Stars, Goddess of Love—please let this information help her.*

"Ankhesenamun," he whispered barely audibly as

he turned to face her. "I found someone today who knew a man named Paaten—"

"Did you find him?" She rolled over and picked her head up to fully engage in his answer.

"It was not him," he said quickly, attempting not to draw out any expectation. At the fall of her eyes, he added, "But I wanted you to know, because it was the first time in a year of traveling through Canaan that we found someone who knew of a man named Paaten."

She looked blankly at him. "We are in an Egyptian Administrative Center." Her whisper wobbled. "There was sure to be someone named Paaten here."

"There was none in Hazzatu, which is also an Egyptian Administrative Center," he countered. "This must be a sign, an omen, we will find them."

A glisten came to her eyes, and she averted her gaze.

What is she not saying? That always means there is something she is not telling me.

"I want to leave this house, Sennedjem." Her eyes closed. "I have comforted Ishat as much as I can, but I can do no more."

"We will." He covered her hand with his, but she pulled away. He sighed at his blunder. *She asked me not to touch her, and I said we should only be a Queen and her Protector. It is to help her heal. Love her from afar, as I would have done in Malkata.*

"I need to trade for a donkey or a camel—" he began.

"When will that be?"

"They are worth a significant amount of trade goods. We do not have trade goods, so we have two options: I can either stop spending part of my days searching and inquiring with the traders that travel through Magidda, and we can leave in a few months, or I can continue to spend part of my days searching, and we can continue onward maybe after a year's time." He watched her brow knit. "I know you said you wanted to leave, but Aqhat and Ishat—"

"I know," she said. "But I do not want to get more comfortable here. I already feel like we are, and I can already picture us having a family with them. But I do not wish to stay in Magidda if Nefe is not here."

She can picture us having a family, but she orders me not to touch her anymore, not even her hand? What am I still missing? How to comfort her?

"I should have the rest of the city searched by the end of this winter. We will not have enough to trade for a donkey, much less a camel, by that time, but we can leave then, if that is what you wish."

He somewhat desired to stay in Magidda; he liked the city. The people were fair traders, Ishat was sweet, and Aqhat had become his friend. He hoped Nefe was here in Magidda; he could see a life here. He traced the outline of Ankhesenamun's face—well, almost a life here. She still needed to heal and to move forward, and he doubted Ishat and Aqhat would help her. He figured if they could have helped her, she would be in his arms by now.

"We do not have much to carry, now that the raiders took our trade goods. Do we need a donkey to continue on our journey?" she asked.

"No, but our trek will be longer. I will tire." He popped his neck, envisioning the weight of the sling and the tent roll upon his back once again. The trek from Tahnaka to Magidda had only been two days with the caravan, but without Ro-en, it was tiresome nonetheless.

"I can help you carry the sling," she offered.

"We will both tire, and then we will both be vulnerable should any raiders, or anyone else for that matter, choose to attack us." He saw a slight shudder come over her.

"Should we find another caravan?"

"We can see. The trade route between Magidda and Hasura is heavily traveled. I am sure there is a caravan we can at least follow," he said.

"Then let us plan to leave as soon as this winter is over." Her eyes closed, and her shoulders softened.

"Yes, my Queen." His back ached at the thought of the coming travel, but Ankhesenamun needed to leave.

I need to do whatever is necessary to help ease her pain. Besides, as I told her before the caravan attack, if we never find Nefe and she feels she has looked enough, we could always return to Magidda.

Near the end of winter, Sennedjem came back with Aqhat after a full day of trading. Kotharat sat at the table with Ankhesenamun and Ishat as they ground grain for the next day's bread.

"Khumit," Aqhat asked, "will you prepare the fish with Ishat?"

"Of course," Ankhesenamun said, standing up and taking Ishat with her. "Will one of you help Kotharat with the grain?"

"I will," Sennedjem said. He turned to Aqhat, knowing that grinding grain was a woman's job in Canaan, and Aqhat would be hard-pressed to do it. "Are you able to put the trades in the back of the house by yourself, Aqhat?"

"Yes, that shall be fine," he said rather quickly, appearing to appreciate Sennedjem's offer to perform the woman's work.

Sennedjem handed his sling to him and knelt down at the table to grind what remained of the grain. He smiled at the old woman sitting across from him. She still had not spoken much to him, if at all. She seemed kind, but she was always intently watching him and Ankhesenamun.

He stole a glance over to Ankhesenamun as she and Ishat walked to the outdoor kitchen. He could see her through the doorway; no smile arose on his lips. *What do I do? I am so lost with her.*

"Why do you call her 'my Queen?'" Kotharat's worn voice snapped him from his thoughts, and she drew his full attention.

How did she know that? Sennedjem pressed his lips tighter and shrugged.

"Is that not blasphemous to your Queen Tey?" Her eyes searched him.

"Perhaps it is." He squirmed under her stare. Although Queen Tey had probably already journeyed west by now. Word traveled slowly in Canaan, it seemed. "I apologize you overheard our whisperings. I try to call her that only when we are alone."

She glanced at Ankhesenamun. "She looks like the statues of the late Queen of Pharaoh Tutankhamun." Her eyes narrowed in thought. "Queen Ankhesenamun?"

A tepid smile arose from his pressed lips. "That is why I call her 'my Queen.' She bears a strong resemblance." A soft relief rolled over his shoulders.

"Well, you are far from Egypt. I doubt word of blasphemy will travel that far." She swayed back and forth as she spoke. A slight tremor lived in her aged hands as she pushed her smooth handstone over its long, curved base stone, grinding the grain to fine dust.

"Yes." He cleared his throat, not knowing what else to say.

"Are you to go back?"

Again he shrugged; he looked up to the woman who curiously stared at him with her penetrating vision. It was as if she were summoning his inner fears forward and out of his mouth. "I am not sure." He found her eyes again, and he obliged their silent command to continue. "I thought this journey to Canaan would bring healing; we both hoped to start our lives anew." He sighed. "It seems it has only brought more division and separation between us."

She pursed her lips and nodded. "But . . . ?"

Again he spoke, not understanding why he was telling all of this to Kotharat. "I love her . . . so much." He fidgeted with his hands on the table, and his eyes fell on them. "I do not know how to comfort her. I know she does not love me as I love her."

She cocked her head to the side. "So young. So naive."

His brow furrowed, and he lifted his gaze to the old woman.

"She is lost and finding her way. You are comforting her just fine. You have stood beside her all the time, no?"

"I have."

"You have let her cry or not cry without judgment? You have let her be? You have been there when she needed you? Wanted you? Allowed her to push you away when she needed to be alone?"

"Yes."

"You have fed her and protected her?"

"Yes."

The old woman's wrinkled lips grew a warming grin. "Then you are comforting her. It is only time. Patience."

He slid his hands off of the table, and they fell

into his lap. He sat thinking about what she said. *Patience. But it has been years.*

"You wish to say something?" Her old voice croaked as she tilted her head at him with a cunning gleam in her eye.

He smirked as she did. "You know my thoughts."

"One does not live as long as I have and not know how to read thoughts." Her head tilted in the opposite direction. "Now, young man, what is it? What advice can this old hag give you?"

He was quick with a reply. "You are not an old hag."

She scoffed and chuckled. "Well, I am not a young siren."

"Still beautiful." He looked at her aged hands that had probably washed and cooked for her family more times than the number of stars in the sky.

"You flatter me." She gestured for him to continue by rolling her hand. "Now, out with your question or concern."

He sat back on his heels and released a deep breath. "I am afraid she will never love me in return. I know she still longs for her late first husband. It has been several years."

"My dear man," her old voice chuckled. "Patience means *long-suffering*. If you were not patient for her, if you never suffered for her, worked hard for her, sacrificed for her"—Kotharat's old voice strained as her hand curled into a fist and light lit in her eyes—"you will never know the depth of appreciation or love you have for her."

Her words replayed in his mind as his gaze drifted to Ankhesenamun. "While that is true, she . . . she pushes me away."

"She is your wife. You are her husband." The old woman bounced a finger on his forearm. "You are faithful to your gods?"

"She has lost her faith," he whispered.

"Then help her see the way."

He rubbed his neck. "How?"

"By being the example: Pray, worship, do whatever it is you Egyptians do. She will see. In time, she will see that you have never left her side. Out of all the chaos running through her mind, you will be the only constant that always stood beside her. You and your faith never wavered. She will see your *long-suffering* . . . "

He chewed his lip in thought. Kotharat had ended her sentence as if there were more she wanted to say but wanted him to ask for it. "And then what will happen?"

Her dark eyes brightened. "She will make a choice."

His gaze shifted back to Kotharat. "What choice will that be?"

The old woman smiled and paused before she answered. "She will either love you . . . or she will not."

He paused and winced. He could guess the

outcome, yet he wanted to believe the other was still possible. "I remind her of the past—one she wants to forget. She will never love me."

She chuckled amid Sennedjem's dismal tone. "She cannot forget the past."

I know that, but . . . "She wants to."

"Again, it is the same," Kotharat said, lifting both hands toward Sennedjem. "She will have to make a choice: Either accept her past and move forward, or reject her past and live in limbo the rest of her days."

"Limbo," he repeated. That was a good word to describe their entire journey thus far.

Kotharat reached over and patted the side of his arm. "One day, she will make that choice. When she makes her choice, you will have to make a choice too."

He shrugged, not understanding what she meant. "What choice will I have to make?"

"If she loves you, do you keep loving her in whatever state she is in? Or, if she continues to live in limbo, do you continue to love her, knowing she will never truly love you, or do you leave her in her limbo and continue on with your life?"

His mind drifted to his many prayers to Hathor and Isis. His longtime request was to have a future with her. Yet, that future could consist of keeping his role as her Protector. He had given Ankhesenamun his word. "I have already made my choice," he said and locked eyes with Kotharat.

"It will be a hard road for you," she said, understanding his implied decision.

"I know," he whispered. "I would give my life for her. I promised her I would protect her and stand beside her all of my days."

"Good." She nodded her head. "Good," she repeated in a whisper. "She is lucky to have such a good man for a husband."

His chest swelled with gratitude. Even though he had not asked her to be his wife directly, it was the same as if he were her husband. He gave her his word, and he would see it through.

"Thank you, Kotharat."

She shooed away his sentiment. "I am just an old hag doling out advice."

They shared a smirk and a soft chuckle while Sennedjem softly shook his head in disagreement. *I will miss this woman when we leave.*

CHAPTER 20

SEEKING CANAAN

ANKHESENAMUN WATCHED AS SENNEDJEM PASSED over the inner home's threshold. He no longer wore the thick robes for winter, and the cold no longer stung her face when she went outside.

"Khumit?" Sennedjem scanned the room and found her kneeling at the table grinding grain. Aqhat followed Sennedjem with a slight upturn in his lips. He patted Sennedjem's shoulder before exiting to the outdoor kitchen, joining his mother and Ishat.

Sennedjem slowly approached; there was something in his eyes.

"What is wrong?" A sudden dread stilled her hands. *Please . . . I cannot endure much more,* she thought.

He knelt down beside her and dipped his head as if she were seated on a royal throne.

"What is it, Sennedjem?" Her gaze fell to the grain in front of her as she continued to push the stone back and forth along its curved partner.

"Ankhesenamun," he whispered, lifting his gaze. "Word has come from Egypt. Both of your grandparents have passed. Your grandmother a year ago; your grandfather a season ago. Horemheb sits on the throne."

A heavy weight settled in her chest as she considered his message. She had expected her grandparents would journey to the afterlife soon. They had lived long lives and were ready to see her mother and sisters again. They would be happy. But the last part of his message caused her to pause.

"Horemheb?" She pressed her eyes shut. "Was not Nakhtmin appointed Hereditary Prince by my grandfather?"

"Master of Pharaoh's Horses Nakhtmin was killed." Sennedjem's voice trailed off as if there was more he did not wish to tell her.

"Killed in battle?"

"Please do not ask," he whispered and placed his hand over hers atop the handmill.

The thick lump in her throat slid down her belly like a rock, adding to the weight already there. But she guessed an answer to her question anyway: "Horemheb had to kill him to take the throne as the rightful successor appointed by Tut." Her shoulders hid her neck from the truth; Sennedjem did not need to confirm. He squeezed her hand, but she slid it into her lap and out of his grasp. She had brought an end to Nakhtmin's life. If she had remained, none of that would have happened. She could have married

Horemheb or Nakhtmin. The appointment would have been sealed without the spilling of more blood, yet she was here with Sennedjem.

"I see," she said, devoid of feeling. Her eyes opened, and, with thinned lips, she continued her task. Back and forth with the handstone. Back and forth. It was easy work. Mind-numbing. It was exactly what she needed.

Sennedjem knelt beside her in silence until Aqhat called him. "I want to help you," he whispered. "But I do not know how."

She said nothing. *I wish he could erase my memory.* She moved the handstone back and forth with a vacant stare. *And I will never see my family again. I cursed the gods. I will have no afterlife; my heart is heavy. If I did not remember them, then perhaps it would not hurt so much never to see them again.*

"Sennedjem, could you please help me with this ibex?" Aqhat called from the outdoor kitchen.

His hand followed hers to her lap, but at her recoil, he dipped his chin. He breathed in anticipation of saying something else, but instead, he said nothing. He left her by herself when Aqhat called to him again.

Her gaze shifted to his frame walking away from her. *I wish Sennedjem could leave and go back to Egypt. He could then be with his Sadeh and child and not be affected by my burdens. I would be alone, and I could . . . look for Nefe.* She had forgotten her quest when the caravan had been attacked, but it returned over time. *Nefe. You are my future, Nefe. I will find you, and then I will have peace. We will live the life Mother wanted for us: away from the strife of Egypt.*

Kotharat came into the home and sat down on the woven rug next to the hearth. She stared at Ankhesenamun, but Ankhesenamun ignored her incessant observation, like she had done all winter long. Kotharat had been kind to her, but Ankhese-namun did not understand why she watched her with such intensity.

"That is the finest dust of grain I have ever seen," her old voice traveled to Ankhesenamun.

She lifted her eyes to the wrinkled woman. "Coarse grain does not bake well." She threw some more grain on her base stone and began to grind a fresh batch. "You told me that, did you not?"

She chuckled. "You are a good listener."

"You are a good observer," Ankhesenamun muttered under her breath.

Kotharat nodded with a smile, her dark brown eyes still watching her attentively. She shakily stood up and came to sit beside Ankhesenamun, helping her replenish the grain as she ground it.

Even as she did so, her stare upon the side of Ankhesenamun's face did not waver, until finally Ankhesenamun had had enough. She sat back on her heels and laid her hands in her lap. Before she spoke, she rolled her shoulders to appease the ache from the day's worth of grinding. She took a deep breath to appease the ache in her chest from Sennedjem's news and pointedly faced Kotharat.

"Why do you stare at us?"

"You are Egyptians in Canaanite clothing—working and living as Canaanites." Kotharat tilted her head. Her old voice shook but held a sweetness about it. The same sweetness Shapash had in hers. Precious Shapash. Why was it easier to remember Shapash than to remember her own daughters? Even when Shapash reminded Ankhesenamun of them?

"Yes, and?"

Kotharat chuckled behind closed lips with a little, smug half-grin on her wrinkled lips. "You seem to be in pain, my child."

A crushing wave took Ankhesenamun's breath away. "Of course, I am in pain. Cowards killed Shapash and Arsiya. I miss them. I want them here." Her shoulder lifted as she explained herself.

Kotharat's half-grin faded. After a short pause, she spoke again. "I believe it to be more than that, my Queen."

A cold chill initiated in her belly and spread to her still countenance. "What did you call me?" she whispered in a rushed, low breath.

Kotharat leaned in close to Ankhesenamun's face. "You are Queen Ankhesenamun," she whispered while patting Ankhesenamun's cheek.

"You are old and are mistaken." Her body's muscles drew tight as she guided Kotharat's hand away from her face.

"I know," she whispered and sat back. "Your secret is safe with this old woman."

Sennedjem. He is the only one who could have told her. But why did he tell her? She narrowed her eyes at Kotharat. "I am not she."

"Then why are you in so much pain, my Queen?"

"I am not in pain," she said and looked away. Her fingers began to fidget in her lap, until, with nothing else to do, she went back to grinding grain.

"Pain ends, Ankhesenamun. You have not realized it yet, but one day you will."

"I am not Ankhesenamun. I—"

"Pain is a funny thing. It can bring the mightiest to their knees. It can spread easily from one to another, especially when the other loves—"

"I am not she."

"The joys of life will return . . . Khumit," she said with a sparkle in her eye.

Ankhesenamun slowed her grinding and peered at Kotharat with a side glance. "I know you still think I am the former royal wife of Pharaoh Ay, but I am not she."

Kotharat ignored her. "But you have to choose to let go of your pain and let the ones who love you help you grieve."

Ankhesenamun picked up the pace once again. She would let go when she was able to forget. "I grieve only Shapash and Arsiya."

"You wish to forget them too?"

The answer volleyed in her mind: *No. Yes. No. Yes.*

Ankhesenamun pushed the handstone harder into the base stone. "Please leave me, Kotharat."

She reached out and patted Ankhesenamun's forearm. "As you wish, my Queen."

They had to leave soon. No one could know she was there, and she did not trust Kotharat with this secret. Tomorrow, she would tell Sennedjem that they were leaving. He would have to ask Aqhat where else they could go. She no longer remembered Panhey's map of Canaan.

Kotharat still sat beside her, watching and staring at her in silence.

Where are you, Nefe? Ankhesenamun changed her thoughts. *I will find you, and then I will be healed. Everything will be at peace once I find you.*

AQHAT DREW A ROUGH MAP IN THE DIRT IN HIS courtyard the next morning. "You can go up through the port cities, Acco, Surru, Sidon, Berytus, Kubna, or you can go inland. I would take the path to Hasura. Then, from there you can take the path through the valley between the two mountains. There, the cities are Kumidi, Migdal, Baal-gad, Khashabu and Labana; follow the river. After you reach Kadesh, you will venture into Hittite land. I would not suggest Egyptians do such a thing, even though there is a peace treaty between the two empires."

And Paaten would not do such a thing. Ankhesenamun tried to remember the map Panhey had
shown them before they left Per-Amun. It blurred in
her mind, and Aqhat's scribbles did nothing to
refresh her memory. She peered at Sennedjem,
hoping he remembered better than she did.

"You can take the path on the other side of the
mountains. It is the furthest inland path, and it will
take you to Damaski. There are no cities along that
path, and the terrain is rough. Once in Damaski,
there is a path to Baal-gad through the mountain
pass, or you can venture onward and head into the
Mitanni lands. But we have received word that King
Tustratta has been killed, and the Hittites are closing
in on his brother's remaining army. The Babylonians
and the Assyrians are following Egypt's example and
not coming to their aid. That land may be in turmoil
here soon. I would not venture past Damaski. South
of Damaski is sparse, with desert and rocky hills. The
main city-states are Astartu, Yanoam, Qanu and
Bezer."

Ankhesenamun glanced at Kotharat, who was
inside the house and seated on the woven rug by the
hearth. She was holding Ishat as she cried; Beth-
shadon played nearby. The poor girl did not want
Ankhesenamun to leave. Ishat had seemed to be
adjusting to life without her mother and sister, but
Ankhesenamun did not want to continue to grow any
closer to her, only to leave later on and cause even

more heartache. Thankfully, Ishat had her grand-mother still.

The justifications did not take away the heaviness in her chest.

Sennedjem pointed at the route. "We shall take the caravan route to Hasura. From there, I do not know what we will do."

"Word of warning: King of Hasura, Abdi-Tirshi, has patrols throughout the area east of the Jordan River. They were the mightiest city-state in the lands before the Habiru took them. Even today, they are known for their military might, though it is not as great as it once was. They like to trade with the empires: gold for wanderers they find. They are like the raiders. They rarely kill, but they do enslave."

Ankhesenamun stared at Kotharat, who stared back at her. *Should we stay in Magidda? Nefe could be a slave some-where. She could be dead. Am I searching in vain?* She wanted to ask a god or goddess to answer her and show her the answer. She needed an indication of what to do, but she had cursed them and left the great land of Egypt. Her long tunic sleeve brushed Sennedjem's. *And I have made a faithful man leave as well.* They would not listen to her.

"What do they look like, so we know to avoid them?" Sennedjem's question cut through her thoughts.

"They have armor. Usually ten to twenty hupshu in a company. They follow their leader, called a Muru-u." He held up a finger. "They have horses and chariots, though. The best thing you can do is pack up quickly and try to find a place to hide."

Sennedjem nodded. "That should be easy."

"No," Aqhat shook his head and placed a hand on Sennedjem's shoulder. "If you go to Astartu and the others, there is no place to hide. It is barren desert and rocks. You might be lucky to find one large rock, but they will look there. If you are spotted, my friend, your life as you know it is over."

Aqhat leaned in close and placed a hand on Ankhesenamun's shoulder as well. He looked both of them in the eye before he said, "Are you sure you need to leave and journey on? My home is always open to you. I had started to enjoy the small family we had become. I know my mother and daughter feel the same." A slight strain overcame his voice.

Sennedjem looked at Ankhesenamun before responding. "We must continue on." He studied her face for any indication that he should say something different, but she held a vacant stare.

Am I searching in vain, Mother? Her ka cried out to the one person she knew might be listening. The sun rose the day after she was entombed, so she must have made it to the barge of Re. She must have made it; otherwise, the sun would not have risen. *Mother!* Her ka called out. *Am I searching in vain?*

She waited for an answer that she knew would not come. Her mother might hear her, but all she could do was watch from Re's great sun barge and hope her daughter made the right decisions.

"Well then, be safe and travel well, my friends." Aqhat patted their shoulders before his hands fell to his sides. "If you ever journey through Magidda again, know you are welcome here."

"May your gods bless you and your family, Aqhat. May Arsiya and Shapash be well in the land of Mot, and may your hearts find peace." Sennedjem picked up the travel sling full of the trades he had garnered throughout the winter. A modified lighter-weight tent and cot were wrapped up and already strapped to his back. Ankhesenamun picked up the travel sling of essential items they would need on the journey.

"You as well, Sennedjem." He dipped his chin as Sennedjem and Ankhesenamun began to walk away.

They almost reached the door of the courtyard.

"You could stay until you are able to trade for a donkey," he called out in one last attempt to persuade them to stay.

Sennedjem again peered at Ankhesenamun, but she remained lost in her thoughts, staring at the home's exit and the narrow street beyond its gateway. He turned back to Aqhat. "One day, we may have a donkey, but we are ready to keep searching for a new way of life out in Canaan before returning to Egypt."

"Very well, travel safely." Aqhat's voice wavered, and his shoulders drooped.

They stepped out into the street, and a harsh "Khumit!" sounded behind them.

Ankhesenamun turned around as Ishat slammed against her waist. "Please, Khumit. Please, do not go," she cried, squeezing her arms around Ankhese-namun's waist. "No one will understand as you do."

Ankhesenamun placed the travel sling down and knelt down to Ishat. "I still do not even understand, Ishat." A sad half-grin slipped on her face. She cupped Ishat's face in her hands. "If remembering your mother and your sister helps you to heal, then remember them every day. Your mother told me when she lost your brother, the one you never knew, she healed by realizing he lived through her." Her forehead pressed to Ishat's. "Your mother and your sister will live through you and Beth-shadon. He needs his sister, Ishat. You are the woman of the house now. Help your grandmother; she needs you. Be there for your father, he needs you the most."

She placed a soft kiss on Ishat's cheek. "I am still grieving. I need to search in order to heal. I need to seek my future. It is hard for me to explain, Ishat, but I hope you will never have to be as I am." She kissed her other cheek. "Dry your tears. Do not shed them for me."

Ishat wiped under one eye as Ankhesenamun wiped the other. "Will I ever see you again?"

Ankhesenamun's half-grin faded. She would find Nefe, or she would die trying. That was the future my mother wanted for her. That was her answer. The realization dawned on her. After all the many ques-tions, she finally realized her mother's answer. *Find Nefe. Live your life in Canaan together.* **That** *is her answer. I must keep searching. I cannot stay in Magidda.*

Ishat's eyes searched hers for an answer, which she forced from her lips. "No, Ishat, and do not wish to see me again. Do not even pray for it. Rather, pray for peace. Pray for healing. Pray for . . . "—she glanced to Kotharat, who stood next to Aqhat in the courtyard—"the joys of life to return."

Ishat wrapped her arms around Ankhesenamun's neck. "Then I shall miss you, Khumit, my friend."

She enfolded the young girl in one last embrace. "And I shall miss you, Ishat, my friend. I shall remember you always."

Ishat buried her face into Ankhesenamun's neck. "And I, you."

CHAPTER 21

SEEKING HASURA

THE GREAT STONE WALLS OF HASURA TOWERED over them as they walked through its multi-chambered gate. Hupshu, the Hasuran soldiers, stood on the top of the walls looking down at them with arrows resting against their bows as they walked the walled avenue into the city. They had been granted entry by the guards at the gate, and Ankhesenamun forced her eyes to stay focused on the path before her.

"They said we could find an inn at the back of the city," Sennedjem whispered as the last of the sun's rays cast their long shadows down the avenue.

Ankhesenamun envisioned a full bed, a bath basin, food, and fresh linens as they trekked down the long city road. The sun had fully set, and they came upon the inn. It looked like a small house, and they walked through the gateway and into the corridor. A man greeted them. "Welcome, travelers. I was about to close the gate."

"Greetings. Might we find a room to stay for the night? Perhaps a few nights?"

"You are in luck. We have one room available for you. I see you have no donkey, so you will not need the courtyard. The kitchen is available for your cooking needs. There is a well in the city center for water. It will be one shat copper for three nights since you have no animal."

"Done," Sennedjem said and pulled a shat copper from his belt. He handed it to the innkeeper for weighing. They walked through the main house and into the kitchen in the back. There were four small shacks around the kitchen, and the innkeeper led them to one. "Here is your room. Have a good evening. I will allow you to go to the well quickly before I close the gate."

"You are most kind," Sennedjem said with a dip of his chin. He gestured for Ankhesenamun to enter as the innkeeper left them to their room. Sennedjem followed behind her and placed his items down; he took the buckets for filling and left for the well.

Ankhesenamun looked around the small shack— the moonlight only fell so far into the room from the open door. Its perceived emptiness and the cool spring air sent a small shiver through her limbs.

A knock on the door made her jump. The innkeeper's shadow fell beside her before she turned to see what he wanted.

"Traveler's Wife, I apologize for not giving this to you sooner. Here is a candle for your stay." He handed her a small, lit candle. Its flame flickered in the breeze.

"Thank you," she said and protected the flame from the breeze with her hand.

"Sleep well," he said, eyeing her before leaving for the main house.

She scanned the room, holding the candle up to see. There was a small table in the corner with a basin upon it; a cot lay in the opposite corner. An empty ceramic clay pot sat by the door. She half smiled at the memory of holding Sidon's miniature clay pot and Arsiya helping her clean the baby boy, but a sadness washed it away.

She closed the door and set the candle on the table before unwrapping the bread she had made earlier that morning. She ripped it in half and set one half aside for Sennedjem. Next, she pulled the salted meat out and ate her half, leaving the rest for him.

Her knees ached as she knelt by the table. *A long day. A long year. A long life.* A heavy sigh fell out of her mouth as she waited for Sennedjem to return. She glanced at the door. *Why did I not go with him? He could be beaten or robbed, or he could have fallen down the well . .*
.

Her thoughts plagued her, imagining every horrible situation Sennedjem could possibly be in. She stood up, deciding to leave the room and look for him, but he pushed open the door as soon as she rose.

His gaze snapped to her and then to the cot. "I thought you would be asleep by now." The two heavy buckets of water were filled to the brim, and he tried not to spill them as he entered.

I had to make sure you were safe. But her eyes averted with the thought, and her lips instead spoke, "I wanted a bath."

"Yes, my Queen." He entered and closed the door behind him, leaving one bucket by the door for the morning. He poured some of the water into the basin and pulled their linen cleaning cloth from the travel sling. He handed it to her. Their fingers brushed in the handoff. "Shall I bathe you?"

"No," she whispered. "Eat."

She stood and began to disrobe while he sat to eat, forcing himself to stare at the table. Her hands stopped in the middle of taking off her belt. It had been almost a season since they had bathed in this way. Baths in Magidda were in segregated bathhouses in the main square, and before Magidda, before Tahnaka, they were not as they were now. *I should not wash where he can see me. It is not fair.*

She laid her belt on the table. The hidden dagger in its folds plopped on the wood as she studied Sennedjem. *So loyal. So true. Does he stay for me? Or does he stay for his oath to me? I have taken him away from Egypt. My heart will weigh heavy on the scales of Ma'at, regardless.*

Sennedjem glanced up at her. He opened his mouth, seemingly to ask her why she stared at him, but she held up a hand. "I am only thinking. Please do not ask."

He nodded, and his gaze fell back to the table. He sighed before he began to eat.

She took the basin near the clay pot, finished disrobing, and cleaned herself. She washed her garments in the water and hung them up to dry before pulling on the clean sleeping tunic she grabbed from the sling. She emptied the dirty water into the clay pot before refilling the basin for Sennedjem.

"You did not have to do that," he said.

"The water was filthy. You need a clean bath too," she said as she finished replenishing the basin. She set it on the table for him, and he glanced at her.

"Thank you."

She nodded and slipped past him, restraining the urge to draw a soft hand over his strong shoulders as she walked. She reached the side of the wool-wrapped cot and sank into its thick, straw-filled plushness.

Sleep came easily, but she heard the *plop* of water and opened her eyes to slits. Sennedjem stood next to the table, naked and facing away from her, running the wet cloth down the side of his body. His form had thinned since Panhey's house, but he still held the same attractive physique. She had been almost giddy when she peeked at him during baths at Panhey's house. At Gibeon, she had anticipated something more, but those cursed hauntings made her sick. In Magidda, she could not bear his touch, knowing it could be nothing more. She wanted what she could not have. Her nightmares became real in his tender touch.

He had advised her their roles should be only Queen and Protector. It was for her own good, she reasoned, but to both of their detriments. And now in the small inn at Hasura, her heart was too dark and too heavy to think of anything more. He washed his other side and down his front. *Why can I not love him and be with him? Why do I care about the rumors that mean nothing anymore? I am a widow; my husband, my grandfather, is gone now. Why do I still remember Pawah and all of his scheming and evil deeds?* Her eyes averted. *Sennedjem is a reminder of that time. I cannot be with him.* She traced the outline of his body with her eyes. *I may never be with him.* The thought brought a glisten to her eyes. *I want to be, though. I want that life with him.*

She chewed her lip as she watched him clean his clothes and hang them to dry alongside hers. *I want him to be happy. He will never be happy with me. I am haunted, and no matter what I do, I will always be haunted until I find Nefe. Then I will be free from Pawah and my past. Then I may be able to be with him.*

He girded his waist with a clean loincloth and slipped his sleeping tunic over his head. He immediately scratched his back and rolled his shoulders. She almost chuckled but could not expend the energy.

He lay down beside her as she opened her eyes.

"I did not mean to wake you," he whispered.

"You did not wake me," she said. *He is the kindest person I know.* Her hand ached to reach out and cup his cheek, but she drew her fingers into a fist and held it by her chest.

"I thought you would be asleep," he said and laid his head on their blanket roll.

"Do you not know by now," she murmured as she closed her eyes, "that nightmares plague me?"

She felt his hand hover over her temple as if he wanted to touch her or pull her into an embrace, but then it was gone. *I had asked him not to touch me anymore. It is for the best.*

"If you ever wish to speak about them, I will listen," he offered. "You do not have to endure them alone."

I do not want to burden you any more than I have, she thought.

"It may be good to talk about them—"

"Do you wish to turn back and live at Magidda?" she asked. It seemed to her that he had wanted to stay. They were only a four-day journey from there.

"You know my wishes, Ankhesenamun. I want you to be at peace. I have always wanted that for you." His hand moved closer to hers.

"Would you have peace at Magidda?" she asked. She would only find peace when they found Nefe.

He shook his head. "I will not be at peace until you are. Will you have peace at Magidda?"

"No." Her heart fell the second time the realization presented itself to her.

"Then no, I do not wish to turn back and live at Magidda." At her lack of movement, he pulled his hand away.

"Where do we go after we search Hasura?"

He sighed and rolled to his back. "Well, it would not be like Paaten to stay in the valley; that is a common route for the Egyptians to travel to the Hittite lands. When he left twelve years ago, we were at war with them. The valley and the route by the sea were the two main paths Pharaoh's army took to the borders. He would not have lived there. The passing army would have recognized him. Labana and Kadesh are too close to the Hittite border to be safe for your sister. He would not have chosen those, either."

"That leaves east of the Jordan River, south of Hazzatu, south of the Salt Sea, and Damaski." She closed her eyes. "What about Damaski? The Mitanni were allies then. That city-state would have been on the trade route to Egypt."

Sennedjem was silent for a moment, thinking. "It is heavily traveled. I do not think he would live there, but we could still search the city-state."

If that was the case, then they should brave the patrols now while they had supplies, food and vigor rather than after the long, harsh journey to Damaski. Aqhat had said the terrain was rough; there were no cities and little water on that trade route. They could search east of the river first; then, depending on their supplies, they could decide whether to go to Damaski or not.

"Shall we then go to Astartu, Yanoam, Qanu and Bezer first?"

He yawned as he answered. "Yes, and then, if you desire, we look in Damaski. After that, I suppose we will journey south, perhaps to Zoar and Addar and the other cities that we missed south of Hazzatu and the Salt Sea." His voice began to slur, as if sleep was overtaking him.

"What of the Hasuran patrols?"

"We both can fight."

"The patrols have ten to twenty hupshu."

"Nefe and Paaten may be here in Hasura," he offered. "We will start our search tomorrow. Do not lose hope, Ankhesenamun. She is out here somewhere. We just have to look."

His chest rose and fell into a rhythmic pattern.

But Ankhesenamun stayed awake thinking. *I hope she will be here in Hasura. If not, we will have to brave the Hasuran patrols if we are to search east of the river before we journey on.*

An uneasy feeling rippled through her stomach. *Or it may be as Sennedjem said: She is here in Hasura.* She smiled before sleep took her. *I am coming, Nefe.*

CHAPTER 22

SEEKING PROTECTION

HASURA, ASTARTU, YANOAM, AND BEZER YIELDED nothing, and Bezer was nothing but a sanctuary for murderers. Now Ankhesenamun and Sennedjem trekked on the long path to the city-state of Qanu. Its vast stone walls came into view.

Another military city-state . . . just like Astartu. During their search of Astartu, they had been almost taken captive and enslaved for being nomads.

"Almost," she said as her eyes traced the sheer height of its walls. Not as tall as Astartu's walls.

"What did you say?" Sennedjem asked her.

"Nothing." Her sleeve brushed his, but then she crossed her arms. His eyes studied her profile in response. *I miss him.* She glanced at Sennedjem, locking her gaze with his. *His eyes long for me, but this is for the best. The nightmares have almost vanished now. Maybe this is a sign Nefe is in this city. I am getting closer to her.*

"I know nothing about Qanu," he said as they stood on a small hill of red dirt and rock. "It looks to be like Astartu."

Part of her heart feared another city like Astartu, but the other part of her needed to press on. "Do you think Nefe could be in there?"

"She could be; I do not know, though." Sennedjem shifted on his feet under the weight of his sling.

Her sling dug into her shoulder, so she readjusted it, only for it to dig into another part of her shoulder.

"The only way to know is to look," he said.

"Then I suppose we look." She rolled her shoulder to appease the ache.

"Yes, my Queen." He offered his hand to her as he took a step off of the small dirt rise. His strong hand beckoned her to take it, but she knew after looking into his longing eyes, she would want to keep her hand in his. She almost took it before he dropped both his hand to his side and his gaze to her feet. "I apologize; you told me not to touch you."

She chewed her lip, unable to respond. *I want his touch, though. Even more so, I miss him. Just him. I have pushed him away; he no longer holds a gleam in his eye or a quip on his tongue. I want my friend back. I want us to be able to speak as we did. But I have pushed him away. I have become cold to him. He is only here because of his word to protect me. If he could leave and return to Egypt, he would.*

He searched her eyes, clearly wondering what she was thinking.

"Shall we enter Qanu then?" she said, unable to

endure his penetrating gaze. She looked toward the city walls. The winds were not as scorching as they had been to the south, and the sands were not as red nor as fine. Rocks and small brown trees abounded in the dirt.

He nodded, and they walked side by side down the dirt path and up to Qanu's main gate. The guards halted them. "Lay your slings down; they will be searched before you enter the city of Qanu."

Their words were spoken in a heavy dialect, one she had never heard before. Ankhesenamun peered at Sennedjem to see if he understood better than she did.

He slid his sling off his shoulder, laid it out in front of them, and dropped the tent roll from his back. She followed his lead. One of the four guards kept a sword raised toward Sennedjem, but his eyes slid over to Ankhesenamun.

"Tell me, guard," Sennedjem said, drawing the guard's attention away from Ankhesenamun, "what are the laws in this city?"

Ankhesenamun watched as three guards searched their slings, each stealing a piece of gold. "They took our trade goods," she told Sennedjem and pointed at the guards.

The guard holding Sennedjem at swordpoint sent a rough backhand to Ankhesenamun's face. She saw it coming; she could have blocked it, but she forcefully kept her hand down to protect them both from more trouble, as women do not fight. The force of his slap caused her to fall to the ground. The burgeoning red blossom upon her cheek stung as she shook off the coward's strike. She peered up at Sennedjem, who stood with fists by his side and his jaw taut.

The guard laughed at her before returning his face to Sennedjem. "The first law here is to obey the King; death will surely follow those who disobey." He gestured toward Ankhesenamun, who was pushing herself back up. "The second law here is to control your women, or else, another will control them for you."

The guards thrust the travel slings back into Sennedjem's and Ankhesenamun's arms. "You are free to enter, travelers," one said as they shuffled them along the path to the city. Kanu's hupshu lined the walls, eyeing them as they walked through the double gate.

Ankhesenamun leaned close to Sennedjem after noticing the hupshu's stares upon her. She spoke low and through her teeth, hoping not to attract any more men who wished to control her tongue, like the guard. "Should we even try to look here? It does not seem like a very friendly city. Do you think Paaten would take my sister here?"

Sennedjem watched each guard as he walked along. "We need to trade for water and food at the very least, but I agree. Let us leave before the sun sets today, and"—he peered down at their travel slings—"we shall hide our more valuable trade goods in our belts to avoid the thieves at the gate."

"Good thinking," she murmured.

———————

THE MARKET MERCHANTS AT QANU WERE JUST AS dishonorable as the guards. Ankhesenamun had stood by Sennedjem in silence. She carried the bulk of their load as Sennedjem traded for the essential goods they would need until they came across a caravan or small spring.

He stuffed their gold, silver and copper trade goods into their belts while they walked along a nearly empty side road. After everything was hidden away, he ushered her back toward the main path out of the city. "We are done here. I can hardly under-stand what they are saying, and anytime I mention Paaten or tell them my name is Sennedjem, they spit at my feet. I do not think they like Egyptians."

But as soon as they stepped onto the path, a string of chariots entered the gate, followed by hupshu marching behind them. Sennedjem pushed Ankhesenamun to the side of the street, where the citizens of Qanu pressed against them to look at the spectacle. A jeweled litter was borne by servants and surrounded by hupshu and guards; its soft fabric canopy floated in the small wisps of winds.

The crowd of people around them suddenly disappeared, and she looked around to see what had become of them. They were all kneeling prostrate on the ground. She and Sennedjem were the only ones left standing.

He yanked on her sleeve. "Kneel down, quickly."

She hoped they had not been seen standing in front of this royal person who demanded all the citizens kneel before him. The company marched along. "Keep your head down, Ankhesenamun," Sennedjem whispered.

"I am."

But it did no good; they had been seen and spotted. Two guards came over and yanked them to their feet.

"The King of Qanu sees that you are not from Qanu, as you did not kneel when you first saw the King's Transport," one guard said as they both gripped Ankhesenamun and Sennedjem's arms.

Ankhesenamun's sleeve brushed Sennedjem's. She kept her face down, but she could see the feet of the servants carrying the litter of the King.

"Her," a voice bellowed.

The guard who held her grunted in a low growl, "Move." Her legs quaked in the moment. *Why did I make us come here?*

A shallow breath escaped her lips as she glanced at Sennedjem. *What are we going to do?*

The guard stripped her sling from her person and then half-pulled, half-dragged her toward the royal litter; she tried to keep her sight on Sennedjem. *Help me. Please. I am afraid.* But all he could do was scan the men and formulate some sort of plan. Some had spears, and some, swords.

"Show the King of Qanu her face," the voice bellowed again.

The guard yanked on her head to show the plump-bellied King her face. Her brow knitted, and a scowl impressed upon her lips.

"Such a beautiful woman. So dirty, though. Must be why you are sad." The King reached down and swiped his hand just above the skin of her cheek. The gold of his rings barely skimmed her flesh. "Take her to the King's harem."

Her jaw dropped, and her gaze snapped back to Sennedjem. *No.* The guard picked her up, and a scream barreled out of her mouth while she reached for the man she loved. *What is happening? No. This cannot happen. I will not let it.*

She pretended to squirm in the guard's grip, hiding a few well-placed elbow strikes to his stomach. On the second hard strike, he lost control of her, and she ran back to Sennedjem, who had stepped toward them after wrenching free of his guard's grip and knocking the guard back into his company.

The King's disgust at his guards' ineptitude sounded behind her while she flung herself into Sennedjem's arms. Over his shoulder, she scanned the citizens, who had moved away from them, and then peered to the long line of soldiers that stood along the path to the gate. *There is no way out of this. And I have spent my last days with him in self-isolation and withdrawal.* Her eyes lifted to him. His gaze was not on her but on the men behind her. "Do not fight," he whispered to her. "Even if I die, you still might live." He maneuvered her behind him as the King's guards drew their weapons.

She held onto his shoulder, hiding in his shadow behind his back. *I cannot bear to watch you die.* But fear gripped her tongue.

Sennedjem held up both hands to show he was unarmed.

"With all respect due the King of Qanu," he bowed his head, "this woman is my wife. We are but travelers here, and she is with my child. We only ask to leave in peace."

The King laughed and cocked his head at the blatant request. "The King of Qanu does not care if this woman is the wife of another man or carries his seed in her womb . . . " He gestured toward her and Sennedjem with a flick of his wrist.

These are not Egyptians, Ankhesenamun thought. *They care nothing about whether a woman is already married. The judgment by their gods must not be as pure as ours.* Ankhesenamun's forehead lowered to the base of Sennedjem's neck. While the King was speaking, a prayer passed through her teeth in an incoherent mumbling: *Hathor and Isis, I have cursed you, but Sennedjem has given you only praise and worship. If someone is to die today, let it be me. Let your brother god, Anhur, return Sennedjem to Egypt, to Horemheb's palace, and let him see his wife and child again.*

" . . . The King shall simply kill the man and enslave his seed once it is born." He snapped his fingers, and another guard approached Sennedjem with his sword drawn, ready to strike.

"Sennedjem, you do not even have a sword," Ankhesenamun's hushed whisper shook as her fingers dug into his shoulder. Images of Sennedjem's dying and blood-splattered body flashed through her mind. She scanned the length of the King's military company lining the main pathway into the city. How would they escape?

"Stay behind me, Ankhesenamun," he whispered over his shoulder. He pushed her away just as the guard brought his sword up into the air and sent it slicing down.

Sennedjem jumped back, and in the moment during the guard's next windup, he drew his hidden dagger from his belt, lunged for the man, and stabbed him through the neck. The brute of a guard fell with a *thud* at his feet. He caught Ankhesenamun's eye. His quick glance at her was accompanied with a reassuring smirk.

"I have a sword now," he whispered to her while he watched the man gurgle and writhe on the dirt. He threw a challenging gaze toward the other soldiers, who were shifting on their feet and twisting their swords and spears in their grips.

But her heart beat fast in her chest, pulsating behind her eyes; she could only nod. Visions of Pawah resurfaced in her mind, and his evil sneer seized her in the present moment. *You weak little girl,* Pawah's words came to her in an instant. *You could not save your family from me. You could not save your friends from the raiders, and now you will watch Sennedjem die. You left Egypt only to warm another's bed.* He laughed. *I gave you the choice to marry me. Because you did not, Sennedjem will die now in a foreign land with no possible way to journey to the Field of Reeds.* Pawah shook his head. *Tsk, tsk.*

Tears pricked her eyes as Pawah vanished; the heat of the day settled upon her brow once again. All eyes were on her and Sennedjem. She glanced at the path to the gate, still full of soldiers, but the King's words drew her attention.

"The King of Qanu is amused at these travelers." He pursed his lips, tapping his adorned finger to them.

"Let us leave Qanu in peace. We will not return," Sennedjem said as he turned his dagger down as a sign of respect to the King. "My deepest regards in taking the life of your guard."

But the King ignored him. "You are a soldier too, I see, or at least trained as one. I need more men like you in my ranks. You can take his place," the King said, gesturing to the dying guard on the ground. "I will let you live under that condition."

Sennedjem scanned the King's men, who gripped their weapons with even more fervor now that one of their own had been cut down. "And what becomes of my wife?"

"She becomes one of the harem of the King of Qanu." He laughed. "I shall polish her up and scrub the dirt from her face. I will make her truly shine like the golden dove that she is—something you could never do for her. She will be happy in my harem and in my bed as my concubine."

Sennedjem peered up at the King. "No. She is mine alone."

"You are a fool." He waved again. The men with spears pointed the tips toward Sennedjem and drew their arms back, preparing to release death upon him, but the King halted them with a quick raise of his hand. "The King of Qanu shall have a show before his dinner." He flicked his wrist, and five guards approached Sennedjem, their swords drawn and ready to attack. "If you survive this, you may go in peace."

"If you are true to your word, then we shall be leaving soon," Sennedjem said under his breath. Applying his seemingly useless trick, he spun the dagger in his hand to a fighting position. He stooped to grab the dying man's sword with his other hand. His fingers securely clutched its handle as he swung the blade through the air, testing its weight and balance. The soldiers soon surrounded him as the citizens moved even further out of the way, taking Ankhesenamun with them.

The King laughed. "This will be a good show." His clap signaled the guards to attack.

Ankhesenamun held her eyes wide open, despite the arid sandy breeze, to behold what would become of her love and her Protector. *He is willing to die for me, even after I have rejected him. Could it be his oath to me, or does he still love me? How will he best five men, five trained soldiers? Will I lose him like all the others?* Her shallow breaths made her mouth as dry as the land beneath her feet.

The clang of bronze against bronze rang throughout the silent city as all watched the traveler fight five Qanu soldiers.

"Now is your chance to run," a man's whisper brushed her ear. "While their attention is on your husband."

Her head shook no. "I will not leave him to die," she said with a tremble on her lip and a plea to the god and goddesses of war in her mind: *Anhur, Sekhmet, Pakhet, give him strength. Protect him.*

Sennedjem solidified his stance and blocked one strike with his sword. Spinning, he blocked the two strikes from behind and stabbed his dagger into one man's eye in the process. The soldier stumbled backward and fell to the ground, dead. Sennedjem ducked a swing meant to take off his head and responded with a lightning-quick strike with his fist, a deep punch to the man's throat. An audible crack reverberated through the crowds, and that soldier reeled backward as well, gasping for air that would no longer be his. As the man stumbled, Sennedjem grabbed the hilt of the man's sword and stripped it from him. The swoosh of air that precedes a blow whistled in the near distance, and Sennedjem raised his first sword to block the strike. He ran a man through with his second sword just as a foot sailed into the side of his back. His jaw grew taut as he let out a grunt and stumbled sideways, losing his balance.

Ankhesenamun's nails dug into the palms of her hands as she searched the ground for a rock—anything—she could use to help him.

The first attacker saw that Sennedjem was off-balance and raised his sword to attack again.

Her hand clutched her belt and felt the smooth handle of her dagger beneath its folds. But by the time she looked up again, Sennedjem had used the man attached to his second sword to block the first attacker and had slashed him down. He let go of his second sword, allowing that soldier to fall dead to the ground with the sword still in his gut. The last man swung at Sennedjem's head, but Sennedjem rolled and picked up the first attacker's sword. He blocked a second strike that came from straight overhead by crossing his swords to catch the blade in a "v" of bronze. Both men's eyes locked with each other as Sennedjem pushed himself to stand.

Ankhesenamun saw the last soldier's hand sneak to his belt. "Dagger!" she yelled, and Sennedjem jumped out of the way before the small bronze blade could even touch his tunic.

The two men circled each other, stepping over the bodies of the slain, before the last soldier cried out, "For the King of Qanu!"

He lunged with sword and dagger blazing through

the air, but Sennedjem retreated, letting the man's momentum be his pitfall. Sennedjem blocked the strike, stepped to the side, and with one fell swoop of his sword, took off the soldier's head.

Sennedjem's chest heaved as he lowered the swords to his sides amid the five fallen soldiers. The men with spears raised their weapons to their throwing positions once again and waited for the King's order to kill Sennedjem where he stood.

Ankhesenamun's lip bled from where she had unknowingly been biting it. The bitter taste of blood soiled her tongue. *He took on five men and lived. He fought for me. He could have been killed for me. He could have left me. But he did not. He stayed. He lives.* The tightness in her chest and in her shoulders lessened as she watched his exchange with the royal.

He peered up at the King of Qanu. "The King said we could go in peace. Will he be true to his word?"

The King's ringed fingers tapped his bottom lip in rapid succession. "The traveler bests five of my men," he said at last. "You shall stay and teach my men to fight."

"And what of my wife?"

"Your wife?" The King threw a furtive glance at Ankhesenamun. "She will be a concubine in my harem."

"The King's word was that we were to go free if I survived the attack of your five men."

"Fine. You may go free, but your wife stays."

"That was not the King's word."

"You dare call the King of Qanu a liar?" The King's eyes turned red, and he stood up straight in his litter. His hand rose to give the order to his spearmen.

No. Ankhesenamun pulled her dagger from her belt and sent it flying through the air, just as Sennedjem had taught her.

Thunk.

The King's eyes grew wide in surprise as he looked at his chest; his body froze before a grimace came over his face. "Where?" His breaths barely escaped his lips. "Who?" His eyes scanned the crowds as he pulled the dagger from his chest. Blood pulsed out from the wound similar to a rapid heartbeat.

Ankhesenamun trembled, having retracted her throwing arm as soon as she could. Her eyes darted, knowing for certain someone had seen what she had done, but only silence came from the crowds and from the men in the company. Did no one see her?

Sennedjem stood still while the King teetered upon his litter. The color drained from the King's skin. A few of the soldiers near the King barked at the servants who carried him to lower the litter to the ground. Others pointed their long spears and swords toward the crowds, looking for the assassin.

"This must be the doing of Astartu," the King yelled out in one last powerful breath. "Avenge me," came the command through a coarse gasp. He stumbled until he fell backward out of his litter to the ground and lay motionless. His crown had fallen, and it rolled to a stop just before it touched the toe of the litter servant.

Silence ensued. The soft fabric of the royal litter's canopy softly waved in the breeze.

All eyes were upon the plump-bellied King, whose head was crownless. Jaws fell agape. Soldiers at the two ends of the marching line peered around each other to see.

"The King is dead!" a citizen cried out, and all at once, shouts and clamoring filled the streets of Qanu and fighting ensued: citizen against soldier, soldier against soldier, citizen against citizen.

Sennedjem swiped the dagger from the headless soldier and his dagger from the other soldier's eye. He pushed through the crowd that had come upon him and locked eyes with Ankhesenamun.

A whisper from the same man as before tickled her ear: "Come with me." A firm grip took hold of her arm as someone pulled her through the crowd.

"Let go of me," she said and yanked out of the grip, only to find a young man staring back at her.

He pulled her close. "If you want to live, you will follow me. You will be killed if you go through the gate."

"I will not leave my husband," she said again.

"I am here." Sennedjem's voice gave her relief; his touch upon her back made her realize she had almost lost him.

The man led them down a side street covered in

shadow and around a few corners, until he came to a small hole in the outer walls. "The water for the city comes in through here. You must crawl out and then not be seen as you run. Qanu does not have archers, as we are still waiting for Egypt to send some to us—"

"Why are you helping us?" Ankhesenamun asked as she glanced toward the small, dark hole in the thick wall.

"The King needed to die." He bowed his head to Ankhesenamun. "Qanu is in your debt." Pointing to the hole, he said, "Go now while the commotion is within the walls of the city."

"Thank you," Sennedjem said, placing a heavy hand on the man's shoulder.

"I picked up your slings as well," the man said and handed them to Sennedjem. "Journey well on your travels. I shall join my brothers in overtaking the throne. We shall have a good King again."

"May peace come swiftly." Sennedjem nodded his head to the man, and then he stooped down to lead the way through the hole.

THE SUN WAS SETTING BY THE TIME THEY REACHED the other side of the thick city walls. Sennedjem strapped the tent to his back and put both slings over his shoulders. "We have no choice. We must run," his hushed whisper came. "Do you still have the trade goods in your belt?"

"Yes," Ankhesenamun said, still in awe that he was alive, yet slightly in shock at the life she had taken.

"Then if the soldiers see us and overtake me, keep running. Leave me. You will come across a caravan sooner or later; trade with them what you need and find your sister." Sennedjem's hard stare fell upon her. It dipped once to her lips before rising again.

"You could have been killed," she whispered. "You could have left me and returned to Egypt."

"Have you such little faith in your Tutor and your Protector?" He leaned in close. His hand hovered beside her cheek but did not touch her. "I will give my life for you, Ankhesenamun."

Does he love me still, or is he simply performing his oath to give his life protecting mine? I have rejected him for so long; have I already lost him?

His fingers recoiled into his palm, and his hand lowered.

"And thank you for saving me in the end."

I had to; he was going to kill you, she thought. But she said nothing; they simply locked eyes until he adjusted the slings once more, securing them across his chest.

"Shall we run?" he asked.

She could only nod in response before they fled the city of Qanu under the setting sun.

CHAPTER 23

SEEKING DESIRE

Sennedjem rubbed his neck and rolled his head around to stretch away the exhaustion of the day. Ankhesenamun's hands slid onto his shoulders as she sat behind him. A light smile appeared on his lips as she massaged the ache away; it was the most she had touched him since Tahnaka, before the raiders came.

The interior of the tent was lit only by the small fire outside the opening for a door. He sat near the tent's main pole and faced their small sack of trade goods he had brought inside just prior.

His hand slid to the bruise on his flank. The dull ache flared with the memory of fighting the five men two days earlier. They were not Egyptian soldiers, but one of them still managed to get a kick in. He winced, knowing he had been several months out of practice. His eyelids fell heavy over his eyes. It had been a long time since he had felt they were safe from harm. Now, they were out in the middle of nowhere, somewhere east of the Jordan River and north of Qanu. At least he thought it was north of Qanu; perhaps it was west, or was it east? He was lost. *Oh well, it will be something we figure out tomorrow. But tonight, we are safe. We lost the Qanu soldiers that came after us. They turned back. We are alone out here.*

He dug the heels of his sandals into the naturally reddened dirt to remove them and popped his feet onto the thin, lightweight cot. He pulled on Ankhesenamun's hand to give her a kiss on her fingers but refrained since she had asked him not to touch her in Magidda. "Thank you, my Queen," he said, gently patting her hand instead.

"I am no longer your Queen, Sennedjem." She kissed the top of his head as she knelt behind him. "Although . . . a Queen's bath sounds good right now."

Sennedjem pursed his lips, wondering what had changed and why she had turned her affections toward him this night. "I heartily agree." He pulled his tunic up over his head and placed it under the blanket roll along with Ankhesenamun's. "I never knew how little the Canaanites bathed." He looked at his sleeping tunic. He did not want to put it on. It itched, but in the previous nights, he felt he needed to since they were only a Queen and her Protector. Yet that night, it stayed where it was; he made no movement to grab it.

"And in a river or a small pool, of all places. I could not live as a nomad forever. I want a bath chamber with a bath well." Ankhesenamun shuddered at the thought of the cold spring water they had bathed in the prior decan.

Sennedjem tried to tie the days together. Had they bathed a decan ago? Or had it been two . . . or three? He shook his head, giving up on deriving the timeline.

"Well, Pharaoh's Army bathed in river water when we needed to, but even in war, we made sure always to bathe at least once every few days." He shook his head and rubbed his face. Their basin of water rested near the cot. "But it is easier when you come upon a river or creek every few days instead of one every few decans." He grabbed the linen cloth beside him and dabbed it into the water to wash his face and chest.

"At least it is cooler here than in Egypt," she said, taking the cloth from him and running it down his back. "Somewhat." With a tender caress, she dabbed it along the bruise on his flank.

He allowed himself to wince. "Were you able to wash?" he asked. *I did not even ask her before I took the cloth first.*

"Not yet."

His chin fell to his chest. "I am sorry, Ankhesenamun. I do not want you to have to wash with my filth—"

"Do not be sorry," she said, kissing the back of his neck. Then she leaned over him to rinse the cloth in the basin. "We are both repulsive anyway." The water droplets plopped into the basin as she wrung the cloth out and began to wash what she could of her body, which was still behind him.

Why is she kissing me? What has changed? His brow knit as he pondered. *Is she ready for a relationship with me again?*

The *plop* came again, and he heard her put on her sleeping tunic and lie down. Her hand reached up to his shoulder and guided him down next to her. The ache in his side drew his hand as he rested on his back. Sleep beckoned him in the silent night.

"Thank you," Ankhesenamun's soft whisper came.

"Thank you for what?" He wondered if whatever reason she was thanking him was behind her renewed affection. *Are her many touches this evening a sign that she is healing? Perhaps she can see a glimmer of the life she wants with me now.*

"For protecting me from living the rest of my life in the King's harem in Qanu." Her fingers grazed the length of his arm. "I have never thanked you since it happened."

His body sank into the thin cot as a small disappointment overcame him. *I had thought she maybe wanted to be with me again.*

"I gave you my word, my Queen. I will give my life protecting you." He stared up at the slight spiral swirl in the tent ceiling before he closed his eyes. "You do not have to thank me."

Her hand covered his; it renewed his hope. "I am not your Queen."

He smiled a sleepy smile. "Ankhesenamun, you

will always be *my* Queen," he said, turning his head to face her. His smile faded at her silence. "But if you do not want me to call you that, I do not have to."

More silence.

He studied her face. *Why will she not talk to me? Am I that horrible of a reminder for her? Has everything I have done thus far meant nothing to her? I have prayed to have a future with her, but she pushes me away. Even tonight as she . . . I cannot think anymore.* But as they locked eyes, he remembered Kotharat's questions to him: *You have let her cry or not cry without judgment? You have been there when she needed you? Allowed her to push you away when she needed to be alone?* His answers had been "yes."

She seemed to need him. *Should I prod her?* The last six or so months—he was not sure how long—had been frustrating and exhausting. *And tonight, she kisses me, she touches me, she washes me . . . what am I to think? I must ask. I am too tired to try and guess or to wait.*

"What are you feeling, Ankhesenamun?" he finally whispered. "Why do you not speak to me as you did before the attack on the caravan?"

Her hand withdrew, and she turned away from him.

Do not push me away again. I cannot bear it, he thought and asked the questions on his mind:

"Have I done something wrong? Have I hurt you? Have—"

"No." She curled away from him. "You have done nothing wrong, Sennedjem."

He sat up and stared at the curve of her back.

277

Then what was it? Why was she pulling away from him again?

The thought came out in full force, as he lacked the strength to hold it in: "Then why are you rejecting me?"

A momentary pause came, and she wrapped her arms across her chest. "I did not realize you only wanted my body."

What? He sighed, releasing his anger at the ridiculous accusation. His head fell back as he stared at the fabric of the tent above his head. His chest expanded with a full breath to help him absorb her lashing. "No, Ankhesenamun. I want you—all of you. I love you, yet you will not even talk to me. Now you do not even look at me. What have I done? What can I do?"

"Nothing."

He rubbed his hair with his hands. His scalp itched. He was going to have to keep hair on the top of his head for the rest of his life. It was an errant thought, but, in the moment, he longed to take a razor to his entire body. He hated the small beard he had on his jaw and over his lip. He wanted a bath. He wanted his natron, oil, susinum, kohl, and shendyt. His hands fell into his lap.

But more than anything, he wanted Ankhesenamun to be happy. He thought she was almost there. He thought she might be accepting what had happened to her and leaving that behind her. He thought she might be able to see this future with him. Was he wrong?

He squeezed the amulets around his neck. Their smooth carved edges pressed into the palm of his hand. *No. She kissed my neck tonight. She washed me. She caressed my hand and my arm. I must prod her. Why did she do that?*

"Ever since the attack at Tahnaka, we have stopped speaking about important matters." He debated gliding his hand over her back and shoulder in an attempt to turn her to face him. *One step at a time. I would rather she speak to me about what she is thinking and feeling than push her further away from me by touching her.*

Still no response. "Do you want me to sleep outside, so you can be alone?"

No answer came, so he assumed she wanted him to sleep beside her. *I suppose I will have to wait until she will speak to me again to know why she did what she did tonight.*

The weight of the day forced him to lie down again on his back. The days had been long as they fled Qanu. His feet hurt. His back hurt. His bruised side once again drew his hand. He looked over to Ankhesenamun. *I should probably make some time for sparring so both of us can keep our training fresh in our minds. I should have done that in Hasura . . . and Astartu . . . and Bezer . . . and the other city-state we went to . . . whatever its name.*

His eyelids fell heavy over his eyes, and his breath steadied. Nothing moved. Nothing stirred. Nothing sounded outside of their tent. The soft rise and fall of his chest and her soft rhythmic breath almost captured him in sleep's relaxing embrace. Sleep had come or almost come when he heard a small whisper: "When did you fall in love with me, Sennedjem?"

Did she say something, or am I dreaming? His eyes lazily opened, and he turned his head toward her to confirm or deny his question. She lay next to him, snuggled against his arm, looking into his eyes.

"I am sorry to wake you. I had hoped you were asleep." She kissed his shoulder with a soft brush of her lips.

He instinctively placed a small kiss on her forehead before he realized his action went against her wishes. "I should not have done that." He turned his face away from her to avoid further tempting himself in his groggy state.

What woke me? He blinked, trying to remember. Her question. Hope lit in his heart, and some of the grogginess faded. *At least she asks a question of substance. When did I fall in love with her?* He cleared his throat as he thought back to the courtyard in Malkata's royal harem. She had been married to Pharaoh Tutankhamun then.

"You will think me dishonorable with my answer."

"Dishonor?" she scoffed. "Why would I ever think you are dishonorable when I am the Queen of dishonor?"

His brow furrowed. "You are not the Queen of dishonor." He closed his eyes. Sleep called him, but he forced his eyes open. He needed to hear her. She needed someone to listen. After almost six months —*or was it seven months?*—of her not really speaking to him since the caravan attack, he needed to stay awake for this conversation.

Her grip upon his arm tightened. "I am the Hereditary Princess. Yet, I am selfish. I chose to be selfish. I wanted to live a secret life of exile with a man of my choosing—a man with whom I was accused of being unfaithful—instead of staying and ensuring peace for Egypt when the crown transitioned to the next Pharaoh. My absence plunged Egypt into civil unrest and the killing of Nakhtmin. I brought that burden to Horemheb's shoulders. I have killed a King of one of Egypt's vassal states. His death will surely have consequences for Egypt. I have . . . " Her voice trailed off as one of her fingers lightly traced the side of his face.

She said she wants to live a life with me—the man with whom she was accused of being unfaithful? Is the guilt over what Panhey and that rumormongering Fleetsman said causing her grief? Or does it stem from Pawah and Tut? He tried to focus his mind on the substance of what she had said instead of wondering what she thought about him. Her feelings toward him could wait. *She feels guilty for leaving Egypt in a state of unrest.* He reached across his chest to rest his hand over her grip on his arm. "The affairs of Egypt are no longer your concern, Ankhesenamun."

"I am the Hereditary Princess. My father and Tut were divinely appointed. I was their blood, and I had a divine duty to Egypt. I forsook it, and Horemheb had to kill Nakhtmin." Her lip quivered. "Consider my mother. She loved Egypt more than I do. To ensure peace, she was willing to live a celibate life, as a priestess of Isis, for the rest of her days, having a man she loved within arm's reach. Yet I choose myself. How can you say I will think you dishonorable?"

She may be right, but surely the gods knew her pain and her suffering. They released her. Pharaoh Ay released her. The duty was no longer hers.

"You are not your mother." He squeezed her hand. "Your mother wanted this life in Canaan for you and your sister. Is that not what you told me? She wanted you to leave Egypt and not to live as she did. That is why we are in Canaan looking for your sister."

Wet tears splashed near his neck. He debated holding her while she cried, but she had told him not to touch her. The awareness of her hand in his became ever-present, though. *This one time I shall not do as she commands.* He turned to his side and wrapped an arm around her. "And the position of Pharaoh of Egypt was always going to fall to either Horemheb or Nakhtmin. Either man would have led Egypt into prosperity. They were both skilled and diplomatic; both were trained in Pharaoh Amenhotep III's army. They both knew what the position of Pharaoh should be in the eyes of the people. Your presence probably would have done little to keep the peace. Nakhtmin still would have been killed because he did not release the throne to the rightfully appointed. And you killed that dishonorable King to save my life. I am forever grateful to you for that."

She has not chided me for touching her, but her shoulders still hold burdens. He rubbed her back as she cried.

"What more do you wish to say, Ankhesenamun?"

"Nothing."

He paused again, debating another action. Should he press her? Should he accept her answer? Should he stop comforting her? "Do you agree with what I said?"

"Yes," she said with an aversion in her gaze and a glisten in her eye.

That always meant there was a half-truth in there. *Should I dig it out? Do I let it be? Should I let her answer stand alone?*

"With what part do you not agree?"

"I agree with everything you said."

"Then why are you still crying?"

"I am not." She wiped her eyes.

He rubbed her shoulder, and the closeness of their faces became apparent. In a moment of weakness, he grazed her lips with his as he stared into her eyes. "I will never harm you, Ankhesenamun. Tell me what is truly bothering you. Why are you not asleep? What changed after Tahnaka and the caravan attack? Did the slayings of Arsiya and Shapash cause it? Should we not have stayed with Aqhat? I thought it would help you to heal, as well as them. Or was it me and my suggestion to be only a Queen and a Protector? I tried to do what I thought best for you. I thought it would help you heal. I will do whatever you need me to do to help you."

After a moment, she cupped his cheek and drew him into a soft kiss.

One burden lifted and gave him renewed energy. She still saw a future with him. She still wanted his touch, even though she commanded differently. *I have missed these lips.* His mind raced into hope so quickly that he almost forgot about the question he had posed to her. *Perhaps after this kiss's end?*

She pulled away and smoothed his cheek. As if knowing his thoughts, she asked, "You never answered my question. When did you fall in love with me?"

He pressed his lips into a sad smile. *When she is ready to answer my questions, I will be here for her.* He rubbed her back. He opened his mouth to tell her but did not know if speaking Tut's name would hurt her, as it had in the past. "Quite a while ago."

"That is not an answer." Her hand fell to his neck and ran down his chest.

She has to know how her touch makes me feel. He covered her hand and pressed it still against him. "It is a time you want to forget; shall I still tell you?"

"Yes," the answer came a short while afterward.

"The day I told you about Sadeh and my child. On that day I told you that I was with you until I journeyed west. On that day I told you that you are never alone. Do you remember that day?" He chewed his lip. *Why did I ask the question at the end? She wants to forget, you fool.*

After a moment of silence, she whispered, "I do. I had asked you if your wife was as selfish as I was. You said I was not and she was not." Ankhesenamun slid her hand out from underneath his. "It was the day Tut told me he could not believe me when I said I did not murder my daughters." Her hand pressed against her forehead, and she turned onto her back.

I am losing her again.

"And Hori and I told you we believed you," he added quickly to press forward.

She said nothing in response.

Do I prod? Do I leave her be? Hathor, Isis, please guide me.

Her soft rhythmic breathing could have fooled another man into thinking she was asleep. The gentle tickle of the cool night air came in through the light weave of the tent fabric as he waited for her to speak. His gaze was firmly fixed upon her; sleep could wait.

"What are you thinking?" The question came out in a hushed tone, as if he were afraid to be heard. *She is so fragile, yet so tough. She has endured so much and still stands.* Her hand slid down her face until it plopped down beside her.

"You were always on my side, were you not?" Tears pricked her eyes as she turned to face him once more. "In the training yard. In Aketaten. In Malkata's corridors. In the harem's courtyard. In my sorrow. In my confusion. In Per-Amun. In Urusalim. In

Magidda. In Qanu. And now." A new admiration bloomed in her eyes as she slid a hand around to his back and pulled herself closer to him, closing the void between their two bodies. "You helped me when I had no one else."

"I am your friend," Sennedjem whispered as he pushed a lock of hair behind her ear. "Even if you do not want a life with me, I will always be your friend."

Her face drew closer to his, and her eyes shined and softened at the same time. A flush came over her cheeks. "I miss you, Sennedjem." The words barely made it over her lips. Her touch lingered on his back.

"I miss you, too." His fingers ached to caress the soft, smooth skin of her cheek. A tingling spread over his body as they locked eyes in a deep gaze. He teased his ache by skimming her hairline at her temple. As he breathed, she breathed, together in unison, growing faster and more audible in the silent night.

She finally spoke. Her words flowed along her breath: "I want a life with you." Her parted lips pressed against his mouth as her hands ran in long strokes down his back.

A semblance of rational thinking took hold of him before he could allow himself to relish the fulfillment of his desires. Her breath rolled upon his lips as he tried to form the words he wanted to say. His mind was blank. He could only envision wrapping her in his arms and cherishing her acceptance of him.

"Do you not love me anymore?" she asked at his inaction.

That question he could answer with ease. "I will always love you." He relinquished control of his hand and cupped her cheek, smoothing his thumb over its soft gleam in the dimming firelight that fell into the tent.

"Then why do you not kiss me in return?"

Why did I stop her? He could not think. He touched his forehead to hers. *Why am I hesitating? This is what I want. This is what she wants. Or is it? Has she healed? Has she moved past what has happened to her?*

"Sennedjem?"

"I am your Protector, my Queen." His lips brushed hers, and he almost lost control again. "You said you want a life with me, but can you *see* your life with me, after everything that has happened?"

She gave a slight nod and ran her fingers down the soft hair of his jawline. A slow smile built on her lips and beamed in her eyes. "I am ready to be with you, Sennedjem."

Had he heard her correctly? Had she finally chosen him? His breath betrayed the fluttering in his chest as he matched her smile. *Is this a dream? Is this true?*

She nestled against him; every curve of her pressed against him. "I am ready to be with you, Sennedjem," she repeated and ran a firm hand down his chest and belly.

His body craved her demanding touch, becoming instantly addicted. Elation dilated his pupils, and a new breath blazed through his chest. He had heard correctly. It was not a dream.

Their heavy breathing mimicked each other in anticipation of what was to come before he sank his lips upon hers. He tasted her and gripped the base of her neck to pull her closer to him. A soft moan left her. The primal urge within him surged through his hands as they roamed over the warmth of her body. Her grip upon his back grew more possessive and intense. The tingling sensation of her tongue and lips ignited a new fervor in his exploration. His heartbeat pounded in his ears as he anticipated that telling hitch of her breath. It was the one last test to see if what she said was true.

But it never came. She had made her choice—the choice of which the old woman Kotharat had spoken. She chose to love him. She chose him.

And I choose her. Forever.

THE MORNING SUN TRICKLED IN THROUGH THE entry flap of their tent and through the light weave of the tent's fabric cover. He took a deep, peaceful breath and opened his eyes to look at the woman he loved lying beside him.

He had expected to see her asleep or smiling with a joyous gleam in her eye, but instead, her eyes welled with tears. Her face held a grimace.

His brow knitted as he grasped her waist, pulling

her close so their bellies touched. "What is it?" his whisper wavered.

Her mouth fell slack as a tear escaped. She rolled to her back with a despairing sigh and then to her side, facing away from him.

What happened during the night? Did I say something in my sleep? What could I have said? I only dreamt of her. I love her.

He sat up to lay a hand on her shoulder. "Did Bes send you a bad dream?"

"No," came the almost inaudible whisper.

His eyes narrowed in thought, darting from the seemingly peaceful day outside the tent flap to their travel sling on the other side of the tent pole. *What happened? Why is she crying?*

Her breath hitched, and his heart sank. Color left his face. A twinge of pain itched in his throat. Any happy future he had dreamt of in the years prior fled from his mind. That was the hitch he had come to dread.

Was I blind last night? She said she was ready. I thought she chose me. I thought she had accepted the past. He chewed his lip. *This is not what I had planned. This is not what I foresaw. This is not what I wanted.*

He drew in a deep breath, as if to ready himself for what was to come.

What was to come?

He swallowed the painful lump in his throat and braced himself for whatever future the gods were to bestow upon him.

"What is it, Ankhesenamun?" His question was thick in his mouth.

"I am hurting," she whimpered and curled into a tighter ball.

"Have I hurt you?" he asked, tears already welling in his own eyes.

"No," her expected answer came.

He rubbed her arm, and she pulled away.

"I feel guilty."

"You feel guilty for lying with me?" he asked, more as a confirmation to himself than a question for her to answer. It soured his tongue as it left his mouth.

"I am sorry, Sennedjem. I was so happy until I woke this morning and realized what I had done."

"What have you done?" It was as if, in lying with him, she had committed a crime and broken a marriage vow, neither of which she had done. *I thought she chose me.* He rested his head in his hands.

"I made the rumors true. I—"

"But they were not true. They were never true."

"They are now. Pawah was right. He won this game. Always. He always wins." Her body tensed, and she pulled her tunic over her nakedness. "He takes everything from me."

His hands clenched to fists. He tried to follow her line of reasoning but came up empty. "Pawah is dead, Ankhesenamun."

"I know that," she said through clenched teeth. "You do not understand."

He peered over at her frame. "I am trying."

Silence.

He leaned over, stroked her arm and tried to kiss her cheek, but she turned away from him.

"Sennedjem . . . please do not speak to me anymore. Do not touch me. Please leave me alone," she whimpered and put her hand over her head as if to push something out of her mind.

"What?" he asked, not believing his ears. "Ankhesena—"

"Please," she begged with a cry in her voice.

Her plea crushed his chest. A paralyzing wave took his body. Numbness gnawed his gut. His mouth turned bitter as he whispered barely audibly, "Yes, my Queen."

She released a small cry at his response. "I am sorry," she kept repeating over and over as he girded his waist with his loincloth and left their tent.

He scanned the vast nothingness: some sand, some stone, some gravel, and some small rocky hills. The hot wind seared his face, cooled only by the tears glistening on his cheeks. In that moment, he realized how far from Egypt he was; the realization trapped his breath in his chest. Sadeh and his unborn rushed to the forefront of his memory. He had held his first wife as she began her journey west, and now he would never see her again. He peered back at the tent where Ankhesenamun lay curled up inside. He had had his life with Sadeh, and then, he wanted a life with Ankhesenamun.

He had made himself believe she would love him one day. She had told him she would one day. He told himself it was enough just knowing he could protect her and love her, but, in the back of his mind, he had believed she would return his love at some point. But his very presence caused her pain.

Is this my life? Will this be my life? His hands clenched to fists as he kicked some of the gravelly rock and sank to his knees, the thoughts fighting to come out. *Was I wrong? I cannot live like this. Sadeh, forgive me. Ankhesenamun, forgive me.*

An indecipherable yell burst from the depths of his belly. Every muscle drew taut when he finally took a breath. He ripped the amulets off of his neck and wound his arm to send them sailing over the barren landscape, but at the point, he would have let them go, he did not. Their smooth, carved edges pressed into his palm. He dropped his hand into his lap while the vigor he had held only a moment before disappeared.

He peered at the amulets of Hathor and Isis before sticking them into the gravel rock, standing them upright.

"Hathor—Goddess of Love, Lady of the Two Lands; Isis—Goddess of Marriage, Mother Goddess, I have nothing to open your mouths." He pressed his eyes shut. "I have no offerings to give you." He fell forward prostrate before them: his forehead to the ground and his hands on each side of his head. "I can only give you praise and pray you grant me blessing and favor. Goddesses of love and marriage and of children and of women . . . help me see."

A crippling wave of nausea passed over his stomach as the rest of his prayer was silent. *Why can I not understand Ankhesenamun? Why can I not help her heal? She will not let me. She will never let me be her husband.* His brow furrowed at the thought, and an ugly grimace covered his face.

"Help me be content." The cry flowed over his lip. "Help me find peace in this life."

Pain coursed through his limbs and stabbed his ka as a new realization entered his mind: When they found Nefe, he would have to leave Ankhesenamun for her to fully heal from all that she had endured. He was her last reminder of the time she did not want to remember.

"I am an eternal reminder to her; I realize this now." He shook his head. "Forgive us for leaving Egypt, the land under your protection and blessing."

He chewed his lip. "I wanted another man's wife. I stayed true until her husband, Pharaoh Ay, put her off. I justified it to myself. I thought this life would grant me a future with her. I now see my folly."

His fingers curled into the gravel rock and dirt beside his head. "She wanted to leave and to forsake her divinely appointed duties to Egypt, and I enabled her. Forgive me, goddesses of love and marriage, Goddess of Stars and Mother Goddess. I have prayed to have a future with Ankhesenamun for so long, but

I see it will not be as I requested. It was foolish of me to make such a request."

A shaky breath left his mouth as his brow smoothed.

"If this be true, then please, Goddess of Stars and Mother Goddess, grant one last request . . . Let it be enough for me that I love her and can protect her in this life." His tears wet the rocks under his face. "Let it be enough for my heart not to weigh heavy. And when the day comes for this life to end, please let Anhur bring me back to Egypt so that I may see Sadeh and my child once more."

CHAPTER 24

SEEKING ACCEPTANCE

THEY WALKED IN SILENCE. SENNEDJEM CARRIED THE heavier travel sling and tent roll on his back. They pushed through the headwinds that slowed their progress. The daylight waned. Her feet tired. Her ankles ached. Her arms hung lifelessly by her side. She peered to the east and then to north, but not to the west. She could not bear to look at Sennedjem.

What have I done? The question had replayed in her mind for the last decan. Sennedjem had tried to comfort her that morning, but she had pushed him away and asked him to remain silent. He obeyed her, and as the winds swirled the rocky gravel around her toes, she wanted nothing more than for him to speak.

He is the most perfect, forbidden reminder of the past I am running from.

In their long shadows that stretched toward the east, Tut's tar-plastered body lying in his sarcophagus flashed before her. In the winds, her mother's muffled scream haunted her ears. The rustling of the gravel sand tossed by the winds became the whispers she had endured at the palace and on the barge to Per-Amun. She had made the rumors true. She had proved the Fleetsmen right. She had finally lost Pawah's game.

Her eyes closed, and she stopped walking. Sennedjem did as well but did not speak.

I am haunted. I will always be haunted. I must do as Mother told me to do. She wanted me to find Nefe. That is the answer to my questions. I must continue to search.

Her eyes opened.

Mother . . . I wish you were here. I wish you could tell me what to do. I wish you could protect me from Pawah. He haunts me. I do not know how to escape him and all he took from me.

Sennedjem stared at the ground by her feet, awaiting her command.

"I do not think the winds will let up," she said. "Perhaps we should make camp here?"

He dropped the travel sling and removed the tent and cot roll from his back. He placed the wooden poles in the ground and secured the tent fabric with rocks as she took out the contents of her sling to start a fire and prepare dinner. They had found a caravan and traded with them for food, but when they asked to join them, they had been rudely rebuffed.

She put a handful of beans in the cooking pot, making sure to ration what they had so that it lasted.

Sennedjem rolled out the lightweight cot and put his travel sling of trade goods in the tent before he came to stand by the fire. They would have beans and bread again tonight.

She stood by the fire as well, watching him stare at the ground by her feet. He had gone about his routine in sorrow—not anger, not resentment, just sorrow. It hurt her heart because she was the reason he was in pain. He had not laughed, teased, joked, or even said one word since they had been together. She could take no more.

"Please say something." Her voice traveled on the winds.

"You asked me not to speak, my Queen." His gaze never lifted.

She took three steps and folded into his chest. "I am sorry I have caused you torment."

His arms tensed, but they did not enclose her.

Her gaze rose, and she found his eyes. "Please say something."

He gently lifted her from his chest so that she stood alone before dropping his hands back to his sides.

"What do you want of me, Ankhesenamun?" Sennedjem stood before her as he once did in his training yard: his body, like that of a sentinel; his eyes, longing. Yet this time, there was exhaustion in his voice.

I want you not to remind me of what I have lost. Her lips pressed closed and did not speak her thoughts. *I want to be with you. I want to love you. I want you to go back to Egypt and leave me in my misery alone.*

A boil kindled in her heart at the injustice in her life and in the lives of those she loved. Her ears burned at the pain she had caused Sennedjem. Hot tears pricked her eyes at her own struggles and frustrations. That night with Sennedjem had been everything she wanted it to be. *Why can I not be at peace? Why? Why? Why, Mother? Why?* The question caused her pressed mouth to open and something to spill out in response to Sennedjem's pleading question.

"I want—" She yanked her headdress off and threw it in the ground. "I want—" A fisted hand slammed into her thigh. Her lips bubbled with unspoken words.

His eyes moistened as he watched her.

"I want to forget, Sennedjem!"

"You cannot forget." His voice broke as he took a step toward her. She pushed him in the chest, but again he advanced, grabbing the sides of her arms. His gaze bored into hers. "You cannot forget."

She parried his hold, knocking away his loose grasp of her arms, just as he had taught her. He did not try to touch her again.

"It is too painful to remember." She jabbed him in the chest with a finger. "With Nefe, I will be able to forget."

"How?" Sennedjem asked her, pushing her finger away but keeping his voice from rising with hers.

"She is my sister."

But he was quick to refute: "How will you forget when you are with Nefe? She was there when your mother was killed. She was there when your father was murdered by your mother. How will she help you forget? Will she not be a reminder as well?"

Ankhesenamun's arms shook, as did her roiling stomach. *My mother gave me the answer. I must find Nefe. I must find her.* Yet his questions threw her thinking into reverse, and she second-guessed herself for a moment. But she could not let her foundation slip.

"You know nothing," she yelled in his face.

His hand clutched his chest. "Then tell me."

"I cannot." The cry weakened into a semi-yell.

"Why?" he responded with the same timbre as she used.

Her breath fell heavily out of her mouth. *Why?* It was such a simple question to ask, but she could not answer it. She had no answer. There was nothing to tell.

He spoke during her momentary pause. "Do you want to know why I can say Sadeh's name and not feel pain?"

Silence. She had asked that question to herself many times but always feared the answer.

"Because I remember," he whispered.

She shook her head vigorously. It was not the same. "Sadeh was not murdered. Everyone I loved was *murdered*."

Again, he was quick to refute: "But they lived, and

you loved them. To forget them is to erase them. Do not forget them."

"But how can I live with this pain, Sennedjem?" She threw her arms in the air. Her tears ran in long streams down her cheeks. "How can I live like this? Remembering my mother's scream, seeing her lying on the floor . . . holding my murdered daughters . . . imagining Tut as he was ambushed . . . envisioning my mother being forced to take poison to my father . . . my father realizing he was poisoned . . . Meritaten being killed in her bed . . . my sisters struggling to breathe from the plague . . . Everyone, everyone I loved is gone. *Taken*. It hurts. It is painful. It never ends. How can I live like this?" Her hands fell once again to her sides.

She took a step back and away from him. "How, Sennedjem? How?" Her yell belied her proud chest.

He stood silent with a glisten in his eyes.

"My life was a game to Pawah, and I have lost everything I ever wanted to that man. Every time I am with you, the accusations and the depth of turmoil Pawah placed upon me rush upon me. I begin to recount them one by one. I remember each horrific murder and each painful death, and every time it ends with the burn of his hands around my neck or his lips seared against mine or his grip upon my body, in place of yours. It was that way up until the night we were together. That night, I was happy, but in the morning when I woke, the memories overwhelmed me. I do not know why it happens . . . " Her voice trailed off.

He remained silent for a few moments, but then he spoke in a low, hushed tone as the winds around them faded, along with the sun. "Because you left your home with me. With the rumors and accusations, Pawah made me a part of his game. You want to forget your past, but I"—he pointed to his chest— "I am your past, along with everyone else you loved. But I can be and want to be your future too." He drew near to her once again. "That is why you cannot forget them. You have to remember them and the way they lived and loved. When you can do that, then you can move forward."

"I do not want to, Sennedjem. I do not want to remember." She clutched her collapsing chest as he wrapped his strong arms around her. "I cannot. The pain is too—" Her incipient cries choked her words, and an open-mouthed sob burst forth from her lips.

CHAPTER 25

SEEKING SAFETY

HER STOMACH ACHED, AND THE SMELL OF FOOD made her physically ill. A second month had passed and a third drew near since Ankhesenamun had experienced a monthly purification. She knew then that a life grew within her womb. Fear struck the depths of her soul. For nights on end, she only dreamed of her daughters' faces and their limp, lifeless bodies. Even the daytime was not safe from those dreams.

She sat on a small rock facing the campfire while Sennedjem knelt beside it, cooking their dinner in the pot set atop the ring of rocks encircling the flame. Its light crackle drew her out of her mind's wanderings of holding a third stillborn daughter. The imagined baby's tiny frame disappeared in her open palms atop her lap.

Ankhesenamun's stomach gurgled. Sennedjem had put the last of the beans they had into the cooking pot and poured the last of their drinking water in to help warm them before they had set up the tent. She closed her eyes and shook her head. "I have doomed us by deciding to look in Astartu first. We have been to all of the city-states east of the Jordan River; no one has heard of Atinuk, Aitye or Paaten. And now, we are hopelessly lost."

Sennedjem stopped what he was doing and crawled closer to her. His warm hand covered her open palm as he sat down next to her. "We will find her."

Her fingers enclosed over his hand. A release of tension came as a momentary reprieve. At least he and she were speaking again. She would be a liar if she said she did not find comfort in his touch. With a sudden graceful moment, she swept his hand to her lips, and she placed a soft kiss there. Their hands fell with a thud into her lap. He seemed so optimistic, and she appreciated his encouragement, but she glanced to their dwindling travel sling. Two deben gold and a few shat copper were all that remained. They had one amphora of beer and two pieces of salted meat left. No grain, no bread, no water, no beans . . . at least starting tomorrow.

"But, Sennedjem, we cannot find her if we die from starvation and thirst in these vast plains." She scanned the landscape—not one trading post or caravan in sight. Nothing. Just the large rock a few cubits away—the only protection they had in the nothingness. "We are lost. I do not even know what city we are to come upon next."

"All will be well." He cupped her cheek and brushed aside her hair from underneath her linen head wrap. "I still have my bow and arrow. I can hunt, and we still have some beer to drink."

"The winds are beginning to have a slight chill in them. It will be winter again in a few months." Her head hung. "And we are lost; where will we find shelter? We cannot live without water, and we cannot live in a tent in the winter."

"We will live. It never fails—we always come upon a spring or creek or caravan whenever we are low on supplies." His soothing pass of his thumb over her fingers sent a small grin to her lips. "And winter, as you said, is a few months off. We should find someone and know where we are going in the next decan. We always do."

He patted her hand and saw the sun's shadow had passed the line in the dirt he had marked. "I think the beans are ready." He slid back over to the fire to plate their beans and bread.

He handed her a bowl and made himself one before he slipped back to her side.

"Thank you," she said in a low voice while her smile faded.

"You are welcome, my Queen." He leaned forward to give her a kiss, but she pulled back.

"I am sorry. I thought . . . " He recoiled and removed his hand from her knee. His gaze averted, and he seemed to wait for her to speak. But after some silence, he studied her again.

Her lips trembled as she wanted to speak what lived in her heart, but how could she form such sweeping gratitude into words? He had given up his life for her. He had jeopardized his afterlife. He had stood by her since the day she stepped into his training yard at Aketaten. He had comforted her in her sorrow and in Tut's rejection and anger at her. He had kept her from a sin of murdering that raider. He had comforted her when she pushed him away, even now after being with him. He had been faithful to his promise to her. What words could convey what her heart wished to say? How else to show him what she felt for him?

Tears formed in her eyes as she stilled her lips and pressed them into a straight line.

"Ankhesenamun," he said, his eyes searching her. He placed his bowl on the ground and hesitantly slid a hand behind her neck. "What is it?"

"I never told you," she began and swallowed.

I love you. Those words never came, though. *What else shall I say? I am grateful. Yes, I am grateful.* But it did not hold the same meaning that she wanted to say.

His gaze locked with hers, asking the question for which he longed to know the answer. The same question he had asked her before the caravan was attacked: *Can you see a future with me? Do you or will you ever love me?*

Her eyes pressed closed; she was not able to respond to his silent plea for an answer. She wanted to scream a resounding "yes" from every high place, but fear or guilt or shame or pain kept her from answering.

"Sennedjem, I . . . "

The words were easy to say: I love you.

"I . . . "

Her voice trailed off. He was the embodiment of everything she needed and everything she wanted. She searched his eyes. How to answer his unspoken question?

Why am I afraid to speak what I know to be true?

He drew her lips to his and left a soft kiss there.

"It is enough for me," he whispered as he moved a strand of hair from her face. He brushed her cheek and then her neck before he picked up her bowl and handed it to her. He pressed his lips to form a reassuring smile that did not reach his eyes before he turned to his food once more.

They ate in silence until their bowls were empty.

Everything he said and did made her want to tell him how she truly felt about him, but it could not get past her tongue. So instead, she asked a question that had plagued her mind since she stepped foot on the private barge at Malkata with him.

She dropped her empty bowl on the ground to create some sort of noise in the deafening silence between them.

He startled and looked at her. "What—"

"Why are you doing this, Sennedjem?" she blurted out. "I have done nothing but make life miserable for you. You could be in Malkata, sleeping on a bed, with food every morning and night, gaining honor and prestige in teaching the future officials of Pharaoh's Army. You could be safe and—"

"Because I love you, Ankhesenamun," Sennedjem whispered. His eyes searched hers for any response.

A twinge of guilt pinched her beating heart. This man had given up everything for her, protected her, loved her, fathered the unborn child in her womb, and yet she could not say the words in return. In her deepest truth, she knew she loved him, but the words could not pass her lips.

She wrapped her hands underneath his linen headdress and ran her fingers through his hair at the base of his neck.

"Everyone I have ever loved . . . " Her voice trailed off, and a glisten came over her eyes. Perhaps if she did not accept she loved him, he would not leave her. He would not die. He would not be murdered. And if he were to leave her, she was unsure where she could run to this time. The only place left to go was to wherever Nefe was living out here in the vast lands of Canaan, and even then, would her past truly be behind her? It seemed to her she could not escape the past—no matter if the past was in Egypt or in Canaan. It stayed and tagged along, pestering her like a swarm of flies.

Her jaw grew taut as a shaky breath filled her chest. She pressed her forehead to his, unable to continue her statement.

A rustling sound approached from the distance.

He pulled away and looked in the direction of the sound. "Patrols," he whispered.

Her eyes grew wide as he grabbed the two daggers and her hand. "Patrols?" she said, looking in the same direction he did. "The Hasuran patrols Aqhat spoke of?"

He looked at their campsite. She followed his gaze. "There is no time to hide it," he said, grunting and looking at the dust coming for them in the distance.

A fluttering beat in her chest gave rise to a waver in her voice. "What are we to do, Sennedjem? We cannot outrun them."

"We hide." He pulled her to the nearby rock and pushed her inside. He scattered the sand and rock to cover their tracks and rounded the corner of the cleft just as the horses' snorts could be heard on the breeze.

His body pressed against her; his steady heartbeat calmed hers. He looked around the small cleft and whispered in her ear, "This space is only big enough for one to hide well."

She curled his tunic into her fists. "Let us hope they do not look here." She laid her cheek against his chest, but Aqhat's warning became clear in her mind: *There is nowhere to hide; and if you are lucky enough to find a rock, they will look.* The thought bristled the hair on her arms. She pushed it away and gripped Sennedjem's tunic even tighter. She stayed quiet while the sound of the Hasurans and their horses reverberated in the small cleft.

"Whoever was here must not have traveled far," a gruff voice said, followed by the clang of their bronze cooking pot hitting against the small rocks in the gravelly ground. "Fire is still ablaze."

"They must have heard or seen us coming," another said.

Sennedjem turned his head, straining to locate them or determine how many of them there were. Ankhesenamun pulled him closer, wishing their hiding space were bigger. Her sweaty, flushed skin fixed her tunic to her body.

Do not search the rock, she pleaded with them. *How did I not see them coming? How did we not hear them sooner? The winds were pressing against them. Their sound was carried behind them and not toward us. That must have been it, but it does us little good now. Why did I not turn around and look?*

The top of her head fit against Sennedjem's tightly drawn neck in their contorted position within the rock cleft.

"But where did they go?" Another rummaged through the travel sling. "They left their bow drill and hunting equipment here. They cannot get far without it."

"There, that rock. Look there."

Ankhesenamun tensed even more, as did Sennedjem. *They are going to find us. What are we going to do?* Sennedjem shoved the two daggers into Ankhesenamun's belt. *Are we not going to fight?* He pressed the remainder of his two deben gold into Ankhesenamun's palm.

The heavy footsteps crunched on the sandy, gravel-covered ground.

Sennedjem gripped the sides of her arms and stared into her eyes. He leaned forward and pressed his lips to hers in a lasting kiss.

This is it. We shall be captured. He gave me his weapons. They will not think an attack will come from a woman. It will be our advantage. I am ready to fight. I am ready—

He ended the kiss, hovering his face over hers and cupping her cheek. "It is enough for me," he whispered on her lips, almost inaudibly. "Stay hidden. Find Nefe. Forget." His dark brown eyes turned soft as he spoke her wants for her life.

Her eyes searched him in the moment that seemed to stretch for eternity. *What is he going to do? Why would he say that? We are going to be caught . . .* Then he pulled away. Her eyes grew wide as she realized his intention to save her. Her fingers dragged along his bicep as he left her in the hiding place. A bloodcurdling scream bolted from her belly but smashed into her pressed lips and instead pushed tears from her eyes. Her chest wrenched tight around her heart and her knees wobbled as she fell deeper into the rock's cleft. She pressed against the darkness and turned her face from the little light that fell into the dark place.

"Sennedjem," she mouthed. The urge to pray came over her, but to which god, she was not sure.

She shut her eyes tight as the harsh Akkadian orders sounded in the evening.

"You there," one of the Hasuran hupshu said.

Ankhesenamun pulled her dark cloak to hide her head and knelt down to make sure it also hid her feet. She prayed to Amun-Re and the Aten, to any god who would hear her. *Please do not take him from me. Please. Hathor, Isis, do something! He prays to you every morning and night. Do something to save your faithful worshiper.* She pushed Tut from her mind. Tut was their divinely appointed, and they did nothing to save him. Who would Sennedjem be to them? Who was she to them, that they should hear her pleas? She had deserted Egypt and cursed the whole panoply of gods and goddesses. But still, she had to try. *Please,* she begged in one last plea. *Do something.*

Tears blurred her vision, and she forced her breath to come out in a shallow, silent sweep through her nose.

"Easy with the spear, my friend," Sennedjem responded just at the cleft's entrance. His shadow from the dying sun's rays fell against the rock at a point that Ankhesenamun could see from the slit of her linen cloak over her head.

"Who are you?" The shadow of two spears pointed toward him.

Sennedjem raised his hands. "I am a traveler. My name is Sidon."

"Why were you hiding?"

"I became afraid when I heard the horses and

chariots, and I hid. I did not know if the approaching party was friend or foe."

"You travel alone?"

"Yes."

A hupshu grunted at his response, and the clank of bronze sounded. The heavy footsteps of a second hupshu drew near, and he stuck his head into the cleft to quickly peer around. Ankhesenamun held her breath.

She saw the shadow of the soldier nod to his apparent leader and allowed herself to breathe once again.

"Where is your tribe?" the leader asked Sennedjem.

"I am traveling home to my family, but I seem to have become lost. Might you know the way to Damaski? I will need to pass through there to return to Labana."

One of the soldiers began to circle Sennedjem. Ankhesenamun closed her eyes, unable to bear witness should they run him through. She wanted to cover her ears with her hands but feared they might hear the rustling of her cloak.

"See the northwest mountains in the distance? You can barely see their outline. Go to their base; follow it north. You will come across a river. Follow the river, and it will take you to Damaski."

"Thank you," Sennedjem nodded his head. "My brother in Labana will be most glad to see me again."

"Where did you say you were going? Your dialect is not from around here."

"Labana."

"Ah, Labana. Well, Labana is not an ally to Hasura. I am afraid your brother will not see you again, traveler Sidon."

Ankhesenamun braced her heart to hear Sennedjem moan from a spear jab to his chest. She pressed her eyes tight and bit down hard on her tongue to keep from crying out. Aqhat's words came back to her: *They are not known for killing.* She hoped what he said was true as tears ran in wet paths down her cheeks.

"But you have told me the way," Sennedjem's voice came.

"But we have found you, and so we will take you to be a servant in the King's court. The King of Hasura pays well for strong men to build his temples or to trade with the Babylonians."

"Please, I have a family and ailing parents. I must be allowed to return home."

"Then you should have thought twice before traveling alone."

The soldiers behind him drew their blades and approached him.

"On your knees, traveler."

Her hands pressed over her mouth to hold in the shattering scream coursing through her chest. She watched the shadow of Sennedjem kneel before the soldiers bound him. He allowed them to tie his hands and tie his feet.

Why does he not fight? Why does he not do something? There must be too many men for him. There must be . . .

As they yanked him up to standing once again, he glanced at the rock as if to say one last goodbye.

To save me. He does nothing to ensure I am safe.

"Walk, servant," one hupshu ordered Sennedjem.

The handles of each of the daggers pressed against her ribs. She envisioned jumping from the cleft and perhaps taking one man by surprise, but how would she deal with the others? She had heard at least three different voices. Two had spears; her daggers were no match for the long spear. She chewed her lip as she listened to them prod Sennedjem, who walked away without incident.

At least they did not kill him.

From the clangs and thuds and grunts, she assumed the hupshu were throwing their items into the travel sling and dismantling their tent, only to load all of it up on their horses.

She closed her eyes until the horses' trots sounded in the distance. Their clattering gave away the direction they were heading. When the sun's rays gave up the sky, she emerged from her hiding place.

She stared out toward the direction of the trotting horses through the dying haze of smoke rising from their extinguished campfire into the dusk of night. The patrolmen's torches ignited one by one—the only indication of their distance.

They had taken everything except the gold in her hand and the daggers in her belt. She now knew the way to Damaski, but instead of facing in the direction of the northwest mountains, she looked in the opposite direction at the diminishing torchlights. She closed her eyes and wiped her tears. The gurgle in her stomach silenced at the sudden weight that fell there.

"He told me to find Nefe and forget." Her shoulders dropped. That had been her goal all along, yet standing there alone, she questioned that purpose.

Was **this** *the life you wanted for me in Canaan, Mother?*

There were at least three men, soldiers; how could she possibly rescue him? A tear ran down her cheek at the inevitable outcome—both of them dead or both enslaved.

"But they took him."

The warm winds whipped around her, pushing her both forward and backward. "Nefe is my sister. Nefe is what my mother wanted for me in Canaan." She stared at the gold in her hand. It would be enough to get to Damaski and more, but . . .

She lifted her gaze once more to the torchlights in the distance. "Would life with Nefe be worth a life without him?"

The rumors encircled her with the winds: the rumors from the Fleetsmen, the rumors from her people, and the rumors from Pawah.

"You will silence," she told them with the confidence and vigor she had possessed as Queen of Egypt.

Her father, her mother, her sisters, Kiya, Tut, and her lifeless daughters flashed before her eyes.

That was the end of this life for them, but that was not their whole life.

Her eyes burned as she heard her mother's scream and saw her mother's lifeless, murdered body lying on the floor. Her cheeks boiled with anger as she sensed Pawah's face near hers, his breath upon her lips, and his hands upon her neck and waist.

Pawah is dead. I will not let him hurt me anymore.

The words of comfort she had spoken to Ishat became clear in an instant.

Only I can change. I hold the memories, not Egypt. It does not matter how far I run, whether or not I find Nefe, or whether or not I love Sennedjem—only I can change myself. The past will always be a part of me, and my future is not written. Only I can change. I, alone, can determine when I have peace and when I am healed. I decide when the joys of life return. Only I can change.

As a break came in the winds, Sennedjem's wish he imparted to her the last day they had expected to see each other at Malkata resounded in memory: *And most of all, I wish you to find peace in whatever life the gods give to you.*

The future had seemed bleak, but she knew she would persevere.

"I shall always attack," she had said.

A fire rekindled in her heart and in her mind as she readied herself for whatever was to come.

I will no longer be haunted.

The validation sent a surging power through her limbs. It ached to be freed. Her hands by her sides abruptly curled into fists as the winds blew into her face and beat against her chest.

"No one shall ever take from me again." A fierce determination swirled around her as the wind's slight pricks of chill tickled her cheeks and revived her strength. *I will face whatever is to come. I will own my life. I will take back what was taken from me. I shall always attack.*

Her eyes popped open as she emerged a new woman. A long, slow and steady breath pushed back against the winds in strong defiance of their will.

Nefe, forgive me. I hope you are safe, as I have always hoped. She clasped her fists over her womb. *Be our mother's legacy for me, should I fail tonight.*

With a hard-set jaw, she tucked her gold in her belt alongside her two daggers and darted forward against the winds in a silent jog, following the specks of torchlight.

CHAPTER 26

SEEKING RESCUE

Six. Seven. Eight. Eight soldiers. Two archers. She counted the soldiers once more. The intense campfire blazed in the middle of the ten hupshu sitting around it, speaking in friendly banter. *Ten hupshu. How am I going to do this?*

The light cast down from the stars paled in comparison to the fire's light, and thus she remained unseen in the shadows just where the darkness met the firelight.

At least the night is to my advantage. Her gaze drifted to Sennedjem, who knelt outside of their circle, tied to a stake by a lone one-man tent; he was still greatly lit by the blaze.

The men chuckled. One spoke to the other: "Yes, *Muru-u.*"

Ankhesenamun's ears perked up at the man directly in front of her. "He must be their commander," she whispered under her breath.

"Do not mock me, boy," the Muru-u responded.

The young hupshu settled, but his beady eyes darted around their group. His back straightened as a gentle hue of red sprang upon his cheeks.

"So, Muru-u, will you share your bounty for the Labanian with the rest of us?" another hupshu said and threw a rock at Sennedjem, pelting him in the arm.

Even though her attention remained on the conversation, her gaze lingered on Sennedjem. His defeated shoulders burdened and bent his usually straight back. He barely reacted to the rock. He sighed and then shook the pain away. His hands and feet were still tied, but when the men's attention turned back to the Muru-u, he quietly snuck the rock into the palm of his hand. *What is he going to do with that?*

The Muru-u leaned back and scratched his beard. "Perhaps I can share. You are my favorite men."

"So I am a man now? I thought I was a boy?" the beady-eyed hupshu said with a sharp, mocking tone.

"That is because you are my boy, Son." He reached over and placed a hand on his boy's shoulder and shook him back and forth.

Ankhesenamun eyed the large Hasuran Muru-u in front of her. *The patrol sits in a circle. Ten of them.* She recounted a third time. *What to do?* If she were to reveal herself and step into the light, the archers would definitely shoot her before she could reach the Muru-u in time. If she were to sneak to Sennedjem, they would most likely see her. She stood in the shadows, silently swaying in the crisp gentle breeze as she planned her next move. It would be either life or death, and she needed careful consideration of each proposed action.

Should I wait to attack until the company is asleep? She eyed each man's physique and standard-issue linen uniform with leather armor. *No, if I know anything about military men, I know they do not sleep deeply or much at all while out of their homeland. I have been standing here the greater part of the night, and they still do not sleep. I need to make sure they do not attack me. I need to be in charge of them. But how? I am one woman.*

She had debated during the entire jog over to their campsite on what she would do. A plan loosely formed in her mind, and she committed to it as she stood watching them.

No one will take from me again. I will free Sennedjem, or I will die trying.

Her heart was steady now, and the beads of sweat were dried. She picked up a rock by her foot. Her heart began to beat faster. *Steady,* she calmed herself. *The one who panics is the one who dies.*

She would have to throw it far enough to spook the horses to divert their attention there. *Should be easy enough; just like throwing a spear or a dagger.* She bounced the rock in her hand. She put one hand out in front to steady herself and extended her hand with the rock behind her.

She rehearsed her plan once more: *Throw the rock.*

Divert their attention. Hold the Muru-u hostage by dagger. Leave with Sennedjem. Hope they do not follow us in the night. She tried to predict how many bounds it would take for her to reach the Muru-u sitting in front of her. She chewed her lip as she weighed that distance against the time it would take for the archers to grab their bows and arrows sitting by their legs and shoot her.

This could go very badly if not everyone's attention is diverted. She straightened up and clutched the rock in front of her chest. *How am I going to best ten men?* Her toe dug into the sandy dirt as she thought. *I will not best them. Even Sennedjem was kicked as he fought five men. One of their kicks could incapacitate me. Two men is the most I have ever fought at the same time, and Arsiya and Shapash were still struck down.* Her eyes pressed closed in the memory. *What am I going to do?*

"Well," the Muru-u said as he stood up.

No! There goes my chance. Her fingers gripped around the rock. *If I was going to follow that plan . . .*

"I will be asleep. Niqmad, Ibiranu, take watch. The rest of you get some sleep." He marched over to his tent, and, before he ducked inside, he peered at Sennedjem. "Get some sleep too. You have a long life ahead of you, Labanian." Then he chuckled and went inside.

The rest of the men took off their armor and spread out their blankets in a circle around the fire, their weapons still within arm's reach. The beady-eyed hupshu and another still dressed in his armor stood up, and they took positions at the north and south ends of the circle.

Ankhesenamun walked around the circle in the shadows to where the tent and Sennedjem were. The son of the Muru-u stood guard next to his father's tent. She faced him as he stood staring out into the darkness. The eeriness of his staring at her but not perceiving her gave rise to small bumps on her skin. *Should I kill them? Should I take one out at a time? I have to be in control of them. My heart is already heavy; does it matter on the scales of Ma'at whether or not I am justified in the killing of them all?* A familiar uneasiness passed over her belly. *I would rather not kill all of them, but how will I be able to show them I am a threat? How do I keep them from following us once we leave? Can I distract the Muru-u's son and retrieve Sennedjem without killing any of them, or will that only make the others rise and be on alert?* She turned the rock over in her hand.

The son of the Muru-u called out to his comrade in arms, "Ibiranu, I have to *ezû*."

The men all groaned, signaling that even though they were asleep, they were sleeping lightly. However, the Muru-u's snores still sounded from the tent.

"Fine, go *ezû*. Yassib, get up. Take his place until he comes back," Ibiranu said.

A man groggily stood up, retrieving his sword on the way up, as Niqmad, the son of the Muru-u, walked toward her. She backed up further into the dark night. *Here is my chance. Do I kill him? Do I leave him alive? He is the Muru-u's son. He may be better left alive, in case I need to barter his life for ours.* She noticed the long whip tied to his belt and his long belt sash. *Those will do.*

He walked past her and then squatted. His form disappeared in the darkness, but she followed the sound of his grunts. *Now is my chance.* As she approached, her eyes adjusted to the darkness, and she found his outline under the dim moonlight. She raised the rock in her hand and cracked it against the back of his head. He fell. *Thud.*

No movement. Out cold.

Yassib, the man who had taken Niqmad's place, laughed. "That was a big *ezû*, Niqmad."

Ankhesenamun grabbed his whip, quickly bound his hands, and stuck a rock and some dirt in his mouth. She felt along his body, grabbed the dagger within his belt, and added it to her growing collection. Then she tied his feet with his long sash.

"Niqmad?" the man shouted in a whisper.

Ankhesenamun went back to her place just outside the ring of light as Yassib began approaching with his sword drawn, tip down.

Should I kill him? She noticed the other men had not stirred, and this Yassib had not alerted Ibiranu he was leaving his post. *In Egypt, killing is not preferable, but we are in Canaan now. My heart is already heavy. I will not have an afterlife. Does it matter?*

The rock turned in one hand as she drew one of her daggers with the other.

I will kill him if I have to, just as I did with the King of

Qanu. She steadied her breath even though her heart beat in her ears. The King of Qanu had been a tyrant and seemingly had abused his power; the citizens and soldiers were divided, and half wanted him dead. This man, Yassib, was simply a soldier looking for his comrade.

"Niqmad?" his hushed whisper came again as he slunk closer. Ankhesenamun let him pass by her before she began trailing him. He stopped in a full halt as if sensing her presence, but it was too late for him. She sent the rock flying into the back of his head too. Only he stumbled and did not fall. Again, she took the rock toward his head, but he spun around, dodging her strike. He opened his mouth to call out as he thrust his sword. She blocked his attacking hand while thrusting the rock over his temple in a wide sweep of her arms.

Thud. She stepped on the hand that held his sword and hit him again over the head with the rock as he groaned.

Out.

She took his belt and bound his hands and feet behind his back. Then, as with Niqmad, she took a smaller rock and stuffed it in his mouth along with some dirt.

She turned around and looked at the campsite. The Muru-u's tent was left unguarded. Ibiranu still stood on the opposite side of the campfire. *How do I get rid of him without alerting the others? Perhaps I can now sneak to Sennedjem since there is no guard by him anymore. I shall make no sound. I will not let them rise. Do not look at us, Ibiranu; otherwise, I will be forced to kill you in the same manner I killed the King of Qanu.*

She came to the ring of light on the ground. If she stepped into the circle, her sanctuary in the dark would be no more. She would no longer have a hiding spot; if Ibiranu saw her, that would be the end. They would surely either kill or enslave both of them.

If I try to distract Ibiranu, he may alert the others. He seems more tenured than the rest of the men. Should I sneak around and throw a dagger to his chest? And hope no one notices his body lying in his lookout spot? And hope that he does not yell out before he dies? I could try to aim for his throat, but I am not that accurate with throwing daggers like Sennedjem is. The chest is the best I can do. She shook her head as Ibiranu's short pacing took him out of her sight. The Muru-u's tent blocked him from her vision. *At least the tent provides me some cover from Ibiranu's sight line. Maybe I do not have to kill him.*

The consequences of any further action she made bounced back and forth in her mind, until she made her decision and stepped from her sanctuary of darkness.

She snuck along the shadow of the tent until she was almost close enough to Sennedjem to touch him. She lightly yanked on the rope that held his feet. He peered over his shoulder and his eyes grew wide. His mouth turned down and he shook his head, but she crawled to him and began cutting his bindings from his wrists. The rock he had in his hands had already cut through some of it, but it would have taken him days to cut through all of it. She quickly sawed the dagger back and forth over the fibers of the rope. *I have to work quickly and hope Ibiranu—*

"Labanian!" a shout came from across the fire.

Her gaze snapped to Sennedjem's face just as the rope broke in two. He pulled Niqmad's dagger from her belt and sent it sailing toward Ibiranu, hitting him dead in the throat. "Run," he told her.

"No."

The men frantically awoke and began looking around, and the Muru-u crawled out of his tent and stood. She took her chance during the momentary disorientation of the sleeping men and sent one of her two remaining daggers for the leg of the Muru-u. He yelled out and fell to his knees while she ran and slid behind him, placing one dagger to his throat. She yanked the second one from his leg and held it to his manhood in one swift motion.

"You will do as I say, Muru-u, or I will first cut it off and then slice your throat," she whispered hotly in his ear as the six remaining hupshu now were up, frozen still, gaping at their commander under hostage. "Tell your men to stand down."

His hands lifted in surrender as his men stood, their eyes darting between Ibiranu and their Muru-u. Some reached for their weapons.

"We are under attack, it seems," the Muru-u told them after releasing a groan of pain.

"Do it," Ankhesenamun said again, pressing the dagger's blade hard against the Muru-u's skin.

The six men stood around the fire: all were without armor, and only three had weapons in their hands.

"Or what?" the Muru-u said, his hand halting his men's advance of her. "A woman comes alone. My archer there"—he pointed at one of the armorless and weaponless hupshu—"only needs to retrieve his bow at his feet; then, he shall pick you off." He laughed and, with a chuckle, repeated, "A woman." The other men laughed along as well—one even lowered his weapon.

He underestimates me. My advantage.

Ankhesenamun tightened her grip upon the daggers in her hands and pressed his back to her bosom. His laughing abruptly stopped.

"You have stolen my husband," she whispered in his ear. Then to the men she announced, "And I am not alone. Do you think me a stupid woman? Our tribe stands in the shadows with their arrows drawn and pointed at each one of you. My tribesmen hold the son of the Muru-u."

Again she addressed the Muru-u, but loudly enough for all to hear: "If you do not cooperate, they shall kill him and pick off your men one by one. Once they are dead, I will kill you, after you know you have failed them."

The Muru-u scoffed. "This man said he had no tribe." But at the slight tension in his jaw, Ankhesenamun deduced he did not wholly believe she was bluffing.

Sennedjem had untied his feet and entered the Muru-u's tent. He emerged with the Muru-u's sword and dagger and came to stand behind her.

Ankhesenamun continued once she felt the command had fallen to her in light of the Muru-u's duress. "Now—"

The man the Muru-u had identified as an archer reached for his bow and quiver, but Sennedjem raised his dagger to throw. The hupshu's gaze turned toward Ibiranu; he paused in mid-reach, realizing he could not complete his task without feeling the strike of a thrown dagger.

A commandeering grin seized her lips. "Our tribe are all skilled with bow and dagger; we kill only when necessary." She turned her mouth to her captive's ear: "You have a chance, Muru-u, to save what is left of your men." Ankhesenamun forced her voice to stay low and firm. "Order them to stand down."

The Muru-u's eyes darted about the darkness, searching. "I think you come alone, woman. You do not have my son."

Ankhesenamun slid the dagger closely to his jugular. "Do not be prideful. See Ibiranu across the way. He is dead. Where is Yassib? Where is your son? I believe you said his name was Niqmad?"

A quiver overcame his jaw. The men shifted on their feet with a hesitant dart of the eyes between their Muru-u and the purported tribesmen in the shadows. "Prove to me your tribe stands; have them shoot an arrow into the flame," he said. A slight strain tainted his voice. "Prove to me my son lives."

"And give away their position by shooting an arrow? Do you think my tribe is made of fools?" She pressed the dagger just above his manhood to draw a tiny amount of blood on his white linen garment.

"Stop, stop, stop," he grunted through clenched teeth. The hupshu all shifted on their feet as they watched where the tip of her second dagger rested.

"Now, I will take your life, and my tribe will take the rest of your men's lives if you do not do exactly as I say."

He lifted his head. "What is it you want us to do, woman?" He groaned again, and his injured leg trembled under his weight even though he knelt.

"Order your men to throw their weapons into the fire, one at a time."

He chuckled amid another groan. "Our weapons are made of bronze. This fire will do nothing to them."

"It will keep you from wielding them until the metal cools." She adjusted her grip on the daggers to hold her weapons still as his men eyed her and him. Their gaze fell to the way she held the daggers—like a military man.

"I will slit your throat, Muru-u, just as we will do to Yassib and Niqmad." Ankhesenamun made sure the others could hear her. "We do not wish to spill more blood this night, so do not force my hand. I will not be called a liar again."

She pressed the dagger a bit more into his jaw until a slow dribble of blood rolled down his neck, spreading like the Nile delta into the fibers of his white linen garment.

He grunted. "Fine, demoness." His hands curled into fists and slammed them to his sides. "Throw your weapons into the fire," he ordered.

"One at a time—starting with the men who already hold their weapons," she added.

Sennedjem knelt, his dagger poised to throw at each man who held a weapon; his eyes stayed glued to the archers.

The men threw their weapons into the fire pit. The archer's bows gave new life to the flame.

"Now have your men tie each other up with the ropes they use to bind men like my husband," she said and pressed the dagger once again along his jawline.

"Do it," he muttered.

Once they were all tied, the last man having tied his own hands in front of him, Ankhesenamun spoke to Sennedjem. "Get our travel slings back, my love."

Sennedjem untied their slings from the chariot horse, grabbing extra water and a bag of beans and salted meat, before he slapped the horses on their flanks, sending them running off into the night. A slew of grunts and groans followed from the hupshu.

"No sense in leaving and then having you hunt

down our tribe," Sennedjem told them and walked around the circle of men to stand beside Ankhesenamun. "I know you probably did a poor job of tying yourselves."

"You will do well to stay here until you believe we have made good distance and our tribesmen and women no longer hold your lives at arrowpoint," she said to the group of hupshu.

Sennedjem took the dagger of the Muru-u and held the tip to his neck while Ankhesenamun whispered to him. "I am glad you chose your life and the life of your men tonight. Do not follow us. Do not take another of us again; otherwise, we shall spill all of your blood. As you have seen, we are not liars."

She slid her daggers away and stood up. "Be grateful you have your lives tonight."

"We know you live in Labana, fools." The Muru-u's voice bellowed into the night, seemingly so the imagined tribesmen would hear. "We will hunt you down, Sidon and his wife. You will pay for this incursion with your lives. And if my son is dead, I will make you beg for death."

Ankhesenamun laughed as she wiped the dagger's bloodied tip on the Muru-u's garment. "You are the fool. We are nomads. Did you think my husband would tell you the truth under duress? Sidon is not even his name." She chuckled. "Good luck taking all the city-states of Canaan to find two ghosts."

He growled, and his muscles tensed. "Do not

cross us again," he bellowed as he fell forward from his injured leg.

Slight grunting and muffled yells came from the place where she had hit Niqmad and Yassib over the head. *I am glad they live. Hopefully they see our mercy and stay away from us.* She laid the flat of her bronze dagger against the Muru-u's cheek.

"That is your son, Muru-u. He lives. Do not cross us again, Hasuran. A woman snuck up on your group of hupshu, disarmed them, and left them for dead; that shall be the story we tell to all the tribes of Canaan. Save your faces and remain in Hasura. That is, after you gather your horses in the morning. You shall think twice before you steal a man again, you dirty thieves."

"*We* are thieves? You steal from us!" The Muru-u gripped his hurt knee with white knuckles. "You murdered Ibiranu. We do not kill as you."

"Yet you enslave." Sennedjem threw the Muru-u's sword into the flame. "We have spared your lives, instead of killing all of you as you slept. You should be thankful."

"Now remain here until morning, and do not pursue us. We will not be this merciful again." Ankhesenamun slipped the point of her dagger from the Muru-u's back, and the two of them slunk away into the shadows. They circumnavigated the firelit circle and ran deeper into the darkness toward Damaski.

When Ankhesenamun peered back, the Hasurans

remained as they had been. The hupshu were standing around the flame: a few tending to Ibiranu's body, a few bandaging the Muru-u, and a few venturing into the darkness toward Niqmad and Yassib. But they did not follow them, and a victorious smirk grew upon her face.

I did it. I took back what had been taken from me.

She grabbed Sennedjem's hand and quelled a squeal, not wanting the Hasurans to know in which direction they actually went as the breeze swept away their tracks in the sand. Her feet beat the ground faster, in tune with her heartbeat, as she ran with Sennedjem toward the dark outline of the northwest mountains in the far distance.

CHAPTER 27

SEEKING PEACE

THEY RAN IN THE DARKNESS AS THE CRISP WIND whipped around their faces and caused the sand to stir around their ankles. They ran until Ankhesenamun's legs gave out under her and she fell to her knees. Sennedjem stopped, bending over and breathing hard.

The odor of sweat attacked her aching lungs, so she pulled her tunic off, wiping her face and hair free of the stench. She threw it away from her with both hands before collapsing and rolling to her back with her arms splayed out.

Sennedjem lay down beside her. Their travel slings fell to the ground.

"I thought you would help me up," she whispered between breaths.

"No," he laughed.

She tried to calm her pounding heart. Her legs twitched. She had never run that far that quickly in her life. But she loved it: the wind whipping through her hair and in her face. The utter freedom with every step. Would the Hasurans follow them? Would they seek them out in the morning? Perhaps, but tonight was their victory. Her victory. She had refused to let someone take a loved one from her. For once, she had fought back and won. The warmth of Tut's embrace and that of her daughters sunk into her chest; they would be proud of her. Her mother and father would smile down at her when the sun shone the next morning—wherever they were, on Re's barge or in the Aten-disc, whichever was truth. The child in her womb jumped at her elation, or at least she perceived it as such.

Sennedjem chuckled and drew in deep gulps of air. He grabbed her hand and rubbed his thumb over her fingers.

They stared up into the dark night pinpricked by sparkling spots in the sky. "So many stars, Sennedjem." She gulped air to ease the burn in her chest. "I never noticed how much light they give when you have no fire to take away their light."

He turned his face to look at her. His breathing had calmed, and hers did as well; although, her heart still pumped rapidly, but now for a new reason.

He squeezed her hand as he rolled to his side, pulling her to her side as well so that they faced one another. He smoothed a hand over her brow. "I told you to find your sister. You were supposed to leave me."

She grinned and placed a hand on his cheek. "I will never leave you, Sennedjem."

"But those men could have killed you. I could not bear for my life to continue if I knew you had been killed for my sake." He wrapped a large hand behind her neck and ran the other down the length of her back. His long-wished-for touch against her skin sent a different type of quiver down her body.

She curled his tunic into her hand, as she had done in the cleft of the rock. "I could not bear for my life to continue if I knew I did nothing to save you." Sweat once again dripped from her brow, plastering her hair to her face and neck. Even her linen head-dress did nothing to help it. "I was ready to fight, Sennedjem. In the rock. I was ready to fight with you. I will always fight for you."

He pulled her as close as he could, intertwining his leg with hers. "Please do not ever do that again."

His warmth felt good against her aching legs. "If you promise me the same." Her lips moved closer to his.

"I promised to protect Pharaoh and his family at all costs," he said, nudging her nose with his.

She gripped his arm as he held her. "But I am not Pharaoh's family any longer."

"Then I promised Horemheb I would protect you with my life." He cupped her face; his whisper tickled her lips. "I promised you I would be your Protector, my Queen."

She snuggled into his chest; her breath grew

heavy. "And you cannot do that if you are a servant in Hasura or elsewhere."

"I guess I cannot." He grinned and pressed his forehead to hers. "Thank you for saving me again."

As if he had reached down and pulled out her innermost secrets, she spoke her gratefulness in the softest whisper she could muster. "No, Sennedjem. Thank you. I lost my light, and you helped me rekindle it. After losing Tut and my daughters, all to Pawah"—speaking the name soiled her tongue, but she did not shudder at its mention—"I thought I could never crawl back out of the darkness I had found myself in."

His shoulders relaxed, and he tilted his head. "I only showed you that you could." He cupped her cheek. "I told you, you are a fighter. Remember? Even the fiercest of warriors needs to rest."

She smiled with a small nod.

"This is your rest—this life away from Egypt. You do not have to forget in order to live. Do you not think remembering the past makes the future mean that much more?"

Her chin quivered. "I have no answer."

"Your past, with all of its hardships, all of its pain, and all of its turmoil, will let you appreciate the events and the people"—he lifted her chin—"so much more deeply."

Her heart stilled at the peace that suddenly set in her ka as she locked eyes with him.

"I love you, Sennedjem."

The words finally escaped her, and they freed her from her fears.

"I have all this time."

She pulled his tunic into her chest and impressed her lips upon his in a permanent seal of commitment. The sweetness of their embrace spiraled within her until he pulled away, breathless.

He grinned. "I never asked you," he whispered with soft eyes as a new light shone deep within them. "Will you be my wife?"

She drew in a deep breath, savoring it. "I thought I already was."

He chuckled and placed his parted lips upon her neck, making his way back to her mouth as she laughed in glee. "I had thought so, too," he murmured.

A FEW DAYS LATER, IN THE PREDAWN LIGHT, Ankhesenamun slid her tunic over her head. Sennedjem's hands warmed her waist, and his lips kissed her belly. A small flutter moved in her womb as she sat up.

"I was not finished with you," he whispered as her tunic fell over his head.

"The sun will be rising soon."

He popped up from underneath her tunic and looked off into the distance. No torchlights followed them. No sounds of horse hooves were near. He returned his gaze to his wife. "We can be with each other a few moments more."

She leaned into him, propping her chin on his chest.

"What is it, Ankhesenamun?" He ran his fingers through her hair and lightly tugged, lifting her lips to his.

"I have withheld the truth from you," she murmured and slid her hands up his back to grip his strong shoulders that called for her touch.

He traced the outline of her face. "And what have you withheld, my love?" he asked with a smirk.

A wide grin crossed her lips, but a small fear lingered in her eyes.

Just out with it now.

She hesitated. The smell of blood filled her senses as she remembered Tut holding their limp baby girl born too soon. There was so much blood.

Pawah is not here anymore, she thought. *No one is here to give me silphium. No one is here who is fearful of that cursed man. No one is here to kill for him. No one is here to do his bidding. I will not be haunted.*

His smirk lessened. "What is it, Ankhesenamun? Is something wrong?"

She shook her head, but her breathing shallowed. *How will he respond?* He had seen her take care of Hurriya's child. He had whispered he hoped that they could have a child like that someday, but did he mean it? Or had he only said it to help ease her frustrations? But he also had a wife who had traveled to the afterlife during childbirth.

"Tell me, my love," he whispered, his eyes locking with hers.

"I am with child, Sennedjem." It came out like a quick jab to the face.

His breath cut off, and his gaze turned vacant. He blinked. He swallowed. "You are with child?" The question flowed on his breath.

She nodded. Her grin fell flat.

He wrapped his arms around her and buried his face into her neck. His usual steady heartbeat raced in his chest as he squeezed her in his embrace.

She needed not to ask him what he felt. No doubt, memories of Sadeh and his unborn child filled his mind, just as her two daughters filled hers.

He guided her to lie down underneath him, and he kissed her shoulder, her neck, her cheek and her lips before he pulled away to caress the side of her face. A tepid smile hid on his lips.

"Please say something, Sennedjem." Her plea was not only to know his thoughts but to placate her fears as well.

His lips quivered, but held a smile. "I am a happy man. I am happy the gods bless us with a child."

Tears filled her eyes. "What if I bear a third still-born?" She remembered all of the accusations and distrust from Tut. Pawah had turned him against her. He had told him their daughter was that of Sennedjem's. She closed her eyes as another twinge of guilt pressed upon her. Now the child was Sennedjem's. *Stop,* she told herself. *Only I can change myself. I will not be haunted.*

He gripped her shoulders and leaned close to her face. "A person can become lost in a world of what-ifs. What if you are to be like Sadeh? What if we are captured again? What if the child lives and you do not?" His head shook slightly. "My memory of Sadeh passing in my arms came to me. I will not be dishonest; I fear the same for you and our child." His hand grazed her belly. "But all we can do is pray to Hathor and Bes and Tawaret——"

"I cursed them, Sennedjem." The truth flew out of her mouth. She had doomed them. She had doomed her child. The gods would not hear her prayers. They would not save them from the spirits seeking to take their lives from this world. "In my anger of losing Tut . . . after losing everyone else, I cursed them all—all the gods and goddesses. They would be happy to leave me and let me die an eternal death——"

"Ankhesenamun, *shh, shh,*" he calmed her and ran his hands over her cheeks and brow.

She could not bear his stare, so she turned her face away from him. "I have condemned our child, have I not?"

He rested his forehead on her temple. "Surely, they saw your pain, my love."

"It does not matter. I still cursed them. If our child does not live, I will be to blame."

"No." He kissed her cheek. "It may just be life, Ankhesenamun. The gods have blessed me with a life with you. They bless you with a second life away from the horror of your life in the palace. If our child does not live, if you do not live—it could just be life. Women and babies travel to the Field of Reeds during childbirth, sometimes even before the baby comes. It is a dangerous thing to have a baby. Those fortunate enough to live should count themselves blessed."

His words made sense. Tut's mother traveled west at his delivery. Her own grandmother passed after birthing her mother. The thought of her own demise made her shudder, though. She had cursed the gods. Her heart would weigh heavy against the feather of Ma'at. She would not have an afterlife.

"But I cursed them, Sennedjem."

"Ask them to forgive you," he whispered, as if it were that easy. "Find your faith again."

She shook her head. The path seemed long, hard, frail and unachievable. "I feel so lost."

He turned her face to his and kissed her with a soft, chaste kiss on the lips. "You have been running, Ankhesenamun. Your life before this one was riddled with every unhappiness. You did not want to remember your family because it brought you unending pain. You tried shutting them out, forgetting them. Now, you have to face your past once again, just as I have to."

"How do we find our way?" The question triggered a deep fear in the pit of her belly.

His eyes lit with a flame of determination. "We find it together."

Ankhesenamun smiled, and two tears escaped. When she had stood in front of Mut almost three years ago, she had believed she was free—free to forget her past life and all the pain it brought with it. The unknown future with Sennedjem, where nothing was clear, put a giddy fear in her heart, but she knew that was what she wanted. She had found love again. Her family was now there: the three of them lying together.

"We will find our way together, my love," he repeated and brushed her hair away from her face. "Just as we will find Nefe."

CHAPTER 28

SEEKING DAMASKI

THE CITY OF DAMASKI SAT ATOP A LARGE HILL; A long river, rumored to have the freshest waters in Canaan, ran through its center.

Ankhesenamun walked hand-in-hand with Sennedjem but stopped before the city gates came into view.

She swallowed the lump in her throat. "What if she is not here, Sennedjem? We have been to every—"

"Then we shall journey to the south of Hazzatu."

Ankhesenamun cupped the bottom of her four-month baby belly. Her gaze fell toward the unborn child growing in her womb. "What if we cannot journey there? We almost lost our lives several times so far."

He stood in front of her and rubbed the sides of her arms. "I will journey wherever you want to go, Ankhesenamun."

She lifted her eyes to him. "Sennedjem, we have been robbed, raided, kidnapped, desolate, cold, and hungry." She rubbed her hand over her belly. "Our family will suffer if we do not try to settle down somewhere."

He peered over his shoulder at the city-state walls of Damaski before returning his gaze to her. He opened his mouth to speak, but she spoke first.

"We have no tribe for protection. We have the little gold and copper we carry on us and a sling of essential travel items. What if Damaski takes what we have left? We will have nothing."

He pulled her into an embrace. "We will have each other."

"Will we ever find her, Sennedjem?" She searched his eyes. "Be honest; be plain. Am I forcing us into a nomadic life for nothing? She could be long buried. They could have been killed or captured by raiders or traveling soldiers, like we almost were. She could be a servant in a palace or a concubine in a King's harem. Am I leading us on a fool's errand?" She chewed her lip, already knowing the answer.

He lowered his forehead to hers. He ran a hand down her cheek, neck, chest and belly but remained silent.

"Tell me," she pleaded.

"We will search Damaski. We will find a place to stay. I will find work to replenish our trade goods, and we will have our child here. If you want to stay in Damaski, I will stay. If you want to live in Magidda like we had once discussed, I will go with you. If you want to search more, I will search with you. But above all, Ankhesenamun, I want you to be happy in whatever life you choose. Is searching for your sister a fool's errand? Maybe; maybe not. If she will bring you happiness, if finding her will make your life complete, then I want you to search for her until your last day."

"What of our family? Where will our child's home be?" A tear rolled down her cheek. "Am I being selfish?"

"No." He smiled. "If Nefe is not here and we continue to search, we shall grow our own clan; we will start our own tribe. We shall press on if that is what you truly want."

"I am afraid of making the wrong choice. What if she is one city north, and we stay here?" She covered her mouth with her hand. "What if we never find her?"

"We all make choices, Ankhesenamun." He pulled her close, allowing room for their child between them. "And I choose you for the rest of my life, as I have told you. Wherever you are and I am, our child will be with us, and we will be our child's home."

She nodded, hoping Nefe was in Damaski. She would make the decision to continue or not after the baby was born. "I shall think on it tomorrow then." But in her heart, she knew this would probably be the last city they searched, and even then, Sennedjem had told her in Hasura, they were probably not here.

When their child was old enough to make the journey, they would return to Magidda.

I tried, Nefe. I hope you are well in whatever life you have found for yourself.

He kissed her before he led her to the city walls. They entered without incident, noticing the lack of military presence lining the city. Only a few guards stood by the gate, but they waved them along, as they did the other travelers and traders.

The city elders were gathered by the inner gate.

"Greetings," Sennedjem said, returning his hands to his sides so as not to dishonor Ankhesenamun in their eyes.

"Greetings, traveler and his wife," they said in return.

"We are wanderers seeking family. Do you know of a man named Atinuk or a man named Paaten or a woman named Aitye?" His question hung in the air as the city elders shared small glances between each other.

"Family?" one elder asked.

"Who are you? What is your relation?" another elder asked.

Ankhesenamun's head snapped to Sennedjem and studied his expression to see if he interpreted their response with the same inference: They knew people with those names. Was she allowing her hopes to become too high?

"So they are here?" Sennedjem asked.

The elders eyed the two of them before one

responded. "Follow the river. Ask the master of the largest estate at the edge of the city about the persons whom you seek." An old finger pointed them in the direction they should go. "There will be many houses on the land."

Could this be? Could it be her—them? Are they servants to the master of this estate? Why, then, would the city elders know their names?

"You are most kind. Thank you." Sennedjem dipped his chin to them as he led Ankhesenamun away in the direction they were told to go.

The city elders waved goodbye to them and greeted others who came to seek their advice and judgment. Her trembling hands gave way to sweaty palms. Sennedjem brushed her tunic sleeve and held a warm smile on his lips.

What would her sister look like now? Would she recognize her? Was she married? Did she have a child?

Ankhesenamun followed the river as the questions swirled in her mind; Sennedjem kept pace beside her. Once they were out of view of the bustling center streets, he took her hand in his.

"The largest estate, with many houses," he said, repeating the elder's instructions.

As they followed the row of estates, each was larger than the last, until they stopped in front of the largest one. Several small houses were scattered over the vast estate, and three large houses sat far off. Rows of cotton plants lined the fields, and women and children were stooped over as they plucked the plants' fluffy seeds in the harvest.

"What is this place?" Sennedjem asked as they surveyed the land.

She brought his hand to her lips. "I am afraid to have hope, Sennedjem."

"Without hope, we have nothing." Sennedjem brushed her thumb with his fingers.

"Thirteen years, Sennedjem. Almost thirteen years since I have seen her. If she is here, will I even recognize her? Surely news of my passing has reached Damaski. Will she believe I am truly myself?"

"Answers we may find at the middle house." He pointed toward the three largest houses situated in the back of the estate.

He shook her hand to goad her forward. "We have endured much, you and I. Shall we find out together?"

She nodded, and her feet took her through the fields. Her breath became shallow as she tried to cage her hope. As they passed through the rows of cotton plants, each laborer looked up at the two strangers and whispered to each other. One rose up to stop them.

"Who are you, and why have you come?" Her smooth voice echoed the smooth river water gushing behind them. A small half-smile held distrust as she examined their faces and then their hands.

Sennedjem cleared his throat and opened his palms, showing he had no weapon. "We heard of a man named Atinuk who lives here. Is there also one named Paaten and a woman named Aitye?"

She cast a wary eye upon them as she scrutinized them from head to toe. "Who are you?" The smoothness in her voice was gone, and her eyes grew dark.

Ankhesenamun shifted on her feet. *They must be here. Why else would this woman be acting so strangely toward us? We are not intimidating. I am with child, Sennedjem has no visible weapon, and we do not even have a donkey.*

Sennedjem gestured to Ankhesenamun. "We are travelers. Can you take us to the master of this estate? The city elders said he would be able to answer our inquiry. We are searching for a long-lost relative and have run out of supplies. We also have a child due in a few months. If our search is in vain, I will also ask the master if I may work here and perhaps earn a place to live for a short time."

The woman glanced at Ankhesenamun's small belly. She chewed her lip as her eyes narrowed in thought. Finally, she spoke: "My father is the master of the estate. I shall take you to him. He shall decide."

"You are most gracious."

Ankhesenamun barely heard her response. She was so sure this time. She tried not to hope, but in her heart, she yearned to be right. But as her eyes focused on the young woman's body in front of them as she led them to the middle house, she wondered why the master's daughter worked the field like a laborer.

She thought the woman would lead them to the house, but instead, she went to the stables behind the house. A large shadow heaved a bag of feed from within the donkey's stables.

"Father?" the woman called out.

"Panna? Is all well?" The shadow stepped out into the sunlight. The voice was deep and lacking a full timbre, but a certain warmth was behind it.

Ankhesenamun studied the man's face. A full white beard accompanied dark eyes. He took a large step toward them.

"These travelers would like to ask for work. They are searching for a lost relative and have run out of supplies . . . Father?"

"I heard you," he whispered. The master stared at Ankhesenamun as if she were a spirit. He leaned toward her; a slight reflection of the sun glimmered in his old gray-brown eyes. He squinted, as if trying to focus on her face.

"Father?"

"Panna." He held up his hand to silence her but kept his eyes locked on Ankhesenamun; his stare caused her to shift on her feet.

Why was he staring?

Sennedjem slightly pulled Ankhesenamun behind him. "We can find work elsewhere, Hurriya." He took a step backward, keeping Ankhesenamun behind him. "We are grateful to you for allowing us to tres-pass on your land. We will leave now."

"Hurriya." The master blinked once, as if pulling himself from a dream. He stood up straight, and his gaze shifted to Sennedjem. "There is no need to be wary, traveler." He shook his head. "I mean no harm. I am but an old man who has lost some of his vision. I could have sworn I had seen your wife once before, a long time ago." A polite smile came over his lips. "You are free to stay and work and gather up your supplies before you continue on your journey." He gestured to the lands. "This estate is a sanctuary for those who need it."

Ankhesenamun stepped forward in front of Sennedjem. A newfound courage overtook her. A calling in her heart urged her to speak. "We were told men named Atinuk and Paaten lived here, along with a woman named Aitye. Is there also a woman here named Neferneferuaten Tasherit?"

"No woman by that name lives here," Panna said as she stood next to her father, but the master's mouth fell slack, and a small chuckle escaped his upturned lips.

"Ankhesenpaaten?" the master whispered.

Ankhesenamun's heart lifted at the sound of her birth name. Had they found them?

"Ankhesenpaaten?" the master whispered again.

Sennedjem looked the man up and down; recogni-tion swept over his face. "General Paaten?"

The master laughed with a wide smile. "I have not

been called that in a lifetime." He wiped a tear that ran down his eyes. "You live, Queen of Egypt?"

Panna's jaw dropped. "This is Queen Ankhesenamun?" She stepped forward, raising a hand over her mouth. "We received word of your passing."

Paaten wrapped Ankhesenamun in his arms, embracing her like his long-lost child. He pulled away and placed his hands on her shoulders, kneeling to one knee before her. "You look so much like your mother." His finger brushed her cheek. He lifted his hands to the Aten-disc and lifted his head to the sun-disc god. "Thank you for allowing me to fulfill my promise to my friend Nefertiti before I travel to the Field of Reeds."

Ankhesenamun wanted to ask about her sister, but Sennedjem wrapped an arm around his wife. "Pharaoh Ay did this for her."

Paaten stood once again, with the help of his daughter and Sennedjem. "And who are you?" Paaten asked, taking note of Sennedjem's dark black beard and squinting once more to study his face.

"I am Sennedjem."

Ankhesenamun's question bounced on the tip of her tongue, but she remained silent, not wanting to be rude to her mother's former General.

He pursed his lips in thought for a moment. "Sennedjem . . . Overseer of the Tutors?"

Sennedjem smiled. "Former."

"You are alone with her, then?"

"Yes. I am her husband."

Quickly. I have to know. Is Nefe alive? She wanted to yell.

A warm smile came over Paaten's face as he glanced to each of them. "You have come. You have found us. Welcome. We shall build you a house next to your sister's."

Ankhesenamun's ears tingled. "Nefe is here? She is alive?"

"Yes." A beam shone brightly from his old, worn eyes.

Tears broke free and ran down her cheeks. All at once, every color her eyes beheld became more radiant: the grass seemed more green and the sky more blue. The sound of the river in the distance became all too comforting. Her face and neck flushed with peace under the sun's warming rays.

"May I see her?" The question flew off her tongue in a weightless whisper.

Paaten stole a look at Panna.

"They are still in the home." Panna pointed to the third home.

Ankhesenamun took off running toward the third house, holding the child in her womb as she ran, ignoring the yells that trailed behind her. Her sister was steps away. After two years of searching since they had left Per-Amun, she was almost there. The pain in her feet left her. Her ankles grew strong in her one last triumphant sprint. Her last sister grew closer with each footstep.

"Nefe?!" she yelled out as she ran toward the

home. She burst through the main door of the third house. "Nefe!"

A middle-aged woman carrying a bronze pot of hot water stopped in front of an open door in the back of the house. "Hush yourself." She looked her up and down. "Leave."

Ankhesenamun ignored her and continued toward the sound of a child crying.

"Who are you?" the woman said again.

Ankhesenamun glanced at her. "Where is Nefe?"

"She is in the room." The woman's eyes darted to the open door before resting upon Ankhesenamun.

She advanced, but the woman cut her off. "I said, 'Leave.'"

A long shadow appeared from the front doorway; the woman glanced over Ankhesenamun's shoulder. "Panna, who is this?"

"Let her enter, Donatiya." Panna's soft voice carried through the quiet four-room home, and Donatiya stepped aside.

Ankhesenamun peered into the room. A woman with long white hair coddled a quieting child and smiled down at the babe. A young man held another woman in his arms as she rested against him.

Could it be her? Could that be her husband and child?

Ankhesenamun stepped into the room, immediately garnering the attention of those inside.

"Please leave. This room is for family," the old woman told her.

She took a moment to stare at the old woman: long white hair, green eyes.

Family?

Her gaze drifted to the woman reclining in the man's arms. "Nefe?"

The man's countenance held a pensive stare as he gripped his woman's arms. "Who are you?"

But the woman sat up straight and tilted her head. "How do you know my name?"

"Nefe," the man whispered in a strained tone.

Ankhesenamun drew near and dropped to her knees before the woman who could be her sister. They locked eyes. Neither of them wore kohl or vulture headdresses. They did not smell of lotus blossoms, and their sandals were not jeweled in Egyptian splendor. They had been separated for thirteen years. They were only fourteen and sixteen when they last saw each other, but the woman in front of her was undoubtedly her sister.

"It can't be," Nefe whispered as she pushed out of the man's arms and crawled to her knees. "Ankhesenpaaten?" A tremor came over her hands as her breath caught in her chest. A well of tears built in her eyes; her mouth opened in wonder. "Sister?" The question rasped out of her throat.

Ankhesenamun nodded. "I found you, Nefe," she whispered in Egyptian as she grasped her sister's hands. "I finally found you." The words could barely escape past the rapid heartbeat that pulsated through her body.

"Queen Ankhesenamun?" Her husband's eyes grew wide.

Nefe fell into her sister's arms. A surge of youthful laughter burst from her lips. "You are alive." She pulled back and ran her fingers along Ankhesenamun's face. "*You* are alive!" Tears streamed down both sisters' faces as they held each other.

"We are finally together again," Ankhesenamun whispered, wiping her little sister's tears from her cheeks. Her quest was complete; her hope had stayed alive as long as needed. She held her sister in her arms and heard Sennedjem's murmur in the main room; all at once, in her spellbound state, she realized everything she wanted had been fulfilled.

THE DAY WANED, AND NEFE AND ANKHESENAMUN sat in Nefe's room by the hearth, detailing what had become of their lives over the past thirteen years. Nefe's husband, Paebel, was in the main room of the house with Sennedjem and Paaten, along with Nefe's one-month-old son and her mother-in-law, Niwa.

"We had heard you were taken with an illness," Nefe said, smoothing her hand over Ankhesenamun's.

"Grandfather had to declare I journeyed west. Pharaoh does not simply let wives go; especially the sole Hereditary Princess." A sad smile commanded her mouth. "After"—she swallowed her pain, but it did not taste as bitter—"after Pawah took mother and Tut, I was to be married to the next Pharaoh after Grandfather. He let me leave, granted me freedom; he let me escape that life."

They cupped each other's cheeks, and Nefe traced Ankhesenamun's face. "And you came to Canaan just like Mother wanted you to all those years ago."

The happy flush in Nefe's cheeks gave color to her tanned face. She had lived a good life thus far in Canaan with her husband and four children. Nefe had done what their mother had wanted for them, and soon Ankhesenamun could do the same.

Tears fell down Ankhesenamun's cheeks as she saw the joyous gleam in her sister's eyes that shined as bright as the stars on that night she had overcome her past. Her hand cupped her small pregnant belly. Her children and Nefe's children would grow up together. Age would come upon her, but Sennedjem and Nefe would be by her side. They would live together free and in peace on this estate away from the strife of Egypt.

"Yes, just like Mother wanted for us."

EPILOGUE: SEEK NO MORE
THREE YEARS LATER

ANKHESENAMUN LIFTED HER EYES TO THE ROWS OF pink and yellow that billowed up into purple and dark-blue clouds. "Remember when you wondered if the skies would be as beautiful in the evening here as they were in Egypt?" Sennedjem asked her.

She pressed her lips into a smile. *Egypt.* Egypt felt like a lifetime ago. Her father, her mother, her sisters, her Tut, her two daughters, Kiya, Shapash and Arsiya, they would all live through her, here in Canaan, in Damaski. She carried them in her heart and on her mind. They gave new meaning to each new day. They gave a renewed sense of peace to her Damaski home. She glanced inside and saw their shrine wall with Hathor and Isis standing in their niches. A woven prayer rug lay before them. The evening's incense to open the goddesses' mouths was reduced to a single stream of smoke rising before them.

Sennedjem kissed her temple, and she leaned into

his embrace. Her faith had been restored. She glanced at the little girl in her arms. "Zanya-tati," she whispered her Akkadian name, along with its meaning: "Beauty come."

He wrapped his arms around Ankhesenamun so that he brushed his daughter's little head of hair. "She is beautiful like her mother." His words tickled her neck.

"Named for her grandmother, the great Nefertiti, 'the beautiful one is come,'" Ankhesenamun whispered.

His hands slid along Ankhesenamun's arms, and he turned her to face him.

She saw the waning sunlight in his eyes, lightening them to a honey brown. "The skies are more beautiful here," she whispered, answering his first question.

A warm smile overcame his lips. "I agree."

"Aunt Ankhesenamun!" Nefe and Paebel's oldest son, Shacar, ran up to them. "Uncle Sennedjem." His arms waved. "It is ready. Come now. Come. Come." He danced on his toes with excitement as he urged them to follow him. Their three-year-old son, Hasāsu, followed. His eyes lit with joy, and his hands curled into fists as he jumped up and down. "Come now, Mother and Father. We are ready for Zanya-tati!"

They glanced at each other and shared a peaceful smile before following Shacar and Hasāsu to the back of the estate as the sun set in the west. A large fire blazed as their dinner cooked over the top of it.

Everyone from the estate came to eat and to share in each other's company. There were many Hittite women, saved from the land of Hatti, who lived there. Some had taken husbands; some lived with their children. They all passed their blessing to the new child, Zanya-tati.

Sennedjem had been adopted by Paaten and Niwa so that he would receive a share of the estate when they passed from this life. He joined their children in the inheritance: their son-by-blood, Paebel, their daughter, Panna, with her husband, as well as their adopted son, Atinuk, and his wife, Aitye.

Once the food was gone, the other families on the estate slowly returned to their homes. The sun's glow had disappeared, and pinpricks of starlight swept across the night sky. The firelight encased Paaten's five family units as they sat around the fire to enjoy time with each other.

The warm winds from her past brushed against Ankhesenamun's back. With it, she felt her mother's embrace and Tut's kiss upon her neck; she heard the laughter from her long-passed sisters on the breeze. The warmth of the fire pressed against her chest: her future. She glanced at Paaten, who was like a father to her and Nefe. He and Niwa held hands, and he kissed her ever so softly, pushing her silver locks behind her ear. Their wrinkles from age creased as they smiled at one another. Paaten had provided for them, all of them, to be entombed in Egypt when the time came. He had kept his promise to his family and her mother. He was the protector of their small clan.

Her gaze shifted to the children of Atinuk and Aitye, playing and running around with Shacar and Hasāsu and their cousins, the children of Panna and her husband. Hasāsu's squeal made Ankhesenamun think of her brother, Horemheb's child, who never knew life outside her mother's womb, her two daughters, and the unborn child of Sadeh and Sennedjem. They would live through Hasāsu. After all, his name meant "to remember."

Aitye laughed and pulled Ankhesenamun's attention toward her. Atinuk's hand fell on Aitye's knee as he murmured something in her ear and kissed her cheek. Aitye would never replace her mother, but she had been like a mother to her once, as Queen Kiya had been. Their memory would live on through them.

Nefe sat next to Aitye. "My sweet Nefe," Ankhesenamun whispered to herself. Her chest swelled at the happiness and carefree glimmer on Nefe's wide smile and the enraptured beam in her eyes and on her cheeks. Paebel kissed Nefe's shoulder and wrapped his arm around her. Their fourth child, a son, only six months older than Hasāsu, lay asleep in her arms.

Sennedjem's hand caressed hers, and she turned her attention to him. The man who had stood by her through every trial, every sorrow, and every happiness . . . he had endured next to her as her friend, her Protector, her comforter, and her lover. He was her husband. The thought caused her eyes to prickle with tears. Holding their sleeping daughter in his arm, he buried his nose in her tiny naked body, whispering his love.

Nefe and Ankhesenamun had found a life away from the strife that had plagued their mother, thus fulfilling her wish for them. Her mother had wanted love and peace—things she could never have. She chose duty and Egypt above all, so her daughters would not have to. Ultimately, she gave Ankhesenamun and Nefe the life she had always wanted. She endured and kept them safe, providing for them even in the direst of circumstances.

The firelight danced on the happy and carefree faces that surrounded her. This was her family. This was her past. This was her future. Tears of joy finally came to fruition and ran down her cheeks. A smile arose on her lips. Her heart lifted, and she knew it would not weigh heavy on the scales of Ma'at. There would be an afterlife for her. She would see them all again. Their memories would live on forever, and this life would be good, as would the next one. A soft, unheard whisper escaped her smiling lips: "I understand now, Mother."

Did you love *The Lost Pharaoh Chronicles*?
Then return to beginning of the 18th Dynasty of
Egypt with ***Egypt's Golden Age Chronicles***.
Start with Book 1: *Warrior King*

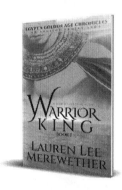

***Expelling the foreign kings of Egypt is proving
costly.***

1575 BC. Surrounded by her enemies, the future of
the rebellion is in the hands of Queen Ahhotep as her
husband's body is laid at her feet.

To unite the divided kingdom, Ahhotep must be
the commanding leader to those still loyal to her
family, a guiding voice her children require, and meet
the impossible expectations of her mother, the Great
Wife Tetisheri. Feeling alone and finding no consola-
tion in the palace, Ahhotep seeks counsel with a man

she loves but cannot have, inviting conflict into her family and her heart.

With obsolete weaponry, inferior resources, and the royal family's divided front, their supporters dissent and leave. To keep their borders secure, Ahhotep must find a way to consolidate power, raise a capable army, and mold her son into a Warrior King before death comes for her and her people.

Warrior King is a beautiful ode to the powerful women behind the crown and how their love, determination, leadership, and sacrifice propelled the once-called Kemet into a golden era of ancient Egyptian history.

EXCLUSIVE READER OFFER

Did you miss *A New Dawn*, the bonus ending to *King's Daughter*?

A New Dawn is exclusively free to Lauren's email subscribers.
Visit www.LaurenLeeMerewether.com
to read Nefe and Paebel's story.

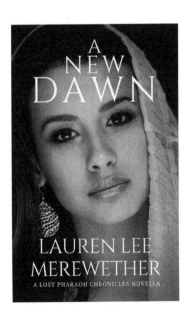

A LOOK INTO THE PAST

Nefertiti's Legacy is a complement of *Silence in the Stone*, the last book of the series, *The Lost Pharaoh Chronicles*. This series occurs during the end of the 18th Dynasty of the New Kingdom of Ancient Egypt. *Nefertiti's Legacy* specifically occurs during the end of Pharaoh Ay's reign and the beginning of the reign of Pharaoh Horemheb.

This story is a part of a complement collection that is mostly fictionalized, but based in historical fact of that period. The following are a few examples:

Pharaoh Ay married the Hereditary Princess Ankhesenamun, the widow of Pharaoh Tutankhamun. By the second or third year of his reign, she was not mentioned again in the historical record and had seemingly disappeared. *Silence in the Stone* and *Nefertiti's Legacy* took liberties in having her leave Egypt. Ankhesenamun's voluntary exile was probably not what actually happened, as royal wives usually fulfilled the role of celibate priestesses of Isis if Pharaoh did not lie with them.

Sennedjem was the name of Tut's tutor. A tomb for Sennedjem, an Overseer of the Tutors, was excavated by Boyo Ockinga[1] in Awlad Azzaz (Akhmim). He notes it appeared Sennedjem's name was deliberately erased from the tomb's decoration. The tomb was heavily damaged, and it is uncertain anyone was ever entombed in it.

The term "Canaan" was used in the 16th to the 11th centuries B.C. as a reference to the land in the Ancient Near East when it was an Egyptian colony. The usage of the term "Canaan" ceased around 1200 B.C. The hieroglyphic translation of "Canaan" is "Ka-na-na."

From the Amarna letter translations, the author used the Akkadian names of the cities and kings/chieftains found in the story.

- The Amarna letters call Jerusalem "Urusalim." This was the name of the city before it was conquered by the biblical King David in 1000 B.C.
- The Amarna letters mention pleas for help and aid made to King Amenhotep III and/or King Akhenaten, citing attacks from the King of Sidon (who did not make it into *Nefertiti's Legacy*); Abdi-Tirshi, King

of Hasura (Hazor); and Labayu, King of Sakmu (Shechem), who had sided with the Apiru/Habiru in the capturing of the Canaan lands. [From the Amarna letters, the city-state of Hasura was conquering the cities of Astartu (Ashtaroth) east of the Jordan River, which led the author to write up the fictional Hasuran patrols in *Nefertiti's Legacy*.]

- The city of Gibeon avoided conquest and enjoyed peace and continued prosperity. Its rich and fertile lands and springs supplied it with a good economy. Scholars suggest the people who lived there were most akin to the Canaanite Hivites.

- The author took liberties with the attitudes toward Egyptians in the city of Sakmu (Shechem) because of the Amarna letter claims of Sakmu's attacks on fellow city-states and also because of an insurrection that occurred there during the reign of Seti I twenty or so years after *Nefertiti's Legacy* (if Horemheb's reign is assumed to be 14 or 17 years rather than 27 years).

- Egypt had administrative centers in Hazzatu/Azzati (Gaza) and Magidda/Makedo (Megiddo) and most likely in any other city-state of notable size. These centers maintained a staff and were led by a Weputy. They acted as economic and political oversight as well as suppliers of information back to Egypt. Magidda controlled the Wadi Ara (also Nahal 'Iron) and the Jezreel Valley and was situated on the trade route from every significant empire in the Ancient Near East.

As an aside, the Apiru/Habiru mentioned in *Nefertiti's Legacy* are sometimes referenced as the Akkadian Habiru or similarly translated as "Hebrew." However, whether or not the Apiru/Habiru are the biblical Israelites has been long debated. For reasons that will be explained in her next series, Lauren's books assume the historical timeline aligns with the proposed biblical Hebrew Exodus in 1446 B.C. There are three main theories on when the Exodus took place, taking into account both biblical and secular scholars (those who do not believe the Exodus is a myth):

1. Early Exodus (New Chronology): King Neferhotep I or King Dudimose
2. Early Exodus (High Chronology): Pharaoh Thutmose III or Pharaoh Amenhotep II
3. Late Exodus (High/Low Chronology): Pharaoh Ramses II or Pharaoh Merneptah

With the second timeline theory, Othniel would have been the judge over Israel during the time of *Nefertiti's Legacy*.

There was limited research the author found in regards to Canaan before it became Ancient Israel. Most of the information available came from tablets found in the ancient Canaanite city of Ugarit. From these, she assumed Canaanite women could do little without a man of blood or marriage to speak for them. The author took liberties in creating the distinction between public displays of affection in Egypt versus Canaan. In Egyptian reliefs of the time, there are people depicted embracing and, in some interpretations, kissing noses. From the Ugarit tablets, Canaan seemed to be a rigid patriarchal society in which women had very little say about their futures. Typical women (nonroyal) seemed to be in charge of the household. But in every instance, women remain nameless. However, each city-state had its own rules, customs, and culture, so history may yet reveal how women were treated in the rest of Canaan during that time.

Because women were nameless, the only known female Canaanite names are those of goddesses and women from Ugaritic legends. The author used these names in *Nefertiti's Legacy*. The names in the story align with the known Canaanite goddesses:

- Arsiya is the name of the Canaanite goddess of earth.

- Kotharat is the name of the seven Canaanite goddesses of marriage; Kotharat plays the role of marriage advisor to Sennedjem in the story.
- Shapash is the name of the Canaanite goddess of the sun.
- Ishat is the name of the Canaanite goddess of fire.
- Hurriya is not the name of a Canaanite goddess but rather the name of King Keret's wife in an Ugaritic legend. The author wanted to name Hurriya's character Ashima (Ashima is the name of the Canaanite goddess of fate) but thought there would be too many "A" names in the story.

Canaan and Egypt had dissimilar beliefs about the body after death, although both customs held that the body should be entombed or buried with grave goods, food and drink. In Canaan, this was done so that the dead would not haunt the living. Their bodies remained shells, but the "nps," or soul, went to the land of Mot. Mot was "Death" but was also the name of the god of the dead.

In contrast, the body was very important in the Ancient Egyptians' beliefs of the afterlife. During this time period, they believed everyone had a ba—not just the Pharaoh, as in earlier times. The ba and ka would be released after death but would need to journey back to the body every night to rest. Without a body laid to rest in Egyptian lands and/or without a name on their grave, the ba and ka would be lost, forever in a state of restlessness. This state is similar to our modern-day "hell." The same state would occur should Ammit devour the person's heart on their journey to the afterlife. Ammit would only devour the heart if it weighed heavy against the feather of Ma'at, meaning the person had committed unjustifiable crimes against the human and divine order, as judged by forty-two gods.

Gold was considered in the 18th and 19th dynasties as the skin of the gods, and some sources say it could never have materialized into a trade commodity due to the symbolic importance placed upon it. Silver, similarly, was considered the bones of the gods, and, to a much lesser extent, bore the same symbolic importance.

The author loved diving deeper into this fascinating culture and hopes you did too. If you enjoyed Lauren's debut series, *The Lost Pharaoh Chronicles*, and its prequel and complement collections, visit her website for more information on her other series and subscribe to her newsletter or follow her on one of her major social media platforms (Facebook, Instagram, Twitter, or BookBub) to stay updated on new releases.

www.LaurenLeeMerewether.com

1. Ockinga, Boyo. A Tomb from the Reign of Tutankhamun at Akhmim. Aris & Phillips, 1997. ISBN 0-85668-801-0

WHAT DID YOU THINK?
DID YOU ENJOY NEFERTITI'S LEGACY?

Thank you for reading the last complement for my debut series, *The Lost Pharaoh Chronicles*. I hope you enjoyed jumping into another culture and reading about Ankhesenamun's fate in the series.

If you enjoyed *Nefertiti's Legacy*, I would like to ask a big favor: Please share with your friends and family on social media sites like **Facebook** and leave a rating or a review on **book retailer sites, BookBub**, and on **Goodreads** if you have accounts there.

I am an independent author; as such, reviews and word of mouth are the best way readers like you can help books like *Nefertiti's Legacy* and the series, *The Lost Pharaoh Chronicles,* reach other readers.

Your feedback and support are of the utmost importance to me. If you want to reach out to me and give feedback on this book, offer ideas to improve my future writings, get updates about future books, or just say howdy, please visit me on the web.

www.LaurenLeeMerewether.com
Or email me at
mail@LaurenLeeMerewether.com
Happy Reading!

GLOSSARY

EGYPTIAN CONCEPTS / ITEMS

1. Ba – a person's personality
2. Chief Royal Wife – premier wife of Pharaoh; Queen
3. Deben – measure of weight equal to about 91 grams
4. Decan – week in Egypt (ten-day period); one month consisted of three decans
5. Field of Reeds – Egyptian afterlife
6. "Gone to Re" – a form of the traditional phrase used to speak about someone's death; another variant is "journeyed west"
7. Ka – the spirit or life force of a person
8. Khopesh – a standard military-issued bronze, sickle-shaped sword
9. Kite – measure of weight equal to one tenth of a deben, or about 9.1 grams

10. Medjay – police or policeman
11. Natron – perfumed soda ash soap that scented bath water for cleansing
12. Nomarch – a governor-type official who oversaw an entire province
13. Pharaoh – the modern title for an ancient Egyptian King
14. Season – three seasons made up the 360-day calendar; each season had 120 days
15. "Set up a house" – a phrase used to speak of marriage
16. Shat – measure of weight; twelve shat equaled one deben
17. Shendyt – apron / skirt; a royal shendyt worn by Pharaoh was pleated and lined with gold
18. Sistrum – a musical instrument of the percussion family, chiefly associated with ancient Iraq and Egypt
19. Vizier – highest royal advisor to Pharaoh who oversaw state affairs
20. Weputy – political officer in a vassal state

CANAANITE CONCEPTS/ITEMS

1. Bēl – Sir
2. Hupshu – Soldier
3. Mot – death; land of the dead
4. Muru-u – Commander

EGYPTIAN GODS

1. Ammit – goddess and demoness; "Devourer of Hearts"
2. Amun – premier god of Egypt in the Middle Kingdom
3. Amun-Re – name given to show the duality of Amun and Re (the hidden god and the sun, respectively) to appease both priesthoods during the early part of the New Kingdom
4. Anhur – god of war; protector of soldiers
5. Aten – sun-disc god of Egypt (referred to as "the Aten"); a minor aspect of the sun god Re
6. Bastet – cat goddess and protector of the home, women, women's secrets and children
7. Bes – god of dreams and of childbirth
8. Hathor – goddess of joy, women's health, and childbirth, among other aspects of love and life
9. Isis – goddess of marriage, love, fertility, motherhood, magic and medicine
10. Pakhet – wildcat goddess of war
11. Re – premier god of Egypt in the Old Kingdom; the sun god

12. Seshat – goddess of the written word and records; consort of Thoth
13. Tawaret – goddess of childbirth
14. Thoth – god of the mind; associated with knowledge, thinking, reason and logic

CANAANITE GODS

1. Anat – goddess of war
2. Baal – lord of the gods
3. Chemosh – god of war
4. Mot – god of death and drought (not worshipped or given offerings)
5. Qadeshtu – goddess of love, lust, pleasure and desire
6. Shalim – god of the setting sun

EGYPTIAN PLACES

1. Aketaten – city of modern-day area of El'Amarna
2. Malkata – palace of Pharaoh Amenhotep III located west of Waset
3. Men-nefer – city of Memphis; located south of modern-day Cairo
4. Per-Amun – ancient port city; modern-day archaeological site of Pelusium
5. Waset – city of modern-day Luxor

CANAANITE PLACES

Where available, place names are in Akkadian form taken from the Amarna letter translations; all of the city-states at this time were tributaries to Egypt and under Egyptian rule.

1. Astartu – ancient city of Ashtaroth located east of the Jordan River in what is now Syria
2. Damaski – modern-day city of Damascus, Syria
3. Gazru – modern-day site of Gezer, Israel
4. Gibeon – modern-day archaeological site of Gibeon, located on the southern edge of the Palestinian town of Al Jib
5. Hasura – modern-day archaeological site of Tel Hazor, located north of the Sea of Galilee in Israel
6. Hazzatu – modern-day city of Gaza; "Azzati" in Egyptian; Canaan administrative center for Egypt (under Egyptian rule)
7. Labana – ancient city of Lebo-Hamath; location is suggested at modern-day city of al-Labwa (Laboueh), Lebanon
8. Lakisha – most likely the biblical city of Lachish and modern-day archaeological site of Tell Lachish, Israel
9. Magidda – modern-day site of Megiddo, Israel; "Makedo" in Egyptian; Canaan

administrative center for Egypt (under Egyptian rule)

10. Qanu – most likely the biblical city of Kenath, which is believed to be the modern-day city of Qanawat, Syria

11. Sakmu – modern-day archaeological site of Shechem, near the Palestinian city of Nablus

12. Salt Sea – ancient name for the modern-day Dead Sea

13. Silo – modern-day archaeological site of Shiloh, near the Israeli settlement of Shilo

14. Surru – modern-day city of Tyre, Lebanon

15. Tahnaka – modern-day Palestinian village of Tel Ta'anach

16. Urusalim – modern-day city of Jerusalem

EGYPTIAN PEOPLE AND ANIMALS

1. Akhenaten – prior Pharaoh; father of Ankhesenamun and Tutankhamun (Tut)

2. Ankhesenamun – former Chief Royal Wife of Pharaoh Tutankhamun; former royal wife of Pharaoh Akhenaten and Pharaoh Ay

3. Ay – Pharaoh; grandfather of Ankhesenamun and Neferneferuaten Tasherit (Nefe)

4. Horemheb – General of Pharaoh's Armies; husband of Mut
5. Khumit – the false name of Ankhesenamun
6. Kiya – deceased royal wife of Pharaoh Akhenaten
7. Meritaten – deceased Chief Royal Wife of Pharaoh Smenkare; sister to Ankhesenamun and Neferneferuaten Tasherit (Nefe)
8. Mut – wife of Horemheb; aunt of Ankhesenamun
9. Nefertiti – prior Pharaoh Neferneferuaten; mother of Ankhesenamun and Neferneferuaten Tasherit (Nefe)
10. Neferneferuaten Tasherit – sister of Ankhesenamun
11. Panhey – Per-Amun noble
12. Pawah – former prophet of Amun; former Vizier; deceased murderer of Akhenaten, Smenkare, Nefertiti, and Tutankhamun, among others
13. Ro-en – donkey of Ankhesenamun and Sennedjem
14. Sadeh – deceased wife of Sennedjem
15. Sennedjem – former Overseer of the Tutors; resigned Captain of the Troop
16. Smenkare – former Pharaoh; uncle and brother-in-law to Ankhesenamun

17. Tutankhamun ("Tut") – previous Pharaoh; deceased husband of Ankhesenamun

CANAANITE PEOPLE

1. Abdi-Heba – Chieftain (King) of Urusalim
2. Abdi-Tirshi – King of Hasura
3. Arsiya – wife of Aqhat; sister of Hurriya
4. Aqhat – husband of Arsiya
5. Biridiya – King of Magidda
6. Beth-shadon – son of Arsiya and Aqhat
7. Heth – husband of Hurriya
8. Hurriya – wife of Heth; sister of Arsiya
9. Ishat – daughter of Arsiya and Aqhat
10. Kotharat – mother of Aqhat
11. Labayu – King of Sakmu
12. Shapash – daughter of Arsiya and Aqhat
13. Sidon – son of Hurriya and Heth
14. Ug – son of Hurriya and Heth

ACKNOWLEDGEMENTS

First and foremost, I want to thank God for blessing me with the people who support me and the opportunities he gave me to do what I love: telling stories.

Many thanks to my dear husband Mark, who supported my early mornings and late nights of writing this book.

Thank you to my family, production team, beta readers, and launch team members, without whom I would not have been able to make the story the best it could be and successfully get the story to market.

Thank you to the Self-Publishing School Fundamentals of Fiction course, which taught me invaluable lessons on the writing process and how to effectively self-publish, as well as gave me the encouragement I needed.

<u>Finally, but certainly not least, thank you to my readers.</u> Without your support, I would not be able to write. I truly hope this story engages you, inspires you, and gives you a peek into the past.

My hope is that when you finish reading this story, your love of history will have deepened a little more—and, of course, that you can't wait to read the next series, *Egypt's Golden Age Chronicles*!

Sign up at www.laurenleemerewether.com to be notified of release!

ABOUT THE AUTHOR

Lauren Lee Merewether, a historical family saga fiction author, loves bringing the world stories forgotten by time, filled with characters who love and lose, fight wrong with right, and feel hope in times of despair.

A lover of ancient history where mysteries still abound, Lauren loves to dive into history and research overlooked, under-appreciated and relatively unknown tidbits of the past and craft engaging stories for her readers.

During the day, Lauren studies the nuances of technology and audit at her job and cares for her family. She saves her nights and early mornings for writing stories.

Get her first multi-award nominated novel, *Blood of Toma,* for **FREE**, say hello, and stay current with Lauren's latest releases at www.LaurenLee-Merewether.com.

ALSO BY LAUREN LEE
MEREWETHER

The Lost Pharaoh Chronicles Prequel Collection

Visit www.llmbooks.com to order.

Discover how Tey came to the house of Ay in **The Valley Iris**, why Ay loved Temehu so much in **Wife of Ay**, General Paaten's struggle and secret in the land of Hatti in **Paaten's War**, how Pawah rose from an impoverished state to priest in **The Fifth Prophet**, and the brotherhood between Thutmose and Amenhotep IV in **Egypt's Second Born**.

The Mitanni Princess and **King's Jubilee** are available for free via sign-up on Lauren's website.

Note: King's Jubilee is the short-story version of Egypt's Second Born.

The Curse of Beauty, Ancient Legends Book I

What if Greek Mythology was based on historical events?

Before the Muses sang of Medusa, a woman inspired the myth.

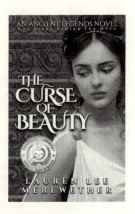

The *Ancient Legends* collection will merge with the Hyksos period of Ancient Egypt and feed into the ***Egypt's Golden Age Chronicles*** series starter, ***Warrior King***.

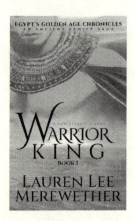

Blood of Toma

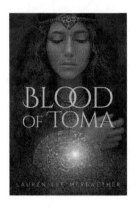

**Running from death seemed unnatural to the High
Priestess Tomantzin, but run she does.**

She escapes to the jungle after witnessing her father's
murder amidst a power struggle within the Mexica Empire
and fears for her life. Instead of finding refuge in the
jaguar's land, she falls into the hands of glimmering gods in
search for glory and gold. With her nation on the brink of
civil war and its pending capture by these gods who call
themselves Conquistadors, a bloody war is inevitable.

Tomantzin must choose to avenge her father, save her
people, or run away with the man she is forbidden to love.

Get this ebook for free at www.laurenleemerewether.com.

Made in the USA
Columbia, SC
20 September 2023

23131337R00243